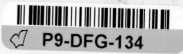

P9-DFG-134

Saint Peter's University Library
Withdrawn

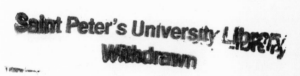

Tales of Manhattan

by Louis Auchincloss

The Indifferent Children

The Injustice Collectors

Sybil

A Law for the Lion

The Romantic Egoists

The Great World and Timothy Colt

Venus in Sparta

Pursuit of the Prodigal

The House of Five Talents

Reflections of a Jacobite

Portrait in Brownstone

Powers of Attorney

The Rector of Justin

Pioneers and Caretakers

The Embezzler

Tales of Manhattan

Tales of Manhattan

Louis Auchincloss

Houghton Mifflin Company · Boston

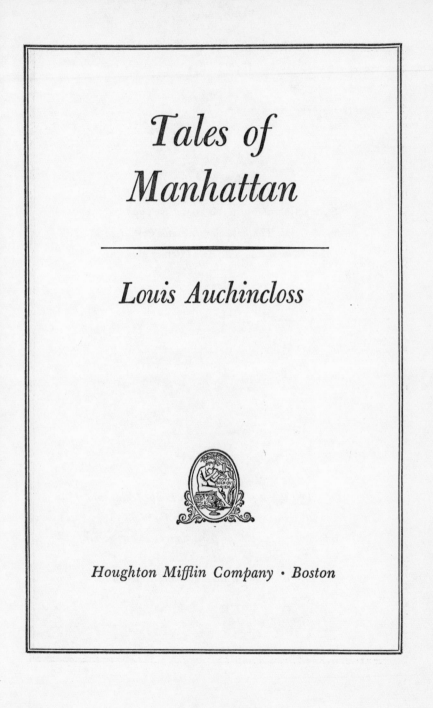

Some of the stories in this book have appeared in *Esquire, McCall's, The Saturday Evening Post, The Virginia Law Review,* and *The Yale Literary Magazine.*

Copyright © 1964, 1966, 1967 by Louis Auchincloss
All rights reserved including the right to reproduce this book or parts thereof in any form

Printed in the United States of America

For my son Andrew

Contents

Memories of an Auctioneer

Stirling's Folly

When I first went to work for the ancient auction gallery of Philip Hone & Sons, at the corner of Park Avenue and Fifty-seventh Street, I was entranced by the endless succession of "things" that passed through its portals: the lavalike stream of house decorations, from Rembrandts to Rothkos, from Thomyres to Calders, from medieval triptychs to Tiffany glass. I found that I was depressed by the cupidity in the flitting eyes and feral faces that crowded through the exhibition rooms and that for a time I preferred the things to their would-be appropriators, seeking that minimum sense of serenity and purpose so essential to a New York life more in the beautiful permanence of porcelain, paint and enamel than in the less lovely and less durable human beings whose function seemed simply to become their brief custodians. But this was only a phase. Both as auctioneer and as humanist my first attention had ultimately to shift from the display counter to the heads looming over it, and from these, perhaps too intensely present, to the heads and souls of past collectors, until the field of *provenance* became as fascinating to me as that of artifacts, until I could have told you more of William H. Vanderbilt than of Corot, more of Louisine Havemeyer than of Manet, more of Benjamin Altman than of Chinese ceramics.

My great game in *provenance* was to deduce the personality of the collector from his collection. Sometimes, of course, the things added up to nothing more than a portrait of vanity, but more often their combinations suggested less common traits: fanaticism, mysticism, megalomania, narcissism, sadism. Sometimes I could make out the taste of persons behind the collector, of his wife, or of figures less legitimately connected; sometimes, as with the mighty Morgan, I could simply see, in the vast scope and eclecticism of the things, the splendid outline of the dimensions of the man. Some collectors were interesting because they were always right, others because they were invariably wrong. But the one who presented me ultimately with the most fascinating of my mysteries, the mystery, indeed, whose unravelment became my principal hobby, was Grant Stirling, who had erected "Stirling Castle" (or "Stirling's Folly" as the public had called it) on a lonely island off the coast of Maine to house his fabulous collection and who had suffered the agony of watching it all go up in smoke in 1911.

The remnants of this collection, things that had been in warehouses or out on loan at the time of the fire, were numerous enough even in 1965 to supply Hone's with occasional reminders of its vanished glory: icons, Chinese jade, Fabergé, illuminated manuscripts, medieval reliquaries, Etruscan jewelry, Aztec figurines. Yet what Grant Stirling's essential purpose had been in collecting them, even what his basic taste had been like, was the slippery quarry that kept eluding me. Only very slowly did I make out certain guidelines. He had scorned the academic painters admired by his family and been an early patron of Whistler, Redon, Moreau. Yet he had had no interest that I could discover in the great classic impressionists: Monet, Manet, Renoir. His library had contained manuscripts of George Moore, Anatole France and Huysmans, but nothing of such greater contemporaries as James, Conrad or Zola. In architecture he had rejected Richard Morris Hunt, respected Louis Sullivan but had been totally unable to fathom Frank Lloyd Wright. Like his castle, he might have been the spirit of *art nouveau,* had he not been obviously aware that *art nouveau* was an insufficient answer to the cultural horrors of the twentieth century.

The theory toward which I at last began to grope my way, because it seemed to fit what I conceived to be the facts, was that Grant Stirling had been a born artist who had tried to make an art out of collecting and had discovered in the end that one could not create a creative act. Stubbornly, remorselessly, his artifacts had remained individual works and had refused, in whatever combination of them he tried, to become, collectively, a work of art. Now this might have seemed obvious enough to any ordinary collector, but I speculated that it was precisely Grant Stirling's genius that would have made him deny the obvious. And coming in the end to face it, pacing the vast and glorious chambers of his mutely rebellious empire, brought up inescapably against the conclusion that the sum was *not* greater than its parts, that perhaps he should have all the while been creating a part himself and not a whole, might he not have set that mysterious fire himself?

Well, what of it? What did that make him but another casualty in the sorry chronicle of American superfortunes? But Grant (as I came familiarly to think of him) was not so very rich, at least by the opulent standards of his time. Oh, the Stirlings were rich, yes, richer than anybody, but they had European ideas, and he was a younger son. Philemon, Grant's grandfather, had started piecing together farms in Queens and Brooklyn as early as 1812; by his death in 1875 he was reckoned the wealthiest man in America. But he had been a miser, and during that long lifetime the children and grandchildren had been forced to live in mere middle-class brownstone respectability. The explosion of spending that followed the probate of his will had created the architectural era that some have called the American Renaissance. Grant, despite his relatively modest inheritance of five millions, set out to outdo the others and outdid them. But in outdoing them (oh, how I made it all fit!) did he not prove himself, more than any of them, Philemon's grandson? And *could* Philemon's grandson be an artist?

His likenesses seemed to bear out my burgeoning theory. The earliest was in the Eastman Johnson group portrait of the Giraud Stirling family, showing them, about 1872, in the parlor of their Fifth Avenue house. It is just before the "Renaissance," yet one feels it on the way; we see them in cluttered, comfortable brownstone elegance, with many tassels and heavy curtains and with walls covered with bad academic paintings of Eastern bazaars and historic scenes. The parents look stout and stiff and homely, a simple, good couple very conscious of being in their Sunday best; the daughters, tall and handsome with the thick dark Stirling eyebrows, seem more assured; some of them have husbands whom they indicate by such proprietary gestures as allowing a glove to be buttoned or a cape to be arranged. The older brothers are languid, faintly bored, on their way to becoming aristocratic. But Grant, though very much the junior, still a little boy, dominates the center of the painting, sitting on a velvet stool and staring out at us, strikingly pale, with straight dark hair and large dark eyes that see far beyond that crowded family scene. "Oh, yes, these are my nearest and dearest," he seems to be telling us, "and of course I love them very much, but they won't *do.* No, indeed, I'm afraid they won't do. You'll have to suspend your judgment till you hear from *me!*"

I see him next, by Boldini, a young dandy, with a cane and top hat, to whom Paris has just become a second home. The picture is silly, for Boldini *was* silly, but it is still exuberant: one senses the young man's joy at finding that the great world outside that Fifth Avenue parlor was as shimmeringly filled with beautiful things and beautiful people as he had dreamed. But with the Whistler portrait, ten years later, in early middle age, the somber note appears. We now see him as a slim, elegant, darkly garbed figure, the epitome of the connoisseur, the collector. He holds in one hand, casually raised to the level of his shoulder, a red volume on which one can just make out the gilt of an armorial bearing. A white tapering forefinger is inserted between the pages as if to serve for a bookmark, but we feel that it is a pose and that the artist means us to feel that it is a pose. The malicious Whistler flared (or thought he flared) the dilettante in his sitter, the man who preferred the fine binding to the content, the rich accumulator who thought he could absorb beauty with his dollars. The face, still handsome, had now a pallor and a sharpness that is almost haggard, and the thin, delicate lips have a disdainful curve that might ultimately turn into cruelty. Yet one imagines that even Whistler doubted this. The more likely eventuality would be the growth of petulance, of a child's disappointment at broken promises.

And finally there is the tragic drawing of Sargent's, a rough sketch made while artist and subject were both visiting James Deering at "Vizcaya," in Miami. It shows a prematurely old man, with humped shoulders and hands plunged in knickerbocker pockets, a pipe clenched between his teeth, leaning against a column on the terrace, gazing out to sea, with an expression of utter resignation, of utter hopelessness. It is a terrifying little thing, Sargent in his latest and best style, when he was learning to face age and death without color or splash.

My theory, of course, was esoteric. New York had a much simpler one. All the Stirling friends and relations subscribed to the legend that Grant's young cousin and wife had enchanted him, enslaved him and destroyed him. They said that she had flung her lovers in his face, that she had spent his money and hoarded her own, that even the children were not his. Yet I was perfectly well aware that all these scandalmongers were on the friendliest terms with Countess Pozzi, as Grant's aged widow was now called. Was this a modern callousness to past evil or a hint that they did not really believe their own scandal?

Certainly, in support of the last of the rumors, none of the

Countess's daughters were collectors; indeed, they were quite the opposite. Rich as they all were, they were not rich enough for their budgets, and even forty years after their putative father's death they would occasionally fish out of storage some remaining treasure and whisk it down to Hone's. It was in a French eighteenth-century secretary, so exhumed by Mrs. Stirling Landon, a glorious piece of oak veneered with tulipwood and set with green-bordered Sèvres plaques, that I found an accordion file of old correspondence which had probably not been opened since Grant's lifetime. I took it eagerly home and spent several evenings sifting through it, and my reward was the charming love letter that here follows, traced by a young lady's careful hand on lavender stationery that had undoubtedly once been scented.

Newport, R.I. July 7, 1905

My own heart's darling:

I am sitting at the desk by the window in my bedroom looking out on a shimmering moonlit sea. Was there ever a more romantic sight? And the calm, the hush, the velvet breeze — no sound but the occasional ripple of laughter from Mamma's guests on the terrace below. What foolish thing can they be laughing at? Who did what or didn't do what at Mrs. Who's? Oh, how I *see* them all now, my dearest, since our wonderful talks at Sands Point! How can I ever see them otherwise again? Mamma is cross with me for leaving her party, but I pleaded the eternal headache, and I am supposed to be in bed. "Don't forget to write your thank you notes to Aunt Daphne and Cousin Grant," she warned.

"*Cousin* Grant"! How I hate that "Cousin"! What does it mean, anyway? Because, like everyone else, I had to have four great-grandfathers, and because one of them had to be called Stirling and had to be *your* grandfather, is that to mean the man I love is lost forever in the miasma of cousinship? In old Spain the kings could marry their nieces. You and I are only cousins — and once removed at that.

And as to age, my angel, never think of it. I am an old nineteen; you are a young forty-four. I felt at Sands Points that *we* were the young ones. Great-aunt Daphne seemed more like your grandmother than your mother. Oh, I know she's the darling of darlings, and I adore her and always will, but, sweetheart, what I say is true! And as for your sisters, they might be your aunts!

You will be glad to know that I have taken your advice about reading, and all my Kipling has gone to the church book fair. When Father protested, I made him furious by quoting what you said about the rich burghers and rug salesmen of New York getting a titillation out of identifying themselves with the British Raj. I am now in the midst of the novel you told me to read: *Illusions Perdues.* Do you think New York society has any such glamorous affairs or demonic conspiracies? Can you imagine Mamma developing a passion for a beautiful young poet from the provinces? I would I could!

Please, my beloved, let me tell her *before* you come here. I cannot bear to have her monopolize you and relegate me to the children's table. And I yearn to see the saucers that her eyes will become when she hears our news. "What, *you,* child, to marry Cousin Grant!" What a hubbub! She's always discussing you and your brothers and sisters and boasting that she was born a Stirling. Now she will be the mother of a Mrs. Stirling. Like Agrippina, the daughter and mother of Caesars! Isn't she comical? Aren't they *all* comical?

But you and I, my angel, will be far from all these absurdities. I used to wish I had been born poor enough to escape from all the silliness of Mamma's and Papa's world. But I won't need to escape it now. It will have ceased to exist for me. I will have taken off into the cerulean sky with you on the "viewless wings of poesy." Come *soon.*

Your only truest love,
ARIETTA

It was perfectly obvious who "Arietta" had to be, but I still reached for the Social Register (textbook of the auctioneer's trade) and, looking up "Pozzi" read: "Pozzi, Ctsse Lazlo (Stirling — Arietta Morse)." My mind told me that it was still conceivable for the writer of that enchanting epistle to have been unfaithful to its recipient, but my heart denied it. Holding it in my hand, I felt that I could feel something of the exhilaration that Grant must have felt six decades before. And then, with a fine, hot scorn for New York gossipmongers in my heart, I sat down at my desk and wrote "Arietta" a respectful love letter (as respectful as forty-five can be to eighty!) and sealed it in an envelope with her own.

The apartment occupied by Countess Pozzi was in a large, solidly constructed building on upper Fifth Avenue opposite to the Metropolitan Museum, one of the first of those designed in the early 1900's to wean the rich from the drafty stone town houses to which they had become so attached. The Countess's living room, into which the butler ushered me, was of noble proportions, with furniture and materials so splendidly maintained as to be gleaming, but it struck me almost at once that there was not a good thing in it. It was simply a decorator's dream, all green and white, with twisted gold columns and enormous eighteenth-century flower paintings and permeated with the odor of incense. But just as I was turning away in disappointment to the great window view of the park, my eye fell upon a little painting, to the side of the mantel, of sea anemones. As I leaned over to examine it I heard a high, clear voice from the doorway saying, in precisely articulated syllables:

"So *you* are the young man who pokes about looking for ancient love letters hidden away in French porcelain tables! An auctioneer and a Cupid — what do *those* add up to?" And I turned to face a marvelous little old lady, exquisite in every detail from her silvery blue-white hair and light, mocking blue eyes down to her silver shoes and stylishly high heels. It was difficult to credit that fine alabaster skin, that perfectly chiseled aquiline nose, those neatly formed scarlet lips with the years they must have reached. The Countess was ageless, like a great actress across the footlights, the Marschallin in *Rosenkavalier,* or even an actress acting an actress, an *Adrienne Lecouvreur.*

"You were very good to let me come, Countess," I replied with a bow. "I was taking the liberty of admiring your little Redon. I suppose it was one of your husband's finds."

She looked at me musingly, as if trying to fix the degree of impertinence of which I might be capable. "It was," she answered in a tone that may have covered a chuckle. "*One* of my husbands. But perhaps not the one you're thinking of. It was Lazlo's."

"Oh." I blushed. "Did Count Pozzi have other Redons?"

"He did not. That was his first and last. One collector was enough to be married to in one lifetime."

"You don't like collecting?"

The Countess seemed the least bit disappointed at my flatness. She seated herself and motioned me to do likewise. "No, Mr. Jordan, I do *not* like collecting. Can I give you tea or a cocktail? Or shall we have both?"

When I suggested the former, she rang, and almost at once the butler and a maid wheeled in a huge silver tea service and proceeded to pour and pass. The Countess took no part in these mechanics and paid no attention to them.

"Tell me," she said, "what you want to know about my letter."

"Do you remember writing it?"

"Remember it!" she cried. "Why, I remember as if it were yesterday. My generation was not as fickle as yours, Mr. Jordan."

"I'm sorry, Countess. All I meant was that it seems so long ago."

"Time, my dear young man, is measured by feeling. That was the most important letter I ever wrote. It brought Grant to the point. You see, I had to be sure that he hadn't been just flirting with me at Sands Point when I was visiting his mother. And he hadn't. Oh, no, he hadn't! He came up to Newport the very day he got that letter and asked Father formally for my hand."

"Which was freely accorded?"

"Not quite as freely as all that." The blue eyes rested gently on me, with a hint of amusement, of rebuff. "After all, Mr. Jordan, I was born a Miss Morse, and the Morses weren't exactly nobody in the New York of those days. Besides, Mamma was a Stirling herself, if only of a cadet branch. And then there was the age difference. But nothing could separate Grant and myself. We were much too deeply in love."

I entirely believed it, as she said it. There was an extraordinary depth in the gaiety of the Countess's tone. She made an instantly personal relation with her listener; I would have bet on her to subdue the sullenest Marxist. I even wondered if she did not affect, in her general *mise-en-scène,* the airs of a great lady of fashion simply to create a prejudice that she might then triumphantly dispel. Like so many beautiful women (or at least like so many former beauties) she was instinctively, pointlessly if you wish, a politician, with no visible goal beyond the compulsion to please.

"And were you as happy as you hoped to be?" I asked.

"We were very happy."

"Did it last?"

"Does anything?"

"What happened to it?"

For a moment, when she was silent, I was dismayed by the idea that she might not be aware that anything *had.* Might she not really believe that Grant Stirling's promise in life had been fulfilled, and, if so, would my question not seem inexcusably brutal in its insinuation? But in a moment the shadow of her smile showed that she was playing with me.

"You have been talking to too many people, Mr. Jordan," she reproached me mildly. "Has it never occurred to you that 'people' don't know everything?"

"Yes, but whom else, besides 'people,' was I to learn from?"

"From me, of course. Isn't that why you're here? You should have come earlier. You should have come as soon as you became interested in Grant Stirling."

"But how did I know that you'd tell me the story?" I demanded. "How did I know you wouldn't toss me out on my ear? How could I think that you'd welcome a nosy investigator who came bursting into your apartment asking: 'What *really* happened to Grant Stirling? Why did he give up collecting? Why does he look so *spent* in the Sargent picture?' Why, of all people, would you tell *me?*"

"Because, my dear young man, nobody else has asked me," she replied with a peal of laughter. "And I've been sitting here for years, just dying to tell!"

When tea had been taken away and we each had a cocktail, and the butler had poked up the fire, the Countess, in the course of the very comfortable next hour, with a smoothness and a cohesion that made me suspect that her story was neither unrehearsed nor told for the first time, related the tale that follows.

"Grant and I were married in the fall of 1905. The honeymoon was all I had dreamed of and a long dream, too — it lasted over a year. Most of it was spent in the Far East, as exotic as a Beardsley drawing or a tale out of the now despised Kipling. In Cambodia we rode elephants to the Angkor Wat; in Peking we bowed before the dragon throne; in India we visited a Maharajah who had a thousand servants. We reclined on house boats, sliding through steaming jungles filled with brilliant vegetation and fantastic birds; we visited ancient and mysterious shrines and held hands in dark, eerie temples; we consulted oracles and hunted tigers. And everywhere Grant bought: jade, jewels, carvings, scrolls, drawings, screens, idols, in one town a whole temple. I wondered if, like Wordsworth's Venice, he would not end up by holding 'the gorgeous East in fee.'

"How can I convey what those months meant to me, Mr. Jordan! It was paradise on earth, a selfish paradise, to be sure, but who wants any other kind? I may have written long, girlish letters home to Mamma and Papa, but never once did I miss them. My youthful egotism was too great. I had Grant, and I had the beauty of the ancient world. What did I care if I never saw New York again? My husband was all that a lover could be: kind, gentle, attentive, infinitely generous. I had only to look at a thing, and it was mine. Oh, yes, Grant spoiled me to death, but it was a *liebestod!*

"People have said unkind things. That is the way of the world. I know, for example, that one of Grant's sisters in later years used to imply that I had found the difference in age a weighty one and that Grant had been wearied and depressed by the energy of his young bride. Nothing could have been further from the truth. Grant was never a strong man, and I made it a sacred rule that he must not overtax himself. In the Orient I delighted in the idea of becoming an Oriental woman. Had Grant taken other wives I would have submitted to it; had he died I might have committed suttee.

"We were happy, but we were serious, too. In every country we had guides who were professors, sometimes famous ones. We spent our evenings reading aloud from books about what we had seen or were going to see. Grant turned his interest from city to city, from country to country, with a renewed freshness that in the first months dazzled me. Was there anything which that agile mind could not encompass? But as time passed this very facility began to arouse other thoughts, even apprehensions. Could a mind that changed so eagerly to welcome each new impression hold any one of them long enough for the serious critical work Grant professed to contemplate? When I asked him on our houseboat at Abu-Simbel about his long-planned book on American nineteenth-century painters, he looked startled.

" 'It is a bit hard, don't you think,' he asked, waving an arm toward the monumental figures of Ramses II that loomed above our anchored vessel in the twilight, 'to consider the charming naïvetés of William Sidney Mount and G. P. A. Healey before those mighty conceptions of the human physiognomy?'

"Well, that was all very well and no doubt perfectly apt, but I was a woman, and women do not lose sight of their practical goals because of the immensity of those of others. The human female, like a squirrel, is always ready to remind the mountain that it cannot crack a nut. Unfortunately for Grant's future work, however, my sex also provided my vulnerability, and I was too pleased that his interest in *me* did not change to chide him unduly for his inconstancy to two American painters of whom I had never even heard.

"Indeed, his interest in me seemed to wax as the honeymoon progressed. I had the gratification of feeling like the star of a musical revue. The backgrounds changed, even the chorus, but I always remained in the center of the stage. My husband would not buy things now unless I went with him to the bazaars; he would look first at me and then at the object coveted as if the latter was only a prop to be added to one of my sets. When I became ill of a fever in Morocco he sat all day by my bed, and when in Lisbon I discovered that I was pregnant I had to restrain him from attaching a permanent doctor and nurse to our retinue.

"My condition, however, interrupted our wanderings at last. I had hoped that we would spend the winter in Paris or Rome and go to Moscow in the spring; we had even talked of spending several years abroad, but now, it appeared, we had to go home. Grant could be very firm when he chose. He wanted me to have the best medical advice, and like all New Yorkers he believed that this could be obtained in only one city. Besides — and he added this in all seriousness — if the child should be a boy, he would have to be born in the United States to qualify under the Constitution to be President. Poor child — he turned out to be Edith! Do you know my oldest daughter, Mr. Jordan? Well, you know *about* her." Here the Countess lowered her voice and raised a finger to tap her temple significantly. "Just a touch, you know. But I must hush, for she sometimes listens at the door. My first surprise on arriving back in New York in 1907 was to discover that Grant had purchased and furnished a house by correspondence without even consulting me. I concede that it was a very comfortable house, with an intriguing Italian rococo façade and filled with fascinating Venetian furniture, but I had not supposed that we had decided to live in New York. When I pointed this out, he simply waved it off by retorting that a house committed us to nothing and that it had been an opportunity to get his Venetian collection out of storage.

" 'I could not have you bothered about housekeeping at such a time,' he concluded gravely. 'Let me handle these few petty details of living, my dearest, while you concentrate on the great ones of a new life.'

"I did not quite like this. It was all very well to be worshipped, Mr. Jordan, but not as a father worships a child. Grant seemed to take for granted that he would attend to our housekeeping, down to the very ordering of meals. All I had to do at a dinner party was to appear and look beautiful. It was as if my husband, having no regular office to go to (other than the Stirling estate office), felt that his manhood required him to take over the direction of the home. It only made matters worse that he did it so well.

"My second surprise, also not entirely agreeable, was his intimacy with his family. I had assumed that being intellectually so much their superior, he would not want to dine with them beyond what was decently required. I found, on the contrary, that the Stirlings delighted in each other's company and that Grant was no exception. In that first season I occasionally wondered what they would have done with their evenings had Grant and I, the 'newlyweds,' not been there to be feted.

"They were dull, Mr. Jordan. So good but so dull! My mother-in-law was a Brooklyn pastor's daughter who had been perfectly content to read books of sermons and gently gossip with her neighbors in the 'best parlor' when she was not harassing her maid of all work until old Philemon Stirling's death had made her hugely and uselessly rich. And my husband's two older brothers and three older sisters, although more sophisticated and elegant than their mother, still led basically bourgeois brownstone lives in their hideous pseudo-Renaissance palaces. They filled their months and years with moving large households from one huge house to another, always on the same date, from New York to Long Island to Newport to Aiken to Maine. No wonder they felt virtuous! No wonder they felt tired! Now that they are all long dead and the relicts of their remaining mansions are convents or schools, people look at their dusty grandeur and think what splendid parties must have once been given under those moldering gables. Huh! And yet Grant, the easily bored, the carping critic, would never turn down a family invitation. He was still their baby brother!

"I was too absorbed, however, in my own baby that year and in the next in another, to be unduly concerned about my in-laws. I had four children in as many years. I had to trade in culture for domesticity and reconcile myself to becoming a young society matron in the socially busy New York of that era. It was not what I had dreamed, but if that was what my husband wanted, why then, that was what I would be. I have always been an adaptable creature, and I prided myself on being able to make the best of any life. But I worried about Grant. The kind of moneyed American existence into which we seemed to be slipping was more insidious to the male than to the female, and I had given up hope for that book on American painters. Was Grant to spend his *whole* life at auction galleries and Stirling family parties? It seemed a dismal enough prospect.

"We never know when we are well off, Mr. Jordan. Little did I suspect that Grant had a very definite project in mind all along, and that I would come in time to look back with nostalgia on the days when he had seemed so aimless. When he first began to talk about Stirling Castle, I assumed it was only another whim that would be soon executed. For years he had owned a lonely, uninhabited island of five thousand acres off the coast of Maine, and what could be more natural than that a Stirling should build a big house on it? But when I saw the massiveness of the plans and their fantastic detail, when I learned that the first drafts were already twenty years old, I had to recognize with dismay that I was face to face with a lifelong ambition and that what Grant had been waiting for, collecting for, dreaming for, was not a site or a plan or even another inheritance, but simply a chatelaine! And who in the name of 'Country Homes and Gardens' was *that* but the poor girl who was just getting used to the crowded, bustling life of New York. What cared *I* for the joyless coast of Maine?

"I cannot speak with detachment, even today, of Stirling Castle. After all, it destroyed the happiness of my marriage. But I honestly do not think I would ever have liked it, even had no emotional issue been involved. I admit that it was much admired at the time and much discussed in architectural magazines, and, of course, it was highly original in a day of copycat building. But originality is not everything, Mr. Jordan. Neither is eclecticism!

"The real architect, as the real landscape gardener and the real interior decorator, was Grant himself. He lived in the superintendent's cottage until the main house was habitable and supervised the laying of every brick and stone. Artists and artisans came and went. Sometimes they resigned their jobs; sometimes they were fired. Sometimes they stayed on and learned to cooperate with their strange but compelling master. Stanford White had drawn the original plan of the house; Ralph Adams Cram and Grant La Farge made later contributions. Yet the finished product looked like none of them. It sprawled over the top of the hill, commanding a peerless view of the ocean and mainland and of its own splendid hanging gardens: a great black and white marble ark with a red porched campanile that soared into the sky like a beacon of the future — or the past.

"Well, you've seen dozens of pictures of it. Mission-Moorish, I used to call it. I could never learn to love the carved courtyards with the ruby iridescent glass tiles, the grinning Chinese lions of turquoise blue that guarded the portals, the gleaming pools with giant rock crystals, the stained glass windows of flamingos and bathing nymphs. Yet it was the background that my husband believed was the perfect setting for *me!* Sometimes I thought that he conceived of me as a fairy princess born for Stirling Castle and sometimes of his castle as having been built for me, but there was certainly a grim relationship between us embedded in the deepest layers of his fancy.

"The attitude of the Stirlings was significant: they thoroughly approved. That Stirling Castle was a madly exotic creation compared to what *they* had built did not seem to bother them at all; possibly they hardly noticed it. What they may have more wisely understood was simply that Grant was solving his problem, like a true Stirling, with masonry. Whether it was good or bad masonry was not the point; he was fulfilling a purpose in life by creating a large number of guest rooms that he would have to keep filled. Indeed, now that that generation of Stirlings has all gone, do not their names evoke a façade before a face? If I say 'Giraud,' do you not summon up in your mind a Genoese palazzo on the Cliff Walk in Newport? If I say 'Adelaide,' do you not picture a Pitti Palace in Lenox?

"My father, George Morse, a wise, discreet and customarily silent old gentleman, one of those wrinkled white-whiskered trust officers of the period who had nursed and swelled Mother's share of the Stirling fortune, was, appropriately enough, the person who awoke me at last to what was going on. He called on me, as gravely as if I had been one of his trust beneficiaries, and asked me if I knew that Grant was spending many times his income.

" 'Maybe old Mrs. Stirling or his brother Giraud have been giving him money,' I suggested. 'I know his mother has often told me that she thought her husband's will was unfair.'

" 'Mrs. Stirling's money is all in trust,' Father observed ominously, 'and on her death it goes to Giraud's sons. As to Giraud himself, while he may be as generous as you suppose, it is not something you should count on. I am afraid, Arietta, that you are not taking in the gravity of the situation. I am suggesting that if Grant keeps this up, he will dissipate his fortune, and that you and your girls will have to depend on what your mother can do for you. Is *that* clearer?'

" 'Very clear!'

"Oh, Mr. Jordan, how I remember that day! A new trait of character, unsuspected by myself, suddenly emerged from the musky depths of my personality, like Athena, fully armed, springing from the head of Zeus. I was tingling all over and spoiling for a fight. My long sleeping Stirling blood began to course feverishly through my veins. Was it really conceivable that Grant did not know what he was doing? Was it really conceivable that he was spending *all* the fortune of our daughters? That they would grow up actually *poor,* cursed with a name that was a symbol of wealth? What a fate!

"It is strange how long we can live out of our natural grooves if we get off to a false start. At nineteen I was convinced that I had the soul of a poet, and Grant had encouraged what should have been laughed away as girlish fatuity. In the violence of my gratitude I had become more his odalisque than his wife; I had obeyed him in everything, to the very dresses that I bought, and when I should wear them. And then, just as I might have normally emerged from this spiritual concubinage to take my place in the world as a normal American wife, I was engulfed by four years of having babies. One might really say that from my engagement to Grant to my financial awakening by Father, I had lived a kind of suspended existence. Underneath, all the time, was my true character, hardening into its present mold. Small wonder that its revelation was a shock to Grant! It was a shock to myself.

"I do not mean, however, when I say that my character was 'hardening,' that I was becoming hard, although poor Grant no doubt found me so. But Nature, Mr. Jordan, had picked me out to be a practical woman. I was much more the great-granddaughter of Philemon Stirling than Grant was ever his grandson, and I showed it the very next day when he came to discuss with me a river bed of almost perfectly rounded pebbles that had been discovered in Guatemala. He wanted to transport them in trucks and place them in the little stream that ran through the great hall of Stirling Castle.

" 'Rather a costly way to get one's pebbles, don't you think?' I observed. 'Maine must be full of rocks.'

" 'To tell the truth, it *is* rather costly,' he answered in sur-

SAINT PETER'S COLLEGE LIBRARY
JERSEY CITY, NEW JERSEY 07306

prise. 'That's why I was going to suggest that we might cut down our household budget a bit.'

" 'Then it's true what Father says!' I exclaimed, in immediate heat. 'You're throwing everything away on that castle of yours!'

"Grant really stared at this. 'What are you talking about?' he asked me coldly. 'I'm not "throwing anything" away. The house is there, isn't it? Didn't I show you last month's *Architectural Record* which described it as the greatest private residence of the new world?'

" 'What good does *that* do if you can't get your money back? And who would ever pay that kind of money for a white elephant on a remote Maine island?'

" 'My dear Arietta,' Grant said in his loftiest tone, 'I do not propose to discuss this matter as a vulgar business proposition. I can't conceive what's got into you. Stirling Castle is the product of a lifetime's dreams. Don't you understand that? Haven't we gone into it together?'

" 'But how will we live in it?' I cried, desperate in my sudden sense of his irrationality and in the fear that he might persuade me to silence. You must remember, Mr. Jordan, the difference in our ages, and how new was this opposition of mine. 'How beautiful will it seem if we have to take in boarders?'

" 'Boarders?' He stared at me now as if *I* were the crazy one. 'Why do you talk about boarders? I'm afraid I don't recognize you in this mood, Arietta. I must decline to discuss Stirling Castle further with you until you have changed your tone.'

" 'You may decline to discuss it, and I may decline to live in it!'

"Grant started as if I had struck him. Never had I seen him so pale! Then he turned on his heel and strode silently from the room.

"A virtual separation followed this scene. When he next left for Maine, I stayed in New York, sending him a strong note to tell him that I would not set foot again in Stirling Castle until I knew exactly where we stood financially. Grant did not deign to answer this, but with his usual aristocratic openness he directed his man of affairs to submit his books to my father's inspection. After a long day in Grant's office, Father called on me again, this time with ashy countenance.

" 'My child, it's far, far worse than I ever dreamed. Outside of his real estate, including Stirling Castle, Grant has hardly eight hundred thousand left. Since his father's death he has spent more than four millions!'

" 'But what could he have been thinking of?' I cried in despair. 'How did he expect us to live?'

" 'So far as I can make out, if he has thought of it at all, he has thought that Giraud would make him some restitution on account of the fortune that he thinks he ought to have had. But I have talked to Giraud, who is not in the least interested. He says that he will never see Grant want for anything, but that he can hardly regard Stirling Castle as a necessity. Old Mrs. Stirling has been helping out a bit, but that, of course, cannot go on forever.'

" 'Papa, what am I to *do?*'

" 'You will leave everything to me, my dear. Never sign anything. Never commit your own signature. It may be necessary to put a notice to this effect in the newspapers. That will seem hard, I know, but desperate situations require desperate remedies. Financially, you will run a household separate from Grant's, sending all your bills to me. There is no other way.'

" 'Papa! I can't!'

" 'My dear child,' he told me in his most solemn tone, 'you are my daughter, and you will find the strength to do what you must do.'

"Six months later old Mrs. Stirling's death brought Grant's

operations to a halt. Already distracted by the loss of his adored mother, he was almost incoherent when he came to tell me of his plans. He paced up and down the living room in New York, snapping out his syllables as if he were giving a dictation to a class of children. Sitting silently in one of his Venetian armchairs with a back shaped like a huge spread peacock's tail, I gradually made out his gist. When he had finished Stirling Castle and sold all his other places, we should have just enough to live there.

" 'Live or exist?' I demanded.

" 'What do you mean?'

" 'Well, if you think I am going to be swallowed up in the maintenance of *your* fantasy, you are very much mistaken. I want my girls to grow up here, in the world they know. I want to be able to travel and see my friends. And I want to give parties, too, right here in New York. What's wrong with all that? I find I'm like other people, after all. If you had taken time off from your beloved castle to spare me a few minutes, you might have observed the change!'

" 'Arietta! Do you know what you're saying? We would have to sell Stirling Castle!'

" 'And whose fault is that?' I cried, jumping to my feet. 'What right did you have to construct a folly that you could not afford to maintain?'

" 'But we *can* maintain it.' Suddenly Grant was very quiet and still. He stood before me, leaning forward now, eager and pleading. 'I'm not mad, Arietta. Truly. I've thought this whole matter through. I was entirely aware from the beginning that I was spending principal, but all along I had a perfectly coherent plan. I was simply going to build the most beautiful house in the world, and when it was completed, you and I and the children were going to live in it. Why wasn't that feasible? And we can still do it, my dearest. You think I'm impractical and visionary, but I know just what my income is, and it will support us very nicely in Stirling Castle. Oh, perhaps we shan't be able to have a big pompous town house and a steam yacht and a lot of bad Rembrandts like all our dear friends and relations, but do we *want* to? Wasn't it precisely our dream that we would build our own world? Wasn't that what brought us together in the first place? Weren't we sick to death of the showy materialism of our friends, even of our dear families? Didn't we want to demonstrate that money could be as potent a force for beauty as it had been in the Italy of Leonardo? And here we are, you and I, on the very threshold of realizing our dream, and you start talking like any ordinary society matron. Arietta, tell me that you're with me!'

"He seized my hand, but I snatched it back. I was too appalled at first by the magnitude of his misconception to see how mortal a blow I was about to deal him. All I could visualize was the horror of being walled up forever in Stirling Castle, fettered with jade and turquoise. The imagined horrors of Philistine New York seemed sudden bliss to me, and fear of losing them made me brutal.

" 'I hate Stirling Castle!' I cried recklessly. 'It's brought us all this trouble, and I'll never live in it! I *or* my daughters!'

"Grant's pallor darkened into a greenish ivory, and he pursed his mouth slowly into a small red circle. His beautiful dark eyes became remote, opaque, and his fingers twitched. Would he try to kill me? Was he mad? These thoughts glided across my mind without really agitating me. I was all alive now, all awake, as I had not been since I had first met him. *He* was the interlude, and I was life. He was the artifacts and bibelots, the books and tapestries, and I was life. He was ill, sad, old, if you want, but I was life. I would take care of him (oh, yes, I would!) but it would have to be on my terms. I was dealing with a lunatic.

"Well, Mr. Jordan, as you can see, he did not kill me. He did not even try. Grant saw in my eyes that he was beaten, and from that moment he never spoke to me again of Stirling Castle. He accepted there and then the change in our relationship; there was something terrible about his silence and the finality of that acceptance. But what else could I have done?

"For two years we lived virtually separated. Grant moved into his castle and completed it with his remaining funds. He gave me nothing, but Mamma and Papa were very generous. I was able to build 'Stirling Lodge' in Mt. Kisco, a delightful French house designed for me by dear Billy Delano, totally unexotic, and to rent this apartment, in what was then the smartest new building in town. I settled down with my daughters to lead the life that I suppose the Stirling gods had all along intended us to lead. It was not a great life, but my girls certainly had a more normal upbringing than they would have had in their father's self-imposed exile.

"Grant would undoubtedly have spent the rest of his days in Stirling Castle, selling off his collection piece by piece to support himself in increasingly shabby solitude and in desolately unpeopled rooms, had he been allowed to do so. But fate had a different disposition for him. Stirling Castle burnt to the ground in the winter of 1911, and poor Grant had to come and live with me in this apartment, a broken man. He had his own room, even his own library, and I saw to it that he had his own car and driver. I supplied him with everything that a reasonable man could need. But he was not a reasonable man, and nothing made any difference. He had lost his taste for life, and he was not to recover it in the few years that remained to him.

"I had thought that I would have trouble with his extravagance, that there would be a constant arrival in the mail of bills from antique stores, but I was wrong. Grant never even entered such stores, much less made purchases there. He spent his mornings with his books, his afternoons walking in the park, his evenings at his club. Sometimes he turned up at one of my dinner parties but more often not, and he was precious little help when he did, for the whiskey that he had consumed between five and eight playing bridge at the Knickerbocker made him a silent and rather ponderous companion for the later part of the evening. His manners with me were always perfect, if ceremonious, as they were with our girls, but I never felt that he was very much interested. The only human relationships that he still seemed to cherish were those with his sisters, who all considered that I was very hard on him. But did *they* come through with any money to continue his sacred collection? Oh, no, that was quite a different matter! That, presumably was up to *me!* And when Grant died, and I, after a perfectly proper interval, married poor Lazlo Pozzi, who had been the most devoted and respectful friend to both of us all during those difficult last years, you would have thought, from the attitude of the Stirlings, that we were dancing on Grant's coffin! Alas, both Grant and Lazlo lie now in the Stirling plot in Ardsley where I will soon enough be joining them.

"Lazlo in the Stirling plot? You look surprised. You forget that I, too, am a Stirling and can have my husbands buried there. Grant, indeed, of the two, is the husband who is most out of place. He had wanted, needless to say, to be buried on the site of his castle, and I would have gladly arranged it, but he had had to sell the island (for a song, Mr. Jordan!) to the State of Maine which had made it a beach resort, zoned against cemeteries. Of course, I was blamed for *that,* too. Grant had to be buried with the other Stirlings. Perhaps, after all, it is the essence of his story."

As the Countess neared the end of her narrative, her tone had grown increasingly bitter, and as she finished now, staring into the declining fire, I thought I could make out a greenish tinge in her blue eyes. When she looked up at me, after a long interval, she was strangely antagonistic.

"And you, Mr. Jordan, what would *you* have done?" she demanded of me. "What would you have done in my place — a young, healthy woman with her life before her?"

"Oh, I'd have gone to live in Stirling Castle," I replied with a shrug. "I could imagine no better life than to be surrounded with beautiful things. But I'm not you, of course. Nor do I criticize."

"Ah, but you do!" the Countess exclaimed harshly. "You're like all the rest of them. And it's so *unfair!*" But she paused here, with a visible effort to recover herself. "I don't really mean it's unfair of *you,* Mr. Jordan, because maybe you would be happy immured in a warehouse. After all, you spend your days at Hone's. But the other Stirlings, for all their criticism of me, were essentially like me. They lived the way I lived. That is the irony of this world: that the more unromantic people's lives are, the more romantic are their daydreams. So long as the Stirlings could have the present as grubby as they wanted it, they were pleased to insist that the past be glamorous. They would hack Mary Stuart's head right off her neck if she came back to life today and hand Cleopatra a box of fresh asps, but so long as these ladies belong to history, they enjoy shedding sloppy tears over their fate. Look what you all do to Grant Stirling, now he's safely dead!"

"But, Countess," I protested, "I only claim he was a great collector."

"Which he was not!" she cried, clapping her hands together in even greater excitement. "And you wouldn't think so either, if Stirling Castle and all *its* evidence had not been destroyed! Sometimes I think Grant's function in history was to carry the extravaganza of his era to its final absurdity. The fire that burnt his castle was a *cleansing* fire, Mr. Jordan. Make no mistake about that. For Grant's taste, even at its best, was basically a Stirling taste. His brothers liked Bouguereau; he liked Aubrey Beardsley. You can't build a life in that distinction. That was his real tragedy, if you *must* have a tragedy: he couldn't get away from them!"

I confess that I sat up at this. Was the Countess right, and did I have to have a tragedy? I suddenly saw the pale face of the Whistler portrait of Grant darkening as the haunted eyes reassessed the endless rooms of the castle. I saw him wandering through the great dusty edifice, uninhabited in its last years except for him and a faithful superintendent, staring with anguish at his treasures and seeing behind every beauty the hideous image of some fatuously grinning artifact in his sister's great stone horror in Lenox. Like the noble prince of an ancient line who, holding a candelabra to a mirror, recognizes the glint of family madness in his own haggard eyes, so might Grant have desperately wondered if his Canova Venus was not a sister of Giraud's "Dying Indian Chief," if his Toulouse-Lautrec horses were really so much finer than his father's Rosa Bonheur.

"Is it possible that your husband himself may have set fire to Stirling Castle?" I asked, with what later struck me as an appalling eagerness. "Wouldn't that have been his supreme act of despair?"

"It would have been a magnificent gesture, would it not?" The Countess's mocking tone had returned: her bitterness was suddenly gone. She smiled at me, a fly in her spangled net. "But, as my grandchildren would say: 'No such luck, Mr. Jordan.' For Grant never knew how deeply he had failed. A mercy for him, if a disappointment for you. No, it so happens that we know exactly how the fire started. The wind brought a small brush fire across from the mainland. At one point Grant's island is less than a mile from the coast. And far from wishing to destroy his collection, he very nearly perished trying to save it. He was going back to the burning tower for his Sung vases when the faithful superintendent stopped him and dragged him to safety. So you see, Mr. Jordan, you dream in vain. Go back to Hone's, to your pots and pans, and leave reality to those who can cope with it!"

At last she had angered me, and I rose, indignant, to my feet. The flash in her eyes bespoke her pleasure at having struck home. But who, in the devil's name, did she think she was to be so superior? Was it her money, or her age, or the legend of her beauty? What did I care for any of those things?

"Has it never occurred to you, Countess," I demanded hotly, "that you were a romantic yourself?"

"But, my dear young man, I was and am! The most incorrigible of them all!"

"No, you *were*. And you blamed your husband for killing romance in you." I drew myself up like a district attorney in a movie. "I suggest, Countess, that you never forgave Mr. Stirling for putting an end to your honeymoon. I suggest that you resented his taking you back to the world you had married him to get away from. The world for which you secretly pined!"

The Countess seemed not in the least bit quelled or irritated by these impertinent speculations. On the contrary, she nodded her head approvingly. "Next time you come we might reconsider the whole story from that point of view."

It was my dismissal, but, after all, it was I who had risen first. In my excitement I had forgotten that our meeting had already gone on long enough to be sufficiently fatiguing for a woman of her years.

"Next time?" I queried. "You mean you would be willing to see me *again* after what I've just suggested?"

"My dear young man, you must think me very thin-skinned indeed. What you've just suggested is the mildest tap on the hand compared to the lurid libels in which my nearest and dearest indulge!"

I somehow stammered out my adieux and was standing alone in the front hall, happy that the butler had not been alerted and that I could fumble my way into my hat and coat alone, when I heard my name pronounced in a hiss and turned to see a plump, elderly woman, with a square red face and small porcine eyes, and elaborately waved, somehow pointlessly dyed blond hair, standing in a doorway that opened into a long corridor.

"I am Miss Stirling," she continued in a rasping tone, moving toward me now to take my hand, "Miss Edith Stirling. I know you found that letter of Ma's and came to see her about it. I know what she's told you. Don't think you've been the first. But I thought you'd like to step back to my study. I have a few things of Pa's that might amuse you. Oh, not to sell, don't worry. I'm the magpie of the family."

"Do you collect, Miss Stirling?" I asked as I followed her down the corridor. After what I had been through, I reflected, the daughter could hardly be worse than the mother. Miss Stirling was strange in manner, but she seemed good-natured. It was no doubt the classic case of the plain old maid daughter trapped for life by the beautiful parent who is perfectly willing to ignore her bad temper so long as she makes herself useful.

"I don't collect. I haven't the means. But I *keep*. Things of Pa's, anyway. And I keep them all here, together, in a room that Ma never goes into!"

In another moment, frozen in the doorway by my own stupefaction, I saw what Miss Stirling meant. The room was simply a shrine to her father! Its walls were covered from floor to ceiling with paintings, drawings, framed manuscripts and illuminated scrolls; its interior was cluttered with cabinets, standing back to back, filled with bibelots, figurines, coins, weapons, God knows what else. I made out frantically in the dim light an Ingres, a Constable, possibly a Cellini. It was suddenly all too much for me. I followed Miss Stirling dazedly to a corner, the only living part of the room, where I vaguely recall that there were two pink Louis XVI *bergères* and a boulle table. My hostess was already shaking a cocktail in a mixer that must have been standing on the table. I reached out my hand gratefully for what turned out to be a warm Martini, half vermouth. But at that point I could drink anything.

"And all this escaped the fire?" I murmured, staring about me.

"All this was simply what he had in *one* storage house," she explained impressively. " 'All this' was my poor share. There's even some question if 'all this' would have qualified for the castle's standards. Does that, Mr. Jordan give you some inkling of what a treasure house was lost to the world in 1911?"

"It does, indeed, Miss Stirling. But then I did not need to be convinced of that. Perhaps you do not realize — there's no reason you should — that I came here in the first place as an admirer of your father's."

"And you still are?" Her small black eyes held me now with a police-like glitter.

"Why should I have ceased to be?"

"You mean, you haven't been brainwashed?"

"Your mother has been most kind, Miss Stirling. She ——"

"Come now, Mr. Jordan!" my stern interlocutor enjoined me. "I am not a babe in arms. I know what my mother tells people about Stirling Castle. Did you think you were the first?"

I murmured something about the Countess having given me to understand that nobody had ever asked her for the real story.

"And you believed her!" Miss Stirling exclaimed contemptuously. "How like a man! You're all putty in her hands. Even at eighty she can bamboozle you. Why, she tells that story to every Tom, Dick and Harry she can induce into her living room, the old spider!"

"My name happens to be Roger," I said with what dignity I could still muster, "and I think that it's high time I took my leave."

"You don't want to hear the *real* story of Stirling Castle?"

"Perhaps another day, if you would be so kind as to give me a rain check . . ."

"A rain check!" Miss Stirling cried. "I talk about truth, and you talk about rain checks! No, indeed, Mr. Jordan, if you want to know what happened, you can learn it now or never. I know from bitter experience that a victim of Mother's poison must be given the antidote immediately. Otherwise he becomes impenetrable to even the toughest fact!"

Having decided, under the impact of this, to give in, I knew that it would be foolish not to do so handsomely. "Miss Stirling," I said, handing her my glass, "give me another of those delicious cocktails, and I will be honored to hear your story."

She eyed me closely. "Was it really mixed right?"

"It was perfect."

"Thank you." She settled herself in the *bergère* as well as anyone so supremely un-Gallic and, to be cruel, unfeminine, could, finished her cocktail at a gulp and replenished her glass with the remnants in the shaker. "It always upsets me to go through this," she explained, "and I need fortification." Then she began.

"Mother could never understand Father's feeling about his family. It was because she has never understood loyalty. To do her justice, she has always been able to stand alone, on her own two feet. But Father, like so many people, was tribal. He needed to feel that he had parents and siblings who were with him, right or wrong. And he had them. Grandmother Stirling was all good and all loving, and her baby, Grant, her last-born, her Benjamin, cared more, in collecting, for the most banal of her appreciations than he did for all the rhapsodies of Mr. Berenson. To this day I picture poor Grandma in black, expensively dowdy, terrified that she is going to say the wrong thing about a Houdon bust, and Father, anticipating her worry, miserable to have her miserable, rattling on about it so that she will not have to say a thing. And the three older sisters, all married to pleasant, faithful, unimaginative husbands, must have naturally turned to their collector brother for any initiation into the world of beauty. Even the two older brothers, less aesthetic even than the sisters, regarded Grant tolerantly as the 'genius' of the family.

"A fortune can disunite a family, but if it is vast enough it tends to pull them together. The Stirlings, staggered by the inheritance that had inundated them, held out hands to each other. Their faith and pleasure in their own company had some of the quaint and touching innocence of a royal family. They sat in neighboring pews at St. Bartholomew's and joined lustily in singing the hymns. Of course, today people would say that Grant, as the youngest, was smothered in this prolonged domesticity, that he grew up wrapped round and round in the maternal apron strings, that he was overprotected from the male world of competition — and from the male's world of women. But he also grew up into a gentle and charming man whose principal wish was to return some of the love so showered upon him and to leave this planet a slightly more beautiful place than he had found it.

"Oh, I admit he had no great love affairs that we know of. In those days one didn't have to. His name was occasionally linked with that of an older woman, usually some famous beauty or former beauty, but for the most part he was considered a bachelor by choice and emotionally self-sufficient. People did not indulge in the disgusting speculations about bachelors and old maids that are the rule today. 'Grant Stirling?' they would say if asked. 'Oh, he's in love with his art collection!' And so he was, until he fell in love with Mother, at the age of forty-four.

"It was one of those total, overwhelming experiences from which a man never fully recovers. Father's interior guards must have been sleeping, or at least they did not suspect Eros in the bosom of the family. When he realized that he had inspired love in the heart of a beautiful nineteen-year-old cousin, an heiress herself, who thus could not be after his money, an enchantress whose hand was being sought by all the most eligible young bucks in New York, he responded first with incredulity, then with gratitude and at last with the most violent of passions. Arietta Morse in a week's time became the whole world to this confirmed and middle-aged celibate. Call me a romantic, Mr. Jordan, but people could still be that way sixty years ago!

"And she? Did she love him? Yes, at first. Mother has always started everything she ever started with absolute sincerity. She is a woman of strong passions, if not durable ones. Her type has ruined many a stronger man than Father. For despite a genius for adapting herself to the status quo, despite having been born the squarest of pegs in the squarest of holes, the most normal, gregarious of creatures, a lover of men, of clothes, of parties, she nonetheless had, with the fatal perversity of her generation of American women, to conceive of herself as a soul apart, a poetess, a priestess of culture, a being hardly made of clay at all. Dear God! It was as if a Roman matron had conceived of herself as a Christian slave and pined for the arena.

"It might have been funny, Mr. Jordan, if Mother's type had been more easily spottable by her contemporaries, or if she and her ilk had been willing to shed their disguise after a brief romp. But that was just the trouble. They clung to their silly roles! Mother was perfectly willing to devote years, passionate, dedicated years, to her pose and then toss it aside, give it, so to speak, to her maid, like an old dress.

"Oh, she started well enough. Brides usually do, I'm told. That's what people mean when they say: 'The honeymoon's over!' The couple comes back to reality. But if Mother had had her way, the honeymoon would have never been over. At least, she would have never come home. After a year of wandering, Father began to realize that he would have to take steps if they were to take up normal life again. He could not bear to disappoint his young bride, and I am sure that he had promised to take her as far as she wanted for as long as she wanted — to the moon, if necessary. What man in love would not? But naturally he had not expected to be taken so literally. He could hardly abandon his old mother who had so little time left to live, his brothers and sisters, his friends, his art collection. Mother might have become the world to him, but a man still has duties.

"She did not see this. She reminded him of all his promises, and what could he say? I do believe that had she not become pregnant (with *me,* Mr. Jordan!) she might have prevailed. But I gave poor Father the excuse that he desperately needed to come home. And once home he found ways to stay. Indeed, if it won't shock you, I will suggest that keeping her pregnant — which he did for four years — was the principal way. We girls may owe our existence to Father's filial devotion. An expanding nursery was the price he paid to see Grandma Stirling!

"Mother behaved bitchily; there is no other word for it. The only excuse I can make for her is that she may have suspected how quickly she would succumb to the temptation of becoming a society queen and may — even subconsciously — have sought to avoid it. She may have dimly conceived of herself as putting up a final fight before the image of being Mrs. Astor was substituted for the image of being Elizabeth Barrett Browning. Unhappily for Father, that fight took the form of being hateful to the Stirlings. She refused to see Grandma at all, on the trumped up charge that she was turning Father against her, and she made herself poison to her sisters-in-law by flirting outrageously with their husbands. There is even a legend that Uncle Eben Potts wanted to run off with her. Father, however, never reproached her, even when her rudeness embroiled him with his relatives.

He always felt that he could never, in a lifetime of devotion, make up for what he deemed her to have sacrificed in not marrying a young buck her own age. What foolishness, Mr. Jordan! As if he had not brought Mother a million times what she brought him — in love, in sympathy, in kindness, in inspiration!

"And *that* is how Stirling Castle came into being. Father conceived it as a substitute for the romantic, wandering life his bride had dreamed of, for his age, for his relatives, perhaps for his very gentleness. He would gather together all the beauty of the ancient and modern worlds so that his Arietta would not regret living in the arid climate of America. The great court would be worthy of Ashurnasirpal, the gardens, of Babylon, the throne room, of the Forbidden City, the cloister, of Mont Saint-Michel. And do you know where the heart of his tragedy lay, Mr. Jordan?"

Miss Stirling's eyes, very small now under her contracted lids, small and suspicious and more piglike than ever, burrowed into me.

"That he failed," I suggested hesitantly. "That his aim too far exceeded his grasp. That what he tried to create was an impossibility."

"No," she cried, terribly agitated now, "that he *succeeded!* That is what people don't know. Because it's all gone. Very few ever saw Stirling Castle just before its destruction, just before its completion. There were hardly any servants in it, so Father did not entertain. But his sister Adelaide did. She told me that the difference, even in the final few months, was staggering. That it was simply the most beautiful house in the world!"

"Were there photographs taken?" I asked eagerly. "I mean *just* before the end? In all that perfection?"

"There were. But they perished, too, in the fire." Miss Stirling shook her head grimly. "And there was another visitor, too.

Besides Aunt Adelaide. You can guess who it was. And she *saw* it all, Mr. Jordan! She saw at once how he had succeeded. She saw, in fine, that he had made good his promise, that he had created the beautiful home where they could lead the beautiful life that they had dreamed of. And how could she go back *now* to the giddy social existence that she had come to love, leaving all that beauty boarded up, rejected, to reproach her? Oh, sure, a rational woman could have, but since when had Mother been rational? So she did the only thing ——"

"Oh, Miss Stirling, no!" I interrupted, jumping to my feet.

"Oh, Mr. Jordan, yes!" she cried, jumping up too. "It was a simple matter. Only the superintendent and his wife, besides Father, lived in the castle, and they were in her pay. She explained to them that his collection was a dangerous obsession, that he might be cured without it. She offered them — God knows what — a fabulous reward. So they did the devilish deed, and the devils even became heroes by rescuing Father from the burning tower!"

"Miss Stirling! How do you *know?*"

"Oh, I know. I have my ways of knowing. Nobody believes me, and they never will, either, until this room, too, goes up in smoke! But there won't be anyone to rescue *me,* Mr. Jordan! I will succeed *there* where Father failed!"

When I finally escaped from that terrible apartment, I walked all the way down Fifth Avenue to my apartment in Washington Square. I took deep breaths of the cold winter air and occasionally tried to solace myself by whistling a tune or reciting a poem. But nothing could stop the shivers up and down my arms and back, and when, at Forty-second Street, I heard the shriek of a fire engine, it was all that I could do not to burst into a run.

The Question of the Existence of Waring Stohl

WORKING IN AN auction room is like working in a funeral parlor: sooner or later everybody comes to you. In the first years of my employment by Philip Hone & Sons, I used to feel like a vulture when, dining out, I caught myself wondering when the Turner over the mantel, or the Dresden centerpiece, or even the monogrammed table cloth itself, would fall under my jurisdiction. But after I moved into the book department, this feeling was greatly diminished. Even if I caught my apprais-ing eye roaming to shelves of my host's first editions, I would reflect that a book is not as personal as a dish or a chair or a picture. A book, in its way, belongs to everybody.

Certainly Professor Nathaniel Streebe had felt so, and when his executors submitted his great collection of Americana to the gallery, I approached the task of preparing the catalogue in al-most festive mood. Streebe had expressly stipulated in his will that his books and manuscripts be sold at auction "so that other collectors may share the joys of acquisition that I have had." It was my biggest job to date at Hone's, and I viewed with misty eyes of appreciation the piles of Morocco cases on the long desk in my workroom. The old man's testamentary order of dispersal seemed to me a noble act, an appropriate recognition of the eternal reconstitution of things, so edifyingly unlike the usual collectors' wills which buried their masters' accumulations un-der a museum tombstone. Museums are all very well for arti-facts, but books? What can they do with books? Streebe's course in "American Lit" had been the high point of my four years at Columbia, and I was proud to be an instrument of his posthumous scheme.

Truly, it was a collection to make the mouth water. Here were all of Hemingway's "firsts," each inscribed to Streebe with an obscenity. Hemingway used sometimes to do this playfully when asked by friends to sign their copies. He meant to reduce the value, but only made it soar! Here was Henry Adams' own copy of *Democracy;* here were Edith Wharton's childhood verses, printed privately in Newport; here was Abraham Lincoln's bookmark. Streebe had never been a rich man; the collection had been made up over a long lifetime of watching and pouncing. And gifts. Oh, yes, many gifts! Hundreds of young novelists had sent their first books to Streebe, and he had kept them all. I had found trunkloads of such in the cellar of his Riverside Drive apartment house and shipped them off, after a screening, to the secondhand market. But the screening had netted me, in mint condition, all of Fitzgerald, all of Wolfe, all of Marquand, and a copy of *Peter Piper,* marked "first off the press," by the young protégé of Streebe's later years, Waring Stohl, who had died before him. On the dedication page, over the glowing printed testimonial to Streebe himself, was scribbled in a large purple hand: *"Homage au Maitre!"*

I could not help the rather sour reflection that it was like Waring to express his effusion in a language that he could never speak. It was part of his mockery of everything and everybody, a mockery of which Nathanial Streebe himself had been a prime target. Back in the winter of 1940, when Waring and I, as seniors, had taken American Lit, he had irked me during those beautiful lectures by passing me notes with such comments as: "The old ham!" or "Do you suppose in heaven he'll be Ruth Draper?" or, more venomously, "I'm sorry; I can't help it; I *like* Streebe."

"Why did you take the course?" I would grumble after class. "After all, everyone knows what Streebe's like."

"Everyone knows but nobody *does* anything about it!" And Waring would open his little gopher's mouth and show two huge front teeth in a silent exhalation of sarcastic enthusiasm. He would even clap his little fat hands. "Why do they call it a course? Why don't they recognize that they've got the last of the great vaudeville stars and share him with the multitude? Nathaniel Streebe, the Painless Parker of *belles lettres!*"

There was some shadow of truth in this. Streebe's golden-toned speech was as much performance as an instruction. Tall, thin, motionless, with batrachian features and hair closely cropped in the Prussian style, perfectly garbed in expensive black or the deepest blue, with a starched collar and a brilliant tie, he would stand by the lectern on which he had deposited the small handful of first editions from which he needed to quote, and wait the beginning of the hour, oblivious of the assembling student body below him. On the stroke of the hour silence would fall; the men nearest the doors would close them (no latecomers were admitted to a Streebe lecture) and the master, after a slight, deliberate throat-clearing, would begin.

Some people, like Waring Stohl, may have sneered, but while Streebe spoke, even the censorious were spellbound. He used no gestures or facial expressions; the trick, or art, was in the rich, full, velvety voice, the dulcet, almost monotonous tone, and the roll of the balanced sentences, recited without pause or stammer. There were no discussions in Streebe's class. One would as soon have risen to one's feet during Gielgud's *Hamlet* as to have presumed to interrupt the flow of his discourse.

And content? What of that? Well, read the lectures; they have all been published now. They are certainly good, but they lack, taken by mere ocular infusion, the ear-tingling pathos with which Streebe's voice could bathe episodes in the lives of lonely and tortured persons of genius. When I think of William Prescott struggling with his blindness, or of Emily Dickinson sitting with a door between herself and a visitor, or of Henry Adams roaming the Pacific after the suicide of his wife, I hear Nathaniel Streebe in the background, and the lump in my throat is as much for my lost college years and the hope of youth as it is for his glorious subjects.

Streebe's hold on the young, however, was not due wholly to his oratory. He was always up to date, up to the very minute. The past, for all the conservatism of his old bachelor's appearance, was no more sacred to him than the present. If he reveled in Melville, it was not at the expense of James; if he adored Hemingway, it was not to slight Wolfe. He delighted in adding pocket supplements to his own *History of American Letters.* Everyone had to have a partner in the past, and Streebe, a sort of literary marriage broker, made it his job to find them.

"Do you suppose he's ever been wrong, really wrong, about anybody?" Waring asked me once. "Do you think he might have said 'Tosh!' when he read *This Side of Paradise* or 'Bunk!' when he read *The Sun Also Rises?* If he did, I'll bet it was only in a tiny whisper until all the reviews were out. Wouldn't it be fun to catch him at it? Why, it might almost compensate for the fatigue of being a genius, if one could write a brilliant, controversial book and squeeze a derogatory statement out of him before the hosannas began to blow in!"

Waring Stohl was certainly the least prepossessing of any member of our Columbia class. He was short and dumpy, pallid and hirsute, with a bald dome across which a few greasy locks were carefully tonicked down. His chin was as oval as an egg, and his upper jaw protruded to give him that rodentlike expression of which I have spoken. His voice was unexpectedly deep and resonant, but just as the thick hair on his arms and legs made one more conscious of the doughy whiteness of his skin, so did the masculine depth of his tone only emphasize the feminine silkiness of his speech. He had a habit of putting his face very close to his interlocutor's as he talked, and he had bad breath.

You will ask: How did I put up with him? The answer is that he had a kind of repulsive charm. His eyes, brown and limpid, were as friendly as his disposition. There was no rebuffing Waring. If he wanted to be your friend, he would dog your steps until he wore you down. I never saw him express resentment at his many rebuffs, much less lose his temper. I doubt if he had one to lose. By the sheer bulk of his flattery, by the irresistible force of his unwavering good will, this odd little epicene figure, who could play no known sport, who engaged in no extracurricular activity and who did not even get good grades, ended up as a friend of all the leaders of the Class of 1940. What is more, he never seemed to find it in the least surprising. As he accepted his own unloveliness, so did he take for granted that the whole lovely world was his oyster.

I must not give the impression that he was a toady. That was precisely his trick, that he wasn't. He was invincibly independent in all his opinions. His flattery was confined strictly to the individual with whom he was talking and not wasted on the individuals about whom he talked. He would not, I think, for the President of the University himself, have admired a book or a play or a picture that he did not admire. On the contrary, he was frequently exasperating in the way he sneered at one's idols, blandly assuming that one would take it in friendly spirit, that all the world shared his own detachment. This was why I hesitated so long, despite all his begging, before taking him to one of Professor Streebe's Sunday afternoons.

These gatherings were held in the library of Streebe's Riverside Drive apartment, amid all the glory of his shelves of Americana. At four o'clock precisely from ten to twenty members of his American Lit class would assemble for general conversation punch of their host's concoction. I do not know just group was formed, but I suspect that the common de- tor was more social than literary. Streebe, like many pr ssors of English, was a bit of a snob. I was included because he could not very well leave out the student with the highest grades in his course, but there was no room for an odd ball like Waring. Waring, however, for some perverse reason of his own, wanted to go, and Waring always got his way. He found out that Streebe allowed the members of his group to bring an occasional guest, and in the end I had to take him. After all, I asked myself desperately, would it kill Streebe to be subjected once to what all the rest of us were subjected to?

That afternoon I was not sure. Waring was gratifyingly silent for most of the session, but toward the end of our allotted two hours, just when I was beginning to congratulate myself that I was quit for my apprehensions, something was said of Thomas Wolfe, and Waring burst into effervescent communication.

"Choo-choo Wolfe, we used to call him at school, because of all that divine tosh about engine whistles. He got it out of Whitman, of course, but at least he didn't go through hospital wards kissing soldiers. Oh, no, nothing queer about the big bad Wolfe! Why, he wrote a million pages of memoirs to prove his virility!"

I did not dare look at Streebe. I simply stared at the floor and prayed. When the latter spoke, however, he was mild enough.

"I did not mean to imply, Mr. Stohl, that I regarded Wolfe as a great novelist. I think that he caught very eloquently the note of nostalgia for the lost small-town life that is so peculiarly the emotion of American cities. No doubt, there are elements of sentimentality, even of hypocrisy in it. Oh, no, Wolfe is no Hemingway."

"No, he never dropped to that."

"I beg your pardon?"

"I mean, he may be silly, but he's not absurd."

"Hemingway absurd?" Streebe's tone showed simple astonishment. "I rate him more highly."

"My dear professor, you can't mean it! A man who's spent his entire life worrying about the most trivial part of it?"

We all waited for the storm, but the storm did not come. Streebe's face was as inscrutable as his manner was ceremonious. "And which part, pray, do you consider the most unimportant?"

"Why, the end of it, of course, the 'stylish death.' The trouble is that death doesn't really have any style. It's too common. No, it's poor old life that has that. Anyway, Lady Brett's the only stylish character Hemingway ever created."

"Which of today's novelists *do* you prefer, Mr. Stohl?" Streebe's "do" was more curious than sarcastic.

"It's hard to say, isn't it? They're all so pompous and all so red." I should insert here that Waring was an early anticommunist. "But I guess old Dreiser's about the best of the lot. At least he admits he belongs to the party. Of course, he doesn't know the first thing about the business world, but that really makes the Cooperwood trilogy more amusing. It's fantasy, but it's fun."

And still God had not said a word!

"I don't see what communism has to do with it," somebody interjected, striking the conventional attitude of the day. "Surely, a man's political affiliations have nothing to do with whether or not he's a good writer."

"That, of course, is what we *have* believed," Professor Streebe announced, rising now to indicate the end of the session. "But I wonder if Mr. Stohl may not be bringing us an intriguing whiff of new attitudes. We mustn't let ourselves become stuffy, gentlemen!" And the final surprise of the afternoon was Streebe's shaking the awful Waring cordially by the hand and adding: "That was very stimulating, Mr. Stohl. May I hope that we can count on you as a permanent member of our little group?"

For the rest of senior year the Sunday meetings were reduced almost to dialogues between Waring and the professor, and some of the faithful, bored, began to absent themselves. But nothing, not even the loudest and crudest of Waring's enthusiasms or condemnations, was able to disenchant his new admirer. Streebe seemed hypnotized. He would ask Waring question after question and shake his head with noncommittal amusement at the remarkable answers that they elicited. Waring even presumed on this new intimacy to ask a question once in Streebe's classroom and received only a modest rebuke.

"I wonder if we could defer that until after class, Mr. Stohl? Otherwise, I lose my train of thought. I'm sorry. It's a matter of advancing years."

It was speculated that Waring had a hidden hold on Streebe, that he had discovered a chapter in one of his books stolen from an obscurer author, that he had surprised him filching a rare volume from the Columbia Library, that he was his illegitimate son. But by graduation we had still not found the answer, and Streebe's grade in American Lit raised Waring Stohl to a totally unmerited *Cum Laude*.

Then came the war, and for years I lost track of Waring Stohl. I knew that he was 4–F, but I never heard that he was associated with any war work. It would not have been like him to worry unduly about world conflict. I did not see him again until 1947 when I started working in Hone's. We met in the display room, where I later found that he was a regular visitor, and he greeted me as pleasantly and as happily as though I had simply missed a week of classes in Columbia. He told me that he was living with his mother in Brooklyn Heights, and he laughed when I asked what he did.

"Oh, mercy me, I don't 'do' anything. Every now and then I have to tell the bank to sell a bond, but they still have a few left. Not many, they tell me, but then I don't need many."

"You mean you just putter around town?" I am afraid that my tone may have contained a note of contempt. It was always a bit difficult not to disapprove of Waring.

"That's it," he agreed cheerfully. "I putter and dream."

"What do you dream about?"

"Why, my novel, of course!"

"You're writing a novel?"

"Isn't everyone?"

"I'm not."

Waring glanced at the long table with the dreary sets of Victorian fiction writers. It happened to be a bad collection. "Ah, you sell them, don't you, the poor dead dears," he said with a sigh. "Some day maybe you'll be selling me."

"You think your first editions will be auction items?"

"They'll be rare, anyway!" And he uttered a loud sputtering laugh that made the browsers look around. "No, but truly, maybe you will. Maybe people will come in here one day and ask: 'And did you once see Waring plain?' "

"Very plain," I reposted.

"Ah, well, you can sneer. You can sit in your morgue of books and sneer. But one fine morning you may wake up to the atrocious discovery that your old friend has become a great man."

"A *great* man? Even if you wrote a dozen best sellers, you wouldn't be a great man. Great men don't write novels. They don't even read them."

"What about Disraeli?"

"All right, I'll give you Disraeli," I said with a shrug. "No doubt Professor Streebe is feeding you these wild ideas."

Waring flung his arms in the air. "Since he's retired, he's really quite impossible. He's always after me, asking how my 'muse' is doing. He's like an officious old midwife poking and prodding a poor girl who's only in her third month!"

But whatever the nature of Professor Streebe's ministrations, they must have been productive, for barely a year after this meeting, I received an advance copy of *Peter Piper,* "a first novel by a brilliant young satirist, Waring Stohl." I confess that I read it with some trepidation, for I could hardly bear the idea that Waring, the idler and dilettante, should make the first signal success of our class. But I need not have worried. The book was quite as bad as any of us could have hoped.

It was really not a novel at all. It was something meant to look like a novel — a fashionable novel of the period. Waring had taken the characters of the popular new Southern school of fiction and moved them up to a brownstone in Harlem occupied by "a great-granddaughter of President Martin Van Buren," who refused to recognize that the neighborhood had changed. You will not be surprised to learn that she was an imperious, highly eccentric old lady whose aristocratic heart was far closer to her poor neighbors than that of her snobbish son who wanted her to move to the Waldorf. The other characters — well, you name them. There was a sadistic, homosexual policeman, a prostitute who read William James, a beautiful young man who wore blue jeans and bicycle boots and wept . . . no, I won't go on.

My opinion, however, was obviously not shared by Waring's publishers, who were spending a considerable sum on advance advertising. By the clever expedient of photographing Waring in profile, with an opera hat and cape, they gave him a vaguely Toulouse-Lautrecian appearance, which was at least amusing. The novel was said to be a "proof that the Confederacy had not, after all, won the War." I was invited to the publication-day party at the Library Room at the St. Regis and found it jammed with the editors of women's magazines. From the corner where I was rather sourly drinking alone, I spotted Professor Streebe. He, too, was alone but he was not drinking. He was studying the crowd like a man who anticipates being called to the witness box to testify as to what he has seen.

It was too ludicrous! Here was a venerable and respected gentleman and scholar almost on his tiptoes to catch the words of Cholly Knickerbocker! I finished my second drink and went boldly up to him.

"Professor Streebe, may I ask . . ."

"Ah, my dear fellow, how are you?" he interrupted me, squeezing my hand with a flattering cordiality. His visits to the book room at Hone's had kept his memory of me fresh. "Could we reverse our old roles for a minute and you be the teacher? Who is that lady in the lavender hat?"

"Somebody you'd do much better to have nothing to do with," I said firmly, propelling the old man by his elbow to two vacant chairs in the opposite corner. "It's taken a world war to give me the guts to do this, but I'm going to insist that you sit down for two minutes and answer a serious question."

Streebe proved perfectly docile, except that when we were seated, he continued to take furtive looks over my shoulder at the tantalizing crowd. "What on earth can I tell *you,* young man?" he asked. "Unless it's something about the poor old battered past which, I must say, doesn't seem to exist in this room."

"It's very much about the poor old battered present that you can tell me. I want to know what you, the disciple of Thoreau and Whitman, can see in the foolish fiction and posing personality of Waring Stohl." Seeing that I now had his attention, I continued: "By what right, you may demand, do I ask so impertinent a question? By the right of the man who introduced this gaudy bug into your uninoculated garden of American flowers!"

Streebe took no offense at my words; on the contrary, he seemed vastly entertained. "Yet you yourself are not reluctant, it seems, to partake of the hospitality of this contagious virus."

"Oh, I'm immune," I said carelessly. "I've known him too long. Besides, I don't matter. I have no reputation to lose. I can show myself promiscuously at any parties that amuse me.

But people believe in you, Professor Streebe. *I* believe in you. So kindly tell me what you're doing in this *galère.*"

"Your generation is terribly direct," Streebe said with a rueful shake of his head. "But you must allow an old-timer to start his reply with an indirection. Let me tell you first about Anatole France and Marcel Proust." He changed his tone, and I had the immediate feeling of being again in his lecture hall. Had I had a notebook, I would have opened it.

"When Proust was young and nobody," he began, "he cultivated the literary patronage of the master of French letters. Anatole France, always gracious, was amused by his youthful admirer, but he could never take him seriously. What, after all, was to be expected of this effete little social climber whose airy discourse was all of titled old ladies and beautiful young men? And when the manuscript of *Les Plaisirs et Les Jours* appeared on his desk, with the author's humble request that he write the preface, was it not precisely the slender collection of lacquered prose and damp sentiments that one might have anticipated?" Here Streebe interrupted himself to shake his head again, this time with vehemence. "I say all this for illustration, dear boy. Please do not imagine that I presume to compare myself to the author of *Thaïs!*"

"I have no objection to *that,*" I assured him warmly. "Indeed, I find it entirely fitting. It is your implication that Waring Stohl has a *Remembrance of Things Past* up his sleeve that staggers me. Does he go home at night after his parties and write up his hostesses in a cork-lined room?"

Streebe, inscrutable again, resumed his lecture. "Anatole France survived his young admirer and lived to see the latter's posthumous triumph. Happily for him, he could not witness the final humiliation. At the sale of his own cherished library by his heirs, it was the copy of *Swann's Way,* with the author's scribbled tribute, that brought the highest bid."

"But that happens all the time," I protested, exasperated by the solemnity of Streebe's tone. "Didn't Wordsworth tell the Brontë sisters to go back to their sewing needles? Didn't Corneille despise the young Racine?"

"But it won't happen to me!" Streebe exclaimed excitedly. "You'll see that it won't happen to me! If I have any niche in American literary history, it will be through Waring Stohl. You will live to see it, my boy!"

"But what do you have to go on, sir?" I protested, caught between the impulses to wonder and to laugh. "Has he shown you some hidden work of merit? Surely, it can't be *Peter Piper?*"

Streebe smiled enigmatically. Obviously, he enjoyed his mystery. "I will say only this," he said as he rose, "and then I must really go and have a word with Waring's dear mother. The facts on which I base my wild surmise are as much known to you as to me. The difference lies only in our processes of induction."

I had to be content with this, but in the year that followed I watched Waring's career with reluctant fascination. *Peter Piper* had a decided success, not so much with the book clubs and ladies' discussion circles as in society and, oddly enough, in the serious literary world. Waring found himself hailed alike in the *Partisan Review* and on the book page of *Vogue;* for several weeks he was discussed in the Pen Club and at charity balls. These two worlds love a first novel as they love a lover, and a brilliant career was predicted for Waring. It was even said that the mantle of Faulkner might fall upon his sloping shoulders. But, better yet, the little book was sold to the movies, and Waring found himself financially at ease.

It did little, however, to stimulate his literary activity. In fact, it seemed to put a complete stop to it. Waring rented a floor of a brownstone which he decorated exotically with looped draperies, large jardinieres, tiger skins and stuffed antelopes' heads. Amid the scent of incense, he entertained at cocktails representatives of the two worlds that adored him. The rich old ladies, with blue hair and blue furs, moved slowly and bravely in and out of the dangerous little box of his self-service elevator and found themselves squeezed against editors with beards, pipes and sports jackets. But it made no matter. In the world of the late 1940's art had come of age, and Waring seemed to be the symbol of its happy majority. We were treated to photographs of Waring at the opening of the opera with Mrs. George Washington Kavanaugh, Waring at a table with the Windsors at the *Bal des Roses,* Waring on the lawn of the "Duke Box" in Southampton. He went out every night and stayed up very late, and, as he had never been strong, he rested in his bed until noon. In the afternoons he visited the *antiquaires* with his old lady friends. When did he write? Or did he?

He told me that he didn't.

"You don't think I'd be ass enough to write a second novel, do you?" he demanded. "The one that everybody's waiting to pounce upon? No, like Phidippides, I shall not sully my little glory. Besides, man, I'm *busy!* Do you realize that as we speak, I'm due in three places? And that one of them is Elsa Maxwell's?"

When I reproved him for his frivolous existence, he smiled without listening. Not only did he regard it as far from frivolous, for he ranked the pursuit of a position in society with the pursuit of one at the bar or in medicine, but he believed that I was insincere. Waring was sincerely convinced that only the envious could sneer at his way of life. Hence he in no way resented my sometimes harsh remarks or even bothered to reply to them. He would even suggest that I go with him to the very party from which I had been urging him to absent himself. For Waring was generous. He was perfectly happy to share his new life with old friends, perfectly willing to extend a hand to help me jump out of the corner into which he conceived me to have been perversely painting myself. It was infuriating.

Only once did he show any emotion at my lectures, and that

was when I suggested how deeply he would disappoint Nathaniel Streebe if he did not produce another book. He waxed even paler than usual.

"What makes you say that?"

"Because he's expecting a masterpiece. He told me so. Or implied as much."

"Oh, the old fiend!" Waring exclaimed, in a unique burst of temper. "He can't let me be, can he? What does he *want* of me?"

"Only to admire you," I replied in astonishment at such unwonted violence. "How can you hold that against him?"

"How little you know him!" he cried with a snort. "He's an old lepidopterist with a net, prowling about a meadow on a sunny day. When I see him I fly away, but he's always following. One day I shall find myself caught in that net and taken out in his pale bony fingers and impaled right through my back with a pin and stuck on one of the ghastly cards of his eternal classifications!"

As I stared at Waring, the yellow shirt and scarlet tie under the small larvalike face *did* suddenly suggest a butterfly. For just a moment I was appalled.

"What can he classify if, as you say, there won't be anything to classify?"

Waring shrugged. "Well, there's my journal, I suppose. I'll bequeath it to him. Will that make him happy, do you suppose?"

"So you *do* keep a journal!"

"Oh, a line a day sort of thing. To keep track of where I've been. It may amuse you to see what he makes of it. What will I care? I'll be playing a harp."

"Streebe's an old man," I pointed out. "Why do you assume he'll survive you?"

"All of you are going to survive me," Waring said with a giggle. "Don't you know that?"

"Are you serious?"

"Oh, my, yes." He tapped his chest proudly. "A weak ticker. The wonder is I've got this far. Now you see why I talk of butterflies. We have our one glorious day. Don't look so gloomy, old fellow. *I* don't mind. Because I'll tell you something. The only serious thing I've ever said to you." He leaned even closer than was his habit. "One can't live forever on a single novel."

He giggled again as he walked off to join his dowager in the main display room, and I was startled that despite his frivolity I was absolutely convinced that he was telling the truth. And indeed he was. In half a year's time he suffered a stroke and had to retire with his mother to a cottage in Florida. Nobody that I knew saw him again. As soon as an active life was no longer possible, he severed his ties with all his friends. He answered no letters, acknowledged no gifts and would see no callers. With perfect philosophy, I was told, he accepted his disability and resolved to die to the world in spirit before he should die in the flesh. Yet it was two years before the end came.

His will, which gave the small balance of his property to his devoted old mother, contained only one other legacy: that of his journal to Streebe. The next time that the great man came into the rare book room at Hone's I asked him if he had had occasion to read it.

"Read it? Bless my soul, young fellow, I know it by heart. I'm going to publish it."

"It's so wonderful then?"

The old boy positively cackled. "Just wait and see!"

And I shuddered at my sudden vision of that long pin through an insect's round little body.

I turned now to a clean page in the copybook where I always inscribed the drafts of my catalogue entries and indicted the following:

Handwritten manuscript of the journal of Waring Stohl. 353 sheets of lined yellow legal-size stationery. The journal was bequeathed by Stohl to Nathaniel Streebe and formed the basis for his final work: *The Question of the Existence of Waring Stohl.* This philosophical essay, which won Streebe the Pulitzer Prize, is now generally considered his masterpiece. Streebe saw in Stohl's journal a distillation of intellectual life in the late 1940's and early 1950's. Stohl was what he termed a "non-author" and his novel a "non-book." In a world that was disillusioned with disillusionment and belonging to a generation that was ashamed to repeat the experience of being "lost," Streebe saw Stohl as the symbol of the young faddists who sought in appearances a reality that they were reconciled in advance to not finding.

I put an estimated price of $5000 on the journal and $1000 on the copy of *Peter Piper.* Had the manuscript of *The Question of the Existence of Waring Stohl* been in the collection, I would have marked it much higher, but that, along with all of the other Streebe manuscripts, had been donated in his lifetime to Columbia. The authorities there hoped to add Waring's journal to the "Streebe Papers," but as it turned out, they were outbid by a Texas university. Waring's account of his pains and parties in Manhattan was sold at Hone's for $10,000. He and Streebe went down together in the ocean of literary archives, tied to each other for the ages like Captain Ahab and his white whale.

The Moon and Six Guineas

ONE OF THE troubles of working in an auction gallery is that one becomes so used to the first-rate, that the second and third benefit by reaction and begin to take on a merit that they do not deserve. In recent years at Philip Hone & Sons, for example, I have become so disgusted by the snobbish stampede of the buying public after a few magic great names that I have gone through periods of almost believing that Bernard and Guillaumin are as good as Gauguin. And then, of a Sunday afternoon, to correct the astigmatism of the week I go to the Metropolitan to see the *Ia Orana Maria.* God! There's nothing like it.

Still, as the masterpieces of art, swept by the inexorable law of the income tax, drop, first one by one, then dozen by dozen, into the great sea of museums, that bourne from whence no traveler returns, it behooves us dealers to develop the public taste in the direction of lesser but more accessible artists. Yeoman's work has been done with Sérusier, with Valtat, with Boggs. Old unfashionable schools have been made fashionable again, and it is not unusual in East Side galleries to see bearded young men in tight pants haggling over an Alma-Tadema or even an Edwin Landseer. But my personal candidate for first place in the second rank, John Howland, has so far not made the grade, and I fear that other dealers, knowing that I once "pushed" him, have been put off by my sudden apparent loss of interest. Yet if this is so, it is most unfair to Howland's reputation, for my failure to finish — or really even to start — the major article on his work whose publication was to accompany a retrospective show of his paintings, had nothing to do with the quality of his art or, for that matter, with my admiration of it.

Before going into the story of my abandonment of this little enterprise, I should explain, for the benefit of those less familiar with the minor American painters, that John Howland (1847–1913) has always, even at his lowest ebb, had a certain attraction for collectors, and that a really first-rate example of his work will fetch today as much as ten thousand dollars. But the accusation that is most commonly flung at him is that he is lacking in vigor. Charming, brilliantly colorful, wonderfully decorative, but not "strong." That is what people are apt to say, people, that is, who are themselves neither charming nor decorative nor strong. What is this twentieth-century craving for "strength" and "vigor" in art but the howling of an anemic child for cod liver oil? Did Napoleon look for vigor in Canova? Did Catherine the Great demand it of Fragonard?

But I must not get off on *that* point. If I do, I'll never stop. I will simply suggest that most art critics tend to find vigor in a coal miner and decadence in an aristocrat and that John Howland was incontrovertibly, irredeemably an aristocrat.

Witness the laconic account of him in Foster's *American Painters:*

> A Bostonian and Mayflower descendant, he was educated at the Dixwell Latin School and at Harvard. After his marriage to Maud Curtis, daughter of a Vermont marble magnate, he moved to Paris where his house became a well-known meeting place for international society. He painted gardens, châteaux and French landscapes in the impressionist style. In his later years, as a widower, Howland roamed the Caribbean on his sailing yacht, *The Wanderer,* and was known for his experiments with color.

Hardly a Bohemian story! Such, however, was the sum total of my knowledge of Howland when I happened to purchase one of his water colors, for a suspiciously small sum, at a rather disreputable Third Avenue gallery. I bought it because it did not look in the least like a Howland and because it was dated 1867, when he was only twenty. Who, I asked myself, would fake a Howland of such an early period and do it in a style that did not even suggest the later ones? It seemed to me I had a bargain.

I took it home, put it on my mantel and lived with it for several weeks. It grew on me uncannily. It depicted a funny, ugly shingle house with an octagonal tower on a long, deserted beach against what seemed to be a gathering storm. But the interesting thing to me about the picture was that the menace was not so much in the storm, which might have been expected, as in the house, which should have been a refuge. The sea, beginning to churn, was still very white and vapory, and the sky over the horizon had the blankness of a void. Only in the darker lines that marked the borders of the beach did the threat seem to begin, and these thickened dramatically as they approached the house, which began to assume the ominousness and dreariness of a House of Usher. It was as if salvation, or at least the safety of cessation, must have existed only in the eye of that storm. Elsewhere, particularly in human habitation, in *that* house anyway, squatted some fetid, sordid danger. I was reminded of the dismal hovels of Vlaminck, of the gloomy fiords of Munch. My little water color certainly did not fit with any of the modern critiques of Howland. It was decidedly "strong."

The biggest projects have often the most inconsequential origins. I doubt if I would have embarked on my task of converting Howland from a "minor" to a "major" figure in American art without my little water color. That ugly shingle tower exercised a hypnotic effect on me; I was determined to find out how it fitted into Howland's polished biography.

I began my research, as we all do now, with his "papers." Howland had bequeathed these to the National Painters' Guild, of which he had been a founder, and they were kept in the Guild's library in New York. The small elderly lady, Miss Neff, who opened the file cabinets in which these were stored was delighted that someone should be doing research on Howland.

"Lots of students come to see his papers," she explained, "but it's always for the letters that people wrote *to* him. He was a great correspondent, you know. Oh, yes, they all wrote him: Mrs. Gardner, Berenson, Edith Wharton, all that crowd."

And indeed they had. Howland seemed to have been on intimate terms with everyone but painters. He had obviously been a highly cultivated man with a rare willingness to place his cultivation at the disposal of his friends. The letters were full of requests: Mrs. Gardner wanted him to look at a supposed Mantegna on exhibit in Paris; Henry Adams had a question about the cathedral at Senlis; William Dean Howells, seeking background material for a novel, inquired about the schooling of a Boston gentleman in the eighteen sixties. It was a civilized but impersonal correspondence.

"I think he must have lived less like a painter than any other painter who ever lived," I said with a discouraged sigh to Miss Neff. Then I brightened as the idea struck me. "Perhaps I might do a piece on just that!"

Miss Neff, as if acting on a sudden impulse, pulled open another drawer and snatched out a folder from the back. "Before you decide that, you should read these!" she exclaimed, holding the folder defensively to her chest, as if frightened by what she was doing. "They must have been torn out of a sketch book that he kept while he was at Harvard."

"You mean they're sketches?" I asked, reaching out an eager hand.

Miss Neff still held the folder back. "Oh, no. We didn't get any sketches or paintings. Mr. Howland's son, who was his executor, determined that the Guild's bequest of 'papers' covered only writings. So he tore all the writings out of the sketch books and turned them over to us. But I don't think he read them first. Not these ones, anyway."

She still clutched the folder.

"Is it a journal?" I asked in a more indifferent tone, in order not to excite her further apprehension.

"Perhaps. Some kind of college journal. I believe Howland lived at home when he was at Harvard. It is mostly about his parents."

In the end she not only let me read the pages; she allowed me to photostat them, and I transcribe below one of the more fascinating excerpts. The handwriting was jagged and straight up and down; it had not yet slanted to the flowing script of the later years. Both hand and content, however, seemed to me to have a direct relation to the hard blunt lines of my water color. This passage, for example, deals with his father:

> I hate him! I hate him! *Why?* For just the reason that there is no he. Like a deer, an antelope, a hunted thing. Nine minutes out of every ten in panic. A conservative? Not he. He cares not a fig for the status quo; he cares not a fig for anything. Except maybe the protective coloration behind which he trembles. The hunted thing again. Death in every bush, every rock. Oh, God, the endless pattern, the endless cheer, the "*Good* morning, old fellow, looks like a spot of rain, or doesn't it? *Hello,* there's jolly round red Mr. Sun!" The anecdote, the gentle chuckle, the wink. If the day can be covered with a sheet of formulas, if the night can be bound up in dreamless sleep, if a wife can become "my better half" and son John a "fine young Harvard buck," can't we get through our allotted seventy years as quickly as possible? Jesus God! When can he go back to the nothing he yearns for?"

I had from this my picture of the senior Mr. Howland, as clear as if a drawn sketch had accompanied the prose one, striding down Beacon Street, a raincoat buttoned up to his chin, a hat pulled down over his brow, an umbrella held close over his head, and three drops of rain in the sky. A man who existed only in reflex actions to minor stimuli. For Mrs. Howland, however, the style became positively Darwinian:

> The desert wasp, in feeding her young, is guided by an instinct as sure as it is terrible. She seeks out the tarantula, for once a victim, and stings it to paralysis but not to death, laying her eggs on its warm abdomen so that her young may have living flesh to feed upon. The Boston desert wasp knows that in destroying her poor tarantula of a husband, she needs neither charm, nor coyness, nor gaiety, nor wit, nor things attractive, nor things generous. No, not even simple good manners. She needs only her sting. And Pa, once paralyzed, goes through the motions of the good spouse, the good parent, like the living dead, to be consumed by his own offspring.

So! I began to think that John Howland had mistaken his vocation. He should have been a novelist.

When I had finished with the papers — and there was very little of personal interest besides the journal — I began the job of running down the known Howland paintings. I discovered straight off that the bulk of these were still in the family, owned by two descendants, the artist's sole surviving child, Miss Millicent Howland, who lived in Manchester, near Boston, and his grandson, Frank Howland, a member of the New York architectural firm of Howland & Howland. The latter received me cordially, when I called by appointment, in the big office on the top of the Flatiron Building that had been his father's before him. The heavy mahogany furniture gave it an opulent Victorian gleam that went well with the drawings on the walls of Italianate summer villas. Frank Howland was a prominent beaux-arts traditionalist, anti-glass and anti-modern, a crusader for decoration and a member of every committee to save every landmark. Like many modern conservatives, he was formidably affable. One could see at once that his technique would be reason and ridicule, that his temper would not be easily lost. He was big and bald and high-domed, with an aristocratic aquiline nose and sensuous nostrils. His voice was dominating, his accent British, and he went straight to the point.

"My aunt and I are both delighted that you're undertaking this work. I talked to her on the telephone after I got your letter. You must understand that with us it is not entirely a matter of sentiment. We have between us some hundred Howlands that we would like to dispose of. If Pont Aven and the Fauves can be revived, why not Grandpa? He could paint circles around any of *them!* I honestly believe that if he hadn't had the misfortune to prefer a clean shirt to a dirty one, and a pair of well-shined boots to some old moccasins, you'd be knocking him down at Hone's for fifty grand a canvas!"

"Maybe I'll be doing it yet," I murmured. Frank Howland was only saying what I had thought, but somehow I liked it less, coming from him.

He looked at me sharply, as if to gauge to what extent my remark was perfunctory. "Well, stranger things have certainly been known. I'll tell you what Aunt Millicent suggested. She said that you couldn't do a proper job on John Howland while working at Hone's. She's offered to match your salary if you can get six month's leave of absence and devote yourself entirely to the article."

I was a bit irritated at the distant Miss Howland's presumption. "How does she know what my salary is?"

"I told her," Frank replied and then blushed to have revealed the extent of his prowling. "That is, I happen to be a shareholder at Hone's, and those figures are available."

"Oh, that's all right," I said with a laugh. I was easier now that the polished Mr. Howland had shown a smudge. "But my object is to approach your grandfather objectively. I'm afraid I must be completely on my own."

"Fine, my dear fellow, fine!" Frank exclaimed, throwing up his hands to reassure me. "As a matter of fact, it's probably better for poor old Grandpa that way. Families have a way of killing the things they commission."

I did not see anything "poor" about John Howland unless it was in the fact that he was dead. "Why do you want to sell his pictures?" I demanded, perhaps a bit bluntly. "Aren't you a collector yourself?"

"Precisely. And my field is the eighteenth century. I happen to believe that Grandpa was as good as the best of the impressionists, but I'd swap the lot of them, even your sacred Monet and Manet, for the Watteaus in the Louvre."

"But even if you don't want the Howlands yourself," I persisted, "wouldn't it be nice to give them to a museum?"

"I detest museums," he said coldly. "The poor pictures hang there, like animals in a zoo, for louts to stare at. Paintings are for artists and for collectors. Nobody else, least of all art critics, understands them. You never really *see* a picture, Mr. Jordan, until you've paid too much for it."

I could hardly agree with him, but as an auctioneer I enjoyed his theory and said nothing. Seeing that I was silent, he proceeded to the little lecture that was evidently meant to serve as the skeleton of my article.

"Grandpa's painting falls basically into three periods. The first is what I call the Hudson River, when he studied landscapes under Church. His work here is romantic, academic — and a bit dull. All those storms and cattle! But remember his conservative family background. The next period, Paris, is the one of liberation and fulfillment. Grandpa fell in love, not only with Grandma, but with the impressionists. His landscapes become more fluid. His flowers are no longer fixed in time or even in space; they begin to have their own world, their own language. There is no question in *my* mind that this is his best work. But Aunt Millicent, you will find, is all for the final period, the Caribbean. She claims that here his liberation became complete, and she touts him as the greatest of the postimpressionists. Well, you must go to Boston to see her and hear some of her spicy tales of Grandpa in the last decade. She tries to make him into a kind of poor man's Gauguin. Or perhaps I should say a rich man's Gauguin. But to me Grandpa lacked discipline at the end. Had he lived any longer he might have gone in for cubism. But the story is still a writer's dream, Mr. Jordan. Don't you see it now? From Back Bay to Antigua! From discipline and snow to a riot of hot sensuous color! Properly written up by *Life* it could bring us a fortune!"

I had had occasion to study the attitude of a good many people toward their illustrious progenitors. But Frank Howland was a novelty. He actually, and in all sincerity, condescended to his grandfather. He, the great architect and eighteenth-century purist, felt sorry for the poor old befuddled would-be abstractionist!

"I would be interested to know what you think of this water color," I asked him, taking from my briefcase my newest acquisition and handing it across the desk. "You see how early it's dated, and yet I see no trace of the academic style which you say is characteristic of the first period. To me it has more a note of Munch. Don't you find it 'strong'?"

Frank took out a pince-nez, carefully blew on each lens, affixed it painstakingly on the thin bridge of his nose and then proceeded to examine the offending picture (for there was no question that it did offend) as a jeweler might examine a questionable stone. When he had finished, he gave a little grunt, and did not answer until he had removed and repocketed the pince-nez.

"My dear fellow," he reproved me, "don't let yourself be converted from so valuable a citizen as an auctioneer into one of the great gaggle of art critics. What you call strength is simply faulty technique. This water color was executed even before Grandpa came under the influence of Church. Hence its unacademic style. It is the work of a very young man, hardly more than a boy, who is not in the least sure that he wants to be an artist. Had he *known* how to paint a cloud, for example, he would never have painted one that way. Munch indeed! But I do not mean to depreciate your water color. As a matter of fact, it probably has a certain value, being so early."

"You think it's genuine, then?"

Frank seemed surprised. "Oh, it's indubitably genuine. That's the old Howland house in Manchester. Aunt Millicent still lives in it."

I was delighted at this unexpected authentication and rose to take my leave. Frank accompanied me politely to the lobby and promised to telephone to the warehouse where his pictures were kept that same afternoon. I was launched on my enterprise.

I was relieved to find, the following day, that Frank had no intention of escorting me and that I was to be allowed to view the Howlands there alone. There were some fifty of them, mostly of the Paris period, for I gathered that in the final division Miss Howland had selected from the Caribbean years while her brother (Frank's father) had been content with the French.

They were certainly very charming. Ranging them about the little room assigned to my use, I had a delicious sense of lightness and ease, almost of gaiety. Flowers and white dresses and marble benches, ponds and lily pads and willow trees, usually under a noon sun, came together and apart again in my dazzled vision. It was difficult to distinguish the flagstones on the path from the light border of dry grass, the red of a hat from the red of poppies, the green of an emerald from the green of shutters. Howland made you want to shade your eyes, to yawn pleasantly, to go inside for a cold lunch and a bottle of dry white wine. The preoccupation with his own villa and his own gardens bespoke a civilized man, a contented man, no doubt a charming man. One did not imagine that he had had much in common with the rough artists of Bohemian Paris. I remembered hearing that his only friends among painters had been Sargent and Mary Cassatt.

Sitting in that room I tried to put John Howland together. What had happened to the angry but guilt-ridden author of those journal pages? Had he buried these feelings in his art? Certainly they had not emerged in this Paris period. I thought of the glimpses I had had of him in the letters at the Guild library: tall and gray-clad and handsome, half-smiling, speaking with quiet deliberation, courteous, grave, formal, mingling in the company of other cultivated expatriates, exquisite in demeanor to his wife, affectionate with his children, intelligent, sensitive, but always uncommunicative about his art, always reserved. Had his youthful soul's rebellion been satisfied by recreating the light on flowers and pebbled streams?

At the hour that was Howland's favorite, twelve, my little room was very warm, and I raised the window. Turning back to the paintings I had a curious feeling. I had the distinct sensation, originating, of course, in the fact that I had placed them on every wall, closely side by side, of being enclosed by a gauze veil. Those brilliant flowers, those sweeping, diaphanous skirts and hats and curtains, those great encompassing willows, the dappled water of those ponds were not so much to *see* as to keep me *from* seeing. If I reached out a hand and plucked that veil aside, might I not behold a starker landscape? Might not there be one as dark and menacing as in the little water color that Frank Howland had tossed aside as juvenilia?

I telephoned to Miss Howland at Manchester, without seeing her nephew again, and accepted her warm invitation to spend the following night. I did not notify Frank Howland that I was going. I felt, no doubt unreasonably, that I could not bear to hear any more of his theorizing. I took a morning plane to Boston and a train to Manchester where Miss Howland met me herself in an ancient Packard limousine, spotless and gleaming red, with immaculate white-wall tires.

Miss Howland was a Boston "character," as lovingly cultivated and tended by friends and servants in this role as some dear old weather-beaten landmark might be painted and preserved by a proud citizenry. In a century of overpopulation, genocide and the bomb, Boston hung on desperately to its reminders of a better day. Miss Howland was a gnarled, stooped, white-haired old lady, aggressively clad in tweeds and shod in rubber-soled shoes, with a splendid lined brown face and pale eyes looming over a huge nose that seemed like a caricature of her nephew's.

"You must be the art man," she shouted from her back-seat window at me. "You have that look of expecting not to be met. Jump in!"

On the way to the house she chattered away without the least regard for any of my murmured responses.

"I'm glad that someone of your generation is coming around at last to an appreciation of Pa. That you're not all of you dedicated to the junk yard. I sometimes wonder if the blessed Cézanne himself came back to earth, if he wouldn't be turned away at the inn. All you young people today, you have it too soft. If you want to be painters, you get scholarships and go gallivanting about Europe. Everyone approves of anything you do. You don't have to fight or learn technique. You don't know what it is to be hungry!"

We were proceeding now down a long driveway, past huge lilac bushes and rhododendrons, toward a large, shapeless shingle house with an octagonal tower. My heart leaped up as I recognized it.

"Surely your father had no money worries?" I could not help but interject.

"Not after he married my mother," Miss Howland retorted with the perfunctory wink of the dutiful iconoclast.

"But even before?"

"Well, not in the basic sense, no," she conceded, irritated by my persistence. "Pa never had to worry where his next meal was coming from. But meals aren't everything. He had to face the iron resistance of a family who couldn't understand how a gentleman could be a painter. Mind you, it was good for him! That was the crucible out of which a great artist was forged. The clash of wills! My grandfather, God bless him, loathed art. He had the character to pound the table and demand that his son go to work respectably in State Street. And his son had the guts to say: 'To hell with you. I'm going to Paris.' They were both *men,* you see, Mr. Jordan. Grandpa wasn't one of your namby-pamby tolerant modern fathers who don't know Jean Jacques Rousseau from Théodore but who think they must support their white-blooded sons in a bit of daubing because the boys are scared of competition in the business world!"

I reminded myself of the journal in my possession and wondered where Miss Howland had learned of this strong-willed grandsire. Or was it just the way women tend to visualize their grandfathers, as Jovean, thunderbolt hurling?

"Did your mother like painting?"

"Never." Miss Howland was positive of this. "Not to her dying day. But she never said so. Oh, no! She was simply silent about it. It was her John's 'little weakness,' never to be mentioned. This was harder, of course, than Grandfather's opposition, for Mother was always ailing, and Papa was an angel to her. Only after she died could he get away to the real liberation, the final freedom."

"And that was the Caribbean?"

"And that was the Caribbean," she repeated heartily. "That

was Pa's end and his beginning. That was where he found his soul at last. In color, in fire, in water, in primitive things. He had come a long way from Beacon Street!"

"Did you accompany him on any of his cruises?"

"Wouldn't I have given my eye teeth!" Miss Howland exclaimed, slapping her knee. "But a fat chance I had, a woman, being taken where *he* wanted to go. No, those were strictly male excursions, if you know what I mean, Mr. Jordan, and I have no reason to think you don't. Father, if it won't embarrass you to hear it, was very much a man, right up to the end." She paused, to give full effect to this ultimate sample of her iconoclasm. "He kept an Indian girl on board *The Wanderer*."

"Really?" It irritated me that I should be blushing to the tips of my ears. "Did he ever paint her?"

"He did. Or perhaps I should say he sketched her."

"And you have the sketches?"

"I have."

"Will you show them to me?"

Miss Howland became inscrutable. "That depends on how we get on," she said mysteriously. "And what I finally decide you're capable of, young man."

We were at the house now, and I was taken up to my room overlooking a white-capped sea. Happy to be alone again, I stood by the window and thought of Howland in his Caribbean phase as he appeared in the memoirs of his friend Winthrop Van Buren, which I had just been reading: the beginning-to-be-venerable sailor in spotless white, with a captain's cap, a pipe always clenched between his teeth, a goatee now on his chin, roaming on his beautiful schooner from island to island, and reporting to his many correspondents, in lucid, faultless prose, on the flora and fauna, on the natives and customs, on his own philosophic reactions to the spectacle of a simpler culture. An Indian woman on board? I could hardly believe it. If Howland had had any feelings for anyone on *The Wanderer,* it might have been for the young second mate, the beautiful Jamaican boy of mixed ancestry, whose yellowish skin and golden brown hair and empty brooding eyes, painted over and over again by his master, made him seem a latter day Antinous.

"What about Alistair Jones?" I asked Miss Howland when I came downstairs, for such had been the boy's name. "Have you any sketches of him?"

Miss Howland gave a snort, but did not answer my question. "That old rotter," she said. "I had a letter from him only last week. Asking for money, of course."

"You mean, he's still alive?"

"Certainly, he's still alive, Mr. Jordan. Why shouldn't he be? He's younger than I."

I decided to probe no further. What did I want to find out, anyway? I had my own surmise. Miss Howland pretended to a certain broadmindedness, but I knew enough of "characters" to know their limitations. She was perfectly willing to give her father a mistress, to invent one, if need be, but that was as far as she would go. With the reporters, the society columnists, the authors of popular books on Boston, all of whom she professed to despise, she would dance out her little public dance to celebrate the myth that there *had* been a past, that titans *had* existed. Had I not seen her in tabloid after tabloid staring out benignly at the reading public like a landmark which has come to believe that tourists exist only for it? Truth, truth, who cared for truth?

"The pictures are all set out in the billiard room," she told me gruffly. "I'll leave you to them."

I spent my afternoon alone with some sixty Howlands, mostly of the final period. It was a curious, uncomfortable couple of hours. As in the warehouse, I found it stifling to be in the presence of so many Howlands. It was as if at window after window a slender, ivory, blue-veined hand had reached out to pull a curtain across my view, a beautiful curtain, to be sure, a splendid decoration, but still a curtain. I finally escaped to the adjoining chamber, which must have been John Howland's study, all leathery and book-lined, and tried to relax with a cigar. But here two more paintings, built into a panel, demanded my reluctant attention. With a sigh I went dutifully up to them.

They were dated 1913, the last year of his life. One was a landscape and one a seascape of Antigua, where he had died. They were a pair that had to be hung together, for one could follow the color scheme only by comparing them. Howland seemed to be trying to convey the sense of living on a small island, the feeling of the enormity of the sea and of the indispensability of the bit of land, by reversing the usual colors. Thus, the hills and woods were a sparkling blue and the sea a rich dark green, the crests of the waves were of brightest yellow and the clouds over the water a dirt red. It was striking and amusing, but it must have seemed more so in 1913 than in 1964. What caught my interest, in pictures so late, was the scrupulous finish of the details, the meticulous accuracy of the figures depicted. For there *were* figures depicted, that was the curious thing. In the very middle of the landscape there was a centaur, grazing in a tobacco field, and in the other a triton was blowing his horn!

The more I studied the pair, the more the curious idea stole over my mind that, except for the arresting unconventionality of the colors and their almost garish brightness, the balance of the execution suggested the Hudson River School. The romantic arrangement of sea, cliffs and reefs, the rather heavy drama of the distant panorama and the introduction of mythological creatures seemed to imply a nostalgia for the calm, bright, lucid days of academic painting. Had not the critics been misled by the pyrotechnics of Howland's later style into thinking that he was voyaging into the future whereas in fact the exact opposite was taking place? Howland at the end of his life was not looking forward to Braque and Derain; he was looking backward to Durand and Church.

Miss Howland and I dined alone that night, fortified by cocktails and wine. The old girl loved her drinks and became a bit thick of speech. I decided that this, if ever, was the time for franker talk and, feeling rather pleasantly fuzzy myself, I embarked on my new theory. For a long time she did not seem to follow me at all, but when she did she became suddenly furious.

"What do you know about painting to have an opinion so soon? You're nothing but a fresh kid! Go back to that notions store, or wherever you came from, and sell your trinkets till you learn respect for your elders and betters!"

This was so rude that I could say nothing at all, and we finished our meal in a dismal silence. Miss Howland, glassy-eyed, breathed heavily and hardly seemed aware of me. After dessert she stamped upstairs, and I retired to the library to spend a quiet if hardly a serene evening. I had assumed that my hostess had gone to bed and could only hope that she would not remember our conversation in the morning, but toward ten o'clock I heard her footsteps on the stairway, and she came in, in a huge red dressing gown and turban.

"Here, take this," she mumbled, thrusting a large portfolio of old leather into my hand. "Take it to bed with you, young man, and see if you can sleep. In the morning you can tell me if you still think my father was harking back in his last years to what Mrs. Wharton called the 'age of innocence.' Hah! These sketches are the *last* work he did!"

I followed her upstairs, and we parted at the landing without a word. In my own room, sitting up in the huge old mahogany double bed, with lamps on on either side, I examined the sketch book. It proved indeed a shock.

The sketches were frankly pornographic. They showed a

naked man and woman doing more things in more positions than I had ever visualized. Their activities were not limited to love-making in any conventional sense; they also embraced the dusky joys of self-humiliation and sadism. Yet the sketches, even at their most sophisticated, their most debauched, had some of the charm of Japanese drawings. The simple lines suggested the Picasso pencil-drawn bathers of the twenties; the figures had the naïveté of children at play, the innocence of a pre-fall Adam and Eve in a garden littered with apple cores and scandalized snakes. They were as sublime as they were depraved, as young as they were evilly old. And as always, when confronted by items of the first rank, I felt the watering of my auctioneer's mouth as well as the twitch of my critic's eye.

I was willingly consigning my whole theory of John Howland to the junk heap of would-be monographs and preparing in good spirit to bow to his daughter's now proven superior knowledge, when that same critic's eye, for all its dazzlement, noticed a peculiar thing. Between some of the pages jagged fragments of paper, near the binding, indicated that others had been torn out. Now why would Howland have removed pages from a sketch book? The very point of the latter is to keep a flowing, developing record of ideas and experiments. No, if pages had been ripped out, they had been ripped out by a later hand, but, again, why? Surely not because they had shocked the observer, for what could be more shocking than what had been left? And then I remembered Howland's bequest of his papers to the Painters' Guild and his executor's decision that these included only *writings*. Had the torn-out papers contained notes that were now at the Guild?

I jumped out of bed, hurried to my bag and slipped out my photostatic copies of the pages of Howland's journal. Taking them to the sketch book, I proceeded, with a slow, triumphant deliberation, to compare their ragged edges with those sticking out of the binding. They fitted, every one, like a picture puzzle.

I then examined the order of the pages and the ink. Was it conceivable that Howland had written the journal, as dated, in 1869, and, decades later, as an old man, drawn his erotic sketches on the remaining blank pages? It was not. Not only were the pages of the journal unevenly interspersed with the sketches, indicating that the book itself had been used for a double purpose, now for a thought, now for a sketch, as the owner's fancy dictated, but the ink used in the journal was the same hard black India used in the drawings. I had before me proof positive that the drawings as well as the text belonged to the *earliest,* not the latest, period of the artist's life.

I felt the thrill that always accompanies the realization that one's inner vision has corresponded with an outward reality. John Howland *had* started, artistically, at the peak of his power. The force of his inner resentments against the Boston of his early years had been sufficiently violent to fling his soul right into the twentieth century! He must have sketched his erotica in a private frenzy, perhaps in an effort to preserve his very sanity. But as the years had passed and as Boston and his family had given him no cause for taking the crimson glove of his hidden fury and dashing it in their calm, twinkling countenances, he must have begun to wonder at last if that fury was anything more than evil, if he were not a kind of devil to so abhor and abominate his poor sad, loving friends and relations. And then — did it not square with every account? — had he not become the conservative of the Paris period, the good Bostonian expatriate in every respect save in the single blemish of the paintbrush, living at Neuilly with his good wife and children as sedately as if he had been back in Needham or Dedham, finding in ceremony, in affability, in rigid habits the same protection from an intruding, violent world that his father had sought before him?

Oh, yes, had I not seen the Howland qualities of playing out with style the hammy roles which they believed inexorably assigned to them by a theater-loving destiny in Frank's pompous attitudinizing, in old Millicent's *enfant terrible?* Had I not read about the old grandfather in the journal? Surely these same qualities had been there to bend and break the genius of John, to drive him back from the future in which he had started to the impressionists with whom he was contemporary, and, finally, in his beautiful schooner, a white symbol of escape, to seek in the Caribbean the calm, the stateliness, the frozen silence of the academicians of his childhood. John Howland must have died like his father, with the answer on his lips: "I beg your pardon?" to the question of the universe.

I fell asleep at last, wondering how best to tell Miss Howland in the morning.

She came down, the old dragon, to breakfast, in the big paneled dining room, looking out on a black Atlantic. The walls were covered with alarming marine specimens and the oars of Howlands who had stroked victorious Harvard crews. Behind her chair were two dark oval portraits with eyes as glassy as those of the fish.

"Well, were those sketches strong enough for you?" she began heartily. "I suppose they're not the kind of thing to show a young man when he's cooped up in a house where even the kitchen maid's over sixty!" Miss Howland winked broadly at the impassive old waitress who was serving her coffee. "You will have to admit *now* that my father kept his interests alive to a very belated hour."

"I have no doubt that he did," I purported to concede. "But if he had interests in his later years, isn't it natural to assume that he had even more in his early ones?"

"Yes, yes, of course, *interests,*" she grumbled. "But they couldn't be more than that until he'd broken away. That's what I keep telling you. Your generation can't conceive what life in a proper Boston household was like. Take a look at my Howland grandparents behind me. Do you think anything much could have gone on while my father was living with *them?*"

I stared up now at the oval portraits, taking them in for the first time. They were actually a rather handsome pair, my painter's parents, he fair and slender, she, dark and meek, but I found myself agreeing with their granddaughter that in their paleness, in the furtiveness of their subdued expressions, in the very quantity of their expensive apparel, there might exist a gentle naïveté before which impure thoughts would scuttle like mice. And then, as I thought this, undoubtedly *because* I thought this, I found myself trying to remember where I had seen, under somewhat different circumstances, a woman's hair-do, as in an Ingres, pulled straight back and parted in the middle, and a man's long curly locks falling romantically half across his high forehead . . .

"No, I must say, I do not," I stammered. "I do not think anything at all would have gone on in your grandparents' household."

I bent over my coffee cup in confusion. For what I had discovered in that blinding moment was that the erotic couple of the sketches was none other than the pair before me in the oval portraits! The hair styles made it only too clear. Miss Howland *thought* she could accept a good deal of truth about her father, but there was a vast difference between what she liked proudly to consider as an old man's erotic memories, based on a magnificent life of amorous experiment, and a neurotic, frustrated young man's psychic revenge on his father and mother. I dared not risk the effect of this truth on her. For the juxtaposition of the journal and the sketches, the former savagely detailing the observed activities of the writer's parents: going to church, going on bird walks, attending family gatherings, and the latter showing them, so *differently* occupied, made it obvious what their son's satirical intent had been. It had been to contrast the outward propriety of their "egos" with what Freud might have later called the fantasy riots of their "ids," to compare their gentle benignity and sanctimoniousness with the denied itchings of their skin.

"And you will correct your monograph or whatever you call it," continued my inexorable hostess, "to show the proper progression of John Howland toward this last, this total freedom?"

"If I write it at all," I murmured.

"What do you mean by that?"

"Well, I don't suppose you will let me reproduce those sketches?"

She stared at me, recognizing the difficulty. "No, I don't suppose I can," she conceded with a grunt. "Not in my lifetime, anyway. Even Millicent Howland has her limits. But you may refer to them, if you wish. And I will bequeath them to the Fogg Art Museum to be shown to students only. I suppose there'll be a lot of people pretending to be students to get in, but I can't help that."

This particular problem of administration never arose for the Fogg, for when Miss Howland died, two years afterwards, the sketch book was not to be found. I went up to Boston to tell her executors about it, and a thorough search of the house was made, but to no avail. One of the maids said that she remembered Miss Howland burning some papers in the dining room fireplace, but no other evidence turned up.

Had she finally made the identification of that busy couple herself? Was that the reason that she chose to burn it in the dining room, as a sacrifice before the portraits of her wronged grandparents? Or was it simply the final triumph of the Howlands over her, the fear of facing in another sphere the creator of their apprehensions, having left evidence on earth of her father's early defiance of him? In any event my dream of ultimately marrying the text and the sketches was over. It was a pity, for it might have saved the artistic reputation of John Howland. Poor Frank has most of his collection still on his hands. It does not look as if he will make now the fortune that he needs to buy Watteau and Fragonard.

Collector of Innocents

PERKINS GODLEY was probably the last man in the world whom I would have expected to find in the display galleries at Philip Hone & Sons, yet in the winter of 1960 he appeared there frequently enough to make me wonder if he might not be harboring visions of becoming a collector. Mrs. Godley, who, as people said, had "had all the money," had recently died, and there had been talk of his "behaving badly" about the will, so it was possible that the old boy had got his hands on some real cash at last. But I could not imagine what a person like that would want to buy. Would he see any difference between a dead fish held aloft in a photograph of himself at his Maine fishing club and a dead fish in a still life by Courbet?

I had known him way back, in the years just before the war, when his three daughters were debutantes, and there always seemed to be some kind of a party going in the Godleys' big house on Seventieth Street. Yet Godley himself was very much on the periphery of these, and the young men who came to the house paid scant attention to him. I had somewhat better manners and made an occasional point of talking to him after a dinner party over the brandy, but although he was always perfectly agreeable, he would take my attention as much for granted as another's indifference and drag out, for my edification, some tired old anti-Roosevelt story that he would relate, quite without conviction (for what did he, comfortably supported, care about taxes?) simply because he thought it the thing to tell the younger and presumably radical generation.

His face, seen now at Hone's, had changed very little in

twenty years. At seventy-five it was the same boyish, unwrinkled, perfunctorily grinning, kindly-eyed host's mask, surrounded by the same high bald dome and flanked by the same long gray hair. But age showed badly in his carriage and his voice. Once tall, thin and straight, he was now long and bent, moving very jerkily with the aid of a cane, and his voice, when he called an attendant or hailed a friend, was embarrassingly loud and somehow irrelevantly hearty. He seemed to be trying to put feeling into his words, not because there was feeling in his heart or even because he wanted his hearer to think so, but simply because his role as an old club man and diner-out seemed to call for it. It was as if he had been given a part to read at a rapid "run through" of a play in a green room.

My interest in him increased one morning when he sat in the ottoman in the middle of the painting gallery for a solid hour contemplating a single picture. It was a small portrait, a "School of Holbein," of a sixteen-year-old lad. I mention the age because the portrait did: "Matthew Pole: Aetatis suae Anno XVI." The face had great charm, despite the fact that, in Holbein's manner, it was shaped like a shield and dropped into a tiny chin. The skin was very white and the large eyes a brooding distant gray, as if this grave boy was looking steadily ahead to the terrible destiny that awaited him. His blouse was of gold thread, his tunic of the richest scarlet, and the tapering fingers of the right hand that held the belted dagger bore heavy sapphire and ruby rings. There was no background, but had a window been opened to the sky I am sure it would have revealed a bright, cloudless Tudor sky. It was an age when men did terrible things and accepted terrible things, unblinkingly.

I went over at last to the ottoman and introduced myself. Mr. Godley sprang into motion with a great deal of jerking and expostulating, but for all his polite insistence to the contrary, it was obvious that he had no recollection of me. However, it hardly mattered. I was sure he remembered none of his daughters' friends.

"Would you like the estimate?" I asked, pointing to the portrait.

"Oh, good heavens, it's obviously way beyond *my* poor means. Why, surely it's a museum piece!"

"It would be, if it were a Holbein. But it's more probably a Luchen."

Mr. Godley looked blank, so I explained that Luchen was an apprentice who had accompanied the master to London and died there of the plague. He gave an exclamation of immediate delight, noticeably more genuine than his others.

"Then I might get it, after all! Imagine caring if it's a Holbein or a Luchen. Isn't it the boy that counts?"

"You mean the painting itself?"

"No, I mean the boy!" He seemed perplexed at the distinction, if indeed there was one. "Isn't he absolutely beautiful?"

"He *is* charming, isn't he?" I agreed, a bit surprised by such enthusiasm. "One hates to think of what happened to him."

"Ah, something *did* happen to him, then?" Godley's eagerness struck me as almost indecent. "I was sure of it. Tell me, did he die young?"

"He perished on the scaffold," I replied, "only two years after the portrait was painted, in 1541. He and his grandmother, the Countess of Salisbury, were beheaded the same day in the Tower. They held hands as they prayed aloud."

"What had they done?"

"Nothing. Except to have York blood in their veins. Henry the Eighth, like a Roman emperor, believed in butchering the royal family. He wanted *his* boy to stand alone."

Godley seemed lost in wonder now as he resumed his contemplation of young Pole. "That fits, then," he said. "I don't like them to grow up."

"Them?"

He smiled as he took in my confusion. "I mean the people in my collection. They're all young, you see."

"The subjects?"

"Yes, of course, the subjects. They're all young people, boys and girls."

"Who never grew up?"

"Well, who never grew up into *bad* people," he qualified in all seriousness. "Suppose Pole here, for example, had grown up into someone like his pig-eyed cousin, the King? Supposing he had become king himself and sent a dear old lady and her grandson to the block? Would you want his likeness on your wall?"

I did not quite know how to answer this. "Oh, I don't think he would have," I hedged.

"You don't *think* he would have, no," Godley retorted earnestly. "But can you be sure? My dear fellow, of course, you can't. Why, Henry the Eighth himself was supposed to have been a charming youth. That is why, in some periods, it's better if they die young. Then those beautiful eyes can never become pig's eyes."

"But are all the subjects of your pictures identifiable?" I pursued in astonishment. "Surely, some of them are simply models?"

"Well, if they're models, of course, one doesn't know what happened to them, and so one doesn't care."

"But if," I continued, intrigued now, "you happened by chance to discover that one of them *had* grown up to be wicked?"

"Oh, out he'd go!" Godley exclaimed with a gesture of prompt dismissal.

We talked a bit more of his novel theory of art collecting, and then he accompanied me to my office where he left a bid for the Luchen-Holbein. Evidently, few dealers or collectors shared his enthusiasm for the subject's personal appearance, and Godley got his painting for a song.

That was the winter I was taken, after a three-year wait, into the coveted Arts & Letters Club, and was able now to lunch at the long table in the baroque dining room with the first wits of the town. It surprised me considerably to find Perkins Godley a member. It surprised me even more to discover that he was treasurer of the club, lived in the clubhouse and frequently sat at the end of the long table in the place of honor. I listened carefully to discover what gifts of subtlety or erudition, hitherto unmarked by me, entitled him to such pre-eminence, but he seemed as banal as ever. Smiling, earnest, with his dry, pleasant, impersonal manner and in the loud voice of the slightly deaf, he would ask the most obvious questions of the most important men. Nothing stopped him. I believe he would have asked Shakespeare if Hamlet had been really mad and Leonardo da Vinci what Mona Lisa was smiling about. And the big men took it like lambs. "I'm glad you asked that question, Perkins," they would say, and then come up, as like as not, with some astonishing new revelation. Indeed, traveling through history with Godley, one might have got a straight answer out of the Delphic Oracle!

I found that I was not the only member who was mystified by Perkins' popularity. One of those wretched creatures who could always be found in the bar (even a literary club, alas, is no stronger than its weakest bar fly), a rambling, buttonholing, gossiping, cheaply cynical name dropper, whose own name I could never remember and whose watery face I kept trying to forget, explained it to me this way:

"Godley is not a bore; he's a tradition, and traditions are sacred here, like the rusty water in the third-floor lavatory and the kitchen smell in the bar. He got in during the depression, when memberships were going begging, and he had the sense to hang on. The trouble with intellectuals is that they haven't the guts to hurt a man's feelings. Everyone considers it a sacred duty to let old Godley talk his ear off. Small wonder he lives here. Nobody would put up with his idiotic stories at home!"

There was more than a grain of truth in this last remark. When I had first known Godley, it had been all too evident that his wife and daughters merely tolerated his existence. I remembered the former as a large, bland, hospitable woman, with a deep voice, and the girls as being like her in girth if higher in tone. I even remembered Mrs. Godley's old mother, from whom the money had reputedly come — from distaff, so to speak, to distaff — as shrill and shrunken but still, in her own squeaking way, suggesting former grandeurs, former hospitalities, so that one's net impression of the rather shadowy host at the end of that ample board was of a silent and rather depleted rooster in a barnyard of cackling hens. Indeed, the only personal possession of Perkins Godley's that I could recall in those crowded chambers was a Zelidov portrait of his later mother, the great actress Alida Kay, in her favorite role of Lady Teazle. Even in his own family, apparently, the female of the species had worn the peacock's tail.

The bar fly now remorselessly filled in the gaps of poor Godley's biography. He had been the sole issue of that tempestuous lady and of some dim, long-forgotten, blue-blooded stage-door Johnnie whom she had briefly married and permanently bankrupted. She had left Godley nothing but the brief, boyish good looks which had secured him the plump white hand of an heiress and a lifelong job of drudgery in the bank that handled her money. But on his wife's recent death, it seemed, our worm had turned. He had spurned his annuity and claimed his widower's third of the estate. True, most of the fortune had been safely tied up in trust, but he had still got his hands on capital that he could spend and *was* spending, on art, of all things! The daughters had been scandalized. There had been a general feeling that Perkins Godley had behaved like a cad. The bar fly here became incoherent with laughter over his story, whether at Godley or the daughters I could not be sure, and I left him, ashamed at having listened so carefully to such a source.

That afternoon I was reading in the library of the Arts & Letters when Godley came over to me.

"You have a briefcase," he said, pointing down to where it rested by my feet.

I nodded. It contained an important letter of Lord Byron's that I had just picked up from a dealer, and I dared not let it out of my sight.

"Bylaw Nineteen has evidently slipped your mind, my dear fellow: 'No business may be discussed by members on the club premises, and all papers and briefcases must be left in the cloakroom.' "

I stared in astonishment that any member should enforce so archaic a rule. But Godley was entirely serious, if perfectly discreet. He might have been calling my attention to a bit of lettuce on my chin. I explained about the Byron letter.

"The rule does not mention any exceptions," he said with a frown of mild perplexity. "But I tell you what we'll do. Let's leave the briefcase with the cashier. There it will be quite safe."

He accompanied me downstairs and took it upon himself to impress the old cashier with the value of the property so deposited. Then, apparently to make amends for what a younger member might consider his officiousness, he offered me a drink.

"Well, it's a bit early for that, if you don't mind," I told him. "But I'd love to see your collection. I understand you keep it in your room here."

It appeared that I had said the right thing, for the old boy became positively radiant.

"My dear fellow, I should love it of all things!"

On the top floor of the clubhouse Godley had a back room, full of heavy mahogany bedroom furniture, including a Victorian marble washstand. In this incongruous atmosphere and aided only by three bare light bulbs dangling from a cord in the middle of the ceiling, I proceeded to examine the extraordinary collection that covered the rather dirty white walls.

"It's a funny place for a gallery," he apologized, "but where else would I see them as much?"

"Where indeed?" I murmured, lost in contemplation.

It took me only a few minutes to pick out the best. There was a Renoir portrait of a little girl in a broad-brimmed hat with big staring eyes, a Mary Cassatt of a little girl in a broad-brimmed hat with sullen, staring eyes, a small Greek marble statue of a nude boy (on the washstand!) and an Ingres drawing of a young soldier whose grave impassive stare made one almost certain that he had died young on a battlefield. But mixed in with these treasures was a great clutter of much less impressive stuff, verging here and there on the cloyingly sentimental: a Landseer of a little boy hugging a terrier, a Gertrude Vanderbilt Whitney of a rebellious girl, overdressed for a party; a dubious American primitive of children weeping by a mother's tomb. I wondered if the presence of the good things was anything more than a coincidence. Yet, as he obviously had money, what a client he might make — with *my* guidance!

"We've just got in a little Moro of the Infanta Maria Isabella," I observed hopefully. "It's an enchanting thing. Why don't you drop in tomorrow and have a look?"

"I've been!" Godley exclaimed. "I saw her yesterday, and I agree she's peerless! But I've looked her up. That's what I was doing just now in the library."

"Oh, did she survive?" I asked, remembering now the indispensable qualification.

"Unhappily, she did. And became Governor of the Lowlands, where she was known for her repressive policies. When she returned to Spain, it is even recorded that she never missed an auto-da-fé!"

"I see she'll never do," I agreed with a smile. "I must keep an eye out for the little princes in the tower."

"Oh, I have them, in storage, by Alma-Tadema, asleep in each other's arms, with a fiend coming in the door." Godley's eyes shone with pride. "But do, please, keep an eye out for other things. I'm here all the time, and I can run up to Hone's in five minutes. I'd deem it the greatest of favors."

Not long after this, a daughter of Basil Zelidov, the rival of Sargent and Boldini among portraitists of the *belle epoque,* died in poverty, and the administrator of her few poor effects asked me to look over some pictures of her father's that she had stacked in a closet of her two-room apartment on West Nineteenth Street. They were a dusty, dreary lot, mostly unfinished portraits of society ladies that had probably not been flattering enough, or rather poor water colors of yachts and summer cottages, but I did find one superb thing, a small oil study of a beautiful boy. It was sentimental, of course, like all of Zelidov's work; he was wearing a sailor suit and holding a toy battleship, and at his feet, on a polar bear's skin, curled up by the open mouth and harmless bared teeth of the poor beast's stuffed head, slept a little Pekinese. But the boy's blond hair and blue eyes, his radiant smile and air of dimpled innocence, suggested Sir Thomas Lawrence at his best or even the great Gainsborough himself. It was a work where genius crashed through bathos. And it reminded me strangely of somebody — I could not think whom.

I told the administrator that I would sell it for him, and it was sent up to the gallery. When it arrived, I had it placed in my office on an easel, as I sometimes did with particularly interesting pictures, to "live with it" for a couple of days. It was not until the afternoon of the second day that I realized of whom the boy's curiously uncommitted eyes reminded me.

I called him up at once. "Don't I remember a portrait of your mother as Lady Teazle by Basil Zelidov?" I demanded.

"Yes, it belongs to my daughter Alida now. Don't tell me she's peddling it at Hone's!"

"No, no. But is it possible that he did one of you at the same time?"

The pause that followed was so long that I repeated the question.

"Yes," he replied at last in a rather faint tone. "Have you seen it?"

"It's right here in my office. And a beauty, too. Won't you come down and have a look at it? It's tailor-made for your collection. A Godley for the Godley!"

He seemed to shove this aside as irrelevant, even as a rather cheap attempt at humor. "But where has it *been* all these years?" he demanded.

"In Zelidov's studio, I suppose. His daughter had it when she died."

I heard some heavy crackling over the wire, as if he were laughing or even crying. Or perhaps, I thought, in sudden horror, having a stroke!

"Are you all right?" I cried.

"My dear fellow, you must forgive me. I'm not myself today."

He hung up, and I hurried around to the Arts & Letters where I was much relieved to find him standing up at the bar. He was holding a long dark glass from which he took rapid sips. He seemed embarrassed at my solicitude and led me to a corner table where we could be alone.

"You're very good, dear fellow, but I'm quite all right now."

He smiled benignantly and pulled a cigar from his pocket. "You must have thought I was crazy. Shall I tell you the story of how Zelidov happened to do that portrait?"

"I think you'd better, after scaring me half to death!"

There was a curious expression on his face as he paused to light his cigar, very slowly and carefully, with a good deal of expert puffing and wheezing. But before he had finished these preparations, or even started his tale, I thought I had diagnosed the expression as simple nostalgia. The memory that he was about to evoke was evidently a tender one, and I had never seen him tender before.

"When Zelidov was commissioned to do Mamma's portrait," he began, "it was understood that he should do it at the house. Mamma considered herself far too grand to go to a studio. I was never allowed in the parlor, where she sat for him, but one afternoon, when she had a matinee, I stole in to have a peek at the picture. Unfortunately, Zelidov was there alone, working on it, and, before I could escape, he demanded in a booming tone what I wanted. I ran away, terrified, but he ran after me and caught me, plumped me up on the piano and proceeded to ask me a stream of questions: who I was, where I went to school, and so forth. He was a big man, very formidable, with a bushy beard and what even then I could see were the friendliest blue eyes. It may sound ridiculous, but we became friends. Real friends. Afterwards, I always went in when he was working on some part of the picture that didn't require Mamma. He used to roar with laughter when I recited bits and pieces of her roles that I had picked up: 'Come to my woman's breasts and take my milk for gall, you murth'ring ministers!' or 'Good Hamlet, cast thy nighted color off.' He would thunder back at me in Italian or Russian, I don't know which, and we would have a terrific time. And then one day he did that little picture of me. I think he must have dashed it off in an afternoon!"

"Did your mother see it?"

Godley's clear brow became puckered with three small lines. "Oh, yes, that's the story. Mamma was very angry. She thought Zelidov was pulling a fast one. 'You were commissioned to do *my* portrait, Monsieur Zelidov,' she told him in what people used to call her 'Mrs. Siddons's' voice. 'If you expect me to pay for two, you are very much mistaken.' Zelidov should have told her that if he were paid for one, he would be quite content, but I guess he didn't know then about Mamma and bills. He drew himself up very straight, like a grand duke and thundered: 'Madame, the portrait of Perkeens (that was how he pronounced my name) belongs to nobody but Perkeens. It is a geeft. The only *free* Zelidov in the world!' "

"So it *is* yours."

"Wait," Godley cautioned me, holding up a hand. "Mamma became very gracious at this. After all, it was something to have two Zelidovs for the price of one, and when his portrait was finished she hung both in the dining room where they were much admired. But I think it must have irked her that mine was admired the most. When Zelidov's bill, like so many others, was not paid, and he called in icy dignity to demand back the portrait, Mamma offered him mine instead. Well, do you know he jumped at it! And then he must have remembered his gift to me, for he insisted that I ratify the transaction. I was summoned, awe-stricken, to the parlor and asked by my friend, in the terrifying presence of Mamma, if I would relinquish my 'title' to the portrait."

"But did you understand what was going on?"

"All I understood was that my new friend wanted to keep my picture, and that was all I cared about. You may find that sentimental, but I had never had a friend before. As a matter of fact, I haven't had as good a one since." Godley's tone was extraordinary. It was purely and simply matter-of-fact. It bore not the faintest detectable trace of self-pity, of bitterness, even of self-dramatization. "Oh, I remember that moment as if it was yesterday! Much better, in fact. I went up to him and put my hand in his and said: 'Mr. Zelidov, I will be proud to have my picture in your studio!' "

"And there it has been ever since," I remarked, moved by his tale. "At least until he died. He must have remembered that day, too."

"That is what caused me my shock this morning," Godley continued with a puzzled shake of his head. "I suppose one of those psychiatrist chaps would say I had uncovered a repressed experience. Except I never repressed it. I simply had always assumed that he would have sold it."

"But why?"

"Because when he left that day, Mamma pointed out that he had not chosen it because it was a portrait of *me*. He had taken it, she said, because it was the more valuable of the two."

"And you believed her?" I asked in horror.

"Of course, I believed her. Mamma was always a realist, and, as I grew older, I saw that it made perfect sense. *Her* portrait was too big, too flamboyant, too special, for anyone but Mamma to buy. Besides it was a bad Zelidov. Whereas mine was not only a good one; it was small and decorative. Everyone likes pictures of children, even of children who aren't their own. Look at me, for example!"

"And yet he didn't sell it," I insisted fiercely, as angry with his old bitch of a mother as if she had not been dead for forty years. "He didn't sell it, even as an old man, when he was bust. I suggest he had *two* reasons for taking it instead of your mother's. One, that he, too, valued the friendship. And secondly, because he knew your mother would have sold it herself at the first opportunity!"

Godley's face became inscrutable, and for several moments he was silent. But I had the distinct impression that some violent emotion was brewing within. At last I thought I could make out a gathering excitement in his eyes.

"Tell me something, my dear fellow," he said quietly, but with a noticeable tremor in his tone. "I suppose that painting is still available?"

"It's in my office for appraisal. You can buy it directly from the estate, if you want."

"Have you any idea what it might fetch?"

"Well, nothing for a man who can buy Holbeins! Shall I tell them you want it?"

He clapped his hands in the air as he gave vent now to his pent-up excitement. "Want it? My dear fellow, I've *got* to have it! Don't you see that portrait is everything I've been trying to express?"

"You mean as a collector?"

"Of course, as a collecter. And as a person! What is a man, my dear fellow, but his own childhood?"

"Unless, as you say, he grows up."

He stared. "Grows up?"

"I mean yourself. You survived."

I saw how wrong I was as soon as I had said it, and Godley at once took in that I *had* seen it, for he simply coughed and looked down at the floor without bothering to explain. I would not have to spend another day in my office with the Zelidov to know what I now knew. Survived? Of course, he had not survived! That radiant child had died as surely as if a Tudor ax had been swung over his crouching figure and crashed down on the bare back of his extended neck.

The Money Juggler

WE HAD, the four of us, two things in common: we were all members of the Columbia class of 1940, and we had bought or rented summer cottages in the Hamptons on Long Island's southern shore.

Townie Drayton, as befitted a Wall Street broker and a Drayton, lived in Southampton; Hilary Knowles, as a popular columnist of manners, good and bad, who had to thread his precarious way between the artistic and the ultrafashionable, rented in East Hampton; and John Grau, a hard-working corporation lawyer who came to the Island only to relax, exercise and see his family, preferred the comparative simplicity of Westhampton. I, vice-president of an auction gallery in the city which collected its treasure hoard from the estates of decedents in all the Hamptons, owned a small, weather-beaten shingle cottage in neutral Amagansett which did not boast a single object that could remind me of those that poured through the doors of Philip Hone & Sons during the eleven other months of the year.

We had been closer friends at college than we were now; indeed, the past was the only real reason for our annual summer reunion at the Dune Club where, after a Saturday morning's eighteen holes, we would sit on the veranda overlooking the ocean and the slapping breakers and drink many rounds of gin. We must have enjoyed ourselves, for we rarely lunched before three, talking with the easy familiarity and bluntness that had characterized our younger days. I believe that the charm of these sessions lay in the very fact that we were no longer intimate, so that our stories evoked a past that had not been blurred by constant familiarity. It was an added advantage that, living so near to each other, our gatherings had none of the forced hilarity of a college reunion.

The great event that had occurred between the summer of 1965 and its predecessor was the failure and flight from justice of our classmate Lester Gordon, the "boy wonder" (if one could still be that at forty-seven) who had made fortunes in one enterprise after another — real estate, magazines, the stock market — only, at what had seemed the apex of a career of miracles, to plummet, a cherub (which he always a bit resembled) from a golden heaven to a most bankrupt hell. Needless to say, such a fall aroused the most complacent feelings in the hearts of those who had envied him, and there were four such hearts around the table at the Dune Club that day.

Hilary Knowles now regretted his friendship with Lester. "How can I write a really candid column about a friend in trouble?" he asked with a moan. "And yet it's the perfect story of our time, tailor-made for my space, a bright, jingling morality tale. Think of it! Everything about Lester was what we were told as children to distrust: he was too glib, too smiling, too quick. He was all glitter and no substance, all hands and fingers and no soul. Do you remember how he was at college: round and ruddy-faced with that thick curly hair and those ghastly shirts and ties, pushing, giggling, unsnubbable? You couldn't get rid of Lester; he stuck like glue. Until he had what he wanted. And then, when he used you as a ladder, he moved so lightly you hardly felt the foot on your face. Aren't we all the better for his fall? The church bells can ring out bravely again, and we can stroll down Main Street in our Sunday best. God *is* in His heaven, and all's right downtown!"

I don't think any of the rest of us would have placed much money on the proposition that Hilary was *not* going to write that column. It seemed to me that it was half done already. Hilary was as thin and sleek and dark as he had been at college, but he was more hirsute; black bushes rustled under his red silk sport shirt, and his sharp, feral countenance was a closely shaven blue. His language was precise, his accent affected, his gestures on the verge of the effeminate. Yet he considered himself irresistible to women, and according to what I heard about him, fatuity must have been half the battle with the fair sex in East Hampton. He had had three famously beautiful wives.

"Lester Gordon was a kind of one-man inflation," Townie Drayton observed. "Almost a one-man revolution. By driving up prices and destroying old values he could make the wealth of the whole community change hands. And in the turnover, of course, Lester would come out on top. Before we knew it, there he was in every club, on every board of trustees, in control of the old institutions, making one welcome in one's own backyard ——"

"Even marrying a Drayton," Hilary interrupted, and we all laughed, for Lester Gordon had married a cousin of Townie's.

"Well, exactly," Townie agreed in all seriousness. "I don't mean to sound overly snobbish, but when I first met Lester at Columbia, I certainly never expected to see *that* in my family."

Townie had only joined us in Columbia after he had been fired from Yale for taking all the radiator caps off the cars parked outside Wolsey Hall on a concert night. He had been one of the handsomest members of our class, but those fine youthful looks had long been buried in the heavy flesh of his middle years. His glassy gray eyes, thick lips and broad aquiline nose would have seemed as coarse as his bulky figure, had it not been for a certain decadent imperial air, the flash of a Caesar, a Nero. Townie, after the Yale escapade, had tried to alter his ways and had tended to pooh-pooh his old Manhattan lineage and land, but as life had developed neither his brains nor his imagination, and had swelled only his girth and the value of his earth, he had come to lean more frankly on these once nominally discredited assets.

"I think that what we all really resent in Lester," John Grau suggested, "is that he understood the heart of our world so much better than we did. Don't you remember his total indifference to the causes that interested us before the war: communism, socialism, pacifism? It wasn't really even indifference; those things actually had no existence for him. What he saw and all he saw was the innate toughness of the capitalist system."

"Oh, come now, John," Townie protested. "There were plenty of us who believed in capitalism, even back in the blackest days of the depression."

"No, Townie, you don't see what I mean," John insisted, in his clear lawyer's voice. "You believed in it, but you didn't believe it would endure. I remember distinctly, when you were first kind enough to ask me to visit your family on Long Island, and we went to some of those fabulous debutante parties, your friends would always say the same thing. As soon as they caught sight of the marquee, the lanterns, the two orchestras, they would exclaim: 'End of an era!' That was the cry to everything, half laughingly, half seriously: 'End of an era!' If I had predicted, in 1938, that, in twenty years' time, the two gubernatorial candidates in New York would be a Rockefeller and a Harriman, each richer than ever before, I would have been laughed out of court. By everyone but Lester."

John Grau seemed at first blush older than the rest of us because his hair was gray. But except for this, which suited his sobriety, his gravity and the legend of his constant toil, he was in the best physical shape and the best-looking of the group. His wide brow, square firm face and broad shoulders gave a formidable backing to his vigorous language, and yet his intent gray-green eyes preserved an enthusiasm that was almost youthful. It was as if the idealist of college days had been better preserved in

John's cell of hard labor than in the more dissipated existences which the rest of us had led.

"Lester perfectly understood," John continued, now with a touch of bitterness, "the modern alliance between capital and labor to load the costs of private wealth and public welfare on the backs of the professional classes. He wasn't fool enough to become a lawyer like me."

"Oh, come, John, you do pretty well," Hilary pointed out. "If I were to tell you that your income would be under seventy-five grand this year, I bet you'd shriek bloody poverty."

"But look at the tax bracket I'm in!" John exclaimed indignantly. "What do you guys know about taxes? Townie here lives off capital gains and tax-exempts, while you, Hilary, swim in a sea of phony deductions."

"Boo hoo!" Hilary cried. "Let's weep for the destitute Wall Street lawyer!"

"Gentlemen, gentlemen," I remonstrated, "to hell with your taxes. Let's get back to Lester Gordon. I want to know much more about him. I want to know *why* this thing happened. What were his origins? So far as I'm concerned, he was born freshman year at Columbia. Do any of us know who his family were or even where he came from?"

"I do," replied Hilary, our always documented columnist. "I got it from his first wife, Huldah. Lester was born Felix Kinsky, the son of a Lithuanian haberdasher in Hamburg. His parents brought him here to escape the Nazis, and both died early. He lived in Queens with a cousin of his mother's, one David Gordon, originally Ginsberg, a minor building contractor. Lester took his guardian's name, or at least his new name, and later married his daughter. You can readily see from that much that he grew up without any of the usual commitments: religious, national or even family. His parents were orthodox Jews, but the Gordons were not, and Lester became a Gordon. He had no ties with Lithuania or Germany, and he took people literally when they described America as the land of opportunity. We four were inclined to be snotty to him at first, when he cultivated us at college. We considered ourselves the big shots of the class, and we didn't want to be cultivated for our big-shottiness. What fatuous asses we were! As if a man starting from scratch should not aim as high as he could!"

"Particularly when our usefulness only *began* at college," Townie added. "Lester made a very good thing out of every man at this table."

"Well, I don't know about me," I demurred. "He bought the usual 'chic' collection of impressionists at Hone's, but that was more our making a good thing out of *him*. You were the one, Townie, who gave him his real start. Tell us about it. Weren't you and Lester together in the war?"

"Just at the beginning," Townie replied, pausing to suck deeply on his cigar. "We were both in the Army Signal Corps and had adjoining desks in Washington. After Pearl Harbor everybody screamed for overseas duty, including Lester. But there are ways and ways of screaming, and it did not surprise me much, when I was shipped off, that he remained, as 'indispensable' to General Miles. Years later, in the Normandy invasion, I saw him again, a smart, blustering little lieutenant colonel, attached to some big brass well behind the lines. Oh, hell, I can't blame him for that." Townie seemed bored, as I think we all felt, at the prospect of reviving the tired old hatred for the desk soldier. "Anyway, he kept things cheerful in the dull Washington days, and he always wrote me afterwards. When the war was over he called one night on Ella and me, and we sat up late drinking and reminiscing. He had a lot of good stories and knew what had happened to everybody in our class. But he seemed particularly interested in where we lived. Father and Mother had moved out to the old family homestead in Queens and had turned over to us the pretty Georgian house in Eighty-seventh Street that Mott Schmitt had built for them in the late twenties. I must say, Ella and I rather rattled around in it, and when Lester suggested a price that was well over the current market, we were interested."

"Where did he get the money?" I asked.

"Oh, he had made use of army connections. He had friends in banks. Besides, he had married that builder's daughter. And there was a big mortgage, of course. But after Ella and I moved out, we never could walk through that street again. It was what afterwards became known as a standard Gordon operation. A cheap front was put on the two lower floors to make it as ugly as the restaurateur who had leased it could wish, and the rest of the building was cut up into small apartments with papery walls. There were plenty of violations but before they were discovered Lester had sold out and was off to bigger deals."

"Is that the way he did it?" I asked. "From house to house?"

"And from corner to corner, from block to block. He and his father-in-law formed a company called Atlas that did a lot of buying in Queens and Brooklyn. They had a reputation for block-busting, probably well deserved. But the most amazing thing to me about Lester was the way he could do the same thing to you twice. He was a bit of a magician: he could show you his hand and then play it. The Eighty-seventh Street house was only a warm-up. What he really wanted was the old Drayton homestead in Queens. You remember it, John. You came out for a week-end once, didn't you? There were sixteen acres and a beautiful white eighteenth-century farmhouse, a landmark if ever there was one. But taxes were high, and my parents were getting older and found it hard to get the maids to run the place. When Lester turned up in my office, with a face as round and bright as a newly minted fifty-cent piece, and offered me a quarter of a million in cash for the property, I didn't see how I could turn it down. Indeed, despite what I knew about him, I thought he was doing me a favor, as there were several other sites that he could have purchased for his veterans' housing development. I wanted to save the family home if I could, and he said it might be used as a clubhouse for the center of the development."

"And you *believed* him?" Hilary demanded.

"I wanted to believe him," Townie replied with another shrug. "It was a good deal. You know how those things are. Of course, once the deed was signed, the old house was wrecked before you could say 'Jack Robinson.' Obviously, Lester had planned it that way, and obviously I should have seen it. Then he leased the land for twenty-five years to one of his corporations, which borrowed the money from the FHA to construct an oval of twelve high-rise apartment houses. The company then leased the apartments to veterans at a rental that covered taxes, interest and amortization, plus a tidy additional sum for the landlord. Thus at the end of twenty-five years, a point of time rapidly approaching, Lester will own — or would have owned — his apartments free and clear, the whole tab being picked up by the FHA. I figure conservatively that an original investment of two hundred and fifty grand will net him a cool twenty-five million."

"But if he was ever to get his buildings back," I asked, "wouldn't he regret having made them so bare and cheap?"

"No. Because the likes of Lester would have built all the other buildings in the area, and there is nothing else for people to live in. And the irony is that he christened the project Drayton Gardens."

"Well, after all," Hilary remonstrated, "the Draytons got a quarter of a million for it. You may sneer at that sum, Townie, but it can still feed and clothe a good many little Draytons. Even if they eat at the Colony and dress at Bergdorf's."

"You can't compare it to twenty-five million!"

"That's the price you pay for being too grand to go into the real estate business," Hilary pointed out scornfully. "But it still took two to wreck the Drayton homestead. And you were one!"

"All right, God damn it, Hilary," Townie rejoined roughly, reddening to the color of real anger, "suppose *you* tell us the story of when you became Lester's hired hand?"

"I shall be glad to," Hilary said coolly, crossing his knees. "Presumably, you are speaking of the time when Lester acquired *Blackwell's Bi-Weekly,* using, no doubt, some of the profits from his coup with the Draytons' 'cherry orchard.' I was then drama editor on that esteemed but impecunious periodical. When the news leaked out that Lester had bought it, the other editors, knowing I was his classmate, scurried to my office to find out what their fates might be under the new management. I could offer them little comfort. What would a realtor of that stripe care for a bleating herd of intellectuals like us? I was surprised, therefore, when our new owner, instead of summoning me to *his* office, came instead to mine. You should have seen him! Short as ever but stouter, red-faced, with that eternal smile and boyishly curled hair, a painted tie dotted with gold balls, a ring with a big diamond, mammoth cuff links with sapphires and a pair of yellow gloves that he kept slapping against his noisily tweeded arm. The King of Philistia astride the throne of Athens!

" 'I suppose you think your money can buy the muses,' I told him. 'I'm afraid you'll find they're not for sale.' 'There you go,' he retorted; 'like all the rest, you're telling me what my money *can't* buy. I know I can't buy the muses. But can't I purchase a little seat from which to see them at work? Is that asking too much?' As he paused for an answer, I had to agree that this might not be asking too much. 'Very well!' he exclaimed, leaning back with folded arms. 'Then here I am watching.' 'And what are you watching?' I demanded. 'Why, my new editor-in-chief, of course!'

"Well, gentlemen, I guess we all have to admit that Lester has charm. It may be a vulgar, repulsive sort of charm, but it's still charm. If anyone had told me the day before that I was going to give up my career as a drama critic to become the amanuensis of Lester Gordon, I'd have called up Bellevue and told the little men in white coats to come and take him away. Yet that is precisely what happened. Of course, he promised me a *carte blanche* and a salary double what I was getting. The picture that he drew of the future of *Blackwell's* was an editor's dream. Everything was to be increased: the circulation, the quality, the illustrations, the text, the advertisements, the staff. Even if one *knew* it was a pipe dream, it was still impossible not to try to believe it."

"But did you succeed in believing it?" Townie interrupted, remembering, no doubt, Hilary's question to him.

"Not really—never really," Hilary admitted. "But I thought I might be able to have things my way with the new *Blackwell's* for a year, and a year's a long time in journalism. The first step I took was to house myself and my staff in sumptuous new offices. Lester was perfectly affable about this, as he was about all the people I wished to hire. He did not bat an eye when I added a music editor, an art editor and an architecture editor to our roster. *Blackwell's* was to be the review of reviews; it was to point the way forward to the best in all the arts everywhere in America."

"But, as I remember it, Hilary, *Blackwell's* did in a way become that," I objected. "For a while, anyway. Wasn't it *after* Lester sold it that it went to the dogs?"

"Perfectly true," Hilary agreed readily. "But that leaves out of the picture *why* Lester sold it. You see, Lester knew from the beginning that a magazine genuinely dedicated to the arts could never be supported by the greater public. He also knew that the town was full of fat cats who were dying to own just such a magazine, but who were terrified of losing their shirts. For this reason he calculated that by souping up *Blackwell's* to look both intellectual and successful, he could make a quick killing. So *Blackwell's* got a large shiny new format, some dazzling photography, a galaxy of brilliant names for one-shot contributions, interviews with such unlikely persons as the Pope, Stalin and Lady Macbeth and a big promotion campaign. By its third issue Brian Longford, a third-generation soft-drinks heir, who was tired of boozing and marrying and wanted to 'contribute' to mankind, was trailing Lester all over town, begging and bawling to buy his magazine. Lester at last, out of the kindness of his heart, agreed to swap *Blackwell's* for a little bottle cap company that Brian happened to own. It also just happened that this little company had a portfolio of vital contracts with Brian's family corporation. By the time the latter had awakened to the necessity of getting the bottle cap factory back, Lester's price was five million!"

"And *Blackwell's?*" I asked. "At least poor Brian Longford had *you,* Hilary."

"Yes, he had me, and a lot of good it did him. I was as much taken in as he was. I had no idea, as Lester had, that four issues of brilliant ideas could not be repeated indefinitely and that the new *Blackwell's* was 'too much, too soon.' I was astonished when subscriptions began to fall off and suggested to Brian, as disaster followed disaster, that we go back to the old format. But the old *Blackwell* subscribers had been alienated by our flashy changes and could not be coaxed back to the fold. Brian kept the magazine going as long as his tax lawyer allowed him and then closed shop and threw his staff into the street."

"Some of them evidently managed to scramble out of that street," John Grau observed dryly.

"And it's interesting, isn't it," Townie suggested, for we were nothing if not critical that day, "that when Lester wanted an editor to give *Blackwell's* the meretricious gleam that would attract the greater multitude, he knew just where to find him."

"And even more interesting," I pointed out, to add my own small bit, "that that same editor went directly from the obsequies of *Blackwell's* to his own greatest triumph as a columnist in *The Knickerbocker Gazette.* Would you have got that job, Hilary, without the fame you acquired in the brief but giddy heyday of Lester's magazine?"

Hilary was not in the least put out. He lit a new cigarette and waved the match slowly back and forth, as if he did not really care to extinguish it. I suppose my word "triumph" made up for everything. "We should be grateful, I suppose," he said with a wink, "that anything at all was saved from so disastrous a wreck."

"Tell us about Lester during the *Blackwell* era," I suggested. "Did he take an active interest in it?"

"Not really. He left the running of it to me. But we were all surprised at how much he was there. I don't think a day went by that he didn't come to my office to chat, to listen in at editorial conferences, to look over galleys. At last it began to dawn on me that Lester had had a subsidiary interest in acquiring the magazine. He wanted to educate himself."

"In art?" Townie demanded in surprise.

"In everything. Or rather in everything fashionable. This was the period in Lester's life when he began to be interested in society, and he took me for his guide and mentor. I considered it a case of symbiosis, or living together for mutual advantage. He would let me run his magazine, and I would try to make him presentable. We started with clothes. I made Lester jettison all his wardrobe and jewelry; I stripped him, so to speak, to his checkbook. Then we took a trip to Europe: to London for suits, to Paris for shirts and ties, to Rome for boots and accessories. But it was a dismal case of *Plus ça change.* Lester remained stubbornly Lester. Dressed by a duke's tailor, he was still the realtor from Queens. Fortunately, that doesn't matter in the fluctuating society of modern New York, particularly in the world of fashion magazines and charity balls."

"Hairdresser society," Townie sneered.

"Society is always society," Hilary retorted coldly, "and as Oscar Wilde so wisely put it, only those who can't get in abuse it. The Draytons and Livingstons and Stuyvesants have had their day. Nobody who really counts gives a hoot about family any more. But I will admit that I could never persuade Lester of this. He was as loyal to the old Knickerbocker families as Townie himself. At least he was *then.* The very ease with which he was accepted by the international set made him suspicious. When he found himself sitting at the Duchess of Dino's table at the Heart Ball, his triumph was clouded by the sad reflection that only a *déclassée* duchess could be the friend of such a meatball as Lester Gordon!"

We all laughed, and I asked: "But where was Huldah in all of this? Did she, too, make the grade with duchesses?"

"Ah, no, even *that* world has its limits. Poor Huldah was left to sulk at home. Lester, with his customary tact, suggested that she take lessons in voice and deportment and learn to be a lady, and she threw a vase at him. Yet he was fond of her in his own way, and when he begged me to intercede and persuade her to grant him a divorce, he wept at the cruelty of a world that made him be so cruel. Napoleon had to cast off Josephine for an Austrian archduchess. Lester Gordon had to have a Drayton!"

"How did he ever pull that off?" John Grau asked, turning to Townie.

"Ask Hilary," Townie replied with a shrug. "He's telling the story."

"Can I speak frankly, then?" Hilary asked Townie.

"Oh, Lord, yes. Gabrielle's only my second cousin. I told her she was a goose to marry him, and she sent me smartly about my own business. That was the last time we spoke until he absconded, and then she came around humbly for my advice. Go ahead, Hilary. I'd like to know myself how she ever talked her father into it. Cousin Bronson once told me he'd rather see his daughter in her coffin than married to a Jew!"

"Gabrielle's father wasn't talked into it," Hilary explained. "He was told. She and her mother, like most women, could be very practical on occasion. Gabrielle, unlike Townie, was a poor Drayton, over thirty and, despite a regal nose and sandy hair, something less than a beauty. She and her mother sneered at Lester when he started calling after meeting them at Townie's, but all sneers ceased together when he made the offer of his hand — even before it was out of Huldah's grasp — and a settlement of a million bucks!"

John whistled. "That's what I call taking a place by storm!"

"Gabrielle and her mother promptly reversed course, and the Drayton aunts were given the family line to spread over town. Lester a Jew? Hadn't people heard of integration? Lester married? Well, was he the first man who had to buy off an adventuress who had trapped him into matrimony in college days? Lester sharp in business practices? Wasn't that what people always said of the successful? Lester not a gentleman? My dear, who *was* these days? By the time Lester and Gabrielle were united, there was even talk that one of her uncles might propose him for the Union Club!"

"And did he?" I asked when Hilary paused to sip his drink.

"He might have, had Lester not lost interest. The same inner principle that made him devalue a charity-ball world as soon as it accepted him, depreciated an old New York that no longer sneered. Lester was oppressed by the stuffiness of Gabrielle's world — as who would not be? — and soon set his sights on higher goals. He was looking now toward big business, the management world, the politicians, control of the human destiny.

He chafed at the mild, softly chatting dinner parties at Gabrielle's mother's. He found that his wife had used all her energy to fit him into *her* world and didn't have an ounce left over to cultivate the people *he* cared to cultivate. Gabrielle was always deploring the low standards of the Social Register, yet to be in it was at least a *sine qua non.* It was only a matter of months before she became an actual liability to Lester."

"Oh, come off it, Hilary," Townie interrupted, irritated at last. "I know things have changed, and the parents of half the people Ella and I see socially today would have been sent to the servants' entrance by our parents ——"

"Thanks!" Hilary interrupted with a sneer. "I guess that takes care of John and myself."

"Don't get huffy," Townie retorted. "I'm only trying to point out that an item can drop in value without becoming worthless. I cannot allow that Gabrielle was ever a hindrance to Lester's social career."

"Ah, but you see, Townie, you *don't* really know how drastically things have changed!" Hilary exclaimed, rising to the climax of his argument. "The social scene has become so diffuse that it's not at all unusual, for example, for a woman like Mrs. Knossos, whose face by Elizabeth Arden and jewels by Schlumberger are known to every reader of the evening papers, never to have heard of the Draytons. I insist that Gabrielle's habit of snubbing people who thought they were simply being kind to Lester's awkward wife did him more damage than all of Huldah's boners. Really, from a purely practical point of view, and leaving aside the moral question, I don't see that Lester had any alternative but to shed Gabrielle. The churning waves of high finance bobbed before him. But that is the tragic denouement, and John's part of the story."

John Grau had been listening carefully as he drank. He was a week-end drinker, for he worked too hard at other times, but when he did drink, he did it thoroughly, like everything else. His capacity seemed unlimited, yet he never showed the effects, except that he very slightly softened. The hard, handsome, regular squarish face relaxed, and the usually pursed, almost censorious lips spread in a half-mile. One was no longer so aware of the gray hair, the humped, about-to-spring quality of that craggy, muscular body. When John smiled and gave one his intense gray-green stares, he had charm. It may have been the charm of the totality of his temporary commitment.

"When Lester threw his derby hat down on my desk and said airily that he wanted a 'Wall Street lawyer,' I practically told him to go to hell," John began. "I don't think I'd seen him more than half a dozen times since college, and I didn't like anything I'd heard. I informed him that we had only a very small, accommodation real estate department, at which he roared with laughter and said that we weren't nearly tough enough to handle his housing matters. No, he was coming to us, he explained, only for his securities work! Well, I got so mad at the idea of our being too soft for one thing and not for the other, that I told him that if we weren't good enough to advise him generally, I wasn't interested. And then, of course, he had me, for he offered me the works: housing, building, finance, and told me to name my own retainer. The upshot of it all was that he took me to lunch, and I had a new client."

"So you *did* do the real estate," Townie interpolated.

"There wasn't much of it left," John replied. "Lester had pretty well sold out of it by then, except for Drayton Gardens. As Hilary implies, he was ashamed of it. He wanted something with more 'tone.' No doubt, he considered that he wouldn't be in 'trade' if he dealt with intangibles, if he sat in a great gleaming office downtown and pushed buttons and talked on the telephone while he bought control of vast enterprises. We always keep coming back, don't we, to the child in Lester, the dreaming, scheming child? I'll never forget the first deal I handled for him. He had figured out that S. & T. Manley's, the old jewelry store on Fifth Avenue, was a ripe fruit to be plucked. Under a gentle family mismanagement the stock had declined in value to a point where it was worth considerably less than the inventory. Swoop! Lester pounced from the sky in the fastest proxy raid I have ever witnessed, closed down an ancient and distinguished firm and sold out the inventory for a spanking profit."

"All handled by you, John," Hilary pointed out.

"Oh, yes, all handled by me, I admit it," John rejoined with a rueful, impatient shake of his head. "What is one to do? I practice law in Arnold & Degener at One Chase Manhattan Plaza. Who am I to turn down high-paying clients with legally honest deals? What would my partners say if I did? For Lester pays well — make no mistake. I've never seen him haggle over a bill. He even once sent me a check for double the amount charged with a note that read: 'I want the best securities lawyer in town, and this is what the best securities lawyer should get.' How many clients do you find who give you that kind of appreciation? Is it *my* job to look out for old mismanaged stores?"

"Of course not," Townie agreed firmly. "You've got to live in the present. We all do."

"Not I," I protested. "I'm an auctioneer. I live in the past and off the past."

"And as a commentator," Hilary insisted, "I live off the immediate future."

John's expression became harder. "I'm not apologizing for myself," he said, "but neither am I praising myself. I knew what I wanted to be when I was in law school, and I'm only sorry that I can't be it more often. I wanted — and want — to be the kind of lawyer who builds, and Lester's genius was always for destruction. If he pieced together a little railroad empire, it was to close it down in favor of his noisy buses. If he laid his hands on a picturesque country inn, it was to replace it with a cheap motel. And his favorite game was the simple taking over and looting of companies, passing on the empty, glittering shell to the unwary public that thought it was protected by a benevolent government. Sometimes I tried to excuse Lester as a frustrated would-be pioneer who had been born too late. What would Vanderbilt or Rockefeller have done with their energy in our century with the frontiers gone? Might they not have torn each other to bits, like so many Lester Gordons?"

"Is that why Lester turned ultimately on himself?" I asked. "Wasn't there an element of financial suicide in the last debacle?"

"I think there was," John agreed, nodding. "Lester was tired of having everything give way before him. He may have experienced an odd kind of relief when he batted his head at last against the hard wall of crime and knew that detection was a minute-to-minute possibility. But first I must tell you about Luella. Let the cold Wall Street lawyer tell you boys about love. True love! "

"Oh, come, John," Hilary protested, "you're not going to try to convince us that Lester was in love with that little tramp."

"Ah, but I am!" John exclaimed. "Lester was very much in love with that little tramp. Or thought he was, and what's the difference?"

"Lester in love," Hilary sneered. "It's a contradiction in terms!"

"But Lester is always in love," John insisted. "And he always was. Lester from the beginning was in love with the whole beautiful world that he wanted to possess. You remember how he was at college: so intense, so interested, always listening, bubbling with curiosity, affectionate, gay? Well, he's still that way, damn him! Lester studied the world because he had to *have* the world. And he had to have it because he loved it."

"Even when he was block-busting for Huldah's father?"

"Even then. Lester doesn't see things the way other people do. He is so totally devoid of any kind of racial prejudice that it strikes him, when it's stuck in front of his nose, as simply another aspect of the human equation to make money out of. People like mountain scenery, so one buys up mountains. Other people don't want Negro neighbors, so one brings in Negroes to induce them to sell cheap. It's market, pure and simple, the supreme law of the market! Lester, you might even argue, was the last of the pure capitalists. He wants to believe that the best of all possible worlds will materialize if the Lesters are only left free to make their profit."

"He couldn't!" I exclaimed incredulously.

"I said he *wants* to," John emphasized. "Of course, he doesn't believe it. Like the rest of us, he sees clearly enough that the world which Lester conquers is an inferior place to the one which Lester assaults. He sees his shoddy houses, his tinsel motels, his soulless stores. He understands that he has made his fortune by swimming in a sea of junk. But hope keeps bubbling. What else keeps him alive? Somewhere, somehow, he has to believe that the brightness and smartness of a good boy like Lester is going to produce something admirable, something permanent, some bit of merchandise that will not fall to pieces before one has got it from the shop down into one's car."

"And that was Luella?" Hilary exclaimed with a snort.

"That was Luella. Exactly. Luella was beauty and sex and love and ideals, like the advertisement of a new car. Huldah, after all, was a bit of a dog, and Gabrielle, saving your reverence, Townie, was no rose, but every man at this table will have to admit that Luella was a dish."

"But a dish for the multitude," Hilary added. "Who has not partaken?"

"Luella was a typically American phenomenon," John continued, again in his lawyer's voice. "Blond, curved, with pouting lip and bad temper. She was the personification of the *appearance* of sex, the symbol, if you like, of fleshly passion. You might say she was a sort of female Lester, a capitalist in love, who gave the least for the most, who wanted a man's soul in return for a wriggle of her fanny. It's elementary psychology to speculate that she was probably no good in bed."

"You needn't speculate," Hilary put in flatly. "I can assure you she was not."

The rest of us were careful not to give Hilary the satisfaction of so much as a cocked eyebrow. As Townie used to say, given enough rope Hilary would prove every hour on the hour that he was no gentleman.

"Very well, then," John went on coldly, "we need not speculate. We know. The importance of Luella in American commercial society is not what she gives her possessor, but what people may be induced to believe that she gives. She is as much a status symbol as a Gauguin or a Rolls-Royce. Everyone seeing Mrs. Lester Gordon can be counted on to envy Mr. Gordon his nights. If this is so, does it very much matter if they sleep in separate bedrooms?"

"But you said he was in love with Luella," I protested. "Surely that implies something beyond impressing his neighbors!"

"No, with Lester I honestly believe it does not. Indeed, I suggest that this is of the essence of Lester. He *doesn't* see the difference between the outward and visible sign and the inward and invisible truth. If Luella is sex to the multitude, then Luella is sex to him. When he came to my office to tell me that he wanted to marry Luella, he was so excited that he could not keep still. He kept jumping up and running about the room, playing with the window shade cord, rustling papers, lighting and putting out cigarettes. Luella was a goddess; Luella was Cleopatra; Luella should be a movie star! Huldah, Gabrielle, all the other women in his life, had been mere shadows. With Luella, at last, he was living!"

"Why was he telling *you?*" I inquired, for John seemed an odd confidant in such matters.

"Because I was his lawyer. And he certainly needed one. One doesn't divorce a Drayton with impunity, does one, Townie? Also, Luella had a rather sticky spouse of her own to shed. I tried to sober Lester down by pointing out that of the eight lawyers who would necessarily be involved — four for each party in New York and four more in Reno — he would have to pay at least six, and if Luella's husband was angry enough, all eight. But nothing bothered him. He was in euphoria! 'I don't care what it costs,' he told me. 'I've got to have my Luella!' "

"How did Luella feel about him?" Townie asked. "Or was it simply a question of dough?"

"Oh, Luella liked him well enough. To marry him for a few years, anyway. I don't suppose even Lester expected that she would be capable of the smallest sacrifice in his respect. I know he was not surprised when she threw him over at the first hint of trouble. But he was a big spender who loved late hours and night clubs: Luella's ideal of a man. And he was willing to take on the trouble and expense of her own divorce — oh, he was worth it. So Arnold & Degener went to work to clear away the legal underbrush that stood between the union of these two passionate lovers."

"I hope you're not referring to my poor little innocent cousin Gabrielle as legal underbrush," Townie intervened with a chuckle.

John flung up his hands. "When it comes to settlements, I'd rather fight a blond gold-digger from the Follies than a brownstone miss from old New York," he emphasized. "When your poor little innocent cousin was through with us, she had clear title to the whole Drayton Gardens project!"

"And I'm happy to tell you that the first thing she did was to rechristen it Queen's Gardens," Townie informed us in all earnestness. "I'm glad to say that the family name is no longer associated with that dump."

"Only the family income," Hilary retorted.

"What a pity," I added, "that Gabrielle's delicacy in nomenclature could not restore the family landmark."

Townie merely grunted as John continued: "Negotiations went on for months. Luella's husband had to be squared as well, for it turned out that he was shattered at the idea of losing *his* status symbol, or at least of losing her to Lester. When the agreements were all signed, Gabrielle insisted that Lester and not she have the bother of going to Reno, although she knew that he was in the midst of the biggest proxy fight in his life and from which she stood to profit: the battle for Atlantic Enterprises." John paused and looked around the table. "But you all know about Atlantic Enterprises?"

"No, John," I answered, "we don't. Or at least I don't. Please remember that we're not all lawyers."

"Atlantic," he continued, "is a holding corporation that controls a string of department stores, a bus line, a theater chain and some three dozen parking lots, all just outside the city limits. Lester was already president of the company, but he wanted control. He had a Napoleonic scheme of uniting Atlantic to his other interests, and to some further ones that he had in mind to acquire, in order to spread a belt around the city. He saw that New York was sliding into poverty and despair and that the middle and upper classes, together with most of the businesses, were fleeing to the suburbs. Out of this hegira Lester would make himself lord of the future. He would put himself in a position where all the insoluble growing problems of our time — overpopulation, racial strife and the growing indigence in the city — would operate to fill his pocketbook. How could he lose? As he once told me: 'Only an ass can be poor these days.'

And I really believe that he might have achieved his goal had he been able to be in New York continuously during the battle. His particular kind of genius required him to be always on the scene. But in the hottest part of the fight he was stuck in Reno, having to check in at court every other day to establish his residence. He had a jet plane in which he tore back and forth through the ether. Never shall I forget the picture of that desperate little man, living on benzedrine, a telephone constantly cradled to his ear, talking, shouting, laughing. For that was the thing about Lester: he was actually enjoying the whole thing. And when I think what he was *doing* all the time, the risks that he was taking, when I think that he knew all along what was hanging over his head, I cannot decide whether he is the bravest man I ever knew or a simple lunatic! "

"But *what* was he doing?" I demanded.

"Man, didn't you read the papers? The market had broken, money was tight, and Lester was always a borrower up to the hilt. I could not imagine where he was getting the money to buy Atlantic stock. I did not find out until Lester's house of cards fell in that he had been using Atlantic's treasury to buy Atlantic stock."

"And that was wrong?" I asked. "Wasn't he president of Atlantic?"

"Small wonder that morals are on the slide," John answered with a snicker, "when the public no longer knows what's right or wrong. Perhaps it's not the public's fault. Perhaps our laws are too complicated. But in this case it would be simple enough even for you, Roger, to understand. The officers of a corporation are not supposed to use its assets for their personal market speculations. Even when they claim, as Lester did, that they are supporting the price of the company stock. But Lester's luck had run out at last. It was no fault of his that he encountered the worst stock market slide since 1929. It was a brief one, but it did for Lester. He ran short of money before he had completed his control of Atlantic, and that was the end. In a single day everyone turned on him. He lost his companies, he lost his reputation, and, needless to say, he lost Luella. In fact, on the rainy morning when he donned dark glasses and boarded the plane for Lisbon, he was not even divorced from Gabrielle."

"So he's still your cousin, Townie," Hilary observed dryly.

"No, Gabrielle went out to Reno after he absconded and got the decree herself," Townie hastened to inform us. "I advised her to do it. How much of what Lester settled on her she will be able to keep is a moot question, but you'll be glad to know she's got a crack lawyer."

Hilary and John and I burst out laughing at the idea of our being "glad" to know this, and Townie's cheeks reddened.

"Speaking of lawyers," I said, turning back to John, "do you still represent Lester?"

"No, I had to give him up. You see, Arnold & Degener are general counsel to Atlantic, and there was an obvious conflict."

"You mean," Hilary put in quickly, "that having to choose between two clients, you kept the best?"

"Not at all," John retorted indignantly. "You don't understand these things, Hilary, and you shouldn't be so smart about them. We dropped Lester because he had deceived us. That was not true of Atlantic."

"But didn't Lester *bring* you Atlantic?" Hilary demanded, and seeing that John was now becoming as angry as Townie, I intervened.

"But I thought you had seen Lester in Lisbon?" I asked him.

"I did see him. I stopped there on my way back from a business trip to Madrid. But I went to see him as a friend, not as a lawyer."

"And what happened when you saw him?"

"We went to a bar and spent a couple of hours together. Lester was nicer than I've ever seen him. Subdued, but far from crushed, and utterly devoid of self-pity. He blamed no one but himself for the debacle and showed no bitterness toward his former business associates who had shrilly reviled him to reporters. As to Luella, he simply said that she had acted as he had told her to act, and even claimed that he had composed her savage press release. Townie and Hilary may sneer at him for being a parvenu, but he was a true gentleman that day. It was an odd background for him: that beautiful, quiet, decadent capital. Possibly some of its ancient style had crept into him through holes battered by disaster."

"You're breaking my heart," Hilary drawled. "Pray tell us, John, before you've sunk to the bathos of a column by our late lamented Elsa Maxwell, what Lester is going to do now. Will he be extradited?"

"It won't be necessary," John snapped. "He's coming back. He's going to give himself up."

"And will he go to jail?" I asked.

John shrugged. "Very possibly. Though he may get a suspended sentence. In any event, it would be a short term."

"And then?"

"Oh, and then he'll go back to business. Lester is far from downed. As I said before, he may even be glad to find that he can't get away with everything. He's like a schoolboy — there I go again! — who has almost taken over the school with his tricks and wiles. Finally, just as he is about to light a fire in the wastepaper basket under the headmaster's desk, he is caught and has his ears roundly boxed. For the first time he respects the institution!"

"And will he make another fortune?" I asked.

"Who knows? He may. But I doubt it." John frowned and shook his head. "I believe there's just so much energy and just so much luck in any man. Lester has drawn heavily on his capital."

Silence enveloped our table now for a minute as we drank and smoked reflectively. Glancing from John to Townie to Hilary, I was suddenly struck by the size of their common denominator. It was in their eyes, in the opaque glitter of their distrustful eyes. They were all prosperous, all expensively and similarly clad. I would have defied John O'Hara himself to have told, in that assemblage of colored shirts, which was the descendant of a colonial governor, which the popular columnist and which the Wall Street lawyer. Over their apparel, which was as beautiful as a *New Yorker* advertisement, glowed the snakes' eyes that saw the world at a snake's level: one inch above the ground. Oh, yes, they saw it whole and they saw it clear — one inch above the ground.

"What a society we live in," I exclaimed, "that such men as you three should all have worked for such a man as Lester Gordon! And you all made a good thing out of him, too. Oh, granted, he made a thousand times more out of each of you, but you've had the last laugh, for you've still got it, while he is bankrupt. What impresses me — or rather *depresses* me — is the fact that you were his agents, that *he* was always the principal. You, Townie, with all your lineage and traditions; you, Hilary, with all your cultivation and sophistication; you, John, the brightest boy in Columbia law, were glad to be the servants of an adventurer whose god was the dollar and whose law was to get it for nothing. Is that capitalism? That the aristocrat, the intellectual and the professional are bound to the chariot of the money juggler? It seems to me that by contrast the Middle Ages, where the priest and soldier ruled, was a time of enlightenment!"

"You talk like a goddam red," Townie growled.

"More like a John Birchite, I would say!" cried Hilary.

"It's easy enough to be detached if you're tucked away in an auction gallery, selling old lamps and pictures," John pointed out. "If you'd been born in your precious Middle Ages, Roger, you'd have scrambled to the nearest monastery and told your beads."

"Not at all," I retorted. "I'd have copied out the *Iliad* and saved it for future generations!"

"Gentlemen, gentlemen," Hilary exclaimed, waving for silence with both hands, "don't you realize that we have in our presence the most gigantic hypocrite of all? When poor Lester Gordon's art collection was placed on the block by his creditors, who do you think sold it, item by item, but our friend Roger here, the same Roger from whom Lester had bought it. And didn't the whole works make a record-breaking price for ultra-fashionable impressionists? And didn't Hone's take its twenty per cent pound of flesh? We three may have been the midwives of Lester's fortune, but Roger was the undertaker!"

In the explosion of laughter that followed this revelation, which, of course, I had known was coming — and would have volunteered myself had I not wished Hilary to have the pleasure of it — the irritation engendered by the afternoon's discussion trickled off, and we were once again our congenial golf foursome. Why should we not, after all, have been the best of friends? What were we but four junior Gordons?

Arnold & Degener,
One Chase Manhattan Plaza

The Senior Partner's Ghosts

THE WIFE of the youngest partner of Arnold & Degener, who had married her husband after his promotion and so had not shared with him the restraining influences of the long clerkship years, had once said of the firm's offices at One Chase Manhattan Plaza that they were as austere as the Escorial and that Mr. Price reminded her, in the center of his dreary labyrinth of closed doors and gray corridors, of a watching, spidery Philip II. A troublemaker repeated the remark to Mr. Price, but the effect was not at all what the troublemaker had sought. Sylvaner Price neither grunted nor frowned; for all his interlocutor could see he might not even have heard the comment. Yet, deep within, his heart had quivered with pleasure, and ever after he liked his youngest partner's wife. For she alone had divined that he was a romantic and that the key to open the high dark gates of his heart's stronghold was not to be found in Blackstone or in Maitland, in Pollock, or in Holmes, but quite simply in Victor Hugo.

Yet, if simple, it was nonetheless a difficult fact to divine, and the young woman's remark might have been a chance shot. Certainly to the world Sylvaner Price created the ever consistent impression of a man who had no existence outside of the famous law firm which had been forged by Guthrie Arnold to be the indispensable tool of the greatest corporations and kept sharp and polished by his more than worthy successor. For although Lloyd Degener had succeeded to the position of "senior partner," being the public and political figure, it was Price who held the old man's clients and still dominated the private councils of the firm. He was a tall, thin, spare figure with a small round belly and a round, almost bald head down the center of which ran a few long dark hairs. His face, too, was round and bore in the center a small hook nose on the thin bridge of which were fastened his spectacles, constantly glittering in the head-shaking movement that expresssed his constant chagrin with human perversity. He was a man of no accessories, no appendages, no stray bits or loose ends. His mild, nervous wife and her little infirm boy had been converted, years before, into two large manila folders marked "Estates of ——," and his big bare Fifth Avenue apartment, with its large dark furniture and small dull prints was simply an annex to One Chase Manhattan Plaza, traveling between which twice a day, in the back seat of his old Pierce Arrow, he made his sole brief contacts with the outside world through window and newspaper.

No, the romantic in Sylvaner Price could not have been surprised by the youngest partner's wife, or indeed by anyone else, unless that person had chanced to observe the furtive little gesture that he made with his right hand every morning when he came into the office, just as he passed the Lazlo portrait of his predecessor. He would glance quickly up at it and quickly down again, and then pass his hand in a rapid half-concealed clutching motion across his chest. One might have almost thought that he was crossing himself. The gesture was certainly reverent, but, more importantly, it implied, unlike any of his others, a certain depth of feeling.

The huge picture hung in the dark paneled reception hall, whose tables, bare of magazines or even newspapers, testified to the sobriety of a client's wait. The late Guthrie Arnold was depicted, standing up, seemingly tall, in a pink coat and top hat, one hand holding a riding crop, the other raised to the bridle of a magnificent bay whose head and front legs occupied more than half of the canvas. One might have assumed that it was an English eighteenth-century portrait, a Romney earl or Lawrence baronet, had it not been for the long oblong countenance of the subject, as equine as its supposed mount, which suggested, with its high intelligent brow, its magisterially dry, thin lips, and its general air of looking down more from a bench than a saddle, the learned profession practiced in the long bare corridors that met at the foot of the frame. One might even have speculated that Mr. Arnold had posed for the artist in unfamiliar garb, with unaccustomed props, that he had, like a visitor in an old photographer's gallery, stuck his head through a hole in a backdrop on which was painted a gaudy scene, had not the lighted glass cases on either side of the portrait and their rows of silver trophy cups testified to indubitable accomplishments in field and stream. The whole group of picture and cases brought to mind a shrine in some barbarous land to a pagan god to whom a greater latitude of behavior was allowed than to his austere and merely mortal votaries. If Mr. Arnold had enjoyed life, that tightly gripped riding crop seemed to imply, it was because Mr. Arnold had been unique. Did any clerk presume to do likewise? Speak up!

Oh, yes, *there* was the romance of Sylvaner Price's life, his memory of Guthrie Arnold, or, more accurately, what he planned to do with that memory. Like all dry, impersonal men, Price was intensely aware that he was dry and impersonal, but this did not mean that he was not proud of the long-hidden imagination which was at last, well past his seventieth year, to explode before a gaping world in all the colors of the rainbow. For what he now planned was nothing less than a sublime work of art — a work of art in the form of a book, a first volume to Lloyd Degener's proposed history of the firm, which would contain a separate biography of the founder that he hoped would rock the downtown world back in its chairs and make it speculate of the author: "Is this our old Sylvaner Price? This Melville, this Whitman, this *peacock?*"

It would be done, too, without the least cheapness, without smirking revelations of discreditable litigations or puerile boastings, in a government-policed era, of what clients used to do in braver, buccaneer days. No, his book would be made glorious simply by its characterization of the great man who had founded and given his name to the firm, a characterization that would reveal him in all the splendor of an individual to an age that had forgotten what such a thing was. Guthrie Arnold in Sylvaner Price's pages would *live,* as a man as well as a lawyer, as a sportsman as well as a philanthropist, as a connoisseur in porcelains as well as in horseflesh, as a wit, as a dandy, as a lady killer, as an iconoclast, in short, as a holy terror. Oh, yes, everyone would gape that Sylvaner Price even *knew* of such things, but that would be just the wonderful fun of it! He had not slaved for his predecessor for four decades without knowing him. And if he, like his other colleagues, had been a worker in the hive all his days and nights, he would prove at least that he had been a worker who had witnessed the flight of the queen bee.

And now, at last, he had actually started on the great work. His mornings from ten o'clock to noon were consecrated to the task. In this hallowed period he was alone with his dictaphone, and Miss Ives, on guard outside his closed door, saw that no calls or callers shattered his peace. Leaning back in his chair and touching the tips of his long fingers together, his eyes resting on the silver-framed photograph of the Lazlo portrait, he would try to achieve what he had heard described as "free association." He would imagine his mind as a white sheet and wait until the unrelated slides of his unconscious memory were projected upon it. As soon as they began to cohere into any definite subject he would turn on his machine. But one day in the third week of his project, an anecdote that he was dictating came out in a very different shape from what he had planned. Indeed, it was so different that the experience quite shook him up.

"Clients," he had started. "Clients and the getting of clients.

Mr. Arnold always said that a job well done was worth a hundred chats on a hundred golf courses. He scorned the idea of the public relations partner to act as a decoy to bring customers to the less charming experts behind the scene. 'Would you go to a dentist because you found his partner good company?' he would ask. The only way, he insisted, that a lawyer could use a social occasion to attract business was by showing off his expertise. And to do that one had to *be* an expert. Mr. Arnold would don his white tie as another man might don his overalls — for work. After dinner, over the brandies with the men, slipping into a seat by the chairman of the biggest company, he might let the talk glide into the channels of the latter's current reorganization. 'I was interested to see in the paper that you didn't use a Section 15 subsidiary. I suppose you wouldn't have qualified under 14-C. Too bad.' When promptly challenged as to the advantages of such a course and informed, perhaps a bit tartly, that the company was represented by Able Fine, Mr. Arnold would raise both hands in prompt disclaimer. 'Ah, my dear fellow, if Able Fine is guiding you, you're all right. Of course, he has some excellent reason for doing as he has done. Depend upon it.' Yet he would shake his head from time to time, as if troubled with a secret, stubborn doubt, and in departing he might reassail his disconcerted fellow guest with the solicitous query: 'Able made a complete recovery from that heart attack, didn't he? Oh, good, good.' "

Price closed his teeth together with a little click as he slowly straightened in his chair. Had *he* said all that? Quickly he adjusted the machine to play back his tape, and there, indubitably, were the scratchy words. Appalled, he took the disc from its pin and dropped it in his wastebasket. Where had such a memory come from? *Memory?* It was no memory, but the rankest fairy tale! Obviously, he was tired or strained or showing his age. He shivered and rang for Miss Ives to tell her that he would start his ordinary day's work and leave the book until the morrow.

But on the morrow the same thing happened. He had chosen for the morning's "free association" the seemingly safe topic of estate administration, and after a rambling start had got into his stride along the following line:

"If there was one thing Mr. Arnold liked it was what he called a 'clean' estate. He maintained that when one had elderly testators it was a duty to start 'cleaning up' in their lifetimes. 'Get rid of foreign property,' he would enjoin me; 'sweep up odd bits of oil ventures, liquidate unnecessary partnerships. When an estate is ripe, it should come off the bough into your hands with hardly a pluck.' Sometimes he carried out his theories with a logic and a matter-of-factness that was a bit disconcerting to his associates. When we got word of his brother Jay's death in Paris, I recall his rubbing his hands briskly together and exclaiming: 'Isn't it luck that we sold that North African mine?' And he actually whistled a tune!"

Price rose slowly to his feet and pressed the tips of his fingers against his lowered lids. There was no need this time to play back the tape; he simply removed the disc and placed it, like its predecessor, in the basket. Then he pulled out his silk handkerchief, carefully daubed his gleaming brow and walked out to the reception hall and over to the portrait of Mr. Arnold.

"What is it, sir?" he whispered under his breath. "Don't you *want* me to write my book?"

He continued to stare until it almost seemed to him that one of those small gray eyes had winked. A mean, mocking, glinting wink. He turned quickly to the receptionist, but she was not minding him. Two messengers, sitting on the bench beside her, looked vacantly at the ceiling. When he glanced back at the portrait, it was as it had always been. The wink had been imagined; he was even conscious of having consciously imagined it. But had he imagined the sudden atmosphere, at once cold and fetid, of the big room?

That day he presided, in Lloyd Degener's absence in Washington, at the partners' weekly lunch, seated at the end of the long oval table in the private dining room of the Merchants' Club. He was as silent as he decently could be, but he felt jumpy all during the meal and could hardly endure listening to the department heads as they reported, with lawyers' prolixity, on the business in their respective charges. At the end of the meal he hit the table sharply with the little gavel that was always left at his place and made a speech that he had no memory of either preparing or conceiving. He could only listen in a kind of stupor to his own harsh voice as it angrily made point after point.

"We've heard, gentlemen, a lot about what's going on *inside* the office, but not a word of what's going on outside. Yet I suppose you all know about Frank Schrader in Dunlap, Schrader & Todd. It's cancer, and only a matter of months. Now I don't think I need to tell anyone, at least anyone in the corporate and securities line, that Frank Schrader is the one man who's been holding that firm together. But on the skids or not, they've still got some beautiful business: Seaboard Trust, Angus Chemicals, and the Stutz family. A lot of that business *belongs* here. Old man Stutz, for example, is a natural for the Arnold & Degener roster. We're perfectly set up for him, and he for us. Now I want to see you fellows move in on that business. Review all your friends in those companies. Check their boards of directors. See which of you belong to what clubs they belong to. Arrange opportunities to meet them. Sometimes I think you fellows think clients grow on trees. Must I do *all* the work around here?"

Wonderingly, as he heard his voice cease, he glanced about the silent, shocked table. They were all staring at him.

"Well, gentlemen?" his voice demanded.

"I've been away for six weeks," came at last the mild, impertinent Southern drawl of the youngest partner, he with the clever wife, the brilliant "boy" with ruffled hair and freckles. "And so perhaps I haven't heard. Have the Canons of Professional Ethics been suspended? Has the Bar Association officially endorsed ambulance chasing?"

Price felt his hand reach for the gavel as the spurt of rebellious laughter started around the table, and he struck the table harder than he had ever heard it struck before. "You can talk to me about ethics when you've paid the rent!" his voice cried out. "There's not one of you who'd be where you are without me. I can hire as many brains as I want, but where do I get the clients? Where, gentlemen? I repeat: on *trees?*" He rose now and tossed the gavel contemptuously on the table. "The meeting is adjourned."

Walking back to the office, Jack Keating, an estates partner, earnest and heavy-jawed, Price's principal pupil, kept up a rather breathless pace with him. "You were terrific, sir," he said. "A reminder like that is a tonic to us all. We get so smug about our big larder of business. Do you know, if I had closed my eyes, I would have sworn it was old Mr. Arnold himself talking!"

Price closed his eyes and gave a little moan. "Oh, don't, Jack, please don't," he murmured.

That evening he worked late, and when he emerged from his office the reception hall was empty. He switched on the light above the portrait and went over to stand beneath it, glancing cautiously to each side to be sure that he was alone. Then he fixed his eyes on the eyes of Mr. Arnold's likeness.

"What do you want?" he asked.

The aspect of the portrait did not change. To his infinite relief it remained an inanimate canvas. But as he continued to stare at it, he felt again that distinct chill in the air about him, a chill that he now associated with this strange communion between himself and the dead. An idea took sudden shape from the misty corners of his mind, flowing together out of Lord knows what long-locked compartments, that there existed an evil spirit imprisoned and imprisoned by *him* right here, where he was now standing, hemmed in to a corner of the great reception room, bound down, so to speak, with the gilded frame of the portrait, with the glass of the trophy cases, confined to that single spot as too dangerous to be allowed to roam. But if it was there, if it always had been there, why was it now felt for the first time and why by him, Sylvaner Price? Why indeed, by all that was unholy, unless it was because he was doing something that he had never done before, and what was that but writing the story of Guthrie Arnold?

"So that's it!" he cried. "I'm letting you out. Letting you out at last. And you think you'll come on your own terms! You think that *you,* the evil genius of Guthrie Arnold, will now prevail — as you never could in his lifetime — over his good, his noble, his magnificent spirit. Well, you won't, that's all I can tell you, my hearty! You'll come into my book, but in your proper place. You want to be wicked, but you'll be only witty. You want to be savage, but you'll be only severe. You want to be slippery, but you'll be merely ingenious. You want to be heartless, but you'll be only just. Oh, I'll *fix* you now, for what you've done to me!"

He was suddenly aware that he was no longer alone, and turning with a little jump he saw a law clerk staring at him with an astonishment that he made no effort to conceal.

"Well, what are you gaping at?" Price demanded testily. "Go on about your business. I'm rehearsing a skit we're putting on at the Bar Association. That's all."

"Yes, sir."

"That's all, I tell you!" he shouted, and the young man fled.

The next morning Price spent his allotted two hours alone with his machine dictating an account of Mr. Arnold's technique in domestic matters. This was to be the basis for what he hoped would be the liveliest chapter of the book, for the late senior partner had known perfectly how to expose fortune hunters, how to keep family money out of the hands of in-laws and incompetents, but it was also the section of Price's proposed book that seemed most to bristle with opportunities for the antic spirit that had now visited him thrice. Price enunciated his words in a hard, graveled tone, as though in uttering them he was nonetheless holding them under his domination, so that he might have resembled some grim old dog-walker in Central Park, moving slowly ahead in the midst of a tumbling mass of canines, each firmly attached by leash to his clenched fist. But everything came out as he had wished, and at twelve o'clock, when Miss Ives knocked, he had completed a full disc of anecdote without the interpolation of his unsought collaborator.

"Is there anything up, Miss Ives?"

"Oh, yes, sir. I almost interrupted you, but I remembered how strict your orders were. Dr. Salter called at eleven. Miss Jenkins died."

"Miss Jenkins! Good heavens, of course, you should have called me. Have you got the will out of the vault?"

"Here it is, sir."

Alone again behind his closed door, he adjusted his features to a fitting solemnity. It was impossible altogether to repress Mr. Arnold's image of the falling of a ripe piece of fruit. Miss Jenkins had approached the perfect client; for eighty-five years she seemed to have been preparing for a neat and orderly demise. Her houses, in town and country, were deeded to her church, subject only to her life estate, and her jewelry and artifacts of any value had been parceled out in her lifetime among her nephews and nieces. There remained, indeed, little enough to bother her faithful counsel: little, that is, but a custodian account at the Standard Trust Company containing fifteen millions of "blue chip" securities. In only one respect had she fallen short of perfection: in her last will (she had made them annually) she had omitted Sylvaner Price as her co-executor with her bank.

"You'll have your counsel fees, Sylvaner," she had gruffly pointed out. "There's really no need for commissions, too, is there? One executor should be quite enough to handle this estate."

He had assured her that it should, but now, as he turned to the last page and contemplated the testatrix's tall strong signature beside the red wafer seal that was stamped over the two ends of the red ribbon that bound the pages together, he felt with his sudden regret a curious itching in his fingertips. Dropping the will to the desk he held up his hands, the palms toward him, and was startled to see his fingers twitching like the legs of two overturned crabs. Repulsed, he let his hands fall to the desk, one on either side of the will and contemplated with shock their immediately quickened movements.

"What do you want?" he cried. "Do you want me to tear *that* up? Do you want to deprive me of my prize estate? Well, go ahead, do your damndest!"

Hypnotized, he continued to watch his waving extremities. His right hand now turned itself over on its palm and slid along the surface of the desk to the drawers on the right and, dropping to the lowest, pulled it open to disclose the pages of another will. For a moment Price stared, and then with a start he recognized it as the next-to-last will that he had prepared for Miss Jenkins and which she had declined to execute because it had provided for two executors. His busy right hand, now flipping the pages expertly, pulled out page eight and brought it up, with the help of his suddenly cooperating arm, to toss it beside the executed instrument. Oh, how he *saw* it now, of course! Page eight was identical in all respects in each will except that the earlier one appointed as executors Sylvaner Price and Standard Trust Company while the later appointed only Standard.

"But what can you do about it?" he demanded, as much now in fascination as in fear of his suddenly quiet hands. "Can you break the seal? Are you trying to put me in jail?"

For answer his right hand soared into the air and then plunged into his vest pocket to extract the gold knife at the end of his watch chain. His left hand moved immediately to open the fine blade, and Price, transfixed, watched as the knife, held between his right forefinger and thumb, deftly and speedily scraped off the red paper seal. Next the ribbon was cut and pulled out and page eight removed and thrown, with the remnants of the seal, into the wastebasket. And all the while his mind kept up with his appendages, explaining, anticipating, almost gloating.

"But there'll be a copy of the executed will in Miss Jenkins' apartment. Oh, no there won't! I remember now, she wouldn't keep a copy. She said the servants might pry. But if I attach a new seal, a chemical test would show that the old one had been removed. Yes, but there won't *be* a chemical test. That's just the point! Who would ever question the fact that Miss Jenkins wanted two executors? Had she not appointed two in thirty previous wills? How it fits! How it all fits!"

His hands appeared to be suddenly at a loss. They sank to the blotter, more like tired doves now than crabs, but the fingers continued to flutter. They seemed to be appealing to him, to be trying to communicate that they had done all they could. . . .

"But naturally!" he cried with near hysteria. "You want ribbon and a new seal. You shall have them!"

He hurried to his door, opened it and found that Miss Ives was not at her desk. Pulling open the drawer where she kept her office supplies, he snatched the ribbon and red paper seal and returned to his room. In a few moments, with a deftness as amazing as the skill with which the first seal had been removed, Miss Jenkins' will with its new page eight had been reribboned and a new seal affixed carefully in the exact place of the old.

Price stared with wonder at the completed document. Nobody would have dreamed that it had been tampered with. It would be probated without a murmur from a single relative, a single legatee. And yet the work of ten minutes would operate to bring to him and his firm, by simple operation of law, a statutory commission of three hundred thousand dollars! It was the perfect crime.

The perfect . . . ! Price came at last to his old senses as he stared, with perfectly immobile body and slowly blinking eyes at the will. The *will!* But it was not a will; it was no more Miss Jenkins' will than his own, lying untampered with in the office vault. It was a rank forgery, and the forger, ghost or no ghost, should be put behind bars. His round gleaming forehead was pimpled again with drops of sweat as he contemplated *who* it would be to stand in that criminal docket. But it was absurd, macabre, unholy! Ghosts could not be allowed to administer estates according to the concealed wickedness of long-buried men. What was done could be undone. He started from his chair to reach in the basket for the removed, the desecrated, the *real* page eight and uttered a little shriek when he saw that he had torn it in two. He snatched up the forged will to rip it likewise in twain but paused just in time. After all, it was, if forged, still the client's only will, and the client was dead!

Sylvaner Price raised his eyes to the ceiling and his guilty fists above his eyes and shook them as he cursed the memory of Guthrie Arnold. But the words were no sooner uttered than his chest was struck by what seemed the impact of a thousand needles, and he fell forward unconscious over his desk and the creamy white red-ribboned parchment on which Miss Ives had so carefully typed the posthumous wishes of the late Miss Jenkins.

In the white hygienic serenity of his hospital room Price enjoyed a dull, doped peace. The proximity to death in which his coronary attack had briefly placed him had left him totally indifferent. He had even been capable of a small smile when Jack Keating, obviously warned to bring to his troubled mind no office news except of the most consoling character, had murmured into his oxygen tent that Miss Jenkins' will had been admitted to probate only two days after her demise, creating what was deemed an office record. It was all right, Price reassured himself. He would know what to do about that. If he should die, he would not have earned the commissions, and if he lived he could renounce them. If there were an afterlife, he could explain to Miss Jenkins, and if not . . . well, he did not really think he believed in anything but nothingness. The nothingness that meant absence of all need of lawyers. The nothingness of total rest.

As he recuperated he began, little by little, to resume his work on the biography, but not at all according to his original plan. Back in his apartment, seated on a couch by a window looking over a wintry Central Park, he dictated for a lengthening period each day to Miss Ives. As the doctor said he was not to exert himself, he consulted no notebooks or records. With his eyes closed and his now innocent hands folded tranquilly on his diminished abdomen, he spoke from memory. From memory or imagination? What did it matter? There were to be no further vividnesses. He was to put Guthrie Arnold back into the legend of the firm, and for this he needed only to consult his own high principles. What did it matter if his history would be like every other firm history? Was there not something restful, dignified, even rather noble about the well-prepared, the well-documented, the well-printed, the well-bound, and the unread?

"Mr. Arnold in his later years was able to delegate some of the detail of his burdensome practice to the shoulders of his younger partners and associates." Price's usual sharp, staccato voice had evened itself out into what was almost a sonorous flow. "This did not mean, however, that he shortened his hours. Whenever he saved time it was to contribute it to the many charitable enterprises on whose boards he so assiduously served. It was the function of younger men, he always maintained, to dedicate themselves wholly to their profession. Every young lawyer, he insisted, should have a hobby — law. But it was the duty of older men to begin to consider the community as a whole. . . ."

Oh, yes, it had all the effect that he knew it would. That other spirit, no longer manifested in the pricking of his brow or the wagging of his fingers, seemed quite at rest, and thinking of the altar of reliquaries in the office reception hall, he wondered if the *cordon sanitaire* with which he was now binding it off might not have manifested itself in the actual apparition of the kind of looped cord used in art galleries to keep back crowds. But evidently not, for nothing untoward was reported from downtown.

When Jack Keating came to report on the administration of the Jenkins estate, Price told him that he had decided to waive his commissions. Keating looked surprised, but it immediately struck Price that there was something factitious about his expression.

"I had a conversation with Miss Jenkins shortly before she died," Price explained gruffly. "She told me she had decided to have only one executor — the bank. Unfortunately I did not have time to prepare a new will. Naturally, under the circumstances, I cannot take commissions."

"Naturally." There was something too quickly conciliatory in Keating's tone, something almost medically professional, nurselike. "One wouldn't expect you to. Was it perhaps like the conversation young Smedburg saw you having one night in the reception hall with the portrait of Mr. Arnold?"

Price gave him a long, hard stare. "Perhaps."

"They're expensive, Mr. Price, your chats with spirits."

In twenty years Keating had never been so familiar. His tone was friendly, as was his rueful laugh, but they were the tone and the laugh that one used to the senile. How well Price knew them!

"You don't believe I had that talk with Miss Jenkins," he said quietly.

"I believe *you* believe it," Keating insisted eagerly. "All of us believe that. All your partners, I mean."

"But you think I've lost my mind."

"Never!" Keating shook his head with a slow, irritating solemnity. "Never. We simply believe you've been under a strain. My God, man, you're not made of iron! You have been running the shop by day and by night, in all seasons, for how many years? How could you expect to get through a lifetime without one crack on the surface?"

A faint smile appeared on Price's thin lips. "What then must Humpty Dumpty do?"

As Keating looked down now at the floor, both hands on his knees, Price suddenly realized that he was embarrassed, mortally embarrassed. All his chuckles and his slow nods had been but a tattered façade to cover his misery. The poor man was suffering as *he* had suffered when he had had to guide old Arnold in his senility. "Tell me," Price said in a gentler tone. "I want to know. I will do anything the firm suggests. What do they think I should do? Resign?"

Keating looked up, his face aglow with relief. "Oh, no, never!" he exclaimed warmly. "We need you much too much. But would you consider . . ." He faltered, wretched again. "Would you consider seeing a psychiatrist?"

"Certainly. Whomever you wish. Whenever you wish."

"There's Dr. Haven. He's the head man at St. Andrew's." Keating's voice shivered with the desire to get it over with. "He's not one of your bearded Freudians. He knows what it's all about. He . . ."

"Make me an appointment, Keating. My doctor says I may go out on Monday. I shall go to Dr. Haven."

"Thank you, sir!" Keating was a clerk again as he jumped gratefully to his feet. "I'm sure it's nothing serious. A couple of talks, and you'll be all squared away."

"Very likely." He coughed, the older partner again, as Keating made his way hastily to the door. "Oh, and Keating," he called.

"Yes, sir?"

"Send me up a renunciation of commissions in the Jenkins estate. And one of the clerks who's a notary with it. He can file it in the Surrogate's Court on his way back."

Keating's face was pathetic in its disappointment. "Won't you wait, sir, until you've seen Dr. Haven?"

"Do as I say, Keating," Price said gravely, "or I shall go to court myself."

He smiled a bit grimly as he heard the whispers in the corridor and knew that Keating was consulting with Miss Ives. But it was all right. His authority still held. Keating would do as he was told.

Dr. Haven made things very easy for him. He was, as promised, not in the least Freudian-looking; he might have come off the golf course, so round, so bald, so tweeded was he, yet withal so friendly, so sympathetic, so oddly wonderful. There was no idea, he quickly reassured Price, of any lying on couches or talking of sex. Price could simply sit, as stiffly as he liked, for all the world as if he were a client in his own office, and tell his story to an auditor whose unique virtue would be his complete attention.

"We're not even thinking of analysis," the doctor frankly told him. "It's not really feasible with older patients. Let's see first what we can do with a patchwork job."

Vastly reassured, Price told him, with less embarrassment

than he would have believed possible, of his strange visitations. Haven seemed not in the least surprised; he nodded as understandingly as if he, too, were constantly bothered by such mischievous sprites as haunted his patient. Yet nonetheless it came as a reassurance and not a disappointment, when, after only four sessions in which they had covered, with a disillusioning speed, the salient events in Sylvaner Price's life, the doctor announced his personal disbelief in the evil spirit of Guthrie Arnold.

"The anecdotes that you dictated were all within your own conscious or unconscious memory," he pointed out. "If they were not actually said by Arnold, they could have been said about him. Or said about someone else and associated by you unconsciously with Arnold. And what happened to the Jenkins will — well, you *saw* what happened to the Jenkins will."

"You think, then, I'm a horror?" Price asked sadly.

"I think, my friend, that you've been a victim of your own deepest fears. All your life you have identified pleasure with sin. That has been very clear from what you have told me of your past. Mr. Arnold was to you a godlike figure who enjoyed a special exemption. He could frolic without incurring the penalties that Sylvaner Price would have incurred. The only way *you* could frolic was by somehow creeping under his exemption. But the moment you tried this, by putting yourself as a biographer in the shoes of your subject — a clever device, I admit — well, of course, you had immediately to sin and immediately to suffer. Clever as it is, the subconscious can't escape itself."

Price considered this for a full minute. "So Mr. Arnold wasn't, after all, that way?"

"What way?"

"Wasn't a crook."

"My dear fellow, I have no doubt that he was every bit as distinguished a member of your profession as your great firm has always proudly claimed!"

"And do you have no doubt, by like token, that, once I have

accepted your diagnosis, I may continue my book in the spirit in which it was originally conceived?"

"No doubt whatever."

Price nodded several times and then, abruptly rising, bade his doctor good day and asked him to send his bill.

"Oh, your firm has taken care of that."

Price looked down at him with the faintest trace of a smile. "I hope they find me worth it."

The next morning, once more in his office, he told Miss Ives that he would revive his isolated biographical sessions, and he addressed himself once more to his dictaphone. Warily, with an eye occasionally cocked at the closed door that led out to the reception hall and its portrait, he began to describe Mr. Arnold as an administrator.

"One of the greatest pitfalls in building a large firm is accommodation business. Every client thinks you can turn over his minor headaches — his wife's fight with the department store, his niece's divorce, his son's traffic violations — to some young clerk and have them lost in the ocean of office overhead. But Mr. Arnold understood perfectly not only that the accumulation of these matters can seriously clog the operation of a law firm, but that being dipped in human spite and perversity they frequently resulted, even when competently handled, in client dissatisfaction. And so he developed his great art of referral. Never has it been carried to more Olympian heights! He could make the unhappy lawyer to whom he entrusted the garrulous old maid with the tangled leasehold think that he was getting a green shoot, the precursor of new business, and not, as in fact he was, a dead branch lopped off the healthy tree of the Arnold roster. 'Don't forget, Price,' he used to remind me with his cackling laugh, 'that a wise referral should accomplish two things: it should clean up your own yard and make a dump of your neighbor's lawn!' "

Price was on his feet now, his fists clenched, his eyes closed in the old agony. Would there be no end to these hideous anecdotes? Would the fiend never let him be? Where would his itching fingers lead him next? Their tips were burning again now, and, opening his hands, he stared at them in terror. Across the white spread sheet of his stunned mind a series of horrible slides were projected, succeeding each other with little clicks. There was the locked drawer of the office files, then the heavy round knob of the office safe. He had a sensation of metal on his finger tips, but *why?* Why in the name of Beelzebub? What horrors could he be seeking there? His right hand began to move up and down, like a dog at the end of a leash, wanting to be taken out, wanting . . .

No, no, what a hell, was there no keeping it out? "Miss Ives!" With a desperate effort he turned and sent the dictaphone crashing to the floor.

Pale and staring, she loomed through the slowly opened door.

"Come in, come in. I've smashed that damn machine. Yes, come in and leave my door open. Always, please, Miss Ives, from now on, leave my door open. I shall dictate only to you. In fact, I'll start right now. Are you ready?"

Miss Ives was always ready. Price walked rapidly back and forth across his room as he continued his reminiscences, and each time that he reached the open door he cast his eyes suspiciously toward the great portrait at the end of the reception hall that gazed so superciliously down at small waiting clients, clutching like immigrants' bundles their small heaps of problems.

"Mr. Arnold," he dictated in his most rasping tone, "always insisted that the Code of Professional Ethics should be more strictly interpreted. Unlike so many of his contemporaries, he never held a share of stock in a corporation that he represented. He would not even allow the firm's telephone number to appear on our letterhead, and it was only with the greatest difficulty that we persuaded him to enter it in the directory."

He paused to glance boldly now for a longer interval at the portrait. Innocuous again, mild, showy, even faintly vulgar, it had dwindled to the more fitting proportions of a piece of interior decoration. Well, if that was the only way! Bitter, dry, determined, Price picked up again his narrative. As he intoned the names of civic institutions and civic honors, as he listed honorary degrees and quoted from testimonials, as he delivered anecdotes to illustrate the wisdom, the common sense, the humanity, the lovableness of his subject, he might have been an undertaker driving in, one by one, the nails of the coffin of Guthrie Arnold — his Guthrie Arnold, Satan's Guthrie Arnold, the firm's Guthrie Arnold, anybody's Guthrie Arnold — what did it matter so long as there was peace?

Foster Evans on Lewis Bovee

I SUPPOSE THAT the most irritating thing to me about Lloyd Degener's decision to take upon his own shoulders the task of writing up the history of Arnold & Degener is that I have no ostensible ground to object. After all, to the clients, the law clerks, even to the members of the firm, nobody could be more obviously qualified. He is our senior partner (only I, with what Lloyd likes to call my "Chinese" reverence for the past, still consider Guthrie Arnold, twenty years dead, as the real boss), and, more than anyone else, he is responsible for the splendid position which we occupy today in the field of corporation law. Lloyd, in his near half century on Wall Street, has developed the firm from what he used rather superciliously to describe as a "gentleman's chaos of prima donnas in high white collars at roll-top desks" to the huge, bright, humming legal machine that occupies two glass stories at Number One Chase Manhattan Plaza. It is not even a detail to him that we may have lost our soul in the process.

Furthermore, like me, he is old, and although, like me, he still comes to the office daily, he has reached the point of making only executive decisions (supposed to be the hardest but really the easiest) and has ample time for the expected pastime of the venerable: reminiscence — or fiction — whichever one chooses to call it. Can't you just see that heavy volume of gilt-edged paper, its title stamped on Morocco leather in gold letters, with reproductions of bad portraits of deceased partners protected from a nonexistent reader by onionskin covers? Can't you picture the chapters of glorious firm history: the corporate reorganizations, the corporate mergers, even the corporate bankruptcies, positively boasting of being unread? Like a marble mausoleum, the volume will be sufficient unto itself.

Lloyd has asked me to contribute my reminiscences of the late Lewis Bovee, and I can hardly refuse, but to fit in with the pompous tone of the other chapters, they will have to be bowdlerized reminiscences, dealing with Mr. Bovee's great court victories in will contests. They will be destined to be read, like Lloyd's own contribution, only by other partners of the firm. But I must give myself the satisfaction of writing a *private* chapter about Mr. Bovee. If I am ever to understand his success and my relative failure, if I am ever to answer the tormenting question of why he, another old bachelor, should have dominated his world while mine dominates me, I had better do so now.

Was the difference in the worlds, or in the old bachelors, or in both? Lloyd would say in the bachelors, but then Lloyd would not really care. It would be no part of *his* firm history. Cardinal Wolsey said that had he served his God as he had served his king, he would not have been abandoned in his old age. I might say the same thing of my God and my law firm. For Arnold & Bovee, now Arnold & Degener, has simply been my whole life. It has been my family, my hobby, my club. If ever a man put all his eggs in one basket, it is I.

A fool, you will say. Of course, I was a fool! But in 1921, when I started to practice law, it was not so ridiculous for a man to put all his heart as well as all his mind into his profession. If the sacrifices were great, the rewards could be sweet. Who knows the joys of Saturday night drinking who has not toiled the preceding six days and nights? Who knows the bond of partnership who has not labored with peers whom he absolutely trusted? In those early days the excitement of the world was provided vividly, if vicariously, by our clients; the office and the courtroom were laboratories in which we could surrender ourselves wholly to the excitement of intellectual combat. And above all there were the friendships. Before the great gray expansion of the twenties and thirties a law firm was like a fraternity or even a secret society. How many times Arnold & Bovee men married into each other's families! How frequently they lived in neighboring houses!

There was always the menace of old age ahead, a sad enough prospect for the unmarried, but I consoled myself by contemplating the splendid last chapters of the glorious old men of the office, particularly that of Mr. Bovee. Lawyers in those days reverenced their seniors, and the downtown lunch hour rang with the admiring tales of clerks of rival firms who outdid each other in descriptions of the eccentricities and brilliancies of their bosses. "The old tartar" and "the old tyrant" were terms of endearment. Was it not so, or did I dream it so? Am I a sour old fool, or have times really changed? Surely I am right that young men in the nineteen-sixties, however hard they may work, and I admit that some work as hard as any of my contemporaries ever did, do not feel the zest for it that we knew. However brilliant they may be, work is work; their "fun" is always home, on the ski trail, in a sailboat, with children, just as their emotional needs are supplied by women, by wives. They have no conception of friendship in the true masculine sense. Their friends are the husbands of their wives' friends. They know nothing of the joy of intellectual work that is really shared. They may have much, but they have missed much.

One thing, anyway, that I have not dreamed is the treatment of the old today. No, indeed, that is no dream, no fantasy, or if it is, it is a nightmare. Never could Mr. Bovee in his seventies have met the conduct that I have met from younger men: the glance at the wrist watch, the stifled yawn, the faked telephone call as an excuse to end our talk. As if they had nothing to learn from my five decades of experience, even from my anecdotes! But Lloyd Degener measures time in work sheets, and he gave me one of his public chidings at a recent partners' lunch for "wasting the time" of the law clerks.

"Foster Evans and I are getting to be a couple of old dodos," he announced with his horrible mock cheerfulness. "I hereby make it the public duty of every partner of the firm to shut us up whenever he catches us telling a story we've told before!"

Very well, Lloyd. I shall hold my tongue, as I pick up my pen.

I must start my account of Lewis Bovee by admitting that my first impression of him was hardly more respectful than would be that of a young law clerk of me today. But the difference is that I am a conventional old crow whom it should be a simple matter to treat with deference, whereas Mr. Bovee was a gaudy peacock who seemed at first blush to invite ridicule. Indeed it struck me that the only straightforward, unaffected thing about him was that he had anglicized the pronunciation of his French name. All else to my inexperienced eyes seemed pose: the slow, measured gait, the elaborate stoop, the inappropriately gay tweeds, the brilliant tie with the huge knot, the exaggerated facial twitching that accompanied the precise articulation, the walking cane with the gold knob, the derby with the hook in the back for a peg, the vast, musty, littered Dickensian office with its door always closed to the rest of the firm, where Mr. Bovee prepared accountings for gigantic fortunes. Could Otis Skinner in one of his famous character parts have been more conscious of his effects than this small, wizened, beak-nosed, agate-eyed, parchment-skinned septuagenarian who changed his black wig every week for a longer one until the end of the month when he would have a much advertised "haircut" and revert to the first? Who in the name of Blackstone and Mansfield did he think he was fooling?

It did not ameliorate my impression, either, that in those first years I saw Mr. Bovee only socially. I did not work in his department, but he would draft the unmarried lawyers as extra men at the lunch parties that he gave every Sunday in his big, cavernous brownstone home on West Thirty-fourth Street, filled with American marble statuary of the Italian school and heavily framed canvases of Eastern bazaars and battle scenes. For Mr. Bovee, the member of an old, prominent and (with the exception of himself) prolific New York family, adored social and cousinly gatherings and loved to preside at the end of a long table loaded with good food and wine, with favors and trinkets and snappers and Lord knows what, surrounded by as many lovely "damsels" as his acquaintance could provide. Indeed, he would hardly allow any general conversation, so busy was he proposing toasts, calling on guests for little speeches or reading aloud some of the *vers de société* for which he considered himself justly famous.

It is hard to convey, in a world of hipsters and beatniks, the peculiar preciousness of those Sunday lunches: the sugary compliments, the "daring" sallies, the effusive praises, the complicated conundrums, the tinkling laughter, the general agreement that Lewis Bovee was the wittiest, the most gallant, the most delightful of older men, a kind of winking Victorian Bacchus who was temporarily on the wagon. Perhaps I can give some conception of it by noting that Mr. Bovee kept a "beauty gallery" of miniatures. It was deemed a high privilege among the fair sex of all ages to be invited to have their likenesses executed by Mr. Florian, Mr. Bovee's commissioned painter, and added, in a gilt oval frame, to the great collection on the red velvet curtain that adorned one whole side of the parlor. This collection was ultimately bequeathed to the Bovee Costume Institute, but on the top floor where it now hangs it does not, alas, enjoy the admiring audience that it did on those Sunday noons of yore.

I assumed, with the cynicism of youth, that Mr. Bovee's value to the firm must have rested largely in his social and family connections, that his function must have been that of a retriever of clients whose legal problems could be threshed out by a competent staff downtown. I had no wish to work for a "front" partner, so when I was summoned one morning to Mr. Bovee's office and asked if I might be interested in transferring to "estates," I did not treat the proposition as the honor that it was intended to be.

"If you'll forgive me, sir," I protested, "I think I'm better cut out to work with corporations and balance sheets than with society people. You see, sir, I'm really just a small-town boy. A bit of a hick, if the truth be told."

"I think, Foster Evans, you had better let *me* be the judge of that," Mr. Bovee replied, shaking his head back and forth, as he perpetually did, and tapping the ends of his fingers together. "I have had several occasions now to observe you in my house, and your manners and deportment have been all that I could ask. You have a head that is stuck squarely on your shoulders, young man, and that is the great thing in dealing with my clients. Never to be dazzled. Never to be cajoled. You must keep the reins at all times very firmly in your hands, however much you may occasionally slacken them."

I was a bit surprised at the firmness of his tone. From what I had observed at those Sunday lunches, I would have thought that Mr. Bovee himself might have been easily enough led by one of his "damsels." But the sudden gleam in those agate eyes gave me to consider for the first time that there might be another side to his nature.

"I think I can promise you some fun," he continued with a dry smile. "I know that I have always found the personal equation the most amusing that our practice affords."

I persisted, however, in my professed devotion to corporations, and Mr. Bovee, suddenly frosty, abruptly terminated our interview. Only when I was summoned to the presence of Mr. Arnold himself did I realize the full extent of my error.

"I should have got to you before Mr. Bovee did, Evans. A word to the wise. One doesn't turn down an offer to work for *him.* I have managed to persuade him to give you a second chance."

And the very next day I was installed in a narrow cubicle that bordered on Mr. Bovee's large office. Here were no bright academic canvases, no vast white images of dying Indian chiefs or babes in the woods. The difference between his office and his home announced the difference between Lewis Bovee at work and at play. Downtown he chose to surround himself only with emblems of his profession: a mahogany bookcase with glass doors for his law reports; black teakwood tables for the heaps of current files, a roll-top desk so littered with paper that he worked at a chair with a desk arm, and on the walls dark engravings of English eighteenth-century chancellors. But whatever the seeming mess, Mr. Bovee and his taciturn, etiolated, dark-clad male secretary, Mr. Banion, knew exactly where everything was. And so, in time, did I.

It did not take me many weeks to discover that Lewis Bovee was a very great family lawyer indeed. He could dictate an entire executor's account, even to the schedule of debts and petty expenses, a job that no self-respecting fiduciary today would dream of taking away from his accountant. Yet figures were never bogies to him. He was not afraid of big ones or overconcerned with small. And he could invest as well as compute; he knew the stock market as intimately as he knew the Surrogate's Court Act. Not only did he guard his clients effectively from will contestants, tax collectors, fortune hunters, borrowers, beggars and other thieves, malicious or unintending, but by judiciously buying and selling he swelled their portfolios as he swelled his fees.

When I say that Mr. Bovee was a "family lawyer," I mean, of

course, a lawyer to rich families. This is not to say that he could not or did not on occasion act for the poor, but his peculiar genius was for the preservation of large properties and their orderly transmission from the dead to the living. In fact, it was sometimes difficult to disassociate his clients *from* their money; it was almost as if they existed so that Lewis Bovee could manage their fortunes. Heiresses had to be protected from unscrupulous husbands, heirs from designing women and gambling dens, parents from blind generosity and the old from their own vagaries, all by the Bovee trusts, terse, clear, cogent instruments, cleverly drafted to encompass every eventuality and reposing broad remedial powers in Bovee himself and in his appointed successors. Yet the system worked. If the people existed for the fortunes, the fortunes nonetheless supported the people. Mr. Bovee was a kind of God at his roll-top desk. The handsome young artist, writer or poet, so effusively greeted and toasted by the Sunday host at Thirty-fourth Street, might find himself described downtown by that same host turned to a fierce lawyer protecting a female client from an improvident marriage, as a "dilettante" or, worse, a "spendthrift."

Small wonder that north of Canal Street Lewis Bovee was much loved and much laughed at, and that south of that line he was often disliked but invariably respected. But searching for a deeper answer, it gave me an occasional shudder to suspect that the discrepancy between the two Bovees might be explained by the fundamental cynicism of the uptown one. Was his idea, or hidden faith, or instinctive evaluation that human life was reducible to coin of the realm and that the rest — love, friendship, art, family ties, adventure, heroism — were all a matter of Sunday lunches served with pink champagne and favors to the sound of dulcet compliments passed to and fro? Did this sere old bachelor really believe that work was everything except for the little bit that was not work, and that that little bit — a kiss, a sigh, a hop, skip and jump, a lilting tune, a mother's love, a Michelangelo — was all summed up in, no better or worse than, a Sunday lunch at Thirty-fourth Street? And I — was I heading to the same conclusion?

He had a first cousin, Edythe Vale, a frequent guest at the Sunday lunches where I was now a fixture. She was considerably younger than Mr. Bovee, but by no means young herself — certainly in her middle sixties. She was handsome, but in a large, horsy way; her face was long, her nose was long, and she wore too much make-up, too much lace, too many beads and bracelets. Her natural pose should have been that of a strong, quiet, gray-haired Minerva. Instead, she chose to dye to a shiny chestnut her high-piled, elaborately waved hair, to smile and sigh and simper, to fuss with a lorgnette, to twist her rings, to imply old sadnesses and spiritual richnesses, to suggest that if youth would only listen to what she had to say . . . but then, of course, she had been born a Bovee. Perhaps she too had a sterner life in another part of the city.

Mrs. Vale from the beginning took a very distinct interest in me. If we were not seated together at table, she would beckon me to join her afterwards in a corner of the parlor, trying to make our colloquy as private as our host would allow — which was never very private. She managed to imply, with many signs and silences, that brilliant as my future might be in her cousin's "great firm," there were things I would do well to learn (as indeed *he* might have done well to learn) from a woman who had suffered.

"Ah, yes, you lawyers," she would murmur. "You carry all before you, all you *see,* anyway. But how much, my dear Mr. Evans, do you really see?"

I have always been a very practical sort of fellow, and there was a personal, insinuating quality to Mrs. Vale's conversation that made me decidedly uncomfortable. Each time I was relieved when Mr. Bovee, who treated her with a rather proprietary combination of testiness and mock gallantry, came to lead her off.

"Now, Edythe, we all know you're too much of a *femme fatale* to be left alone with a young man. What good is Foster Evans going to be to me in the office tomorrow? Why, he'll be mooning about the place like young Romeo and won't know an injunction from a demurrer. Besides, my dear, you're needed as my hostess. You must not forget the high demands of blood propinquity!"

In the collection of miniatures Mrs. Vale had proudly identified her own likeness, if that was the word. For I would never have recognized her in the wide-eyed, alabaster-skinned red-haired girl, frail, almost ailing, pathetic in her intensity, in her apprehension, who stared out at me. One Sunday, after his other guests had left, I asked Mr. Bovee if there had been a tragedy in Mrs. Vale's life. The terseness of his answer confirmed my impression of his dislike of his cousin.

"None but of her own making."

"Aren't those just the most tragic of all?"

"Don't be a sentimental fool, Evans."

"But, sir, misfortunes that are simple accidents cannot be tragic. Consider Shakespeare."

"Shakespeare didn't write tragedies about geese," he grumbled. "And Edythe is a goose. She always has been, and she always will be."

I observed that she must have been a very lovely young goose.

"She *was* lovely," he conceded, "but loveliness in a goose is only a liability. And when it's coupled with uncontrolled generosity, the case is hopeless. Edythe as a girl gave away her dolls to children in the street and her pin money to beggars."

"I find that enchanting!"

Mr. Bovee favored me with his patient, pained look. "I see,

my boy, that I must tell you the facts of life. Edythe at twenty-one ran off with a married man old enough to be her father. In those days that was the end of a woman. But I was determined to keep her real father (my uncle Bertie) from breaking his heart. I followed them and brought her back. I managed pretty well to hush the matter up. Edythe was taken by her mother for one of those extended European trips that needed no explanation in those days. A young lawyer in the office, one Vale, who was very much indebted to me, was willing to marry her for an acquittance. They were divorced a year later, but Edythe at least had a legal father for her child."

"And she never married again?"

"Who would have her? I said the matter was 'pretty well' hushed up. I could not work miracles."

"What a life," I murmured, thinking of Mrs. Vale's distracted eyes.

"Yes, what a life. But when you get to my age, you'll see these things in terms of their alternatives. Edythe, I grant, is a bit *déclassée,* but she has not been ostracized, as she would have been without my interference. And she has had her beautiful daughter to bring up and worship. *That* has been her life. I venture to suggest that it has been at least tolerable, as lives of geese go. If you'll come next Sunday you will meet the daughter. She is married to the Reverend Elias Talbot who has just been called to St. Clement's after two years in Boston. I hope they will be among the faithful at my Sundays now. Oh, you will find Madeleine Talbot our star of stars!"

Indeed, I came, and indeed I found her perfect. Yet so gracefully did Madeleine Talbot blend herself into the Bovee scene that it took my eyes, unaccustomed to her subtle art, more than one Sunday to appreciate her. It would have been a simple matter for one so young and lovely, with such beautiful black curls and such limpid, closely watching, gently curious brown eyes, one so slight and white and perfectly formed, to have triumphed over Mr. Bovee's assemblage of elderly hangers-on, but such vulgar victories were not for Mrs. Talbot. No, she even dressed so as not to stand out, yet in rich subdued colors that gradually stole upon one's notice, in murky claret, or in a purple that was nearly black, with a small velvet toque and perhaps a single bracelet, and a gold band around her neck. Her voice was very low but clear, and she spoke slowly, directing her conversation entirely to her partner as if it could be taken for granted that her own affairs were too slight for discussion.

"I know if I were a man, Mr. Evans, I'd rather be a lawyer than anything else. Cousin Lewis has brought me up on the most wonderful stories of the law."

"Well, of course, a lot of it is pretty dry," I demurred. "Sometimes we seem to be dealing more with companies than people."

"And companies don't have souls?" she inquired.

"Like dogs and pussycats?" I rejoined, beginning to feel very clever under that sober, serene stare. "Why not? Perhaps after dissolution they go to a corporate heaven where there are no stockholders' meetings and no antitrust laws. Where they can merge and monopolize and fix prices to their hearts' content. If they have hearts."

"Oh, if they have souls, they must have hearts," Mrs. Talbot insisted.

"Unlike some humans," I muttered, thinking of the beast who had been this lovely creature's father.

"You're a cynic, Mr. Evans."

"Not necessarily. A Christian must believe in souls. He needn't believe in hearts."

"Now I hear the lawyer talking."

"Or the realist."

"That's your credo, isn't it!" she exclaimed. "Like Cousin Lewis's. That the two are the same. It must come from having to see people in such exposing conditions. After crimes. During divorces. Except Cousin Lewis doesn't handle divorces, does he?"

"Well, not usually. Unless a regular client is involved."

"Oh, would he do it for a regular client? I thought with him it was a matter of principle."

"Principles have a way of dimming when they stand in the way of old and valued clients," I answered, feeling very sophisticated, though I hardly dared to look down the table in the direction of my host.

"Indeed. Then there *are* circumstances under which your great law firm would be willing to put asunder those whom God has joined together?"

Her tone was soft and serious, but there was a reassuring tremor of amusement in her eyes. I had almost forgotten that she was the wife of a clergyman.

"Does that seem very wicked to you?"

"Oh, I'm a woman, Mr. Evans, and women don't make nearly as many moral judgments as men. How does it seem to *you?*"

I did not know why, but I felt suddenly sure that it would benefit me in the eyes of this charming creature if I proved a liberal. "Oh, I'm rather advanced in these matters," I told her, enunciating a doctrine that was not only new to me, but opposed to everything I had hitherto believed. "I see no reason that society — or God Himself for that matter — should compel two persons to live together who no longer wish it."

She contemplated me gravely, but with no hint of agreement. Or of disagreement. "Even when there are children?"

"Even when there are children," I said stoutly.

"You *are* advanced, Mr. Evans," she said quietly, and we turned to other topics.

Such was my first meeting with Madeleine Talbot. But thereafter she appeared regularly, as he had hoped, at her Cousin

Lewis's Sundays, and it became a tacitly understood thing that she and I should always have a little talk. If we were not seated beside each other at table, I would seek her out after the meal, and if foiled — which sometimes happened, as all the old boys were after her — I would be allowed to escort her home, ten blocks away. If her husband was with her, we would make a threesome. In the course of a couple of months I learned very little about Madeleine Talbot, but there was substantially nothing that she did not learn about me. That was the kind of woman she was. Men told her everything. If a man had nothing to tell, he would probably have made it up.

The Reverend Elias Talbot could have been better described by Trollope's pen than by mine. He would be hardly credible to the young of the nineteen-sixties. It is all very well to say that human nature does not change, but certain types exist only with certain types of civilization. The miser, for example, in the old sense of one who secretes and gloats over silver or gold, has not survived into the age of paper currency. Similarly, the unctuous clerical hypocrite belongs to the ages of faith. Talbot was beginning to be an anachronism even in my youth.

He may have been briefly handsome in his twenties, but in his late thirties, when I knew him, he was fair and soft and fat, full of gushing banalities and exaggerated politenesses to the other guests at Mr. Bovee's. It seemed incredible that anyone as exquisite as Madeleine should have married such a man. Some of my incredulity must have expressed itself in the questions that I tried to put tactfully to her mother, for Mrs. Vale became very frank on the subject.

"Madeleine, like myself as a young woman, went through a deeply religious period," she explained to me one Sunday lunch when we were table partners. "Oh, we were all too worldly for her then! She went in head over heels for slums and settlement houses. If I so much as opened my mouth in protest, I was called

Mrs. Mammon. And when she first brought Elias to the house, I will have to admit that he looked like a cherub. Working with alcoholics and other degenerates, he must have seemed as bright and shiny as a boy knight in a painting by Burne-Jones or Rossetti. How could poor Madeleine tell that he would run like a mouse to the first fashionable parish he was offered after they were married?"

I was a bit taken aback by such confidence. "No doubt she enjoys that life also," I responded discreetly. "After all, God is everywhere."

"It has always seemed to me that He's more in some places than in others," Mrs. Vale retorted with a sniff. "My cousin Lewis once explained to me the only kind of fraud that invalidates a marriage. Apparently if a man puts on a false nose, and I marry him, believing him to be someone else, I can get out of it. But if I marry a divine cherub, and he turns out to be a fatuous ass, I'm stuck. That's law for you!"

My throat tightened, so that I could hardly swallow, and the odor of lilies at the crowded table almost stifled me. The sudden new concept of Madeleine as an unhappily married woman made me shiver all over. Young people would not believe it today, but until that moment I had had no notion of what my feelings really consisted. Now in that stuffy dining room with its overdressed women and dark cloth-lined walls I had a giddy sense of covers being pulled off, of nudities about to be revealed.

"Do you mean," I demanded tensely, "that Madeleine *regrets* her marriage?"

Mrs. Vale surveyed me critically. Evidently she had not bargained on so strong a response. "I mean that *I* regret it, Foster," she explained, for so she called me now. "I think you're enough of a friend to be able to share a disagreeable confidence. How would you feel if you were the parent of an exquisite creature like that and saw her limited to the social activities of the fashionable parish of a pious fraud? Wouldn't it make you find arguments in favor of a system that offered second chances in life? Look at him, Foster!" I follewed her eyes down the table to where Elias Talbot was pushing his spoon deep into a mound of strawberry ice cream. "My child needs love. What can she expect of *him?*"

"You mean he doesn't love her?"

"Oh, love her!" Mrs. Vale's shrug was impatient. "He loves her, no doubt, in a pale, pre-Raphaelite way. I mean love her as a *man.*"

I gaped at the territories that seemed to be opening before me as this terrible old woman continued her rampage of tearing away veils. "But they have two children," I protested feebly.

Mrs. Vale cackled. "Twins!" she cried contemptuously, and I blushed furiously as I thought I caught her meaning.

I could not imagine that Mrs. Vale was ever as brutally candid with her sensitive daughter as she had been with me, so my relations with Madeleine were not embarrassed by the fear that she might know what I had learned. But I was certainly more observant now. Whenever she mentioned her husband, whenever she so much as glanced his way, I would study her discreetly to catch any sign of concealed aversion. There never was any.

And if there had been, what did I expect to gain? Did I aspire to be the second husband of Madeleine Talbot? I think I can honestly say that I was too humble for such *hubris.* I thought of myself at most as a knight errant who would be amply rewarded by the mere opportunity to rescue the lady in distress. If love can be pieced together from the elements of such a worshipping championship, then I loved Madeleine. I even consciously tried to keep my thoughts of her pure. Oh, I was in a bad way. No question about that.

If Madeleine failed now to appear at a Sunday lunch, my whole week was ruined. She was the Freya of Mr. Bovee's Valhalla; without her the poor old gods were old and shabby indeed. Their banquet became a kind of ghastly parody of a children's party in which bony hands pulled the snappers and grabbed at the sweets. But when she appeared, the catalytic agent, how promptly did matters right themselves! Then everything fell into order, made sense; then the shrill clamor of egotistical complaints and boasts subsided into equable discussion, and the food and drink were reduced to the role of pleasant props for a civilized interchange of greetings and ideas. I began to see that the entertainment of those lunch parties existed only in and through Madeleine. Without her the rest were animals, and old animals at that.

They all knew it, too. It was not simply the result of my infatuation. The chorus of welcome that greeted Madeleine was a true chorus for a protagonist: now the play could begin. What did it matter if it was a comedy or a tragedy so long as they were on stage? That, anyway, was living, even if death bobbed about impatiently in the wings. And the manager of the whole spectacle, our host, was the most aware of this of all. One could see it in the hasty way in which he rose and waddled to the door, both arms outstretched when he saw her, crying:

"Madeleine, my angel! We had almost given you up!"

With me her conversation remained always on the same level, so peculiarly her own: that of the impersonal personally approached. I had a curious and delightful sense of intimacy with her even when we discussed matters as dry as "Cousin Lewis's" trust accountings. She seemed inexhaustibly interested in all things concerning her cousin and trustee. She never talked about herself, and only once made an indirect reference to her husband that might have been construed as derogatory. It was after I had told her that I took Mr. Bovee for my model in everything.

"I hope not in *everything,* Foster," she protested gently. "I hope, for example, that you don't intend to remain a bachelor forever."

"Oh, I doubt I shall ever marry," I said airily, with what I yet hoped was a tinge of discernible melancholy.

"Don't say that. You were cut out to be an excellent husband. It would be a sad loss to some otherwise lucky girl."

"It's too late," I said gloomily.

"Too late?"

"The only woman I've ever wanted to marry is not free," I blurted out.

Madeleine took it wonderfully. She did not blink; she did not brush it off; she did not reject it. She was simply silent for a moment, impassively silent, as if in formal and dignified recognition of a sentiment that she could respect but to which she could not respond. Then she proceeded with the argument. "Let us hope that time may cure that," she said softly. "And when you do marry, please promise me one thing. Don't make the mistake of excluding your wife from your career. Let her share it. Tell her, for example, all the things you have told me."

"She'd probably be bored to death."

"No. No wife is bored with her husband's career unless he's bored with her."

It was then that I recalled that in all our talks she had never referred to her duties, if any, as a clergyman's wife, and this further evidence of her misery filled me with a wild happiness and an unreasoning hope.

The next Sunday Madeleine's mother, Mrs. Vale, asked me to walk with her to her hotel on Madison Avenue.

"The time has come," she announced mysteriously, as soon as we were out of earshot of the other guests descending the brownstone stoop.

"The time?"

"The time to go to Lewis. I've had a blistering talk with Elias. He is willing to consider letting Madeleine go if the break can be made to seem her fault and if he receives half her income. Of course, he's a beastly pirate, but what other way is there?"

My heart was beating painfully. "You mean he'd give her a divorce? Won't it ruin his career?"

"Not if he doesn't remarry, and what does *he* want with a wife unless to torture her? Besides, it wouldn't exactly help his career if Madeleine were to sue him for a separation on grounds of cruelty."

I shuddered. "She has such grounds?"

"Oh, grounds and grounds! I assure you, Foster, I've been working on this for years. And now, at long last, I've got him almost to the point of letting my poor precious tortured darling out of her gilded cage. A cage gilded with her own money!" Mrs. Vale drew herself up imperiously here, pausing in her walk to strike the pavement with the end of her umbrella. "I've done my end of the job, Foster! But that's only the half of it. The other half is to bring Lewis around. And for that, my boy, we count on you!"

She did not have to explain. I knew all about her daughter's trust arrangements. Mrs. Vale's late father, Lewis Bovee's uncle, had left his daughter Edythe only a small annuity, because of her scandalous early conduct, and had placed the balance of his considerable estate in trust for his adored granddaughter, Madeleine. It was a curiously drawn New Jersey will which provided that the income of the trust could be paid to Madeleine or to any member or members of her family, *or* accumulated, "in the absolute and unquestioned discretion of Lewis Bovee, even though the exercise of that discretion should deprive any beneficiary of his or her sole means of support." The instrument had, of course, been drafted by Lewis Bovee himself. If any income was to be funneled from that trust into the fat, damp, clutching hands of the Reverend Elias Talbot, somebody was going to have to talk Mr. Bovee into it.

"Of course, I'll do what I can," I said, with a heavy sigh. "But you know how he is."

"Oh, I know how he is. But, Foster, you *have* to prevail. My child's very life is at stake!"

"I wonder if all our lives aren't at stake," I said gloomily. For the rest of our walk I hardly listened to the excited flow of her complaints and ejaculations, so intent was I on preparing for the morrow's interview.

It proved even worse than I had expected. Mr. Bovee sat immobile at his roll-top desk without the least alteration of his expression until I had entirely finished my plea. Then he shook his head.

"This is a bad business, Foster."

"I know it is, sir."

"I mean your end of it. You've allowed two women to make an ass of you."

"Sir?"

"And I'm afraid you've compounded your folly by falling in love with one of them. It's my fault, of course. I should have seen it coming."

"Is it a sin to fall in love, sir?"

"I said folly, my boy," he said sadly. "Not sin, folly. Foster, let me ask you something." For the first time in our relationship I thought I detected an actually tender note in his voice. "I have a terrible fear that I have not fulfilled my responsibility toward you. Tell me something. Is it possible, after all you have seen of Madeleine and her mother, that you do not know who Gardner Greene is?"

I closed my eyes and waited, conscious primarily of the sudden searing dryness of my throat. "He is the man Madeleine wants to marry," I heard myself saying in a dead voice. "Is that what you want to tell me?"

Mr. Bovee was not for a minute fooled by my guess. He rose and put a hand on my shoulder and then abruptly took it away. Turning from me to the window, he answered me. "I'm not going to watch your face, my boy, because no man can help another at a time like this. All you can do is listen, and all I can do is talk. I'll make it as brief as I can."

He then proceeded to tell me the story of Madeleine and her lover in his dry, precise court voice. Not seeing his face, as each of his carefully articulated words fell upon the warm skin of my soul like little knobs of hard, cold hail, I had a fantasy that I was being tried for the murder of Madeleine, and that Mr. Bovee was defending me.

"Madeleine, like her mother, was much given to worthy causes. As a debutante she spent her afternoons in poor girls' clubs and her evenings teaching literature to culturally ambitious stenographers. Oh, you will say, how worthy, and I will reply, how *excessive.* No good ever comes from such mawkishness. No, Foster, a debutante should be a selfish, giddy creature. Of such are the solidest matrons made. When Madeleine brought home Elias Talbot, a young parson as seemingly bland and lost in the heavens as herself, her grandfather, who was dying, asked me what was to be done. The marriage could not be prevented; both were of age. So I induced him to leave Madeleine's share of his estate to me with the broadest powers. I hope that I persuaded him that I would be able to look after her. I hope that he died in peace."

Mr. Bovee's tone became rich and level, as the pace of his story slackened. "That trust, my dear Foster, has now been in existence for close to fifteen years. Its principal has doubled under my care. It was not adequate at first to support Madeleine and her family. It is now. And it will be adequate to keep her children out of the gutter into which she and her mother are intent on pushing them. That is what I call fulfilling my word. And that is why I will not give a penny of the trust income to Elias Talbot. No matter what you say he does to her, which, incidentally, I do not for a minute believe."

I stamped my foot and turned to the door.

"But wait, you have not heard all." Mr. Bovee's tone was sharply peremptory. "Madeleine in marrying Talbot had underestimated herself. She had assumed that their shared ecstasy over the poor, the benighted, the unwashed, the ignorant and the obscene was the spiritual sublimation of that impulse which in less exalted folk is known as sex. She had assumed that the delight she felt in hearing Talbot's banal and pompous homilies was a message transmitted from the body that it desired to reproduce itself by a union with this man. This, then, was love: love of God, love of mankind, love of Elias Talbot. And in the due course of time the reproduction of the species was very precisely accomplished by the birth of a son to ensure the continuity of Talbot's evangelicism and of a daughter to guarantee that Madeline's altruism would not be lost to our terrestrial globe."

After a pause, his voice suddenly soared to a high pitch of bitterness. "But where was love? Where had *that* gone? I will tell you where it had gone. It had gone to Gardner Greene, the handsome, dark-haired school teacher who played the organ in the Reverend Talbot's church. He was ardent; she was generous. The profanest love followed the most sacred, and carried all before it. Madeleine is now willing to give up her income to the unhappy Talbot: it is all for love or the world well lost. Unfortunately, the old lawyer cousin is given power to write the last act."

There must have been a silence of at least a minute while I stared at the dark back of the little man at the window.

"Even if it's all true," I said in a strangled tone, "is it any reason she should remain shackled forever to that beast?"

"She chose him."

"Isn't it your duty as a trustee to see that she is happy?" I exclaimed in a louder voice. "You'd buy her a house if she had to have one. Shouldn't you buy her a new husband? Or at least buy off the old one?"

Mr. Bovee turned around now, his thin lips pale and compressed. "You're not yourself today, Foster. You are certainly in no condition to advise me as to my fiduciary duties. I suggest you take the rest of the day off. Get drunk if you want. But please fix one thing in your mind so that we need never revert to the painful topic again. So long as a breath remains in this old body, not a single penny of my uncle's trust will be paid to the Reverend Elias Talbot. You may relay *that* to the old goose, Edythe Vale!"

I left his office without a word and took his advice about getting drunk. Indeed I remained in an alcoholic stupor for three days. Before I did so, however, I telephoned to Mrs. Vale and told her the results of my conference. When she began to berate me hysterically for my failure, I simply hung up. Whatever else I had my doubts about, I was quite sure that I was through with *her*.

When I came back to the office Mr. Bovee made no comment about my absence, but his secretary handed me a clipping from an evening paper that I had missed. It was, in fact, more than a clipping; it was the whole social page with one huge black headline. Only one as drunk as myself could not have been aware that Mrs. Elias Talbot had left the rector of the fashionable church of St. Clement's for his organist! It was the scandal of the season.

I felt no resentment of Madeleine's conduct now. I simply

understood her for the first time. She was an Anna Karenina, a Helen of Troy, a woman capable of giving up everything for a great passion. It was possible that the passion was even enhanced by the accompanying abandonments. Poor Mrs. Vale had known this and had been desperately trying to head off disaster. No wonder she had made use of me; no wonder they both had. Madeleine knew that only through me did she have a chance of marrying her lover and keeping her children. Now that the chance was gone, she had given up the children. That was what Anna Kareninas did. Even with my bitterness I found it in me to admire her consistency and her logic. For Madeleine there were no halfways.

"The old man was in a terrible snit when he heard," the secretary, Mr. Banion, told me in a half whisper, although he had already closed the door. "Then he called Morgan's and told them to remit no further trust income to Mrs. Talbot. She can live on love, he said. He swore he'd accumulate the income until he died or she went back to her husband."

"She'll never do it!" I cried. "She'll starve first."

Mr. Banion's little white mouse face looked askance at my enthusiasm. "What about the children? Who'll support them?"

"Won't their father?"

"How can he?" exclaimed Mr. Banion with a cackle of glee. "He's lost his parish! The Bishop held him responsible for the scandal!"

It was not long after this that I began to see the deadly effectiveness of Mr. Bovee's scheme. The Talbot family were reduced to almost immediate destitution. The boy and girl were removed from private school, the servants let go. Mrs. Vale had to take her granddaughter in with her, while Mr. Talbot and the boy moved into his old mother's three-room flat. Cries of protest were raised by members of the Bovee family, and there was even talk of dragging Cousin Lewis into court. But he remained perfectly adamant and totally cool. The income of the trust would be paid only to Madeleine and only when she returned to her husband. Other cousins talked about helping the children, but the talk came to nothing. To open their purses under the circumstances must have seemed like fostering adultery. And all the while, according to Mr. Banion, weekly reports were sent to the shabby Mexican watering place where Madeleine and her lover were acting out their idyll, of the remorseless reduction in the comforts of the young Talbots.

Mrs. Vale came to see me in the office, risking an encounter with her detested cousin. She implored me to do something, and when I protested that I was helpless, she asked me for money. She did so as if she were demanding no more than her due from one whose fault the whole sorry business indubitably was. I gave her everything I had in my savings account. Young lawyers made little in those days, and I had my own mother to support.

Mr. Bovee somehow got wind of this, for he stopped in my doorway a week later and muttered grimly:

"I think I ought to tell you that your pittance has not delayed my master plan by more than two weeks. You are a fool, Foster, but I stubbornly cling to the conviction that there's hope for you yet."

It was the sale of young Elias Talbot's adored pony, which until then had been boarded with a friend, that brought his broken mother back to New York and to a husband who was at last induced to forgive. Although Mr. Bovee had sworn not to give this clerical cuckold a penny of his wife's income, I think he may have parted with a considerable fraction of his own to attain this result. I also speculate that he may have made a very sizable contribution to the Episcopal Church to obtain the "call" of Elias Talbot to a parish in Honolulu. Such, anyway, was his high concept of duty.

I never saw Madeleine again. I have heard that she is still alive and still handsome, though stout. She apparently accepted her exile in good enough grace and turned her energies to the bridge table. Talbot was always a popular preacher and, so far as one can tell, did not beat her. He is dead, but not long dead. It all worked out rather better than even Mr. Bovee had expected. Anna Karenina did not end up under the wheels of a locomotive but as runner-up in a Honolulu contract tournament. That was as good as Mr. Bovee thought she could possibly do. That was what Mr. Bovee thought of life.

I think it was more than two years before I really made matters up with him. During all that time we worked together daily but formally, and I went no longer to the Sunday lunches. Such a situation might seem impossibly embarrassing to a modern eye, but it was saved by the fact that Mr. Bovee was naturally gruff and brusque, so that there was very little outward difference between his good will and his mere toleration. Yet in point of fact I was at all times aware of his good will, even of his affection. For Mr. Bovee in his old age was seeking a kind of adoptive son, and who else was there but I?

Oh, yes, we needed each other. It does not take long for a lonely, hard-working, disappointed man to become a confirmed bachelor, and it was increasingly clear that such was to be my fate. I was thirty-two at the time of Madeleine's elopement; at thirty-five I fell wildly in love with a seventeen-year-old girl whom I met at a summer hotel in Maine. She regarded me with affectionate contempt as an old man, and that was the end of my love life.

I was made a partner in Arnold & Bovee and gradually took over Mr. Bovee's clients. As he grew older, I acted more and more in his behalf. Our understanding was perfect, although rarely articulated, and our mutual devotion may have seemed deeper than it actually was by dint of never being expressed. But we suited each other very well, and we had the reputation of being a law firm within a law firm. Life lost its color for me when I lost Lewis Bovee.

Needless to say, the resumption of our intimacy had brought with it the resumption of my attendance at the Sunday lunches, and I remained a steady guest at these as long as they lasted. I always tended to smile a bit at them, and only in my own old age have I come to realize their importance. Mr. Bovee never forgot, as I did, that man is innately a social being, that clients, even for the busiest lawyer, have an existence outside his chambers. Those Sunday lunches were life, reduced to the restraints that their host deemed necessary. Well did he know, from his years of practice, that beneath the big plumed hats, behind the soft chatter and the spun sugar and the favors and all the bibelots, were the hot fierce natures of jungle cats. Mr. Bovee at the end of his long table, dispensing compliments and offering little toasts, might have been the man with the long whip surrounded by seemingly docile tigers perched on stools. The whip was the law, and without the law he and I well knew to what a shambles life was reduced. Yes, my tragedy, or at least my bathos, is that I have been simply a lawyer. My guide and mentor was, in his own fashion, a man.

Mr. Bovee died at eighty, as neatly as he did everything else, of a quick pneumonia and did me the honor of naming me his executor. His will, as might have been expected from so consummate a draftsman, was a noble and detailed articulation of an imaginative and generous testamentary scheme. His faithful secretary was given a hundred thousand dollars; his next of kin, who were five first cousins, including Edythe Vale, fifty thousand dollars each, subject to an "in terrorem" clause providing that any contestant of the will would forfeit his bequest. After some hundred other legacies of cash or objets d'art to friends, godchildren, office associates and charities, the residuary estate was bequeathed to trustees to be administered for scholarships in New York City law schools.

I could hardly believe it when Edythe Vale sent back the consent to probate which I had mailed to her, unexecuted, with a terse note instructing me that she had retained Leo Sturman, a notorious shyster, to represent her. I was even more shocked to discover that he intended to contest the will. Recovering from this, I assumed that he would be glad enough to settle for almost any figure over the actual sum of the forfeited legacy, but all negotiations proved futile. He held out adamantly for the full twenty per cent of the residuary estate to which his client would have been entitled in intestacy!

Nobody could understand either his motives or hers. I knew there was no way that the will could be upset. Why would Edythe Vale forfeit a legacy of fifty thousand dollars for the simple satisfaction of making herself disagreeable to her cousin's executor? Why would a lawyer like Mr. Sturman go along with her?

And yet he did.

The case of *In re Bovee* was fought as far as it could be fought, which was to the Appellate Division, which unanimously affirmed the Surrogate's decision to probate the will. The opinion even went so far as to excoriate Edythe Vale's "baseless and vindictive" contest. But thanks to our New York faith that justice is only obtained if the least scrupulous is given the longest day in court, the whole foolish business lasted almost a year. There were depositions, hearings before trial, demurrers, appeals — there seemed no end to it. Mr. Bovee's poor secretary was reduced to a state of nervous breakdown by Sturman's obscene insinuations that his relationship with his employer had been an unnatural one. The Bovee family, some of whom, like sharks roused from domestic lethargy by sanguinary smells, had joined Edythe, was split in two forever, and Lewis Bovee's trust for law students, because of its required investment in unprofitable "legals" during the contest, lost thousands of dollars.

On the day that the Appellate Division at last rendered its

decision in our favor, as I was leaving the courthouse, I was surprised to see the tall, white lacy figure of Mrs. Vale approach me. She raised the veil which she had all along affected in court (not having missed to my knowledge a single session) and showed me the once familiar high powdered forehead, the long, sharp nose, the lined, ravaged cheeks, the haggard, watery blue eyes. She looked shockingly old.

"Would you allow me a word, Mr. Evans? Or can't you find the strength in your stomach to listen to me?"

"I ought not to speak to you at all unless your counsel is present, Mrs. Vale," I replied frigidly. "That is one of our canons."

"Ah, but my counsel is gone; that's all over now," she said with a wave of her arm. "I shan't see him any more except when he comes for my annual contribution to his monstrous fee. I have promised him half my annuity. No, it's not as a litigant that I want to talk to you, Mr. Evans. I thought you might want to know *why*."

"Why?"

"Why all this." She encompassed the courtroom and the departing counsel with another melancholy wave of the arm.

I wanted to turn my back on her, but curiosity was too much. After all, I had spent a year on the wretched case. So I nodded, and we sat together on a back bench.

"Let me say at the outset that I never had the slightest illusion that I could win my suit. I knew from the very first that it had to end as it ended today."

I looked with mingled awe and exasperation at that long, drawn face. She might have been relating the story of *her* martyrdom!

"Mrs. Vale," I warned her severely, "I do not think you should tell me any more. You are rendering yourself liable to a suit for punitive damages."

"Ah, you can sue me for anything you want," she retorted

with a third magnificent sweep of her arm. "I am way beyond all that now. When I have told you what I am going to tell you, Mr. Evans, I will have completed my function here below. Except to live as long as I can to pay back Mr. Sturman."

"It seems peculiarly unfitting," I said in a hard tone (remember my provocation!), "that a Bovee annuity should be used to pay off a lawyer who has done his darndest to tarnish the Bovee name."

"If you had suffered as I have suffered from Bovees," she replied in the same irritatingly superior tone, "you would not be so sensitive about blemishes to that name. My daughter and I have both been left with the wreckage of lives guided onto the rocks of safety by that sinister pilot, my cousin. When I read that 'perfect' will of his that you sent me, that beautiful 'testamentary instrument' as he would have called it, I suddenly saw my challenge. I decided that I was capable of one great gesture in my life. I would defy the shade of Lewis Bovee! I would show the world that his infallible trusts and wills were fallible. That his own splendid estate, borne into the sky on the wings of angel executors, like a ceiling fresco in a baroque chapel, could be temporarily upset and its contents scattered to the heavens."

I stared with more awe than surprise into the now gelatinous eyes of this mad old woman. "And what good, pray, would *that* do anybody?"

"It would give hope back to the people!" she exclaimed triumphantly. "It would show them that they are not quite powerless. It would be a demonstration, Mr. Evans, that life exists as well as law. And I believe in life!"

"And I believe in law," I retorted as I rose to leave her.

"Oh, yes, Lewis got you. I could see that. He has you for life, now!"

I strode quickly away, and that was the last I had to see of Edythe Vale. I am happy to add that Mr. Sturman never got paid his fee. She died in the following year, and her annuity ceased.

There was one further surprise in store for me in the administration of Lewis Bovee's estate. The young painter of miniatures for the "gallery of beauty," the third to be so commissioned since its establishment, called on me in my office. He had finished a portrait ordered by Mr. Bovee in the last year of his life, but, reading of the will contest and knowing the personalities involved, he had hesitated to offer either it or the bill to the troubled executor. Now, however, that the case was over, he wondered if the estate would be interested in completing the collection. He took the miniature out of his pocket, explaining, before he showed it to me, that though he had done it from photographs, he considered it his masterpiece.

Indeed, it was.

Madeleine looked out at me as I remembered her at those early Sunday lunches, very white and spiritual, with large haunting brown eyes. I gave the artist my personal check and kept the painting for myself. It hangs in my bedroom to this day, and it can still, on occasion, evoke my tears. No wonder Mr. Bovee preferred his gallery to the originals!

Is that my moral? Is that all I have learned? Was *that* the triumph of Lewis Bovee? Or have I simply become as garrulous as our present senior partner suggests? Lloyd Degener, no doubt, would point out that I started by talking of the love of law and ended by talking of love. Quite right! I'm an old fool.

I have today added a codicil to my will bequeathing the miniature of Madeleine to the Bovee Costume Institute. It will join the other miniatures of the "gallery of beauty" on the top floor in the big glass case, protected from the sun by a red curtain that nobody ever pulls aside.

Lloyd Degener on Eric Temple

IT IS THE lugubrious duty of the senior partner to go through the private papers of any deceased junior and decide what should go to the office files, what to the family and what be destroyed. It was thus that I discovered the dim little essay that Foster Evans had written on Lewis Bovee, with its nasty preface about me. I wonder if Foster had any grim intimation, on that last night before he went to bed in the grimy old stone hotel on Central Park West where he had stubbornly lived for forty years, of my sitting at his desk, taking in his last venomous attack. What a dry little cackle he must have emitted!

It seems to be a sorry fact that of my thirty partners only the young ones like me. The middle-aged are already restive under the tightness of my administration, and the old, who remember the days when we were clerks together, resent that they should be subject to any laws but their own. Yet if I did not exist they would have to invent me. They all know perfectly well that a big law firm can no longer afford the luxury of democratic rule. We must have a dictator or overhead will bust us.

It may be necessary to their sentimental conceptions of themselves as independent practitioners of the law, as bewigged barristers in nineteenth-century prints with Cruikshankian angularities and eccentricities, living for their briefs, to hate me as a kind of Martian robot sent to destroy the rights and to flout the dignity of man.

Really, they are children.

Oh, yes, I suppose I could handle my administration more

tactfully. I could make more exceptions. I did not have to tell Foster, for example, that the firm would not pay for his completely unnecessary sixth estate accountant. No doubt, it would have been easier, at relatively small expense, to have indulged the old man's vanity. But where does one stop? And isn't it a kind of insult to one's partners to dignify their fantasies by giving in to them? Why should *I* bear the whole onus of a system that everyone knows is necessary? Let them all feel its weight. *That's* their democracy.

I have never been willing to conceal my efficiency, as more diplomatic men do. For example, when I play tennis (and I still do, at seventy-one) it bores me to waste time rallying. I hit the first shot as well as any other. One of my sons-in-law told me I should hide this. "People hate people who don't have to rally," he warned me. Well, let them. I hate people who hate people who don't have to rally.

For all this, however, my discovery of Evans' waspish comments has had one important result. I have decided to give up my project of a history of Arnold & Degener. If Foster Evans has gone to his grave sneering at the idea, if Sylvaner Price has suffered a nervous breakdown simply from working at his chapter on Guthrie Arnold, I must be bucking too much of a tide. I had thought they might all get amusement out of the idea. Each partner was to do a short biography of another. But the facts seem to be against me, and I can only yield.

The little volume was to end with my sketch of Eric Temple and Eric's of me. Eric wanted to do himself, but I was afraid that he would strike the pose of a disillusioned Henry Adams lamenting the failure of his education and life. It would have been amusing to see what he would have done with mine. Now that he is to be relieved of the task, it seems unlikely that my biography will ever be written, privately or publicly. Even as a lawyer, outside of my firm, I have little importance. But Eric, as a member of Franklin Roosevelt's "brain trust," as a political philosopher and former ambassador to Japan and Russia, is a public figure who has already been the subject of many articles. It is almost a duty to history to memorialize what I know about him. It is at least an excuse to save my notes.

So much, at any rate, will have been salvaged from my poor project. At the same time I will be tossing a sop to my injured ego, for the story of Eric Temple is inextricably bound up with my own. Indeed, I may say that a lot of people will be startled to discover how much it *is* my own.

Our relationship might best be described by the biological term "symbiosis." We complemented each other: each lived at the other's expense, yet gave as much as he received. We were as the tickbird and the rhinoceros, the cowbird and the cow. I think, on the whole, that I liked Eric. I am much less sure that he liked me. To tell the truth, I am not sure that he really liked anyone, although it was one of his charms, on occasion, to seem affectionate.

To start with a picture of us together, I offer the minutes of our last meeting, which occurred only a week ago. Eric is recovering from a prostate operation at Greenlanes, Connecticut, and I had driven out to see him on Saturday morning.

A word about his house, for it tells something of Eric. It is beautifully situated, on a slight rise that slopes in a rolling green lawn right down to the sound, and one's first impression is that it depends entirely on its natural advantages. It is a commodious, styleless, white-shingle mansion, with big rooms and cool verandas furnished with well-stuffed chairs and sofas. It is only after one has visited there a couple of times that one becomes aware that it is the home of an archsybarite. Part of the very comfort of the furniture is in the fact that one does not worry about cigarette ashes or slopped drinks. Part of one's delight in the service is that the cozy old maids who render it seem to do it out of friendship. I know enough of maintenance to know there is always an iron hand behind such perfection.

And having mentioned the sybarite, I should not neglect the aesthete. On the walls, in the corridors, in the very bedrooms and bathrooms is hung Eric's peerless collection of paintings, drawings and prints: Segonzac, Matisse, Picasso, Munch, Nolde. It is a subtle enhancement to the beauty of the pictures that they should be seen so completely without competition in the decor.

Sally Temple, no longer the passionate social rebel of the thirties, but subdued by the ego-destroying devotion that Eric always inspired in women to a silent, gray, efficient, faintly grumbling suburban housewife, conducted me to the terrace where her husband was reclining, urging me not to stay long.

"His spirits are very low," she explained in a loud whisper. "I'm told it's a common aftermath to that operation."

"Don't be vulgar, Sally," Eric snapped, without turning his head. "It's so like a woman to attribute a man's depression to any meddling with his private parts. My operation had nothing whatever to do with the present low level of my mood. If it won't embarrass Lloyd unduly, I may add that it merely affixed the seal to an already existing apathy of the sexual appetite." Here he turned his long, lean brown face and crown of gray hair to me. His large light brown eyes, so full of moving and misleading warmth, glinted with malicious humor. "But perhaps you don't know that state of affairs, Lloyd? Perhaps you and Florence are still as sparky as newlyweds?"

"Sally is quite right, of course," I said, taking a seat by his couch. "The operation is notoriously depressing."

Eric looked almost balefully after the retreating figure of his devoted spouse. "Like you, Lloyd, she is of the earth, earthy. Have you ever known a day's illness in your life?"

The elegance of that shimmering crimson silk robe, draped so neatly over the long, spare sinewy figure, right down to the alligator skin slippers, seemed to proclaim that ailments, at least temporary ones, were the expected companions of the romantic soul. As my Florence used to say, with the tongue that had made her feared in the Arnold & Degener family, Eric looked the way Lincoln might have, had Lincoln been born an Italian duke.

"I keep as fit as I can."

"You invest even your good health with a moral quality," Eric retorted dryly.

"All right, then, why *are* you depressed?"

"Because it's a depressing world!" he cried with sudden fire. "Because I'm old and disillusioned! Can't you imagine that? Can't you understand, my thick old friend, that a man might be depressed by things that have nothing to do with his sexual organs or his urinary tract? Good God, have we surrendered all to the physicians? Can't you imagine that a man might be depressed by the H-bomb?"

"Wasn't it Doctor Johnson who said that no man enjoyed his dinner less because of an earthquake in Portugal?"

"Doctor Johnson was an attitudinizing ass! Doesn't it depress you that we can no longer afford to fight any other nuclear power? No matter how wicked and vicious and Hitlerian that power might be?"

I shrugged. "Why should it? I've never shared your enthusiasm for Armageddon."

"But if we can't afford to fight the devil, we must *live* with the devil!" Eric had the capacity of generating his own excitement, and his voice rose shrilly now. "And if we must live with the devil, where has valor gone? You weren't in England during the blitz. Oh, needless to say, you weren't! You don't know what that exhilaration was. But if Hitler had had an H-bomb, would any of Churchill's golden words have mattered? Wouldn't the British have capitulated as the Japs did?"

I decided that his depression was more serious than I had thought. Gently, I tried to move him to less agitating fields. "Well, if the opportunity for valor has disappeared between the great nations," I argued, "are there no battles left on the home-front? Must a great liberal like yourself live only for armed conflict? Think how shocked your public would be? What about poverty and racial prejudice?"

"Oh, don't bore me."

"Bore *you! I've* never been the one to rant about those things."

"I repeat: don't bore me. Those battles are won. Oh, I know, there's a good deal of cleaning up to be done, but everyone's basically against poverty and discrimination. That's what gives protest its dead aspect today. Those crowds of chanting, bearded youngsters with their placards. They won't listen because they dare not listen. In a world of dwindling causes they cling with tight fingers to the few that are left!"

"And in your day it was so different?"

"In my day?"

"In the old brain trust era, with F.D.R.?"

" 'Bliss was it in that dawn to be alive'!" Eric exclaimed with real passion now, sitting up straight in his couch. "Oh, Lloyd, don't disparage a past of which you had no part! Isn't it enough for you to own the present? Where every college freshman is as cool and cynical as the senior partner of a downtown law firm? Can't you leave us poor idealists our one little ragged patch of history!"

There it was in a nutshell: the ancient attitude, dating from the very beginning of the forty-odd years of our association, that I was a Philistine, a barbarian, a man obsessed with ledger sheets of profit and loss, who had sold his soul to some kind of legal Satan while he, Eric, was a Byronic hero whose romantic idealism was comprehensible to only a few sensitive natures. It is an attitude, may I say at last, of which I am thoroughly sick.

And having said it, let that be the purge. There is too much that is important to the history of Arnold & Degener in the story of Eric to be clouded, in our old age, by personal bitterness. As Talleyrand said, "After eighty, there are no enemies, only survivors." Well, Eric and I are a good way from eighty, but the principle still applies. His great career and his great ego go together like the beautiful wings and less beautiful body of a butterfly. And I suppose, now I am playing with metaphors, that it is not impossible that some ultimate reader may decide that Eric and I together constituted that gaudy insect: that he was the beautiful wings and I the less lovely body, that he soared while I could only perch. But what is a butterfly that can only soar?

I had already been a clerk for two years in Arnold & Bovee when Eric Temple joined the firm in the fall of 1923. We had graduated from law school, he from Harvard and I from Columbia, in the same year, but he had spent a year at Oxford studying ancient law and then a year in Paris where he had written a bright but conventionally satirical novel on expatriate society, with some vivid flashbacks to the war, which he had witnessed as an ambulance driver. The leisurely pace with which he was commencing his practice in a competitive era was explained by the security of his job. His father, Roderick Temple, had been a partner and a figure of legendary brilliance and industry. He had died at forty, twenty years before, but his memory was still fresh among the older members of the firm.

Eric's romantic looks and easy charm made him at once adored by every stenographer, and his perfect manners made him respected by the clerks. But I suspected that he condescended and was determined not to be patronized. When he sauntered into the room that I shared with Foster Evans to suggest that we go to the Fish Market or take a sandwich and ride the ferry to Staten Island (he was full of imagination about the lunch hour, which seemed to me a mark of superficiality), I would shrug and plead business. It was not until he was put to work on a tangled corporate reorganization as my assistant that I came to know him.

Let me say at once that he was as brilliant as his father. Even one as grudging as myself had to concede this after a single day of working with him. What I had thought was merely facile turned out to be lucid; what I had taken for detachment was in truth philosophy. If Eric did not "grind" the way the rest of us did, it was because he had an uncanny sense of mental direction that sent him at once to the pertinent paragraph, to the relevant case. He looked before he leaped, and it was a long, cool look.

As soon as I had to recognize him as a peer, I dropped my guard, and we became friends. When Foster Evans moved to the estates department to work for Mr. Bovee, I arranged that Eric should move in with me. That was before the regime, inaugurated by myself, which assigned desks and rooms on a strict seniority basis. We were a smaller office then and could be freer. Eric was glad enough to accept my overture of friendship. For all his superiority, he wanted affection. He lived in a small Madison Avenue apartment with his widowed mother, whose only child he was, in the lofty isolation of the poor but proud. For Roderick Temple had died too young to have made the fortune that had seemed his manifest destiny.

When we had completed our first job together, Eric took me to dinner at a speakeasy where we sat up late over many drinks. We had been friendly; now we became confidential. I told him that I hoped to be a partner in the firm and in my old age to be a federal judge. I think I was even sufficiently inebriated to confess to a boyish desire to sit on the Supreme Court. Eric listened reflectively, and I was again seized with the uneasy idea that he was condescending to me.

"You make me feel out of step, Lloyd. Oh, not that you tell

me anything I didn't know. Of course, I realize that every clerk in Arnold & Bovee dreams of becoming a partner. He has no business being there if he doesn't. But my trouble is precisely that I don't *want* to be a partner."

I was not prepared to accept this. I suspected a pose. "Why then did you drive yourself so over that New Jersey Aluminum job?"

"Because I enjoyed it! Because it was novel. I can love one corporate reorganization. Maybe even two or three. But hardly sixty!"

"Yet that's the only way to become an expert," I pointed out, pouring myself more wine. "And the only truly novel experience comes to the expert. The rest is vulgar stuff."

"But I don't *want* to be an expert. I want to be an amateur, a dilettante, even a vulgar one. I want to know nothing about everything!" He suddenly burst into a roar of laughter as he noticed the way I was savoring my wine. It was a Haut-Brion of a good year. "What a phony you are, Lloyd! You're a gourmet and ashamed to admit it. You love the good things of life and go about pretending that you live only to grind. If you put in ten hours a day you tell the world it's twelve. Whereas I'm just the opposite! I have a sneaking taste for drudgery of which I'm rather ashamed. I like to seem to care more for Blakelock than Blackstone, for Corot than Coke. I leave the office ostentatiously early to go to art galleries and sneak back to work in the corner of the library till midnight! How can I compete with you if nobody knows I'm competing?"

"Perhaps they know more than you think."

Eric gave me a shrewd look. "What a rotten old cynic you are! You think everyone sees through me and what you consider my poses. But I do a bit of seeing myself. And I'm afraid I see how crude you are, old man. If you're to succeed, you'll need a shock absorber between yourself and your public."

I was pleased that the wine should have induced such candor. It was precisely the conversation that I had wanted to have. "Have you any ideas as to what that shock absorber should be?"

Eric seemed surprised at my affability. "As a matter of fact, I have."

"A diplomatic partner?"

"Exactly."

"And have you a candidate for the position?"

"I have."

"His name?"

"His name?" Eric looked blank. "But I'm talking about a wife, you dunce! If ever a man's situation screamed for a clever wife, it's yours."

It was my turn to be taken aback. "And who, pray, have you picked out?"

"Why, the only possible one for a rising man like yourself. The boss's daughter!"

Eric lived apart from the hierarchy of the firm and the toadying which, however concealed, was an inevitable feature of any social pyramid. He treated partners and associates with equal affability. He used to go frequently to the Arnolds' (Guthrie Arnold had been his father's particular intimate), and he took me to one of their Sunday afternoons as easily as if they had been an uncle and aunt and I his out-of-town house guest. It was there that I met and fell in love with Florence Arnold who, after a persistent courtship of two years, at last consented to become my wife.

This is not the place to go into my happy personal life. I was for a time jealous of Eric, but Florence assured me that I had no cause, although she irritated me by suggesting that if Eric had been more attentive, I might have. The fact is that Eric showed little interest in the other sex. He was reputed to be a "mother's boy," but whether because of this, or from simple friendship or out of a desire to protect himself from any designs on the part of

Florence (this will pay *her* back for her insinuations if she ever reads this), he did more than just introduce me. He fostered my courtship throughout. I needed encouragement, too. It was not an easy thing for an ambitious young man to be desperately in love with the senior partner's daughter, and Florence's own suspicions of my possible ulterior motives made it no easier. Without Eric's encouragement I might well have chucked the firm and Florence in despair and gone to seek my fortune in Chicago. Whatever else has come between us, I shall always cherish my debt to him in this.

Through the remaining years of our clerkship Eric and I worked closely together, and by the time we "made partner" in 1929, we were virtually in charge of the corporation department, the most vital in the office. Due largely, I believe, to the fascination of this little factory that he and I ran together, not to mention his interest in my protracted courtship (he loved puzzles), his patience with Wall Street lasted a good deal longer than he had threatened on that significant night in the speakeasy. But it did not last forever, and had I not conceived the bright idea of sending him to Paris to start a branch office there — which he brilliantly did — I might not have conserved his indispensable talent for the firm. When he came back to New York, however, at the nadir of the depression in 1933, he was in a restless mood which he could not seem to throw off.

"Our whole society is about to blow up," he kept muttering to me, "and all we can do is chatter nervously about creditors' rights. No doubt, when the Black Plague was mowing down England, lawyers talked frenetically about detinue and trespass on the case."

Florence and I, in the manner of many happy couples, told each other that what he needed was a wife. After all, he was thirty-seven. And when his mother called us up one night in a great state of nerves and begged us to come around to help her talk Eric out of a "crazy project," we were both in high hopes that it might be a girl. We found him seated by the fireplace in his mother's neat, ancestor-filled little parlor, smiling with a stubborn patience. He simply pointed to his distracted parent, pacing the chamber, when we asked what it was all about.

"Let *her* tell you," he said. "If there's a crisis, it's of Ma's making."

It was always difficult for me to think of Mrs. Temple except in terms of the position in life that she would have occupied had her husband lived — she was so obviously better qualified for it than the smaller one that fate had accorded her. I remember hers as a large, sad, reproachful presence, always in simple, classic robes that managed somehow to "swish," with high-piled gray hair, Roman, yet at the same time in faint disarray, as if from anxiety or maybe simply from exhaustion, handsome in a massive way, with her high marble forehead and aristocratic nose, and tragic, an empress in exile or captivity, Andromache at the court of Pyrrhus, doomed to carry her remnant of imperial trappings through a life of cadging scholarships and market tips for her only child from men who were enjoying the success that his father should have lived to enjoy.

"He's going to throw everything over," she commenced with Delphic solemnity. "He's going to fling to the winds everything that he and I have worked for. Everything that his dear father worked for before us. He's going to give it all up and go down to Washington to work for that *man*."

"All of which, being interpreted, simply meaneth," Eric explained, with a wave of his hand to dismiss the maternal complaints, "that I have decided to go along with Tommy Corcoran's suggestion and go to work for Mr. Roosevelt and the future instead of continuing with Messrs. Arnold & Bovee and the past. Go ahead, Lloyd, get it out of your system. Call me a traitor to my class and have done with it."

"Oh, if you listen to *him,* you'd think he was Lincoln freeing the slaves," Mrs. Temple wailed. "But I know why he's doing it. He's doing it, for all his fancy phrases, to get back at *me!*"

"Now, Ma, don't be tiresome."

"You are, Eric. You resent me for what I've done for you. But you'll find you're cutting off your nose to spite *my* face, my boy. The firm will never have you back if you desert them now. And they shouldn't!"

This prognostication was not quite as crazy as it may sound. Working for the New Deal in those days was like going over to the enemy. Eric's mother, who regarded herself as a kind of vestal virgin of the old order, was sincerely heartbroken. I sat in silence, debating the different positions I might take.

"If big business and big law were the noble things my dear mother deems them," Eric observed sarcastically, "the administration of Franklin Roosevelt would indeed be an impertinence. But are they? *Must* they be?"

"Have you told the firm yet?" I asked him.

"My dear fellow, whom would I tell ahead of you?"

"Then I want you to do me a favor. Let me handle it for you."

"What is there to handle? I simply go to your respected father-in-law in the morning and tell him: 'I quit.' "

"Lloyd," Mrs. Temple implored me, "are you going to let him do it? Can't you dissuade him? Won't you even *try?*"

"Mrs. Temple, I know your son too well to flatter myself that I could talk him out of so serious a project."

"Why should Lloyd cut off *his* nose to spite my face?" Eric asked her mockingly. "Doesn't my resignation remove another candidate for the throne of old Guthrie Arnold?"

I turned on him indignantly. "Do you really think that affects me?"

"Can't you take a joke, old man?"

But I have always believed that if one takes every joke literally one is more often right than wrong. It shocked me that Eric should think me so pettily ambitious. I wanted great things for us, yes, but in a great way. I wanted to conserve his brilliance and energy for the greater good of the firm. It would be to my own greater good, too, of course, but only in so far as I was a part of the firm.

"I tell you what I'll do, Mrs. Temple," I said to his mother. "I'll try to arrange it that Eric can come back to the firm when he's through with Uncle Sam."

"Oh, Lloyd, if you could only do that!"

"Who says I *want* to come back?" Eric demanded belligerently.

"Nobody," I retorted. "But if I can fix it to please your mother, I will certainly do so."

"You think they'd have me back — tainted by heresy?"

"They might."

"Even corrupted by the great white demagogue?"

"Oh, we'll whip you back into shape, never fear."

Eric's tone became almost querulous. "I thought you'd all wash your hands of me."

"No such luck!"

His long stare at this ended in a shrug. "Oh, very well," he said, as if he were doing *me* a favor, "have it your own way, as you always do. I leave the whole matter to you and Mr. Arnold."

The next morning I had it out, hot and heavy, with my father-in-law. I told him roundly that we were moving into a new era and that it would be invaluable to have a partner trained in the councils of the New Deal. The old boy put up such a fearful amount of blustering that I had in the end to hint that Eric Temple might not be the only one to leave. That did it. He came around, and, as always when he did so, he came around handsomely. He even volunteered to give a farewell dinner for Eric at the Knickerbocker Club.

That festive occasion confirmed my initial impression that Eric was less than delighted by my diplomacy. He addressed us, very urbanely and very wittily; he made even the most conservative partners smile by his picture of the chaos of the new alphabetical agencies in Washington. He ended with an eloquent prediction that out of it all might come a new society that would save the best of the old. But there was a lurking note of sarcasm in his smooth phrases, particularly in his humorous references to my role of "killing the fatted calf before the prodigal had even got away." I think he must have felt that I had dimmed the glory of his sacrifice. The crackle of his carefully planned auto-da-fé had become the roar of a welcoming bonfire. The martyr was being feted like a bridegroom!

So it was that Eric joined what all of his partners and most of his associates regarded as the lighthearted and lightheaded group that was taking apart the nation's economy, like children dismembering toys, holding up each broken part for the amused chuckles of their suave leader of the silver tongue and the long cigarette holder. He started as a special assistant to the Secretary of Agriculture and later became a leading administrator of the National Recovery Act. He gained the confidence of the President himself. I was not surprised. It bore out my feeling that a man of his capacity was bound to be even more useful to the addled New Dealers than he had been to us. But it is not my purpose here to go into his political career. There are plenty to write up that.

What I mean to stick to is *my* role in Eric's life — and his in mine. I hope that I gave him as much encouragement with Sally Teriot as he had given me with Florence. Only here things were a bit different. Sally, a passionate young public relations expert with the United Mine Workers, had to court *him*. Eric was certainly attracted to her, but he was far too confirmed a bachelor to be won without a fight. It was a case of opposites. He was intrigued by her violent, redheaded impetuosity, by her unabashed radicalism, by her willingness totally to commit herself to a cause. I believe he had a collector's urge to add her to his *bibelots,* and an egoist's curiosity to see if he could deflect her commitment from the masses to himself. He succeeded only too well. Sally's heat responded violently to his coolness. She found in him the coordinator and controller of her scattered energies that she must have been always unconsciously seeking. Certainly, she never afterwards needed another master or another cause.

It may begin to look here as if my vaunted "role" in Eric's life was confined to giving him moral backing in whatever fancy happened to seize him. But not long after his marriage we had our first sharp disagreement. The President wanted to appoint him to the Securities and Exchange Commission, and Eric wanted to return to private practice. After four years in Washington he was beginning to be restive again. He was tired of agencies, of bureaucrats, of the eternal jargon of national recovery. He was deflated by the public's easy acceptance of what he had deemed revolutionary new principles. Furthermore, with marriage and the prospect of a baby, he needed the larger income of the law. Eric was too old a father to help in the nursery. He wanted servants. He wanted cash to augment the art collection whose growth had been temporarily stunted by his government service.

He was very much surprised when I flew down to Washington to urge him to accept the Commission.

"But I don't want it," he protested. "It's too sedentary, too much like being a judge. Besides, I'm sick of government."

"Do it for a year," I begged. "Do it for a year, and I promise to make it worth your while."

"You shouldn't try to bribe public officers, Lloyd."

"All right, do it because you owe it to me."

"Owe it to *you?*"

"Owe it to the firm, then."

"Are you and the firm the same?"

"We're getting there," I said boldly. "You can depend on any commitment that I make here."

Eric whistled, and the expression in his brown and yellow eyes was not pleasant. "So I'll be taking orders from you, is that it? Behind the scenes, it'll be Lloyd Degener, the kingmaker?"

"Think what your experience will be worth to us," I continued, brushing aside his questions. "Half our business is going to be involved with the S.E.C."

"And what am I to live on in the meanwhile?" he demanded. "It's all very well for you to point out what I ought to be doing while you're pulling down your big percentage. Try living on a government salary for a change."

"The firm will advance you whatever you need."

But Eric could be stubborn, and his tone developed an injured note. "Is it a case of 'must'? Is a year on the Commission the price of my return to the firm?"

"Don't be an ass, Eric. You can come back any day you want. I'm simply telling you how to come back most advantageously to yourself."

"And to the firm. And to *you.*"

"Do you expect me to deny it? Aren't we in business for mutual advantage? Would you like to owe your partnership to my generosity?"

Eric became very dry at this. "No, Lloyd, I would *not* like to owe anything to your generosity."

"I tell you what else I'll promise. If, when you come back, your percentage is a penny less than my own, I'll resign from the firm."

Eric stared at me with a slowly dying smile and then whistled a second time. "Whatever else they may say about you, Lloyd, they can never call you a small man. As an old auction hound, let me compliment a bold bidder." Here he struck his desk with a paper cutter as if it were a gavel. "Gone!" he exclaimed, "to the big man in the back of the room for the highest sum ever paid for a law partner!"

Eric's value to us was as much enhanced by his two years on the Commission as I had hoped. When he came back, I put him in charge of all our securities work, and two of the biggest underwriting firms in the country retained us. I would have changed our name to Arnold, Degener & Temple, but Eric, characteristically, declined this. By keeping his own name out of the letterhead he made me seem a bit pushy to have put mine in. Our relationship never seemed to lose its subtle competitiveness. He and Sally bought their place in Connecticut and rented an apartment on Park Avenue. He started buying pictures again; it was the period when he acquired his famous Redon panels. Except for the start of the war in Europe, life seemed to be turning out exactly as I had planned. It was almost spooky.

And then he left us again. Florence and I had just finished dinner when we received another of those desperate telephone calls, this time from Sally, begging us to come around to their apartment. But unlike her mother-in-law, some years before, she told us what it was about. Eric was leaving in two days' time to enlist in the British Army as a private! He would go to Montreal and thence to London on a transport.

"But he's forty-three," I objected, staggered.

"Well, he's got all that worked out, I don't know how," she wailed. "Won't you please come?"

"Of course, we'll come."

We found them sitting in the library where Eric was finishing a brandy, as cool as if we were all about to set out for the theater. The only difference from that other day of crisis was that he showed more tenderness to Sally than he had to his mother. Of course, her plight was more pitiable. She made no effort to hide her copious tears.

"My wife," Eric informed us in a voice of gentle sarcasm, "has quite forgotten the days when she would have pushed me to the barricades for the rights of man. She used to be always looking for the bayonets of authority on which to impale herself. And now behold her! A middle-class wife and mother who is entirely willing to let the world go hang so long as she can preserve her home." He rose to poke the fire. Then he turned suddenly to face us with an expression of the utmost calm and resolution. "The long and short of it is that I do not choose to live any longer in a world where Hitler even exists. And the only way to get rid of him is with a gun. So I go to England to shoulder a gun. Q.E.D."

"You're only doing it to get away from me and the children!" Sally cried bitterly. "If you'd admit it, I wouldn't mind so much. Why not tell me you feel cooped up and trapped by marriage?"

"Florence," Eric said, turning to my wife, "do take Sally into the living room and see that she has a good stiff drink. We may as well try to get over this hump as smoothly as possible. Lloyd and I have office matters to discuss."

Alone together, he poured me a brandy. "What are you going to do about this one, Lloyd?" he asked with a malicious twinkle in his eye.

"What do you mean: what am *I* going to do?"

"How are you going to turn it to the profit of the firm? I'll be interested to see. Except it's no use. You'll have to give it up. This time I've got you licked."

"Is that why you're going? To spite me?"

For once I had got the better of him. Eric snorted with a disgust that was totally out of key with the lightness of my tone. "I suppose it's too much to expect of the head of a Wall Street law firm to see that his very practice may depend on who wins this war."

"Now you're being pompous."

"Oh, that's right, it doesn't matter, does it?" he retorted with a sneer. "We have plenty of good German clients, don't we?"

"Now you're being offensive. I'm simply here to suggest that if you're really bent on killing Hitler, you'll do it better in Washington than by playing soldier boy at your age."

"But, don't you see, that's just the universal fallacy!" Eric exclaimed in excitement now, slapping the palm of his hand down on the table so that our glasses jumped. "Everyone over here wants to get rid of the devil by passing laws or writing checks. I tell you, Lloyd, the time has come to fight! And thank God I'm still man enough to handle a gun!"

As I listened I felt the stirring of a resentment akin to Sally's. What I think we both minded was the unmistakable glint of happiness in those oddly youthful brown eyes. In all the mish-mash of his romanticism, in all the clangor of his self-dramatization, had he ever had a greater role than this? To leave all, wife family, friends, law, paintings, even his beloved Redon panels, and plunge into the melee of a distant war against Lucifer! What was wrong with our times that they offered so perfect a series of settings before which our hero could strut? Was God Max Reinhardt for Eric's John Barrymore?

"I can't accuse you of irresponsibility," I said in my driest tone, "because it's so clear that you are not leaving anyone un-provided for. Obviously, I can be counted on to take care of your family and your law practice."

Eric contemplated me for a moment before he spoke. He seemed to be debating which of several attitudes he might take.

The one that he adopted at last was at least not antagonistic. He needed me, after all, quite as much as I had said. He laughed, shrugged and held out his hand.

"Very well, Lloyd, let us leave it so. We all know what Milton said about those who only stand and wait."

That winter was the winter of the "phony war," and Eric's hopes of dealing personally with the tyrant were frustrated. He had his training on the Salisbury plains and was promoted to lieutenant before the fall of the Low Countries and the invasion of France. His letters were vivid and amusing, but I thought I could detect in them a note of a fear of having made a fool of himself. This ended, at last, with action. Once he had crossed the Channel, his correspondence took on a lyrical note, as of a latter-day Rupert Brooke. Then for a long time we heard no more, and I could only pray with Sally that he had been taken prisoner. She had long renounced the attitude of injured wife and was now belligerently handing out white feathers to all who did not acknowledge Eric as the model hero.

When the news came of the preparation for the great Dunkirk evacuation, Sally showed me a letter that she had been preparing for the *Times* in answer to the isolationists. Its theme, of course, was Eric's sacrifice. The only trouble was that Sally could not write.

"Let me have it for a day," I urged her. "Let me see what I can do with it."

What I wrote and what Sally ultimately signed stirred up a great deal of comment. I have always been rather proud of the beginning:

"In a day when we hear so many young men asking why they should fight for a distant cause, why they should risk their precious lives for the anachronisms of the British and French empires, it is consoling to contemplate the example of Eric Temple who, over the age of conscription and without deigning to answer the arguments of those who maintain that wolves are lambs, gave up a law career at its apex and went east to join the ranks of those who believe in the dignity of man."

In the first letter that Sally received from Eric, announcing his safe arrival back in England, he asked her if I had helped with the "propaganda" that she was getting out. Apparently we had made him famous even there!

After Pearl Harbor, even I left the office. I went to Washington to act as a special assistant to our great Secretary of War, Henry L. Stimson. I hope that I proved of some use to him, but I know that my utility was not comparable to what he did for me. For it was through Mr. Stimson that I was able to render Eric the service that ultimately changed his public career from one of mere distinction to one of near greatness. The Secretary persuaded General Eisenhower, when he went to England, that Eric, now transferred to the U. S. Army, would be the perfect liaison. What other officer, of comparable skill, had served under two flags?

As I look back on those days, I marvel at how beautifully and how rapidly it all fitted together. After the years of preparation glory seemed to come in a rush. Major General Eric Temple was at Yalta with Roosevelt, and at Potsdam with Harry Truman. His military reputation and the heroic story of his early enlistment was the perfect antidote to his identification with the New Deal, no longer fashionable in the more conservative democratic administration of the postwar years. As ambassador to Japan and to Russia he became one of the great figures of the cold war, and when, between appointments, he returned to the practice of law in Arnold & Degener and occupied the biggest office, just beyond the reception room, filled with signed photographs of great political and military figures and drawings from his postimpressionist collection, he brought us a prestige that was as lucrative as it was gratifying. It was not only the new clients either who wanted the name of Ambassador Temple on their briefs in the federal courts; it was the law review boys from Harvard, Yale and Columbia, so hard to get in those competitive years, who were eager to work for a firm that offered the possibility of such an opening into glory.

By far the pleasantest part of my relationship with Eric was during his ambassadorships. We maintained a steady correspondence, and Florence and I visited him both in Moscow and Tokyo. Through me he used the resources of the firm for research, speech-writing and general assistance with his books and articles. I had a junior partner permanently assigned to his work. I enjoyed pretending to play Father Joseph to Eric's Richelieu, and he liked the steadying support, in a wooly bureaucratic world, of a tightly knit, well-organized capitalist law machine. Never had the cow and the cowbird lived more happily together.

But, less happily, our finally achieved comradeship did not survive the first extended lapse in Eric's federal appointments. The election of General Eisenhower was fatal to his further political ambitions. For all his intimacy with the new President, Eric had identified himself too closely with the other party to expect much from the pie that was being parceled out among hungry Republicans. He professed to be delighted to stay at home and practice law, but I was soon aware that he was again restless. The government bug is a pernicious one. Very rarely, once bitten, can a man return for long to normal life. Eric would interrupt anything he was doing to talk on the telephone to a reporter or to give an interview to an old government colleague. I think if Ike had offered him the job of vice-consul in Zanzibar he would have jumped at the chance.

It was the era of the McCarthy investigations, and I was apprehensive about the violence of Eric's reaction to them. I could see that they offered just the kind of fight that he itched to get into, and I did not look forward to what the Senator might do to poor Sally. I knew that she had been briefly married, as a very young woman, to a member of the Communist party. The marriage had been annulled, two years before she had met Eric, and she had resumed her maiden name, but there it was. It was a secret, but Eric knew it and I knew it, and presumably even the Senator's clumsy but malevolent bloodhounds might uncover it.

On the morning when he came to my office to say that he had decided to represent Ned Rossiter, the liberal editor who had once been a fellow traveler, I could only point this out.

"Oh, but Sally doesn't mind," he replied cheerfully. "Of course, we've been into all that. She has to be ready to be pilloried, poor girl. You can't make an omelet without breaking eggs."

"A pity that Sally has to be one of them," I observed bleakly. "I don't suppose it will do young Eric much good at Harvard, either. Or Eloise at Foxcroft."

"The children have to learn about fighting," Eric insisted. "You'll see. It will do them good. They've had it too easy."

I began to be suddenly very angry. "I'm surprised that even a man of *your* ego should sacrifice an innocent family quite so casually."

"Innocent? What do you mean, innocent? Everyone Joe McCarthy is after is innocent! It's a glory to be one of his victims! And an ultimate guaranty, I assure you, my dear cautious partner, of political respectability."

"Everyone wouldn't agree with you there."

"Everyone *will*. Wait and see. If you'd ever got out of Wall Street and done any fighting, Lloyd, you'd know it's not as terrible as people think. If Sally and the children can't take a bit of going over from the junior senator from Wisconsin, they haven't the stuff they were born with. But, you'll see, I know they *can!*"

At this I blew up altogether. "It was one thing when you left to go prancing off to play soldier in Europe. At least they were safe here. But it's quite another when they have to be dragged into the limelight to satisfy your craving for notoriety. My God, man, will you *never* be tired of play acting?"

Eric stared at me with a smile of surprise that gradually withered into condescension. "It's always been that to you, hasn't it, Lloyd? Play acting. Any smallest concern with the welfare of the underdog, any more than casual interest in the fate of a child stuffed into a gas chamber, is melodrama. You are so independent yourself, so normal, so reasonable, so well adjusted, so self-contained, that you cannot really conceive that other people may not be so, or, if they are not, that it is not somehow their fault. Therefore, any worry about them must be misguided, if not actually fraudulent. And you deem it your job to keep that fraud under control, or better yet, to harness it, like nuclear energy, to useful, money-making purposes. So far you've done pretty well with me, haven't you?"

"You brush aside the little fact that it is *I* who am concerned with your wife and children!"

"Ah, then, let me borrow a leaf from your notebook and call that the most fraudulent concern of all!" Eric was on his feet now; he should have been on a stage. "What you're concerned about, my friend, are the clients who may be upset by a McCarthy smear! Even the great Lloyd Degener, who can get water out of a stone, does not see how he can quench his thirst with *that* one. And yet he's wrong." Eric shook his finger at me mockingly. "You've lost your nerve, Lloyd. The years are telling on you. McCarthy, unlike Hitler, cannot last. He's so ridiculously irresponsible, so fantastically deceitful, that he's bound to blow up. And when that happens people are going to look back on his reign of terror as a bad dream of which they are thoroughly ashamed. And then, you'll find, it will be positively *chic* to have been his victim!"

"No doubt, that will be Sally's consolation."

Eric turned on his heel. "Of course," he flung back at me, "if it will make you feel easier, I can always resign from the firm."

Fortunately, before he had reached the door, I managed to find my voice.

"Please, Eric, not that, whatever you do! We've been through too much together!"

He did not answer, but when he went to Washington to confront the Senator, I am happy to say that he went as a partner in Arnold & Degener.

It all came out, of course, as both of us had predicted. Senator McCarthy was never much of an investigator, but even his staff were able to pick up the red whiff on Sally's trail. Her first marriage and her early radical days were described luridly in every newspaper in the country. Eric always maintained afterwards, in his cheerful fashion, that she had actually enjoyed the rumpus. But Florence and I knew better. Sally suffered deeply at the humiliation of the children. They were an attractive pair, young Eric and Eloise, but they were spoiled and a bit snobbish, and they found the publicity about their mother embarrassing in the smart social circles in which they traveled. They were too wise to tell their father this, but Sally felt it. A mother always does. And the fact that children *shouldn't* be embarrassed doesn't make it any less agonizing for the parent who has embarrassed them.

The person who did enjoy the rumpus was Eric. Poor Joe McCarthy! How much all the old liberals owed to him! Who else could have provided so superb a rostrum for their grandiloquent phrases, their glorious affirmations? It was the last great hippodrome of the New Deal, with its long line of chanting patriarchs parading to a would-be martyrdom at the claws and jaws of ferocious beasts. Amid all the singing and all the orating the admiring crowd never noticed that the lions and tigers were only a small snarling bundle of rather nasty kittens.

Eric called it unabashedly his "finest hour." He and Ned Rossiter emerged from the investigation the heroes of the day. Even our most tory clients came knocking at Eric's door now; law review men more than ever flooded our mail with applications for jobs. The partnership of Lloyd Degener and Eric Temple was evidently foolproof.

Small wonder that our intimacy does not increase with our old age. Small wonder that each is a bit embarrassed by the other. There was a time when Eric could enjoy my success and I his. But not as old men. We have grown too greedy. I envy him the reverence that I see in the eyes of the young law clerks, and he cannot live with the fact that I helped to put it there.

Cliffie Beach on Himself

SOME MONTHS BACK, Lloyd Degener gave me his private account of our partner, Eric Temple, to read. He told me he had given up the idea of compiling a firm history, but that pride of authorship impelled him to show me at least this much of it. Of course, I understood his real motive. He hoped that one day I would write *his* story. He had long regarded me as his apostle and chosen successor, and he liked to think that I would perpetuate his memory to other generations of partners and associates in Arnold & Degener in one of those handsomely printed monographs: "Lloyd Degener, as I knew him, by Clifford Beach." It is something that I might have done then, but that I cannot do now.

For since that day, I *did* succeed him as senior or managing partner, but under circumstances that have destroyed our old relationship. Lloyd will go to his tomb (the ugly mausoleum under the big soaring angel that Guthrie Arnold erected in Woodlawn), convinced that I forced him ruthlessly from his presiding chair to satisfy my ravenous ambition. He believes that I could no more help it than a tiger can help going after a superannuated buffalo. He even told his wife: "That's what comes of thinking that certain wild beasts can be domesticated."

What is more, everyone in the firm is of the same opinion, including the younger partners who took my side. Once the necessary job of toppling Caesar had been accomplished, they were all Mark Antonys to my solitary Brutus. I was branded as a kind of prehensile ape who had reached out instinctively to grab my neighbor's property. It was like my affair with Edie Ward. So long as I had wanted her, what did it matter that she was the wife of a partner and friend? I had simply taken her.

And they are right, by the law. Justice Holmes maintained that a man is judged, not only civilly but criminally, according to whether or not he should have foreseen the probable results of his acts. His motive, his *subjective* motive, counts for nothing. Is not this true socially as well? Are not our standards of appraising our fellow men purely objective? If a man is arrogant to me, why then he is arrogant. Do I care if in his soul he cringes with humility? If he strikes me, do I care that he intended a caress? And if he takes my wife, what does it matter to me that I no longer wanted her? I sometimes think that God, if He exist at all, may be a kind of super Holmes, J., and that on the Day of Judgment we will be graded by our acts and our acts alone.

I am not joking. May I not be close to explaining the "loneliness" that modern writers make so much of? We all have to live in our own little world of private judgment of ourselves from which even the psychiatrist is excluded. For he must find our motives in a subconscious state that *he* must deduce from our acts, so he too becomes a Holmesian, and we are thrown once more back upon ourselves and to those conscious motives that have existence and validity only in our souls, only to our private selves, of which the world is both ignorant and careless.

Of course, I can see why the ordinary observer would attribute my rise in Arnold & Degener to a simple lust for power. I never worked for another firm or even wanted to; I never had another interest or hobby. From the early days when I spent my law school vacations working for Mr. Degener as a "summer boarder" to the unhappy moment of his angry and quite unnecessary retirement from the firm, my life has appeared to be one long crawl up that steeply titled ladder. Yet it still seems to me that a shrewd witness might have noted something peculiar in the total containment of my supposed ambition in a single law firm. Is it a characteristic of self-aggrandizement to be so special? Would Napoleon have limited himself to Corsica?

That same observer might even have deduced (privately, of course, for he would not wish to be hooted down with mocking laughter) that my other possible motive might have been simple devotion to the firm.

Or love — how about that?

It sounds silly, even to my private ears, yet I know it to be true. Indeed, it is the only thing that makes my life make any sense at all.

The first thing that I can remember craving was neatness. My mother was sloppy — in thought, in deed, in habit. Oh, she was well enough got together when she went out — beautifully so — but her loveliness to the world was like a bright pink plaster cover on a garbage pail. I lived in the backwash of her smeared lipstick and strewn underwear. Mother was not a whore in the conventional sense, but it is certainly true that she received cash presents from her admirers in the frequent intervals between her marriages. She had been the adopted daughter of an elderly childless couple in Poughkeepsie and had escaped early to the gayer life of the city. It was, as my adoptive grandmother used to say, a triumph of inheritance over environment.

My father, the first of her husbands, was also the refugee from respectable parents. He was an unemployed actor and an alcoholic, and I never knew him until I was working in Arnold & Degener when he turned up, very shabby, to ask for a loan. I supported him thereafter until his early death, though he never aroused my sympathy. If I am judged by *my* acts, I will judge others by theirs. His marrying Mother and siring me were voluntary acts. So was the relinquishment of his basic duties. I believe that a drunk in the gutter is where he deserves to be. It was only my pride that made me pull him out.

Mother is still alive, in Mexico City. She also is supported by me. She showed me an occasional sentimental affection, in her own trashy way, for I was a good-looking boy, according to my photographs, in a dark, sullen fashion, but she was glad enough to release me at an early date to the care of my adoptive grandmother in Poughkeepsie, a dull, dry, conscientious, just old lady, who brought me up out of a sense of duty and for whom I felt the inordinate affection of a child who has to love someone.

Grandma had a great respect for the law, for her father, of whom she incessantly talked, had been a judge. When Mother was bearing me, she induced her to hang a print of Daniel Webster in her bedroom believing, with the superstition common to many matter-of-fact, literal persons, that this would control the unborn child's choice of career. I do not suppose Mother even knew who Webster was, but she was always good-natured about the presence of gentlemen in her bedroom, and the great orator and advocate was permitted there. At any rate, it worked, for I cannot remember a time when I did not plan a life at the bar. Grandma, after putting me through Columbia Law School, where I was editor-in-chief of the *Review,* was able to chant her *Nunc dimittis* in seeing me safely established in Arnold & Degener.

I plunged into the pool of law like a hot boy on a July day. The orderly, hierarchical atmosphere of the firm, where one knew precisely at all times what was expected of one and where one rose from tier to tier pretty much in proportion to one's efforts, seemed to me to be a tiny civilization in the midst of chaos, a Greek city state on a plain surrounded by barbarians. I loved the law from the beginning and loved the practice of it. I have never believed in the sincerity of those who profess to find it difficult to live within a code.

Yet Arnold & Degener offered me even more than that. They offered me a family. I had no presentable relatives, after Grandma's death, and I worked too hard to have time to make new friends. The firm's bi-annual dinners, its Christmas and Easter cocktail parties, its spring outing at the Sleepy Hollow Country Club, to say nothing of the many evenings offered by the partners at their homes, supplied me with my social life. I have always been awkward at parties, so there was an obvious advantage in belonging to an organization where one was accepted and appreciated for one's legal aptitude as well as one's personality. At Arnold & Degener gatherings I could relax and be myself. Later, when the war came, and I served on an aircraft carrier in the Pacific, the firm's monthly mimeographed news sheet was the mail I looked forward to most eagerly. To tell the truth, it was the only mail I had.

I was made a partner in 1949 when I was only thirty-three, a record in the history of the firm, and I decided it was time for me to marry. Mrs. Degener, who now occupied a position in my life and affections somewhat comparable to my late grandmother's, very obligingly introduced me to a series of girls on a series of weekends at her house in Cold Spring Harbor. From these I chose Rosey Blount.

This, of course, was generally explained in the firm by Rosey's distant kinship to Mrs. Degener. Any connection by marriage to the senior partner was seized upon by the malicious as the obvious reason that I should be willing to overlook the fact that Rosey was plain, dowdy, shy and rather showily intellectual. How little they knew me! I had studied Rosey with the greatest care, and I had figured out exactly why she would suit me.

In the first place, although she may have been plain of feature, with evasive, melancholy gray eyes and messy, sandy straight hair that kept falling over her face, she had a fine strong figure (how few men seem to look for that!) which promised healthy children and a satisfactory, regular sex life. In both these respects my prediction was utterly justified. Secondly, her distaste for social life and love of books meant to me that she would more readily put up with my long nights of working and with the global business trips on which she would not be taken. Here, too, I judged correctly. Indeed I have often wondered if any other woman would have so placidly endured to be placed quite so far behind her husband's career. Thirdly, I assumed that the combined persuasions of Mrs. Degener and myself would be ultimately enough to induce her to play at least the small social role required of a partner's wife. In this last assumption, I proved dead wrong.

Still, one cannot have everything. Rosey was ninety per cent the wife I had wanted. If all this sounds horridly calculating on my part, it was at least as much so on hers. She had looked *me* over and had seen that the bargain offered was a good one. She, too, had wanted physical love and spiritual freedom; she had yearned to be rid of her fussy old parents. It may not sound like a romantic match, but millions are made with no better a basis.

What I underestimated in Rosey was the intensity of her fear of people. Everything she did was designed to avoid them. Even her appalling appetite for reading was in reality a pretext. Left without books, she could just as well do crossword puzzles, or play solitaire, or simply stare out the window or, in later years, look at television, so long as she was not at a social gathering. Busy and preoccupied, I indulged her craving for solitude, always hopefully assuming that boredom would drive her out of herself by the time I really needed her. I allowed her a year to recuperate from the difficult birth of Ella, two more for little Rosey, two more for the death of her ancient father, two more for her mother's, and *still* she looked at me with haggard eyes every time I told her we were dining with the Degeners!

We had been married sixteen years, and both our daughters

were at boarding school, depriving Rosey of her last valid excuse for declining invitations, when the great crisis of my life arose, and I decided that she would have to face it with me.

"I want you to go with me to the Degeners for the annual firm weekend," I announced. I had finished breakfast and gone back to our bedroom where she was starting the *Times* double-crostic. She looked up in immediate dismay.

"But, Cliffie, you've *never* made me do that!"

"This year is different."

Her agitation might have been pitiable had it not been so ridiculous. I hardened my heart by recalling that she never thought of *my* needs. Let this, then, be her call for redemption. To the sound of trumpets!

"They only want you, really," she continued miserably. "All they do is talk shop. Why can't they leave the wives out of it?"

"Because the wives are supposed to take an occasional interest in that 'shop.' "

The Degeners' annual weekend, though not on the official agenda of firm social occasions, was still recognized as a "summit" gathering. It was held in their big black Swiss chalet on a high hill over Cold Spring Harbor and included those nine or ten partners, selected in the sole discretion of the host, who most actively, regardless of age, percentage or seniority, really ran the firm. That I had allowed Rosey, in the first two years of my inclusion, to plead one of her now permanent colds was proof enough of my coddling.

"Why is this particular weekend so special?" she wanted to know.

"Because a very important thing is going to happen during it." I paused to wet my lips. I am not normally a nervous man, but the mere prospect of mentioning the "thing" for the first time outside of the little group of partners who had planned it made my mouth dry. "Albert Ward and I have decided that we are going to speak to Lloyd Degener about putting the management of the firm in the hands of a committee of younger partners."

The enormity of what I was saying was apparent in the astonishment of Rosey's usually indifferent eyes. For a moment she even forgot the weekend.

"You want Cousin Lloyd to do that!" she gasped. "But I thought he was your god!"

"Even gods get old."

I felt suddenly sick as I said it. Until that very moment I had not known the full violence of the struggle between my loyalty to the firm and my duty to Degener.

"But you always said that without him the firm would have fallen to pieces!"

"And so it would have," I replied sharply. My reasons now tumbled out in the rapid, singsong fashion of a child reciting a poem. I became more and more indignant at Rosey for making me go through this. "But because he once saved the firm is no reason it shouldn't be saved from him. He's over seventy, and he's grown impossibly rigid. He refuses to go along with the other big firms in salary raises. He refuses to give the clerks a month's vacation. He even refuses to let them take Saturdays off. He's back in the days when a law clerk was regarded as an apprentice who was privileged to learn a trade!"

"But isn't that how he made the firm great?"

"It doesn't work any more, Rosey! We're not getting the good law review men from Harvard and Yale we used to get. They won't work under these conditions. Why should they?"

"Because they'll be the better for it!" Rosey exclaimed with unexpected heat. "Why should you take men who are thinking only of a few extra bucks?"

I had long been irritated by Rosey's total lack of concern for the firm, but her sudden untimely interest was doubly aggravating. To find an advocate for Caesar, after all the soul-searching that I had been through, in my own bedroom, in my own wife, made me suddenly cutting.

"You're talking about things you know nothing about," I retorted. "*All* men think of salary these days. Besides, it's not only a question of the clerks. Lloyd won't pay the stenographers and office boys enough. And he's even tough with the partners. He won't allow them to buy shares in client corporations, for example ——"

"You said yourself that was a good rule!" Rosey interrupted, showing a memory for which I had not given her credit.

"How else are the younger partners to make any money?" I demanded, furious now. "He keeps their percentages ridiculously low. His general attitude is that lawyers shouldn't think about money until they have one foot in the grave!"

"Well, even if all that were true, it's still not up to you to push Cousin Lloyd around. Why, you owe everything to him, your job, your partnership, even me! To say nothing of my relationship to Cousin Ethel. And you say Albert Ward is with you? Ugh, I think it's perfectly revolting! You're like the wolf pack in *The Jungle Book,* all snarling around the old leader Akela."

A literary reference was all that I needed to put the final touches on my exasperation. It was the last straw that Rosey, who was so scared of the whole world, should be so unafraid of her husband, that she should spend sixteen years giving me no moral support whatever and then, at the one moment when I needed help, throw in her weight on the other side. Psychologically, of course, I understood it. In her mind Cousin Lloyd was always the great lawyer and I simply the poor clerk who had sunk, by marrying her, to the low rank that she deemed her own. But it was still maddening.

"Well, *this* wolf is still expecting you to go to the Degeners' for the weekend of May fifteenth," I retorted.

"Don't expect me to help you snap at poor Cousin Lloyd's heels!"

"Since when have I expected you to help me in anything?"

With this crack I left her. Had I stayed in that room another minute I would probably have pulled her out of bed and given her a good whacking on the backside. It may have been just what she needed. It probably was just what she wanted.

To be told that I owed everything to Lloyd Degener was the last thing I needed to hear. My conscience was always shrieking it at me. Rationally, I knew it was not true. I knew, indeed, that Lloyd Degener owed just as much, perhaps more, to me, but the fact that he was my patron put the obligation otherwise in the eyes of the world, and the eyes of the world and one's own conscience are apt to use the same glasses.

I would have liked him more — I would very possibly have worshipped him blindly (for there was always that capacity, unfulfilled, in my nature) — had he been at all fond of me. But I suppose a man never really likes his successor, even when he has chosen him himself, and it had been obvious from an early date that Lloyd was grooming me for his job. He trusted me; he depended on me, yet he treated me always with an affable condescension, a friendly superiority that almost bordered on contempt. Lloyd liked to think of himself as a philosopher as well as a lawyer, as an observer of great scope who could laugh at the puppet Lloyd Degener arguing a case. I know that he thought me incapable of his flights of fancy. He found me a good work horse, a better companion in a man's office than in his home or his club. In short, he felt a bit toward me as Mr. Temple felt toward *him*. And he resented the fact that, big and bluff as he was, with the high, hailing voice and forced cheerfulness of a great statesman, he was *still* more like me than Mr. Temple.

When I had first urged him to alter his wages and hours and generally to modernize his philosophy of running the office, he had simply smiled and put me off. When I returned stubbornly to the theme, he grew angry and in the end he told me roundly to hold my tongue. "You'll have it all your own way soon enough," he said sharply. "You can leave the present to your elders and betters." Unhappily, I knew that I could not do that. Lolyd was in splendid health; he could hold on as senior partner for another decade, and by that time the harm would be irreparable.

I went to see Mrs. Degener alone. She had, in the past, taken me under her wing, as she was apt to do with the senior associates and junior partners, and I had responded with a devotion of which she took little notice. As with my grandmother, the relationship was a one-way street. She dazzled me with her hard, bright, straight-from-the-shoulder talk, this busy little pretty old lady, always at her needlepoint, always smoking, always in black with big pearls, gossiping, scolding, cutting thread with her teeth, throwing her head back to cackle with laughter. But she did not laugh that day.

"Now you listen to me, Cliffie Beach," she said severely. "You younger men always think the world's coming to an end because a few old folks get a bit set in their habits. It was the same way when my father, Mr. Arnold, was senior partner. Lloyd wanted him to delegate some of his functions, and I made him hold off. And then what happened? When Papa finally retired, Lloyd found that half the things he'd wanted to do away with, he had to continue. That's the difference between backseat driving and being at the wheel yourself!"

How wise she sounded, this Agrippina of Arnold & Degener, daughter and wife of senior partners! All her life she had exercised her wisdom over the destinies of the firm. She reveled in every bit of gossip about every partner and every associate; she dealt out her advice and her reproaches; she lived for the firm as much as did her husband himself. And yet, for all my devotion to her, I had to recognize, realist as I incurably was and always have been, that the empire of this bustling little czarina, this Ethel the Great, was largely, if not entirely, in her own imagination. Wall Street, like Washington, has always been free of petticoat influences. It is why so many readers find our history so dull.

"I thought *you* might suggest it to him," I insisted. "Only for his own good. After all, he's too old to be spending so much time on administrative matters."

"Now, Cliffie, you know you're talking nonsense. Nothing keeps Lloyd going but that office routine. He'd fall to pieces without it in a week's time. You've done all right so far by taking my advice. Don't make the mistake of ignoring me now." She reached over and gave my hand a sharp little slap. "You have only to wait until Arnold & Degener falls into your hands like a ripe plum. And look who's telling you that!"

I looked away because I was afraid there might be tears in my eyes, and what would she think of *them?* To what depths of misconstruction might I not be exposed? A ripe plum? I was more apt to find myself holding a rotten apple!

There was nothing that I could do but go forward alone, with death in my heart, for I saw now everything it was going to cost me. Such few close human associations as I had would be forfeited. But the world is divided into those who live for sentiment and those who live for ideals. Arnold & Degener represented an ideal to me. I did not really have any basic decision to make. I knew that I could not let the firm down.

I sounded out the partners of my own age group, and they were all willing that something should be done so long as I did it. None of them volunteered to speak to Lloyd Degener, nor even to be present when he was spoken to. They were perfectly frank about it. They didn't have the guts.

Then I went to Albert Ward. I had to have at least one partner who would go to Lloyd with me. Everyone had said that Albert would turn me down. He was our star litigator, a man of dazzling intellectual brilliance, but utterly removed from the distasteful routine of administrative matters. He regarded the firm as a kind of dressing room for his performances. Yet for all his forensic ability, out of court he was large and stumbling, big-eared and tongue-tied, with tousled hair and impenetrable blue eyes, a prince turned back into a swineherd, a Parsifal, innocent and gaping. But I suspected what the others did not. After all, the firm was my specialty. I suspected that he had guts.

He did not utter a word until I had finished the whole story. "I get it," he said with a nod. "I see it's got to be done. Very well, let's do it."

He was to be, for the first time, among the favored few at the Degener weekend, and he and I agreed that we would talk to Lloyd then. It would have seemed strange to those who did not know the firm that we should have chosen a social occasion and one where Lloyd was our host, but those weekends were consecrated to the discussion of the highest matters of policy. It was only taking the lion at his word to beard him in his den.

The weekend started badly. I had so much to do at the office that I could not get off before the middle of Saturday afternoon. Rosey had been rather sullenly assembling her courage all week, but it began to drip away on the trip down Long Island, the rate of loss accelerating as the car approached the Degeners'. Had we been operating from the well of her fortitude instead of our tank of gasoline, we would have stopped dead at the entrance of the drive. The last drops at the bottom of her spirit evaporated when, after walking through the dark front hall, we were ushered out onto the sun-bathed patio where the other guests were already assembled and heard Edie Ward's high, clear, mocking tones:

"Well, *now* I feel much more at home. Here's my old pal Rosey Blount, from Lawrence, L. I. Rosey and I used to be inseparable as little girls, Mrs. Degener. Didn't we, Rosey? We went through the 'crush' stage together. Do you remember the terrible mash you had on Alverta Van der Pelt? It must have lasted a year!"

Edie's mauve velvet hat, bulging forward over a face that might have been pretty had it not been so mean, with its crowded little features and large, constantly moving lips, seemed insultingly fashionable. She was the kind of woman who dressed up to the minute with an expensiveness that was aggressive to the point of unpleasantness. "All right, so it's foolish," her twitching shoulders and slanting eyes seemed to sneer, "but when has fashion been anything but foolish? And if *I'm* foolish, what, my dear, do you suppose *you* are?" She had been as plain a guinea hen as Rosey when she had married Albert, but she had spent the leisure hours created by his labor very differently.

Rosey ran from the patio without a word and went straight upstairs to her room. I had to argue for half an hour to induce her to come down for dinner. She treated me to one of those long shocking monologues of hate to which repressed people give occasional vent.

"Edie's had it in for me ever since we were little girls. Sneering at everything I did. Always so superior, just because her family had that big white house while we lived in the old gate cottage. Filling my good straw hat with wet sand! And making fun of things you weren't supposed to make fun of, like Mummie's stoutness and Daddy's stutter. And what made it all even worse was that Mummie and Daddy actually looked down on Edie's parents. Who had Edie's mother *been,* anyway, they were always asking. Did anyone know her maiden name? That was the final turn of the screw, to have them make fun of the people who were turning it! Mummie didn't even want to ask Edie to my wretched little *thé dansant*. Dear God, as if she'd have come! Except, of course, she did, in a scarlet dress, to stay for two minutes and ruin *that* for me, too. And now I suppose she wants her husband to be senior partner, so she'll join with you to push out poor old Cousin Lloyd. Well, if you think I'm going to help *her!*"

The whole house party seemed to share Rosey's tenseness. I suppose enough had been bruited about concerning my project so that people were watching me uneasily. The big, dark, cool house with its eighteenth-century lithographs and framed letters of the great to various Arnolds, its elaborate Victorian furnishings and matted floors, seemed aloof and aristocratic in contrast to its furtive, nervous inhabitants. And everyone drank too much.

At dinner, after a pointlessly extended cocktail hour, people were noisy without being gay. I noticed apprehensively that Rosey, who was seated next to Albert Ward, was talking to him with unwonted animation and occasionally glancing down the table in my direction with an ominous defiance. I was by Edie Ward who flirted with me blatantly, no doubt in the light of her ancient rivalry with Rosey. Disagreeable as she was, Edie was a sexy creature. There was sex even in her bad temper and jerky movements. Then she noticed what was going on across the table.

"What the hell is your Rosey doing to my Albert?" she asked with a sudden change of manner. "Is she trying to get him to make a fool of himself? She'd better watch her step, that girl. How did she ever manage to bag a catch like you, anyway?"

I glanced again at Rosey and saw that Edie was perfectly right. She *was* trying to make a fool of Albert. And what was more, she was succeeding! Was there anything in the world more ridiculous than a scholastic lawyer, unaccustomed to society, egged on after a few drinks to "shine" in company? Rosey, with a boldness that must have been cocktail-bred, was calling down the table now to "Cousin Lloyd" that he simply *had* to hear what Albert Ward was telling her, that it was much too good to be all wasted on her. And now Albert, killing all general conversation with his high, court voice, so condescending in its false humility, with eyes wagging to left and right in confidence that the humor would be appreciated by all, was proceeding into one of his longest and most obscure legal stories, about a judge who had confused the Rule in Shelley's case with the poet, an anecdote so strewn with legal terms as to be totally incomprehensible, yet withal faintly hinting pornography and replete with those cheeky familiarities with the long dead by which the learned apologize for their erudition: a distinguished barrister described as an "old geezer," a beautiful countess as a "filly," the Lord Chief Justice as "quite a guy!"

I began to feel hopeless at the prospect of waging my battle with so giddy an ally. What did Albert's guts count against a few drinks and a little crude flattery? And then I was seized with a violent anger. I wanted to strike hard at Albert, to push my fist into the mushy center of his big white smiling face. I turned to his wife and hesitated. But only for a moment. For only a man like Albert who had resolutely, fatuously, and in the end insanely, refused to face a single fact outside of his law cases, could have walked into the uncamouflaged booby trap of such a marriage. It was catch-as-catch-can in the jungle of the Degeners' weekend.

"You ask how Rosey caught *me,*" I said roughly. "How did an ass like Albert catch *you?*"

Edie's black eyes glittered with excitement as I pressed my knee against hers.

"Isn't he brilliant?" she asked with a smirk.

"Is that what women want?"

"Well, maybe if they had to choose between brilliance and something else, they'd take something else."

"Like who, for example?"

"Like who do you think?"

Mrs. Degener, on my other side, poked me to indicate that the table was changing, and I turned, almost in relief. Seducing Edie would be like shooting cows.

"Don't get too chummy with the likes of *her,*" Mrs. Degener warned me grimly. "She's nothing but a tramp, you know."

"Mrs. Degener!" I exclaimed, feigning to be scandalized. "Is *that* the way you brought me up to speak of partners' wives?"

"I'm looking after you, honeybunch. A little bird tells me you may need it."

"You know you don't have to worry about any other woman so long as you're at the table."

"*That's* better." Sensible as she was, Mrs. Degener always adored the language of mock courtship. "Remember, I'm like the Virgin Queen. I expect my gallants to be absolutely faithful. In return for nothing at all."

"Not even an occasional opportunity to throw one's coat in a mud puddle?"

But something was going on down the table. There was a tinkle of glasses preparatory to a toast, and I saw to my consternation Rosey was rising to her feet!

"Cousin Lloyd has been telling me how old he is," she began in the unexpectedly assured voice that sometimes comes to those who never speak, "and I have been telling him what everyone else at this table is thinking." She paused and looked directly at me. "I've been telling him that we all find him and Cousin Ethel the youngest people present." Here followed the silly burst of clapping that always accompanies any total banality. "Albert Ward was just now explaining to me how meticulously Cousin Lloyd runs the office. How, when he sleeps, he must dream about the size of stationery and the length of coffee breaks. And then I thought Albert summed up the matter quite beautifully. 'So long as he keeps it up,' he told me, 'the rest of us can enjoy the luxury of practicing law.' So I want to drink a toast. I want to drink a toast to Cousin Lloyd's next ten years as managing partner!"

There was a roar of assent, and we were all on our feet cheering. I noted that Albert made more noise than anyone else. The silly ass, in the whorish way of trial lawyers, had talked himself over to the other side! Oh, yes, I knew he was half drunk — he had a notoriously light head — and tomorrow he would be himself again, but what could I do with a first lieutenant who had only the integrity of a boy? If he, if all of them, preferred to lick the toes of the old wizard down the table to facing up to their responsibilities as members of a great firm, was it my function to horsewhip them into a different submission? Wasn't I the Johnny-out-of-step, the driveling sentimentalist who cared more about the pack than the leader, the deluded fool who thought that the whole was greater than the sum of its parts? Who but I had been twisted into a freak of nature that loved a law firm?

Very well, I would give up my plan, and I would give up everything else. I would certainly not continue as a partner of the firm whose future I had failed to protect from a senile leader.

Turning to Edie after we were seated, I proposed that she and I drive into New York later that night. Oh, her eyes really glittered now! What, after all, had she to lose? Childless, loveless, desperate with boredom, independently rich, the world was her own rotten oyster.

"Do you mean what I think you mean?"

"Let me spell it out. I propose that we go to a small, cozy hotel that I know and spend the night together there."

The twitching of her shoulders showed how much she loved crudity. Why not, after the years with Parsifal?

"When do we start?" she whispered, her eyes aglow with the flame of burning bridges.

*

The following morning at ten o'clock I was sitting alone drinking coffee by a potted plant in the small conservatory of the Hotel Naomi when Albert Ward walked in. Edie had gone home to her apartment an hour before in hysteria because I had refused to agree to marry her. Albert stood before me, pale and shaking, a buffoon Othello.

"You're lucky I didn't bring my gun," he rasped. "My first inclination was to shoot you down like a dog."

"Oh, don't be any more of an ass than God made you," I retorted. "Do you think you have any rights after what you did?"

Angry as he was, Albert could still gape. "What *I* did?"

"Bitching up my plan about Degener. Sacrificing your duty for Rosey's cheap toast."

"You compare that to what *you* did!"

"I shouldn't, of course. I didn't take anything from you that you wanted. Edie tells me you haven't made love to her in two years. The poor girl was half out of her mind."

I stared at him coldly as I threw this in his stage-angry face. His reaction was curious. At first his face turned almost olive, and he seemed to be strangling. Then he rubbed his brow and held his head down as if he were going to be sick. At last he took a deep sigh and appeared to take hold of himself.

"Are you feeling all right?" I inquired.

"Listen to me, Beach. There's a lot I ought to say, perhaps a lot I ought to do, but skip that. I left Edie at home just now, under heavy sedation, with her old nurse to watch her. She was in a pitiable state. The only thing that keeps me from committing mayhem on you right now . . ."

"Just try it," I sneered. "Just go ahead and try it."

Albert paused to swallow deeply again. "The only thing that keeps me from mayhem, as I say, is the conviction that came to me in the taxi crossing the park that the one way I can save Edie is by saving our marriage. And to do that I must be sure you'll leave her alone. *Will you?*"

"I've already told her that."

"Swine!"

"Look, Ward, how do you want it? For me to leave her alone or for me not to leave her alone?"

"For you to leave her alone!" he gasped.

"Very well."

"For you never to speak to her again!"

"Fine."

"And for you never to mention what happened to anyone else!"

"Oh, for Pete's sake," I said in disgust, "do you think I'd *boast* about it?"

"There's nothing I'd put past you!"

"Go home."

And he went, leaving me, the injured, to ponder the remarkable standards of the world in judging right and wrong.

When I went back to my own apartment I found Rosey too relieved to see me to be reproachful. She had evidently been terrified that I would never come back. However much outraged, she dreaded above everything else the prospect of having to reorganize her slothful life. Later in the day, when she had become more used to the idea that her marriage was not, after all, over, she ventured to chide me, and I treated her as peremptorily as I had treated Albert.

"So long as you feel at liberty to play fast and loose with my career, I shall feel at liberty to play in the same way with my marriage vows. Is that absolutely and finally clear?"

Apparently it was, for she made no answer.

On Monday morning at the office there was not the smallest indication, by so much as an averted glance or a quickened pace to avoid a corridor meeting, that anyone had noticed anything. I realized, with a dull soreness in my heart, what had happened. Word had gone out from the chief that the episode was to be buried, and buried it would be. It would become, in the phrase of George Orwell, a "non-fact." Life, my life, the firm's life, even my career in it would go on as if nothing out of the ordinary had occurred. I had learned that nobody can create a scandal who does not believe in it himself.

I slammed the door to my office and, slumping forward on my desk, covered my face with my hands and gave way to a few dry sobs. Then I pulled myself together. Nobody, after all, could say that I had not tried. There were things that seemed simply to be preordained. I rose and went to Albert Ward's office. He looked up as I came in, haggard and surprised.

"Don't you think we ought to talk to Lloyd now?" I asked. "And get it over with?"

"About *us?*"

"No, silly, about the new management committee."

In dumb amazement he followed me down the corridor to the old man's office. Lloyd Degener received us grimly, as if he had been expecting the visit. I went straight to work. Albert later told the other partners that I had been like a bulldog going for the jugular vein. When we had finished, Lloyd, as usual, had the last word by saying that he would retire altogether, that he would have nothing further to do with a firm that treated him as the British electorate had treated Churchill in 1945.

This, of course, was hateful of him. I had never asked to be senior partner. I had not even wanted to be. I had never suggested that he give up his title or his percentage of the profits. I had simply demanded that the administration of the firm — universally regarded as a tedious chore — be placed in the hands of younger partners. What could have been more reasonable?

Yet all hell broke loose. There was an outcry of sympathy for the old man, although, be it noted, no suggestion that he reconsider his decision. I received black looks from the older partners and worried telephone calls from clients. But I survived it. We all survived it. Only my home collapsed. Rosey, aghast at what I had done, packed a bag and moved to the Degeners'. Something in her at last proved greater than her inertia. But I knew her too well to hope that it would be a permanent change.

One night when I came home, our old cook told me at the door that Mrs. Degener was waiting in the living room. I found her as grim as her black sequins. She waved away all thought of a cocktail. She would not even sit.

"I had to know how you could treat us this way," she said in a cool, brittle tone. "Call it simple curiosity, if you like. How could a man on whom we have lavished so much of our affection and care turn upon us so? Oh, I know one reads of it in novels and plays. *King Lear* is everybody's favorite theme today. But I just can't believe it. Tell me, *Mr.* Beach, why?"

"You! Lavished care and affection on me!" The tears blinded me, and my voice went oddly high. "You! The one woman I've ever cared about except Grandma! What do *you* know of care and affection?"

And then I let her have it. I told her all about the firm and what her husband was doing to it. I told her of my plan and of my later decision to give it up. I told her how I had gone off with Edie to create a scandal that would blast me out of Arnold & Degener, maybe out of Wall Street. I pointed out that it was her fault, hers and her husband's, that my scandal had been quashed. What more could I do to get out of a firm that I had to save if I stayed? *What,* in God's name?

When I had finished and sat down weeping in a chair, Mrs. Degener seemed very much shaken. She even came over and put her hand on my head.

"Then it's true what Rosey says, my dear boy," she murmured. "You *have* cracked up. One thing, anyway, I *can* do. I can make her come home and look after you."

When she had gone I sat alone in the darkening room and considered this latest twist. Perhaps, after all, it was my best "out" to be considered a trifle cracked. But I wondered if sending Rosey back was not a revenge as exquisite as her husband's melodramatic retirement. Save a bees' nest from a burning bush, and you can count on them to sting you to death!

The Matrons

The Landmarker

CHAUNCEY LEFFERTS had been trained as an "extra man" in a social era when extra men had had still more or less to be men, before the age of the designer, the decorator, the peacock whose cry is as harsh as his plumage is bright. Nobody had minded that Lefferts was drab so long as Lefferts was punctual or that he was dull so long as he was available. Unremarkable of appearance as of opinion, he had been perfectly content to be unnoticed so long as he was present: a slight, round, paunchy gentleman, discreetly dressed, with soft brown hair, all his own and undyed, who never forgot a name or a family relationship and who talked as easily with the men over the brandy as with the ladies in the drawing room.

In his sixties Lefferts began to ask himself the questions that most men would have asked three decades before. Was the New York social game worth the candle? Did the conversation, the food, even the wine justify the effort of getting into a stiff shirt? Now to most people the lateness of such doubts might seem proof of a weak intellect, even of a deranged one, but that would be because they could not comprehend the peculiar combination of Lefferts' sexual inhibition and natural gregariousness, of his fear of competition and his yearning to be identified with those who have competed and won. Only in society can one mingle with beautiful women and successful men and escape unscathed, which was why the opiate had operated so long and so effectively for him. But now, with age, and just when he most needed it, it began to lose its potency, and, catching sight of his black crow's feet and tired eyes in a French mirror, on a grand stairway, he would wonder if the institution of the dinner party, which had once seemed to supply him with the most blessed of veils, did not provide instead a merciless searchlight.

He was sure that the younger people giggled at him, and he hated them for it. He grumbled audibly now when he found himself abandoned at dinner, between two bare backs of partners talking to the men on their other sides, yet, when a lady *was* talking to him, if he was bored, he lapsed into sulky silence. His personal comments became more caustic, his appearances less punctual, his dinner jackets less pressed, his tips to servants less generous, and he was even known on occasion to drink too much. He began to behave, in short, with an independence that was the very opposite of the quality that had made him initially popular. Society will accept any conduct in its inner circles, provided those so conducting themselves have always behaved that way; what it cannot abide is to have its pigeons change their holes. Lefferts' fall was as speedy as social falls always are. He found that he was asked for weekends on Friday night and for dinners on the morning of the party, and soon enough, with the exception of the faithful Bella Hoppin, whose fetish for personal consistency and quasi-royal passion for order fortunately encompassed loyalty to protégés, he was greeted by his old gang with the terrible falsity of the cry: "Chauncey dear! Why do we *never* see you?"

He tried to console himself by saying that society had gone to hell and that he had known, after all, its great days. He tried to consider his years of dining out as a preparation for writing a great novel and played with the idea of becoming a latter-day Proust. He took long walks to recapture the old New York that was dying with him. If he was out-of-date, he was out-of-date like history, out-of-date like the old mansions in which he had dined as a younger man, some of which survived here and there, as boardinghouses or shops, moldering and dowdy, admired only by his faithful self. As time drew on, the façades of these disappearing abodes came to be his sole connection with their former owners, some dead but others merely transplanted and dead now only to him in their distant fashionableness, so that his daily rambles became a sort of social memoir, a retracing in asphalt of his old gay rounds. Living in the past, did people say? Where else *could* he live?

And what a past! He remembered as a young man, before the first war, the exhilaration of riding up Fifth Avenue on the top of an open bus and seeing unfold before him that glorious romp through the Renaissance! He remembered the massive brownstone of the Vanderbilt "twins" at Fifty-first Street, the mellow pink tower of the Gerry château, where the Pierre now stands, and, farther north, the birthday-cake splendor of Senator Clark's and the wide grilled portals of Mrs. Astor that opened to the visitor before he ever touched a bell. And he remembered, too, the long wonderful dinners, to him a peak of civilization, where one arrived happily at eight and departed satisfied at eleven, having spent two of the intervening hours at table over seven courses and five wines.

Oh, people sneered at those parties now, of course. But at least one had known what was expected of one. Today, even at Bella Hoppin's, one never knew how late into the night cocktails might push the battered meal or what ghastly parlor game would be thrust on one afterward. Lefferts lived in a constant secret dread that he would be asked, as a penalty in one of these, to step up on a table and strip before the jeering multitude.

"Well, at least we're *alive,*" Bella had once retorted to his protests. "We don't just sit in a row like a herd of dressed-up swine with our noses in the trough. We use our imaginations. I'm afraid you're getting stuffy, Chauncey."

"My idea of heaven," Lefferts muttered, "is a place where one needn't be ashamed to be stuffy."

"Don't turn into a crank, dearie. You haven't the money for that."

Lefferts sighed. It was certainly true that his income, like his invitations, had dropped off. The old grandfather who had limited the modest family trust to railway bonds had ignored the perils of inflation. Had it not been for Bella, who had been his friend since dancing-school days, and a few much younger couples who regarded him beneficently as a social curiosity, rather like a tattered hansom cab parked outside the Plaza, he might have had to dine every night at the Cosmopolitan Club with his maiden sisters who never made even a decent effort to conceal their satisfaction that he should have been dropped at last by Mammon. Poor Lefferts had plenty of opportunity to consider Oscar Wilde's axiom that if to be in society was simply a bore, to be out of it was simply a tragedy.

Happily for him, however, the past did not prove a sterile pursuit. When there were no longer enough houses to visit on his daily walks, he ventured farther afield to seek out other survivals of the great preceding century. In a curious way his need to retreat to it seemed to have a democratizing effect on his attitudes. Anything that shared now in the dignity and grandeur of that greater age — a church, a station, a hotel or a store — shared similarly in his widening affections. He learned the secrets of the rapid transit to be able to visit even the most distant of his new friends, and the same Lefferts who had once walked by the Lady Chapel of St. Patrick's Cathedral and Commodore Farragut's statue in Madison Square without turning his head was now happy to pass a morning traveling underground to the center of Brooklyn for a glimpse of the Gothic gates of Greenwood Cemetery.

It was as if he and the old by-passed city had found each other in a golden twilight. As he stood looking up at Louis Sullivan's terra-cotta angels with their outstretched arms, high on a cornice over Bleecker Street, or wandered amid the chaste Greek porticos of Snug Harbor, or took in the faded grandeur of Colonnade Row in Lafayette Street, he felt a tremendous upsurge of spirit. This was even more intensely the case when the approach to the landmark was through dingy streets, past yawning warehouses, where Lefferts had to piece his way cautiously and self-consciously, peering ahead until at last he saw, shooting up out of the jumbled masonry, like a nymph rising from her bath, the fine thrust of a Florentine campanile. The very mass of the surrounding city, the engulfing, amorphous, indifferent city, like a huge sow smothering her own offspring, gave to his searches some of the excitement of a consecrating act, as though, a monk in a desperate age, he was solacing his soul by lighting little candles in darkest corners. It even charmed him that the landmarks were frequently merely façades, that the interiors were put to vulgar uses, that bales were stored where there had once been counters of silverware, that dull-eyed lodgers, unconscious of the past and hardly aware of the present, moped in what had once been gilded drawing rooms. The very precariousness of surviving beauty, the mask or shell exposed to a world that never looked up, was analogous to his own threadbare elegance. What was he but a sober, four-story brownstone façade, with Gothic arches and an iron grille, such as one might find in Hicks Street over at Brooklyn Heights?

"Have you ever heard of Tinetti's?" he asked Bella Hoppin, one night before dinner, in her splendid yellow-and-gold drawing room that opened up to the arriving guest like an issue of *House and Garden*. Ordinarily he had the tact not to put such a question to his hostess at such a time, but his new obsession made him importunate. "It was the most fashionable department store in the city in 1850. It stood at the corner at Lafayette and Spring streets. A great square iron palazzo with a hundred arched windows, like the Sansovino library in Venice.

When your great-grandfather, Mayor Brevoort, opened it, he said that the new world need no longer hang its head before the architecture of the old."

The reference to her ancestor checked the incipient frown on Bella's high brow. "Weren't they divine, those old New Yorkers? Like Hudson River primitives. Whatever put them in your head?"

"Because the Tinetti building is still standing. It's a textile factory, a bit beat up, naturally, but the lines and proportions and the old dignity are still there. I thought it might amuse you to give your St. Andrew's Settlement House ball there. It could be cleaned up in a few days, and we could all go in the costumes of the opening." He watched her closely as he paused. "You would go, of course, as your great-grandmother Brevoort."

Oh, he had her attention now! "Why, Chauncey, what a perfectly divine idea. Do you know I still have some of her dresses? But where would we ever get permission to fix the place up?"

"Right here."

"Here?"

"You own the block, Bella. It's up to you. And so is the fate of Tinetti's, which is scheduled to be torn down, come spring."

Lefferts remembered having read that a hippopotamus is dangerous to man only when he gets between it and the water. The same, he concluded sadly, taking in the sudden opaqueness of Bella's gaze, might be said of the heiress and the sources of her wealth.

"I make it a point never to interfere with my agents," she said in a crisper tone. "They do their job, I mine."

"But, Bella," he protested, "their job is to get you the greatest revenue they can. Yours is a higher responsibility. It is to see that for the sake of a few more dollars that you don't really need ——"

"I'm glad you're in a position, Chauncey, to talk of not needing dollars," she interrupted as she moved away to greet a newcomer. "The rest of us find them very useful."

It was not Bella's general reputation that she was a disappointing woman — indeed, if anything, she was deemed to fulfill more richly even than she promised — but to Lefferts this was now her essential quality. He had gone so far, in the bitterness of his recent seventieth birthday, to wonder if his disappointment in Bella was not his disappointment in life. She always appeared so large, so handsome, so full-blown, so fair of breast and straight of carriage, with so noble a brow and nose and such fine luxuriant hair, a Roman mother of heroes, like Cornelia or Volumnia. True, her laugh was a bit too loud, her voice too raucous, her perspiration too quick, but that was even part of the promise. The disappointment was in her ultimate failure to be what she seemed: the perfect mixture of wisdom and worldliness, sentiment and saltiness, horse sense and horsiness, to be instead a Volumnia who blued her hair, a Cornelia who doted on gossip. It never occurred to Bella that "good talk" was anything but a kind of oral album of candid-camera shots of the great, and her world agreed with her. "Isn't Bella wonderful?" they were always saying. Only Lefferts dissented. Bella was not sensitive, but she could sense dissent.

"Chauncey, I'm going to be frank with you," she told him later that night, having beckoned him to her sofa when the gentlemen joined the ladies. "I don't like the way you've been looking. Have you seen a doctor? We're not at an age where we can take chances, you know."

So that was it, he reflected morosely. He was to be "handled." He was to be "fixed." His ears echoed already with the plaudits of the friends: "Bella is really prodigious. She never forgets anyone."

"I have a common or garden variety of arterial trouble," he said dryly. "We can't all have your health. It will kill me in time, but, after all, something must. There are no fountains of eternal youth. Not in New York, anyway. And if there were, somebody'd tear them down."

"I thought you might be looking for one in those rambles you're always taking."

"No, I just go to visit a few old friends. Poor shabby edifices that will probably disappear even before me. And be missed about as much."

"You must stop feeling sorry for yourself," Bella reproached him. "Nothing ages like self-pity."

"I'm not aging. I'm aged."

"Fiddlesticks, seventy isn't old any more. The worse thing you can possibly do is to keep relating yourself to a lot of old tenements waiting for the wrecker. It's turning you into the dullest kind of bore, the one who's always trying to save some shack from a highway or housing development. Mark my words, Chauncey, those people end by losing all discrimination. You'll be wringing your hands over the Third Avenue El."

"As a matter of fact, those Gothic entrances were a great loss!"

"Now, stop! You see? What you need is people. You've got to see more people. It's the only way to stay young."

People! What else had aged him? Surviving to seventy with one's mental faculties intact was like going to a cocktail party while on the wagon. How noisy his contemporaries sounded, how little they listened, how obsessive was their naked concern with their own "pluck" and their trips, their endless jet trips, to Luxor, to Hong Kong, to Tokyo! As though it took pluck to throw their old carcasses into armchairs and be transported from one pleasure to another! No, the only true companions of Lefferts' old age were the shabby, graceful, undemanding façades of his landmarks.

He went down the next morning to visit the doomed, dark,

dusty Italian palace, empty now, with broken windows, ready for demolition, but like a marquise in a tumbrel on her way to the guillotine, her neck bared, her head high, her scornful eyes fixed over the heads of the screeching mob. Lefferts tried desperately to imagine the building a century back; he closed his eyes tightly until amid the stars and flashing he had a sense of crinolines and glittering counters. He seemed suddenly to be losing his balance, and he spread his arms out wildly.

He recovered consciousness in a clean, commodious green hospital room with a dazzling view of the Hudson, and he speculated idly that he might be at last in the heaven of old landmarks, until it was borne in upon him with a shock that he was in the Harkness Pavilion. Could his sisters have possibly played so fast and loose with his funds? Nowadays the poor, like himself, did not expect to leave estates; they simply looked to save enough to cover their terminal ailments. But at fifty dollars a day! He reached frantically for the bell just as the door opened, and Bella came in.

"There's not a thing to worry about," she assured him. "Just a slight seizure. It's providential that it happened where it did. My managing agent was in the building when you were brought in, and when he found the card in your wallet he recognized your name and called me. I had you taken right here, and, of course, you're not even to *think* of the bill. In a way, I regard myself as responsible. It was your worry about that old store that brought this on. And you were right about it, too. It *is* a beauty. I went down and looked at it myself this morning. I've given instructions to preserve it. We may even have it done over. It'll be like the Racketty-Packetty House of Frances Hodgson Burnett, do you remember? I used to read it to the girls when they were little. The old dolls' house that was going to be burnt until the little princess spotted it and recognized its true worth and had it refurbished so that it was even grander than Tidy Castle?"

Lefferts spent the next weeks in a kind of euphoria. When Bella took on a job, she did it thoroughly. After he was released from Harkness she moved him to her apartment where he had a trained nurse and breakfast in bed and was taken out for a short drive in the afternoon in Bella's Bentley. He liked to think that the interest in old buildings that he might have imparted to her would have a softening effect on her, too. It was an odd way to learn humanity, no doubt, but was it not possible, as her interest stretched from interiors to exteriors, from the abodes of the rich to stores and even tenements, that her heart might reach out to *all* who lived under roofs? Or was this merely the loosest kind of sentimentality, the product of what had been — despite all Bella's efforts to conceal it from him — a stroke?

Yes, he was certainly very ill, and, worst of all, the common but deadly disease that had clutched him was at last striking at his memory. He could not remember what he had done the day before, how long he had been at Bella's, when his sisters had last called. He was afraid of seeing in the faces of his nurse and of Bella's discreet, impassive staff just how bad it was, and he smiled vaguely when they asked him questions that troubled him, or affected not to have heard. If only in losing one's memory, one could forget that one had lost it! But the awareness of his growing deficiency stayed with him like a street lamp seen by an insomniac from a darkened house.

He kept reminding himself that Bella had promised to spare Tinetti's, but he could not be sure that he had not imagined it, and he dared not ask her for fear of making her reconsider an act of such uncharacteristic extravagance. It became his fixed idea to visit the old place and see if her offered renovations had been started, but he had not the courage to ask her grand chauffeur to take him so far downtown. One afternoon, however, when the nurse had delivered him to the doorman and returned to the elevator, his chance came. Bella's chauffeur was late.

"Oh, please, tell him I took a cab," Lefferts said eagerly to the hesitant doorman, under orders, no doubt, about Mrs. Hoppin's guest. "Would you be good enough to call me one?"

The cab driver took him down by the East River and turned off at Delancey Street. As he approached the area of Tinetti's down Spring Street under the old dark commercial buildings he felt an excitement that was almost unbearable.

"Please let me out here and wait!" he exclaimed, and getting out of the cab he stumbled along the pavement toward Lafayette Street. He would not look ahead; he would not have the driver witness his shock at what he now realized that he must see. When he had come within visual range of the old store, he closed his eyes, his head still bowed, and uttered a prayer. Then, resolutely, he looked up and opened his eyes.

Of course, it was gone.

On the site was a great pit in the bottom of which a crane was working. The corner was flooded with a new sunlight that made the dull windows of the neighboring buildings blink. Lefferts had an extraordinary and oddly painless sense of inner void, as though a cube in his own mind, comparable to Tinetti's, had been removed by the most competent surgery. But that cube of sensation had nonetheless been the best of him, and he and the departed building were together at the end in his own departing memory. As for the rest of him — well, he would know now what to do with the rest of him.

He was perfectly calm again. He returned to the cab and to Bella's apartment. At tea she asked him, a bit suspiciously, where he had been, and he told her that he had dropped in at the Frick Collection.

"I like to visit the great Holbeins of More and Cromwell once a year. A saint and a sinner, yet they have in common that pale, hard accepting look of Tudor courtiers. They were always willing to gamble, even knowing that they would lose. I sometimes think you're a bit of a Tudor, Bella. But a Tudor queen. *They* always won."

Bella smiled. He would not alienate her now. Obviously she believed that he had forgotten Tinetti's. He would have to be very careful to do nothing to upset that belief. For Bella in the right could be tremendous, but Bella in the wrong might oust him from her apartment. And how he clung to it, that apartment! To be fed and fussed over, to be safe from his censorious siblings, to be able to doze over a drink by a fire while the muted sounds of Bella's social life throbbed from the distant drawing room — it was not to be lost now.

"If you ever have any trouble with Saint Peter, Bella," he continued as he sipped his tea, "just mention what you've done for old Chauncey Lefferts, and he'll whisk you right past those pearly gates!"

Bella smiled again and even beamed; she loved to be thanked as she loved to be worshipped. Her smile embraced him and reassured him. "Trust me, give yourself up and be cared for," she seemed to be telling him. She was nurse; she was asylum; she was the city itself, with its force and possessiveness. She could be counted on to succor the weak, as she could be counted on to destroy the strong. A Tudor, he repeated to himself, with a pale accepting smile. A terrible Tudor queen.

Sabina and the Herd

SABINA FITCH believed in the fundamentals; indeed, she believed in little else. As long as her three daughters did not exceed their incomes by more than her power to supplement, as long as their husbands submitted with at least outward docility to the continuing yoke of matrimony, as long as her many grandchildren were in animal spirits and private schools, what else really mattered? Sabina had a habit of giving "what else" the back of her hand, as she liked to put it. And the reverse side of that plump white appendage was constantly directed to the scattering of such "elses" as permanent waves, interior decoration, world cruises (of the type adored by her fellow widows), book classes, romance, the arts (if they were "arty") and something she called "formality." Seated on comfortable wicker on the porch of "Shingle Eyrie" overlooking the sailboat-crowded harbor of Cold Spring Harbor, on Long Island Sound, Sabina, brown and round as autumnal fruit in her brown tweeds, serene as her bland unpowdered countenance and highly piled gray hair, could contemplate the prefabricated houses of her daughters Gwen and Fran, handsomely stark in their economical utility, and the old gardener's cottage that she had successfully refurbished for Amanda, and reflect that it was very much to her credit, in a day when "interference" was the bogey of the young, that three of her four children should consider that the advantages of having a landlady who charged neither rents for her land nor fees for her baby-sitting should outweigh the indubitable drawback of that landlady's being "Ma."

Sabina pitied her friends who had to spread a long old age over a small card table or project themselves around and around a diminishing globe because they could not adapt themselves to the exigencies of their middle-aging young, but she blamed them for expecting too much. They wanted anniversaries remembered, Sunday lunches attended, summers shared, advice (and anecdotes) listened to and grandchildren who bowed or bobbed as they eternally thanked. Thanked? For what? As if it wasn't the blessed privilege of the old, with lives uselessly protracted by officious medicine, sitting on money that would be far better spent developing young muscles than easing old aches, to give and give and *give* to the posterity that they were lucky enough to have!

Oh yes, if Sabina knew anything, she knew her place. If she had a religion it was her zeal for sacrifices. She knelt daily before the eternal truth of genesis. "Thank *me?*" she would exclaim to any grandchild who might offer her, on leaving, perfunctory gratitude for a party of bobbing for apples that had reduced her living room to a bog. "Thank *you* for coming! Thank *you,* my dear, for giving an old lady the time of her life!" Did Gwen's son need a red sash for a gypsy costume in his school play? Wasn't it luck that Granny had a dress of just the shade that could be cut up? Did Fran's daughter need Granny's old Buick and gardener-chauffeur to take her to dancing school on Granny's Philharmonic day? Of course! Granny's radio was good enough for Granny's aging ears. And as to any gifts to Granny, on anniversaries, even on Christmas, it was a brave descendant who ventured to violate her famous ban. "Land sakes, angel," she would cry, thrusting away the proffered package, "when I'm doing my darndest to get rid of all my fool stuff, do me the simple kindness of not giving me more!"

But the visitor on the porch of "Shingle Eyrie" that autumn day who was engaging all of Sabina's nervous attention was certainly not a descendant. The ample figures of Gwen, Fran and

Amanda could not have been encompassed by that slight lavender print or their shoulders protected by that diminutive mink cape, and the bright sapphire eyes under the dark plucked lashes, the black shiny curls under the little toque could have belonged only to a daughter-in-law, to Cecilia Fitch, Eliot's wife, who lived in the wicked city and cared about "elses" and who could be seen of an afternoon in Central Park with two stylishly clipped poodles and two little dark-eyed daughters with ermine hats, looking for all the world like a Renoir family portrait.

"I know you'll never do anything for yourself, Mrs. Fitch," the quiet tone conveyed to a worried Sabina, "or even hear of anyone else doing it for you, and that is why Eliot and I feel that we must present you with a *fait accompli.* We do not think that November eighteenth can be allowed to pass unnoticed this year."

"November eighteenth?" Sabina queried insincerely. "Bless you, child, you mean my poor old birthday? But after seventy we mustn't notice birthdays, must we? Do you realize I shall be seventy-one?"

"No, Mrs. Fitch, you will be seventy," Cecilia retorted smoothly, smiling at such clumsy tactics. "Eliot has all the family birthdays entered in a little book, and Eliot, you know, never gets things wrong. He and I are in perfect accord that so important a milestone must not be passed over like the others. We want to give you a real party with all the trimmings!"

A little tremor of pain passed over Sabina's heart as she contemplated the lovely creature before her. It was caused by the recollection of another pain, a greater one, inflicted by her husband just before the stroke that had extinguished his brilliant legal career and, a terrible year later, his life. It had been after Cecilia and Eliot's engagement party, when, in the taxi, she had ventured to confide in Mr. Fitch her hopes that their future daughter-in-law might learn to care about the "right things." "By all means," he had retorted, looking at her through the quivering pince-nez on the tiny bridge of his big aquiline nose, "but let us hope that she may accomplish it without becoming quite so frumpy as our own dear girls."

"I know it's very kind of you and Eliot," Sabina murmured now to her daughter-in-law, "and I assure you that it's a case of the thought being better than the deed. Now that you mention a party, I think you're quite right. There *should* be a party. Oh, I'm not as self-denying as you think! Let there be a party by all means, but let me give it at Cold Spring Harbor. I have so much room, and old Nellie has so little to do and likes to cook, and the girls are all there and won't have to get sitters for the babies and ——"

"Gwen and Fran and Amanda can all jolly well get sitters and hike themselves into town for once," Cecilia interrupted firmly. "It's the only trouble they'll have to take, for Eliot and I will do all the rest. What would you say to a dinner dance?"

A dinner dance! Sabina shuddered at the vision of soaring costs. Of course, Eliot was doing very well in his brokerage house, but it was folly for him not to save any party money for the ultimate debuts of his daughters. A dinner dance for an old hag of seventy! It was too ludicrous. Yet looking at Cecilia now, so calm, so easily assuming, she wondered with dismay if it might not actually come off. She remembered Gwen's saying when Cecilia had first come into the family, "Oh, we'll knock her into shape, don't worry, Ma. She looks the type that can be kicked around." But the figuratively speaking Gwen had broken her big toe on the first assault, and Sabina herself remembered, when she had called once too often at the perfect little *boîte* occupied by the newlyweds high over Park Avenue, bearing flowers and tomatoes and corn from her garden in Cold Spring Harbor, being instructed (and chilled) by the sweet, clear little voice with its message that Cecilia's own mother visited only by appointment.

"I'll talk to the girls," Sabina said in a fainter tone, "and see what plans they have."

"I have already talked to the girls," pursued the relentless Cecilia, "and they have no plans." She gazed for a moment at her mother-in-law's disappointed face and concluded more gently, "I'm sorry, Mrs. Fitch, but Eliot and I feel so strongly about it that I think you really ought to give in to him. Sometimes it's hard to remember that family love can be a two-way street."

Even Sabina could not resist this. She threw out her arms in a gesture of surrender to Eliot's wife. "Bless you, my darling. Of course, I'll come to your party."

Gwen, Fran and Amanda, alerted by telephone, came over in the evening to discuss the crisis. Though a day never passed without Sabina's going to one of them, it was the first time in many months that they had all been under the maternal roof at once. The family resemblance was striking. They were big, like their mother, with heavy chests and buttocks, sandy hair, small fat aquiline noses (a paternal inheritance) and alabaster skins. Gwen was the best-looking and the biggest. Had she emphasized the Valkyrie in her looks, she might have been magnificent. But the Fitch girls took their appearances as much for granted as they took their husbands. They dressed for the country and ate what they wanted. Unanimously, they panned the idea of Cecilia's party.

"So like her to try to take over the party *we* should be giving," Gwen announced. "She thinks we don't know how to give one, so she'll show us."

"I suppose it's a good excuse to invite a lot of her own friends," Amanda contributed. "Do you really want your birthday, Ma, to be the occasion for wining and dining half the trash you read about in the gossip columns?"

"I don't want to seem snobbish," Fran apologized, "but I

can't help being embarrassed at the way Cecilia entertains. All that spit and polish betrays the daughter of the garbage collector."

"Mr. Smythe manufactured incinerators," Sabina reproved her mildly. She did not really mind the injustice done Cecilia. Entirely preoccupied by the vertical relationships between the generations, she was quite indifferent to horizontal conflicts. Not being herself involved in the antipathy between her daughters and daughter-in-law, it did not have to exist for her. "But what can I do about it now?" she asked. "I've promised Cecilia that she could have the party. Do you think I can possibly get out of it? Which of us would dare face Eliot?"

There were no volunteers for this, but Gwen had a more practical suggestion. "Of course we're stuck with it, Ma, as long as you've been weak enough to say yes. But we should still try to exercise some control over the party. After all, we have a responsibility to see that old friends of Daddy's like Judge Fowler aren't drowned in a sea of Cecilia's twittering friends. The main thing is to see that it's kept a Fitch party. After all, it's your birthday, not Cecilia's."

Sabina agreed with this, glad to feel backed up, and she went into the city the very next day to tackle Cecilia while her courage was still up.

It was a bit deflating to have her conditions so promptly complied with. Seated on a sofa of turquoise blue under a Lily Cushing Mexican landscape, Cecilia fixed her lovely eyes on her mother-in-law with an air of faintly amused surprise.

The guest list? But of course, Mrs. Fitch could draw it up herself. The menu? Naturally, it must not strain the digestive faculties of the elderly. As to wines, Eliot had meant to keep the champagne for dessert, after a sherry, a white and a red, but if Mrs. Fitch really felt that her friends would find four glasses "showy," they could have champagne throughout. And as to dancing, well if Mrs. Fitch absolutely insisted, they could have a strolling accordionist instead, but a *trickman?*

Sabina, like many timid people, was a bit of a bully when she got her way. It was why the late Mr. Fitch had never allowed her to have it. She had not thought of the trickman until that moment, but suddenly it seemed a *sine qua non.*

"I thought we'd have to do something for the grandchildren," she pointed out.

"Grandchildren!" Cecilia exclaimed. "I didn't know we were going to have grandchildren. The older ones, I suppose you mean?"

"Oh, no, every blessed one of them!" Sabina cried. "I couldn't think of leaving out a single babe!"

"Even Amanda's twin two-year-olds?"

"Oh, them most of all!"

Sabina felt her hopes rise as she saw the clouding of Cecilia's blue eyes.

"I can cope with a children's party," the latter said in a drier tone. "And I hope by now I can cope with an adults'. But I wonder if the combination isn't a mistake." She paused. "A rather serious mistake."

Sabina pounced on this. Imagine not wanting the children! It just *showed* how right the girls were about Cecilia. "Maybe that's just why I'd better have the party in Cold Spring. You see, dear, I'm set up for it there. Of course, it won't be *nearly* as elegant as here, but ——"

"My dear Mrs. Fitch," Cecilia interrupted in a tone that had more correctness than warmth, "you must, of course, have your party any way you like. I only wanted to make it a pleasant occasion for you."

Sabina contemplated the beautiful creature before her and was startled by the sudden churnings of remorse within herself. "It's only because of Eliot's father," she murmured insincerely.

"In his memory I thought the party should be at his home."

"Then have it there by all means!" cried Cecilia, throwing up her hands.

Motoring home that afternoon Sabina had ample occasion to reflect how unexpectedly nasty it could be to get one's own way.

The girls came over for cocktails to hear about the interview, this time accompanied by their husbands, two bank officers and an insurance salesman, dry serious men, big like their wives, who would be "getting on" right up to the day of their mandatory retirements. They were all rather grimly pleased that Cecilia had abandoned her party, but unanimous in their opinion that Sabina should not be allowed to take it over. It could be given in her house, and even at her expense, if she insisted (and she *did* insist), but it had to be organized by her daughters. Let it never be said, or even suggested that Cecilia could set an example for *them* in filial duty!

Sabina was touched. She found, after all, that she *did* want a party, silly old fool though she might be. Perhaps all she had really minded about Cecilia's project was that Cecilia had thought of it, and not her own dear girls. But now that Gwen, Amanda and Fran were going to do it, she had to admit that it was rather fun. Perhaps Cecilia was right that she ought to let her family do more for her. Now that she came to think of it, she *had* detected of late (though she was ashamed to admit it) a certain casualness of attitude in respect to herself. Fran, for example, had borrowed her car the other day without even telling her. Of course, she had been taking a child to a dental appointment, but she still might have mentioned it. Then Gwen's oldest daughter, the "liberal" one, had called her a "social parasite" to her face, using the term, as she later rather feebly apologized, only in its "technical" sense. And Amanda's children had all giggled when little Timmy had asked her how soon she was going to die. Oh, yes, she reflected with increasing warmth, as more such memories began to march through her mind, perhaps it *was* time that they should all, for once, put on their best bib and tucker and pay their respects to the septuagenarian who paid their bills.

But Sabina had ruefully to admit that the days which followed were not marked by any notable increase in the general respect for Grandma. The girls, whose unity seemed only to have existed as a bulwark against Cecilia, fell apart with the latter's elimination. Gwen, whose children were in their teens and could more or less behave themselves, wanted only grandchildren over twelve at the party. Fran, whose youngest was six, thought six should be the age limit, and Amanda, the prospect of whose twins had daunted even the intrepid Cecilia, wanted no limit at all.

Sabina, to the disgust of her older daughters, agreed wholeheartedly with Amanda. "What," she demanded, "is the point of a birthday if it's not for the children? What may I ask, is the point of *us* if it's not for the children?" But Gwen and Fran were very far from adopting their mother's theory of parental suttee and grumbled that the party was already spoiled.

A further point of dispute was the guest list. Gwen, the traditionalist, felt that it should be limited to her mother's oldest friends. Fran, the social member, insisted that her friends be included, for what fun, she charmingly asked, would a party be if half the guests had one foot in the grave? Amanda, who was the most active in local affairs, thought it should be done strictly on a basis of neighborhood. And then there was the question of wines. Gwen felt that champagne was essential; Fran said that her friends drank only whiskey, and Amanda wanted checkered tablecloths and steins of beer. Sabina, listening to their bickering, began to wonder if she did not wish the responsibility back in Cecilia's competent hands.

But the greatest blow of all was the defection of Gwen. Her husband was unexpectedly ordered by his bank to attend a trust officers' conference in Miami during the week of Sabina's birthday, and he suggested that Gwen blow herself to the trip and come with him. What hurt Sabina was that Gwen never even hesitated.

"Of course, I shall be shattered to miss the party," she told her mother buoyantly, "but the children will be there, and you'll have too many people anyway. Do you realize that Ed and I have never been off on a real trip together? I mean just the two of us?"

Well, what else, Sabina pondered sadly, could she have expected? What could be more neatly in line with everything that she had ever professed? And yet that night, how her heart ached! How she suddenly and ludicrously cared about her silly birthday! When she at last fell asleep it was only to find herself embogged in a hateful dream to which she kept returning despite constant awakenings.

In this dream her family had become a herd of cattle. That she should dream of Gwen and Fran and Amanda as cows was distressing enough, but it had happened before. Sabina had tried to square her conscience for these bovine visitations with the argument that as nobody need ever know of them, they did not really exist. But the peculiar horror of this dream was that the girls were not simply cows but horrid cows; dirty, ill-tempered, pushing beasts, their flanks slathered with manure, black flies buzzing about their eyes and ears, and they kept up an infernal din of mooing as they lashed their tails. And most horrid of all was the fact that Sabina herself was a cow, not the mother cow, but merely another member of the herd. Indeed, there appeared to be no relationships; that was somehow, but very clearly, the meaning of the dream.

Even the calves received only a grudging attention from their mothers. As Sabina watched distressfully, Gwen actually kicked a weaned calf that was seeking its accustomed nourishment. Once a cow, evidently, one ceased to be a daughter. The animal to be pushed away from the greener grass might be one's mother or grandmother or even great-great-grandmother — it didn't matter. The cows showed affection (if one could call it that!) only when they mounted each other in that disgusting way cows have. Gwen and Fran . . . but here, mercifully, Sabina awakened. When exhausted, however, she fell asleep again, it was worse. Eliot, a bull, was approaching, and the dull glitter in his eye, as he surveyed the cows who were his mother and siblings, was decidedly not consanguineous. This time Sabina awoke with a scream, turned the lights on and waited in misery for the dawn.

At eight o'clock the telephone rang. It was Gwen to tell her that her oldest girl, the "liberal," had been asked to a football game at Dartmouth and would have to regret the birthday party.

"Fortunately she need not regret it very much," Sabina retorted coldly. "Because there isn't going to be any silly party. It's too foolish, an old woman celebrating an age that she had far better not have reached!"

"Oh, come now, Ma," Gwen protested in a startled voice. "Don't be that way about it. I'll tell Gwenny to give up her weekend. I hadn't realized you cared."

"I wouldn't *dream* of interfering with her weekend," Sabina exclaimed passionately. "It's not a question of *my* caring. It's a question of nobody else giving a tinker's damn! Why should I ask you all to be hypocrites? It's too grotesque!"

She was trembling all over. Never before in her memory had she so surrendered herself to the churning rapids of self-pity. It was heady, soul-satisfying, dangerous stuff. She knew that she was reckless now, that there was no telling what slimy ugliness she might uncover. But she also knew she couldn't stop.

"That's a bit stiff, Ma," Gwen retorted, taken aback by the

violence of her mother's reaction. "You're just punishing me for my Florida trip."

"My dear, I'm way beyond such pettiness. If you only *knew* how far beyond!"

"Well, you might consider little Gwen, even if you won't consider me," Gwen continued in a voice of hardening anger. "How is she going to feel if you call off your party because she's going to Dartmouth? You keep telling your grandchildren that old people don't 'matter.' But when they take you up on it, you shriek to the skies!"

"I'm perfectly aware that it's all my fault," Sabina said moodily.

"Oh, fiddlesticks, I know that tone. You're burned up, that's all."

"I am burned up, I'm afraid, Gwen, but not in the way you imagine. I'm not feeling at all myself, and if you don't mind, I shall ring off now."

As soon as she had done so, Sabina was very ill indeed. She lay down on her bed and felt her heart pounding wildly. When old Nelly came in with her breakfast she asked her weakly to fetch Doctor Brandon. He came in an hour's time and pronounced that she had suffered a slight heart attack.

Thirteen months later, on Sabina Fitch's seventy-first birthday, her son and daughter-in-law gave a large and decorous dinner party in her honor at their beautiful apartment. In every particular the occasion bore the "Cecilia touch." There were a dozen little tables and two larger ones; there was a three-piece Hungarian orchestra; there were clusters of tall red candles in silver candelabra; there were flaming dishes and flowing wines. All of the children and their spouses were present and all grandchildren over the age of fourteen. Sabina's old friends enjoyed the French cooking and the French champagne with evident relish, and Judge Fowler was a bit unsteady when he rose to make a sentimental toast. Eliot, looking less severe than usual, less like the late father whom he almost comically resembled, recited a bit heavily the comic poem that his wife had composed. Gwen, Fran and Amanda, throughout the party, were at their most gracious. But it was Sabina who was the constant center of attention. Looking remarkably pretty in a new scarlet dress with her hair handsomely waved for the first time, she announced that she was taking a world cruise with the beautiful cash present from her children and friends and quoted Tennyson's "Ulysses" about it being her purpose "to sail beyond the sunset and the baths of all the western stars" before she died. There were tears even in Gwen's eyes when she concluded.

When the guests and family had all departed and Eliot had gone to bed, Cecilia and her mother-in-law, who had become almost intimate in a year's time, sat up by the fire for a last glass of champagne.

"Tell me, my dear," Sabina asked after a long but relaxed silence, "why do you know so much and I so little?"

"So much about what?"

"Oh, so much about life. How did someone as young as yourself ever learn the importance of ceremony, while an addled old fool like me trusted to the human heart?"

"You forget that I had the head start of an unhappy childhood," Cecilia answered, showing by her change of tone that she would take up the discussion at the level proposed. It was one of the delightful things about Cecilia that she was willing to be serious. "We were poor, you know, before Daddy's invention caught on. Grindingly poor. And he and Mummie were most unhappily married. When you have neither the heart nor the manner, it's the manner you cultivate. At least, *I* did."

"While I, as a girl, had both," Sabina rejoined sadly. "My parents were perfect: they honored every anniversary, every occasion, and their love was real. So I, blind child, never saw the dependence between those things. I opted for love alone. I thought it was all I had to give, all I had to ask. And here I am, past threescore years and ten and only too happy to settle for appearances. For forms, pure and simple. While you, dear child, have both."

"Both?"

"Of course, both. Nobody has a life more ordered, more beautiful to look upon. And I have no doubt that within, it's at least as good as without. That *must* be so, for you and Eliot, must it not?"

Sabina reflected afterwards that Cecilia really *was* perfect. She even knew when she was not supposed to answer. She simply cradled her glass in both hands, staring with a faint smile into the few drops of champagne that it contained, and then tilted her head back and bore the crystal cup slowly to her lips as though she were about to savor a rare and precious liqueur.

The Club Bedroom

A Play in One Act

Dramatis Personae

MRS. RUGGLES
MRS. MILES
ELMINA RUGGLES

The scene is a corner of one of the common rooms of a fashionable ladies' club, the Clinton, on Park Avenue in New York City. The time is a midafternoon in October, 1965. In the center of the stage are two Louis XV bergère chairs (modern copies, newly upholstered) on either side of a round table containing a crystal ash tray and a pile of magazines. Above the table and chairs, dwarfing them, is a gilt-framed, full-length portrait of a former president of the club, painted in 1910 and as pompous as only portraits of that era can be. The subject is a lady of erect carriage, broad shoulders and ample girth, with a square, pale, high brow and a large nose. She wears her dress of sweeping black and her big pearls in a way to dominate but not to charm.

At curtain MRS. RUGGLES *is standing by the table greeting* MRS. MILES, *who is coming in.* MRS. MILES *is a discreet, tactful, efficient woman in her fifties, trim, self-assured, quietly dressed, the kind of person who could afford to dress better, to talk louder, to push people around, but doesn't — and knows that she chooses not to. She will always take control of any organization with which she is connected, not because she is ambitious, but because she is willing and able to do detailed work.* MRS. RUGGLES, *nearing seventy, is a plump, bland-faced woman with rather wispy gray hair, who might have been quite pretty in a long-lost youth. Her nervousness is reflected in the twitch of her hands and in the haggard, almost animal fear in her large damp eyes. Her dress is dowdy, fussy. She is obviously afraid of making social errors. Her Clinton Club membership came through marriage rather than birth, and if everyone else has forgotten it,* she *hasn't.*

MRS. RUGGLES. It's very kind of you, Mrs. Miles, to spare me these few minutes. I know the House Committee has my formal request for the corner bedroom on the third floor, but I thought, before you met this afternoon, it might help you to know my personal reasons for wanting that room.

MRS. MILES. I'm very happy to talk it over with you, Mrs. Ruggles. (*They sit.*) But, as I understand the matter, it's not simply a question of the room. It's more a question of our waiving the rule that members cannot reside in the clubhouse for more than six months at a time. Isn't that it? Haven't you been here now since May?

MRS. RUGGLES. I have. And I am hoping *so* hard that you will waive the rule. I do love being here, Mrs. Miles! I really don't know where else I should go. Of course, I suppose I could live more economically in a hotel . . .

MRS. MILES. (*Practical.*) Yes, that room you want is four hundred a month.

MRS. RUGGLES. (*Agitated.*) But I can afford it, Mrs. Miles! I've pinched and saved, and I can afford it, if I can't afford anything else. Oh, the Ruggleses aren't what they were in *her* day. (*She looks up at the portrait.*) No, not by a long shot, but we can still make ends meet if we stretch.

MRS. MILES. (*Placating.*) Well, I can't make you any promises, Mrs. Ruggles, but I don't mind telling you that I, for one, shall urge that the rule be waived in your case. I think we go too far these days in treating everyone alike. I don't see why the committee shouldn't give some consideration to the fact that you're the daughter-in-law of our founder and first president.

They both look up for a reverent moment at the portrait.

MRS. RUGGLES. (*Moved.*) Thank you, Mrs. Miles. She was a great woman. That's why I always like to sit here, beneath her beautiful portrait. It's my own special little niche. Sort of like a chapel, if that doesn't shock you. And now you will see why I want that bedroom. It was the one *she* always occupied when she stayed in the city.

MRS. MILES. (*Sympathetic.*) You were very close to her, were you not?

MRS. RUGGLES. (*Eager.*) Oh, yes, much more like a daughter than a daughter-in-law. My husband was her only child, and my two children are her only living descendants.

MRS. MILES. Well, I think it's very much to both your credits that you got on so well. It's no easy thing to be married to an only son. I know a bit about that myself.

MRS. RUGGLES. Oh, but I knew Mrs. Ruggles *before* I knew Minthorn. In fact, I met him through her. (*There is a pause before she can quite bring this out.*) I was her trained nurse.

MRS. MILES. (*Glancing again at the portrait.*) Really? You mean she was ever *ill?*

MRS. RUGGLES. (*Bowing her head.*) Mrs. Ruggles was one of those splendid women who gave her all to her public life. This had to be paid for, inevitably, by some degree of private collapse. I was what would have been called a psychiatric nurse today. I specialized in nervous tensions.

MRS. MILES. (*Still incredulous.*) Mrs. Ruggles was "nervous"?

MRS. RUGGLES. (*Finding this perhaps a disrespectful term.*) Let me put it this way, Mrs. Miles. I helped her to relax. I read to her; I persuaded her to take little walks; I kept people off. I made her home a sanctuary that her public could not invade. Inevitably, we became very intimate.

MRS. MILES. (*Curious now.*) It must have been a tricky thing to convert that relationship into one of mother-in-law and daughter-in-law.

MRS. RUGGLES. Do you know what, Mrs. Miles? It was as easy as rolling off a log!

MRS. MILES. You don't say!

MRS. RUGGLES. Oh, but I do. Mrs. Ruggles was a really *big* woman. Besides, she had been worried about Minthorn. He never had her constitution. Oh, dear, no. She was happy to think that she had found him a wife who could take care of him.

MRS. MILES. She must have hated having you leave her, though.

MRS. RUGGLES. But, good heavens, there was never any question of that! We all lived together in that big house in Bernardsville. There was plenty of room.

MRS. MILES. (*Beginning to wonder about it all.*) But as the children grew older, didn't you want your own establishment?

MRS. RUGGLES. Well, I did, at times. But my husband was never well enough to work, and the Ruggles money wasn't what it had been, and it seemed hard to ask my mother-in-law to support *two* establishments. Besides, she needed me. And then it was wonderful for Griffin and Elmina to grow up knowing their grandmother so well.

MRS. MILES. (*Less sure of this.*) Yes, I suppose. Why could your husband never work? I mean, what was his ailment?

MRS. RUGGLES. (*After a pause, bravely.*) My husband had a partiality for intoxicating beverages. Perhaps I shouldn't be the one to say it, but I'm afraid it was no secret. Not in Bernardsville, anyway.

MRS. MILES. (*Beginning to be fascinated.*) Dear me. I suppose this was a great grief to his mother.

MRS. RUGGLES. It was, Mrs. Miles. A great grief. But Mrs. Ruggles had great courage. And great philosophy. To those who knew her superficially it sometimes seemed more like detachment. For example, I remember that a doctor, who had come to talk to her about her son, was a bit surprised when she simply said: "Add the Howland moodiness to the Burrill bad temper, sprinkle the combination with a dash of the Herrick hysteria and the Lyman laziness, and what do you get? Minthorn!" But, you see, she was a dedicated student of genealogy. She believed it explained everything.

MRS. MILES. (*Dry.*) How wonderful to be able to take it that way. It disposes so completely of any feelings of guilt.

MRS. RUGGLES. (*Taking this at face value.*) Yes, Mrs. Ruggles was above ordinary fears or inhibitions. When she died, for example, she willed the poor remnants of the Ruggles fortune — after the terrible expenses of her last years — to me instead of to Minthorn. She felt that I would be the better custodian.

MRS. MILES. And how did your husband feel about *that?*

MRS. RUGGLES. Well, of course, it was too much to expect that he would be pleased. But by the time his mother died — she lived, you know, into her nineties — he was in very poor shape. He hardly survived her a year.

MRS. MILES. (*Turning to what she hopes will be a pleasanter topic.*) And your children, what do they do? Are they married?

MRS. RUGGLES. (*With a sigh.*) No, alas, neither of them is married. It was a great blow to Mrs. Ruggles, particularly in the case of Griffin. It was hard for a woman with her family pride to contemplate the extinction of the Ruggleses. At least of her branch.

MRS. MILES. (*Gently correcting the emphasis.*) And hard on you, too.

MRS. RUGGLES. Well, it hasn't been easy. But one gets used to anything, Mrs. Miles. The hardest time, I find, is the Christmas season. When all those cards come in with snapshots of the friends surrounded by clusters of dear little grandchildren. Yes, that's the worst time.

MRS. MILES. (*Sympathetic, perhaps regretting her own Christmas greetings.*) I really think those cards are obscene. The idea that out of *this* came all *these.*

MRS. RUGGLES. You have grandchildren?

MRS. MILES. Twelve, I'm afraid. But surely your case isn't hopeless. Your children can't be out of their thirties yet.

MRS. RUGGLES. No, Griffin is only thirty-five. But I'm afraid he's not the marrying kind. He's an artist — a painter.

MRS. MILES. (*Smiling to cover her real feelings about art.*) And I suppose as incomprehensible as all the others.

MRS. RUGGLES. At times I wish he were. He's rather too comprehensible. In fact, I'm afraid he's unmistakable. He does enormous canvases with a meticulous realism of . . . well, parts of the anatomy that you and I, Mrs. Miles, are not accustomed to seeing treated at all, let alone in such detail.

MRS. MILES. (*With a shudder.*) I see. Or rather I don't want to see. Does he have much success with these . . . these studies?

MRS. RUGGLES. No great commercial success, no. They're not exactly what *House Beautiful* would suggest for your living room. There was some talk of the Museum of Modern Art buying one, but it didn't come to anything.

MRS. MILES. (*Still looking for a better solution than the third-floor room.*) I should think *he* might want to share an apartment with you. Doesn't he need someone to look after him? Or does he prefer to be alone in his studio?

MRS. RUGGLES. (*Honest to a fault.*) Well, he's not exactly alone.

MRS. MILES. (*Embarrassed, but trying to be a woman of the world.*) I see. No more questions!

MRS. RUGGLES. (*Hastily.*) Oh, it's not what you think, not a woman. He has a roommate. Another man.

MRS. MILES. (*Dubious.*) Another painter, I suppose.

MRS. RUGGLES. Well, actually not. This young man — I say young, for he's only nineteen — wants to be an actor. I think he's hoping one of Griffin's theater friends will get him a job. Probably one of them will. Griffin would do anything for that boy.

MRS. MILES. (*Stiffening, changing the subject.*) What about your daughter, Mrs. Ruggles? Does she live in town, too?

MRS. RUGGLES. Oh, yes, she runs a little antique shop on Lexington Avenue. She has the most exquisite taste, if I say so myself. As a matter of fact, she's coming in this afternoon. Could you stay and meet her?

MRS. MILES. (*Ever the club trustee.*) Do you think she might be interested in one of our junior memberships?

MRS. RUGGLES. I'm afraid she's over the age limit. I shouldn't tattle, but Elmina's thirty-six. Anyway, I'm sure she wouldn't join, even if I paid her way. She's not very keen about women's organizations. Particularly clubs. I'm afraid she thinks of us as a lot of old tabbies.

MRS. MILES. (*Not amused.*) I know many of the younger women feel that way. I wonder what we could do to attract them more.

MRS. RUGGLES. Oh, I don't think we should do a thing! I think we should stay just as we are. If we changed, we wouldn't be what they're going to need when they *do* need us.

MRS. MILES. What do you think they're going to need?

MRS. RUGGLES. (*Emphatic, emerging for the first time from her cover of self-apology.*) Niceness, Mrs. Miles. Good old-fashioned, plain, simple niceness. Do you know that I've never once heard an angry argument inside this club? I mean a really angry argument, one of those bitter, insulting ones that young people seem to love. Here we try to look at the brighter side of things. And what's wrong with that? I've seen my share of the darker side, and I don't need to go poking around in closets or turning over stones to find any more of it. I *like* things to be cheerful. And I *enjoy* the company of my own sex. I even distrust women who don't! I'm sorry, Mrs. Miles. I didn't mean to expose you to my credo. But I did want to tell you how I felt about the club.

MRS. MILES. (*Rising.*) I'm glad you told me, Mrs. Ruggles. I think a good many of us feel that way, only few these days have the courage to express it. It's not fashionable any more. I shall be off to my meeting now. And I shall certainly give your application my heartiest endorsement.

MRS. RUGGLES. (*Taking Mrs. Miles's hand in both of hers.*) Oh, thank you, Mrs. Miles. If you *knew* what it means to me!

As MRS. MILES *is turning to go,* ELMINA RUGGLES *enters and walks up to the table. She is very thin, very pale and angular, with long jet-black hair, and she wears a black knitted sweater over a gray skirt. Her attitude toward life, or at least toward the Clinton Club, seems expressed in her sway-back posture, her too high heels, her dangling cigarette, her overrouged, thick pouting lips: she is defiant. Yet there is about her some of the air of a bluestocking trying to look like a Bohemian, of a lady endeavoring to convince you that she is a tramp.* ELMINA *will never get away from her intellectualism, just as she will never quite sever the cables of her good taste. She knows this, and it angers her, even though she is also well aware that it gives her her peculiar style.*

MRS. RUGGLES. (*Nervously introducing them.*) This is my daughter, Elmina. Elmina, Mrs. Miles.

MRS. MILES. I'm so glad to meet you, Miss Ruggles. We were just speaking about you. Your mother was telling me what marvelous taste you have.

ELMINA. (*Glancing about.*) Any time you'd like to do this room over, you can find me in the book.

MRS. MILES. (*Offended, smiling glacially.*) Good day, Miss Ruggles. Good day, Mrs. Ruggles. I've so enjoyed our little chat.

Exit MRS. MILES.

MRS. RUGGLES. (*Bitterly reproachful.*) Elmina, how could you? She's on the House Comittee. They just did this room over!

ELMINA. (*Looking about again.*) So they have. In the very latest nineteen twenty. I must say, it's all too wonderfully typical, from that lampshade to that ghastly portrait of Granny. I'd forgotten how bad it was. Lanza, isn't it? He was almost as vulgar as Sargent.

MRS. RUGGLES. Sargent? *Vulgar?*

ELMINA. But, of course, he was the most vulgar painter in the world! All those burghers' wives puffing out their bosoms to look like archduchesses. Or to look like what they *thought* archduchesses looked like. Still, I admit he could paint, which was something Lanza never learned. But to hell with all that. (*She slumps in a chair and puts out her cigarette.*) I came to talk finances.

MRS. RUGGLES. (*Wearily sitting in the other chair.*) Oh, Elmina. Again?

ELMINA. (*Down to earth.*) Now look, Ma. You don't have to take that tone with me. If Granny had left her money to her own flesh and blood, as she ought to have, I wouldn't be here begging today.

MRS. RUGGLES. (*Lofty.*) Indeed, you wouldn't. There wouldn't be anything to beg about. Your father would have seen to that.

ELMINA. She could have put it in trust for him. That would have been the more normal thing. And then, when he died, it would have come to Griffin and me. And our roles today would be reversed.

MRS. RUGGLES. Except for two things. You and Griffin would have spent it just as fast as your father. And I would never have asked you for a penny.

ELMINA. (*Sneering.*) What would you have done? Starved?

MRS. RUGGLES. (*Calmly dignified.*) I would have returned to my profession.

ELMINA. (*Laughing nastily.*) Don't you think you're a bit old for domestic service?

MRS. RUGGLES. (*Above this petty attack.*) Elmina, your spitefulness is sometimes embarrassing. Just because on occasion I did a maid's work for your grandmother does not mean that I was a maid.

ELMINA. What were you then?

MRS. RUGGLES. You know as well as I. A trained nurse.

ELMINA. Trained? In what school?

MRS. RUGGLES. (*Taking an even higher tone.*) One didn't have to go to a school in those days. Doctor Talmud preferred to instruct his own nurses. And certainly no school could have prepared me for what I faced at your grandmother's. No school could have prepared me to be nurse and companion and housekeeper, as well as mother and wife and chauffeur. Small wonder that your grandmother left me in charge. I always *had* been!

ELMINA. (*Shrugging.*) Oh, I'm not disputing that the money's legally yours. I'm simply saying that morally it's Ruggles money, and I'm a Ruggles.

MRS. RUGGLES. (*Provoked at last.*) And haven't you had more than half my income, you and Griffin? Didn't I buy his studio?

Didn't I set you up in your shop? Haven't I paid the enormous bills of your endless psychoanalysis?

ELMINA. (*Flaring.*) And who should better pay the doctor than she who caused the disease?

MRS. RUGGLES. You and Doctor Leming seem to spend hours at my expense discussing what I did to you and Griffin. But you never tell me what it was.

ELMINA. Do you really want to know?

MRS. RUGGLES. (*Bland.*) Very much. I'd be very much interested.

ELMINA. (*Clinical.*) Well, to begin with, you destroyed Father. Psychically speaking.

MRS. RUGGLES. You don't think *he* contributed to that end?

ELMINA. (*Patient, condescending, later excited.*) You don't understand. I mean, you destroyed him in *our* eyes. In Griffin's and mine. Can't you imagine how it struck us? That big dark dining room in Bernarsdville, with you at one end of the table and Granny at the other, and Griffin and I in between. And the empty place laid for Father — that terrible empty place! Yet it was worse if he *did* come in, much worse, and shuffled to his seat, or upset a glass, or spoke in slurred syllables. How I remember you and Granny and those understanding glances you exchanged! Oh, poor Griffin, what could he think of his sex when he saw his own father caught there, impaled between those two powerful female presences? Those Junos! What was it in the name of God but a mutilation of the father figure? A public castration?

MRS. RUGGLES. (*Looking apprehensively around.*) Please, Elmina! Not so loud!

ELMINA. (*Remorseless.*) And when he was old enough for sex, did he dare go to those dismembering giantesses? Where could he possibly go but to the boys? Poor stingy old nature, after all, only gave us two sexes.

MRS. RUGGLES. (*Stung at last.*) I loved Griffin, and he loved me, too! Then, anyway.

ELMINA. (*Contemptuous.*) Oh, yes, he loved you. But it was the love of a slave for a despotic queen who with the twitch of an eyelid could summon a guard with a scimitar to cut off his ——

MRS. RUGGLES. (*Hastily interrupting.*) Please! Not again! I get the point. And what about you, then? Did I appear as a despotic queen to you, too?

ELMINA. (*Relapsing to her normal tone.*) Oh, I was different. You never cared about me as you cared about Griffin. Perhaps I was lucky.

MRS. RUGGLES. Elmina, I adored you!

ELMINA. (*Shrugging.*) You adored the image of a little girl. As with Griffin you adored the image of a little boy. Except he looked the part. I never did. You wanted a candy box cover, a Miss Muffet, with golden locks and blue sashes, like a fashionable portrait. Like a Lanza! If you couldn't have a proper husband, at least you were going to have proper offspring. And later on I was to be a debutante who would have a whirl at parties and who would ultimately select, from a circle of eligible, swooning swains, the rich young golden-haired stud who was to sire on me all the golden-haired grandchildren you needed for your inane Christmas cards!

MRS. RUGGLES. (*Irked.*) Does Doctor Leming have any grandchildren?

ELMINA. (*Surprised.*) No, I don't think so.

MRS. RUGGLES. Well, I hope he never will!

ELMINA. (*Ignoring this.*) I don't think you ever once really saw me as I was until I was eighteen.

MRS. RUGGLES. (*Grim.*) I saw you then.

ELMINA. Because I *made* you. Because I had to stop the farce. After you'd spent all the money I wanted for my Paris winter on that damn fool coming-out party. Oh, I had to make my gesture! That's why I had to walk out of the party with that waiter!

MRS. RUGGLES. (*Wrinkling her nose.*) Not even a young one, either. He must have been fifty.

ELMINA. (*Aggressive.*) Yes, that's the way it's always been with me. Even way back then. Older men. Tommy Bogardus, after all, is damn near your age. Of course, Doctor Leming says I'm looking for the father I never had. It's almost a cliché.

MRS. RUGGLES. (*Shocked.*) But how could you want to . . . well, how could you want to do those things with a *father?*

ELMINA. (*With a hoot of laughter.*) Mother, you're priceless! I'd like to put you in a jar!

MRS. RUGGLES. (*Stubborn.*) Well, I can't see why, if Doctor Leming has convinced you that you're looking for a father in Mr. Bogardus, he hasn't cured you of Mr. Bogardus. I thought that was the whole point of psychoanalysis.

ELMINA. (*Conceding the point.*) He might have. If he'd caught me in time. But I'm like a terminal case. All Doctor Leming can basically do is make me as comfortable as he can.

MRS. RUGGLES. (*Giving it up.*) Well, it all seems very dismal to me. And I don't see why I get so sneered at for having wanted a better life for my daughter than being the friend of a married man in his sixties who refuses to get a divorce.

ELMINA. (*Grim.*) For "friend" read "mistress." I guess I've earned that title by now.

MRS. RUGGLES. (*Throwing her hands up.*) All right, have it your way, mistress, concubine, kept woman, what you will!

ELMINA. (*Picking her up firmly on the first point.*) No, "kept woman" I won't allow. I have never been kept. I have never taken so much as a jewel from Tommy. Which brings me to the point of my visit. Tommy is going to Paris to represent his bank. He'll be there two years, until he retires. I've had an offer of a job from an *antiquaire* in the Place Vendôme. I figure it will cost me twenty-five hundred bucks to close up here and move to France.

MRS. RUGGLES. (*Dismayed.*) Twenty-five hundred! And where am I to get *that?*

ELMINA. (*Cool.*) You can take it out of principal and charge it against my share of your estate. I assume I *have* a share.

MRS. RUGGLES. But, my child, I swore to your grandmother on bended knee I'd never touch a penny of her capital!

ELMINA. (*Shrugging.*) *She* was not troubled by any such inhibitions. But all right, I'm not fussy. Take it out of income.

MRS. RUGGLES. Out of income! Do you realize that's more than half the cost of the room I'm applying for here?

ELMINA. There must be cheaper rooms.

MRS. RUGGLES. Yes, of course, up under the eaves, much cheaper. But they're not nearly as nice. And I had so set my heart on your grandmother's room!

ELMINA. Well, I don't like to sound greedy, Ma, but every thing in *my* life depends on this Paris move, and I honestly don't see why one club bedroom is any different from another. You spend all your time in the public rooms, anyway.

MRS. RUGGLES. (*Pleading.*) Elmina, dear, when I *think* of all you've sacrificed to Mr. Bogardus, who is several times a millionaire, it *does* seem that it would not be so very bad to let him undertake this one small expense. After all, it's *his* move that has necessitated it.

ELMINA. (*Triumphant.*) *Now* who's the whore?

MRS. RUGGLES. But just *once,* Elmina!

ELMINA. Look, Ma. The only integrity I have left is that Tommy gives me nothing. Don't take that away, for pity's sake. Tommy Bogardus stands for everything in this world I'm passionately opposed to. He's a banker, a Babbitt, a Birchite. He's a howling snob and a social climber. He roars with laughter when I abuse him and shows me off to his friends as if I were some kind of dirty-talking parrot. From the very beginning, he's wanted to keep me, almost as much as he wanted to sleep with me. He's wanted to deck me out with jewels and label me his little captive radical. Well, captive I am not! Put it on my tombstone. It's all I can say of my wasted life, but that much I can say.

MRS. RUGGLES. (*With a shudder.*) I don't see how you can stay with a man whom you feel that way about.

ELMINA. (*Bitter.*) Isn't that what old Maugham meant by human bondage? Tommy asked me to a cocktail party the other day. One of those huge sprawling affairs his bank gives when they open a new branch. I can go to *those* because Mrs. Bogardus won't. Well, I was watching him — across a crowded room — talking to some rich lady depositor — all furs and fat and lipstick like a Peter Arno cartoon. And I was sickened by his oozing unctuosity! I thought for one desperate moment: "This can't go on, this madness. I'll leave him now. I'll walk out and never come back." And then I heard his laugh, that braying, brassy, Philistine laugh. That laugh which would have bounced the stone from David's slingshot right back in David's nose! "Now!" I told myself. "*Now* or never!" And then he winked at me. He winked at me lewdly over that fat minky shoulder. It was a wink that seemed to touch me, to make me a part of the whole sordid scene. And I loved it!

MRS. RUGGLES. (*Maternal again, hopeful.*) Perhaps his wife may give him a divorce, after all.

ELMINA. Never! She hates me too much. That's *her* integrity.

MRS. RUGGLES. But he could get one in Mexico.

ELMINA. Not without her consent. It would be no good.

MRS. RUGGLES. If he came back, yes. Not if he stayed there. I read all about it in the *Reader's Digest*. And why shouldn't he live in Mexico as well as France? His bank has branches everywhere. You could be married down there and have one of those beautiful places in Cuernavaca. And perhaps a beach house in Acapulco. Oh, I begin to see it for you, Elmina! It could be a lovely life. And you might still have a baby, you're not too old . . .

ELMINA. (*Sour.*) And you could have a grandchild for that Christmas card. At long last! No, Ma, you're dreaming. I wouldn't marry him even if his wife was dead. I wouldn't give him the satisfaction. Truly.

MRS. RUGGLES. (*Sighing deeply.*) Oh, I believe you. Ever since you were a little girl you've had a singular talent for looking gift horses squarely in the mouth. And I suppose I shall have to give you the money. (*Pause as she bites her lip.*) I suppose I'll have to take one of the eaves rooms. I'll just have to swallow it, that's all.

ELMINA. (*Embarrassed, at last.*) I'm sorry, Ma. But it *is* important for me.

MRS. RUGGLES. Yes, my dear, I see it is. And, of course, I'm an old fool to care so much about that silly bedroom. (*She takes a deep breath to check an involuntary sob.*) Oh, goodness me, I hope I'm not going to make an ass of myself!

ELMINA. (*Appalled at the sudden vision of how much her mother* does *care.*) Ma! Take that room. I'll manage somehow.

MRS. RUGGLES. (*Shaking her head.*) No, dear, I'm not going to change my mind. I've said you could have the money, and you shall have it. Nothing is going to change that. (*She holds up her hand to quell any protest.*) *Nothing,* Elmina. But I want to tell you why I wanted that room. I want to have my say, too. Even the villain should have a day in court.

ELMINA. (*Embarrassed again.*) Oh, villain, there are no villains, Ma. These things all have psychological explanations. It's not a question of fault.

MRS. RUGGLES. (*Serene again, at her most dignified.*) Perhaps not. I don't have an analyst to make my apologies. I couldn't afford one, anyway, and what does it matter about an old woman? But I wasn't always an old woman, Elmina. When I first went to your grandmother, I was young, and if I say so myself, I was pretty. I wanted all the things a young woman wants: a husband, children, a home of my own. And I was immured in that house in Bernardsville. When the depression started, I had to send my wages home, and I didn't even have the cash to go to New York on my day off. There were no young men in Bernardsville. Not for me, anyway. I was regarded as a kind of servant by the local families, and I held myself too good for the village boys. Perhaps I was wrong, but, like you, my pride was all I had. When your father began to look at me, I couldn't help but be interested. Of course, he didn't mean marriage at first . . .

ELMINA. My God, it's straight out of Ibsen!

MRS. RUGGLES. A country community is never very far from Ibsen. I deluded myself with the idea that I would be the saving of your father. Your grandmother encouraged me. Together, we brought him around . . .

ELMINA. Bound and gagged!

MRS. RUGGLES. (*Severe.*) Women who marry, Elmina, often have to do that. But I honestly thought it would be for his own good. And when I found that nothing was going to stop his drinking, I turned my hopes to you and Griffin. At least I could make lives for you! Well, you know how *that* turned out. And all during those terrible years, whenever things got too bad, when your father was too violent, or Griffin too hysterical or you too sullen, your grandmother would take off to New York to her room at the Clinton Club. She used to say: "Anna, Bernardsville is reality. Bernardsville is family. Bernardsville is the world. But my little room in the Clinton Club is heaven!" And then I would think of her longingly in that bright little chamber with the gay chintz and the Nattier lithographs of French princesses and the view down Park Avenue and breakfast coming in with the *Herald Tribune* and the telephone to ask friends for lunch and maybe a matinee. Oh, yes, you will say it was an escape from responsibility, from men, from sex. And I will say: "You bet it was!" I was never happy until I moved into this club. And what I will never understand, to my dying day, is why your and Griffin's solutions to life are considered serious and mine ridiculous. Why are Mr. Bogardus and Griffin's young man serious and my room silly? *Why?* Aren't I neurotic too? Didn't I have a mother? And a mother-in-law? If sex is the only thing you young people take seriously, then my little third-floor corner room is sex!

ELMINA. (*Moved.*) Ma, I don't know what to say. I . . .

MRS. RUGGLES. (*Agitated.*) Don't say it! Don't say it, dear. Don't say a thing. Anything you say now would make me feel even more foolish. I've indulged myself. Maybe I've even enjoyed it. I don't know. But you've listened, which was all I wanted. Go, now, and I'll send you the check in the morning. Please, dear, *go!*

ELMINA. (*Rising.*) I'll call you tomorrow. Goodby, Ma. And thanks. Thanks a million.

ELMINA *kisses her mother on the forehead and exits rapidly. Her stride is almost exuberant; after all, she has what she came for.* MRS. RUGGLES *watches her go and then rises slowly to turn and face the portrait of her mother-in-law.*

MRS. RUGGLES. (*In a low, tense, curious tone, a blend of deep resentment and reluctant admiration.*) How did you do it, Mrs. Ruggles? How did you have it all your own way and escape the blame as well? How did you have your cake and eat it, right down to the last sweet, juicy crumb? What was the secret of your glorious generation? And why does mine have neither cake nor crumbs? Was it just that you believed so blindly in yourselves? Was *that* your secret? (*She pauses as if waiting for an answer.*) You must be in some terrible purgatory now to make up for your glimpse of heaven on earth. But wherever you are, Mrs. Ruggles, I wonder if you're far enough away to escape my curse. (*Her voice rises to shrillness.*) For if they blame *me,* I blame *you!* You fed on us, you fattened on us, you left us to hell while you stepped loftily toward heaven! Well, look back, Mrs. Ruggles! Look back, like Lot's wife and turn to salt! Look back and see your only grandson a fairy and your only granddaughter a tramp! (*She steps back, appalled at her own temerity.*) All right? No thunderbolt! No divine wrath! Were you only a mortal woman, Mrs. Ruggles? Who would have believed it?

MRS. MILES, *looking very grave, enters.* MRS. RUGGLES, *seeing her, pulls herself together with a start.*

MRS. RUGGLES. Oh, Mrs. Miles, your meeting's over?

MRS. MILES. Yes, but I'm afraid, Mrs. Ruggles, I don't have very good news for you.

MRS. RUGGLES. (*Abruptly.*) The corner room is taken.

MRS. MILES. No, as a matter of fact, it's free, but ——

MRS. RUGGLES. (*Interrupting impetuously.*) It doesn't really matter. I've decided that I don't want it. I mean, I've decided I can't afford it. Not this year, anyway. I'd like one of the cheaper rooms. One of those little ones under the eaves.

MRS. MILES. (*Gentle but inexorable.*) I'm afraid that won't be possible, Mrs. Ruggles. You see, the committee felt that it could not make an exception in your case. That it could not waive the rule that no member can live in the clubhouse more than six months at a time. So I fear we're going to have to ask you to move elsewhere — at least until this time next year.

MRS. RUGGLES. (*Appalled.*) But I thought the House Committee was going to change the rule!

MRS. MILES. So I thought too. But we were wrong. We have a new member on the committee who seems to be very strong for tradition. She even quoted your late mother-in-law as saying: "A club is by definition an undemocratic organization. All the more reason that among its membership a strict democracy should be maintained." She argued from this that we should not abrogate a rule in favor of one member.

MRS. RUGGLES. (*Crushed.*) I see. Then that's it. Of course, I must move.

MRS. MILES. (*Moved.*) I'm sorry, Mrs. Ruggles. I did the best I could. Perhaps we can lunch one of these days. I'd like to know you better.

They shake hands, and MRS. MILES *moves to the exit.*

MRS. RUGGLES. (*Calling after her.*) Oh, Mrs. Miles.

MRS. MILES. (*Turning back.*) Yes?

MRS. RUGGLES. Would you mind telling me the name of the new member of the House Committee? The one who's such a strict traditionalist?

MRS. MILES. Not at all. She's the mainstay of the board these days, probably our next president. I'm sure you must know her — Mrs. Bogardus. Mrs. Tommy Bogardus.

MRS. MILES *exits leaving* MRS. RUGGLES *staring, awe-stricken, at the portrait as the curtain falls.*

The Wagnerians

January 1, 195—

Dear Mr. Styles:

When I told you that I would not "write up" Uncle Ed for your history of opera in the Americas, you implied that I was being stuffy. Privately I have no doubt that you used a harsher word. "What bad luck," you must have said to your fellow editors, "that the only person living who remembers Edmund Stillman should be a prudish niece who is determined to take her sixty-year secrets with her virginity to the grave!" Oh, yes, I can imagine how you young writers talk. I have not always lead the cloistered existence of the New York old maid, bounded on the south by Carnegie Hall and on the north by the Colony Club. No, Mr. Styles, you will be surprised to hear that I had an operatic career of my own! I sang in public — on one occasion.

And that is precisely why I have now revised (not changed) my position. I have decided that my reluctance to write about Uncle Ed must spring from my identification of his failure as manager of the opera house with my own failure as an opera singer. What egotism! To compare his magnificent and catastrophic experiment with ten years of voice lessons ending in a single appearance as Ortrud in a road company *Lohengrin!* And so I have resolved that I will do what you ask and record here my memories of my uncle. But, there is one very stiff condition. You may not publish it in my lifetime. For even though these memories are so ancient that they have ceased to hurt, there are still some that I do not care to see set forth in the impertinence of print: the quizzical, puzzled stare in Uncle Ed's eyes after too many brandies, my father's embarrassment before the devoted ushers at the opera house who he feared were his brother's unpaid creditors, my grandmother's bewilderment at finding herself choosing to side with her own world against her favorite son. But when I am gone (and I am past eighty), you may do as you like with these pages. They will be in nobody's memory then.

I shall start, being old-fashioned, in the time-honored way of Balzac (the only novelist I still read) by saying a word about the position of the Stillmans in the New York of 1890. We were one of those unremarkable families, indigenous to the "best" society of any large city, who seemed to have no particular claim to our position other than the fact that we had always had it. By a claim I mean such an obvious thing as a fortune or a distinguished lineage or simply a relationship to some great man. There are New York families that have their colonial governor as Roman families have their Pope. But each generation of our Stillmans had managed to move gracefully across the social scene without particularly distinguishing itself or particularly disgracing itself and always without leaving more than a modest competence to the succeeding one. They were great believers in the "here and now." So long as their dinners were good and their clothes in style, they did not much care what sort of old brownstone (provided, of course, it was in the right neighborhood) housed them. They found the world as it was a pretty good place. Of course, they didn't go around turning over stones or poking behind curtains. They did not conceive that to be their function. But if a curtain happened to fall and a skeleton was revealed, if a moral issue developed and people started to raise their voices and take sides, if, in other words, the chips were down, the Stillmans, God bless them, were apt to be on the side of the angels.

Uncle Ed, my father's bachelor brother, was the Stillman who came closest to breaking the family rule of "Nothing in Excess," but his excess was of a Stillman sort. In personal adornment he was a bit of a peacock, even in that gaudy age. Look at the photograph of him in Gustav Kobbé's *Complete Opera Book.* The long slim body in the perfectly tailored Prince Albert with the velvet collar seems to flow gracefully upward to the grave bearded face, the reflective eyes and the glistening, narrow-brimmed stovepipe hat. The beard is neatly trimmed to follow the contours of the squarish chin and also those of the gently drooping mustache. It would be altogether the portrait of a dandy of the period, with a bit of the hardness of one of Whistler's *boulevardiers,* a touch of the cruelty of a Paul Bourget hero, were it not for the eyes, large and brown and almost brooding. Oh, yes, the eyes gave Uncle Ed away as they gave my father away. They were eyes that could see the main chance, but beyond the main chance they saw perfectly the price that one paid for it.

A more serious excess in Uncle Ed was his drinking, but this, too, was done with Stillman style. There was never (at least before his final European chapter) anything so vulgar as intoxication. Uncle Ed, as Father used to put it, was like a noble greensward that needed a constant, gentle sprinkling. Each drink had its consecrated hour: the midmorning sherry flip, the noon gin fizz, the afternoon cognac, the evening "cocktail" at the men's bar, the midnight whiskey, without mentioning the diverse flow of mealtime wines that constituted the central river to which the other drinks were tributary. The family used to ascribe Uncle Ed's drinking to his lack of steady employment, and from my earliest years I remember table discussion of how to lure him from his bibulous idleness. Uncle Ed, apparently, was always willing to try anything once, but his jobs had a way of terminating after a few months, always with the remarkable circumstance of his remaining a fast friend of his former employer.

It was my father who first conceived the idea of finding him a job at the opera house. Father was always the most imaginative member of the family. Physically, he resembled his brother, but it was as a guinea fowl resembles a pheasant. Father was much less elegant and, by like token, much more responsible. But he had the kindness of the Stillman men, and when he put his mind on his brother, he thought of his brother and not of himself thinking of his brother.

"Everybody wants Ed to do what *they* happen to like doing," he told my grandmother, above whose sober widow's establishment Uncle Ed maintained a gay top floor. "Uncle Harry wants him to go into the iron business. My boss keeps urging him to become a banker. And Marion Crawford tells him to write novels. We ought to be trying to make a life for Ed out of the things that *Ed* likes doing. Now what are they? Well, first off, he likes the opera. Couldn't Uncle Harry get him something to do there?"

It was the ace of trumps on the first draw! Granny Stillman's older sister, my Great-aunt Rosalie, was married to Uncle Harry Belknap, a rich ironmaster from Troy and a director of the opera. Nothing was easier for him than to secure for his wife's nephew, whom most of the boxholders knew and liked, the position of Secretary to the company, and for the next two years (an unprecedented tenure for him) Uncle Ed attended the board meetings faithfully and ornamentally, kept the minutes neatly and concisely and busied himself about the office, at least until the early afternoon. He even took to dropping in on rehearsals, and with his knack for friendship he soon became intimate with the leading singers and musicians. The opera house developed for him into a combination of hobby and club, and my family breathed in relief at Father's brilliant solution of the problem.

Promotion followed swiftly. In those days the gulf between the owners of the opera house, all New York businessmen, and the artists, already dominated by Germans and Wagnerites, was almost unbridgeable. Neither side could even listen to the other, and opera was produced in an atmosphere of what we would call a "cold war." But Uncle Ed could talk to Mr. Morgan and to Mr. Damrosch and make each feel that he was on his side. When the general managership fell vacant in 1890, the board, after several long, wrangling sessions, was suddenly united by the prospect of this dark but very glossy horse.

There was an outburst of enthusiasm. What did it matter that Ed Stillman was not a musician? Was there not too much expertise already? Were the directors not sick of managers who swore guttural oaths and regarded "opera" and "Wagner" as synonyms? The only trouble seemed to be with Uncle Ed himself who resisted the appointment with a stubbornness that surprised everybody, and, when at last prevailed upon, accepted it with a gravity of manner that seemed almost Teutonic. Had the directors paused, however, to remember how the miter had changed Thomas à Becket (which, needless to say, they did not), they might have consoled themselves with the thought that they were twelve King Henrys to his single archbishop.

One person who had no reservations over Uncle Ed's promotion was his sixteen-year-old niece. I was already a devoted opera fan, with a picture by my bedside of Melba, whose London debut as Lucia had been the great moment of my life. I attended the Brearley School, but books, and even, in holiday parties, boys, hardly existed for me. I lived for the afternoons and my singing teacher, Miss Angela Frith. Uncle Ed, whose courteous demeanor to the young raised them briefly to the paradise of adults, was already my favorite relative. Now he became a god.

Mother, who considered herself vastly more liberal than the

Stillmans, was as one with them when it came to any serious extension of the arts beyond the parlor. She laughed at my musical pretensions, when she was not irritated by them.

"Why don't you take Amy to one of your rehearsals, Ed?" she asked my uncle one night. "I wonder if seeing the opera house in its shirt sleeves wouldn't cure some of her fancies?"

Poor Mother! If she only had known what oil she was pouring on my fire! I waited breathless for Uncle Ed's answer, afraid to ruin my chances by showing my enthusiasm, but his smile recognized my palpitations. He knew that waiting was torture to the young.

"Why, certainly, any rehearsal she wants. We're running through the second act of *Tristan* tomorrow afternoon. How will that do?"

And so, after a sleepless night and a morning at school in which I took in nothing, my dream came true. There was I, Amy Stillman, seated with my uncle in the center of the second row of the orchestra pit in the great dark, empty opera house before a stage covered with cartons and dirty canvases, watching two stout middle-aged persons, a man and a woman in modern dress, sitting side by side on a small wicker divan. And when the conductor raised his baton, and we started right off in the middle of the love duet, I thought it the most romantic setting that I had ever seen. So much for Mother's precautions!

I was familiar with *Lohengrin* and *Die Walküre,* but I had never heard a note of *Tristan.* Its effect on me was ambivalent. I was intrigued and excited by the violence and surge of the music, but at the same time it made me restless, apprehensive, almost afraid. Of what? Of love, of physical love? I have often asked myself since. But I do not think so. It was difficult for a girl in my time to associate love with the portly middle age represented by the two performers. No, there was something else in that churning, seething music, something like being caught in the backwash of a big breaker when surf bathing in Southampton on a visit to Granny, tossed and pulled by the hissing water and borne out ineluctably to sea, to be smothered, perhaps to be drowned in a terrible peace beneath that tormented surface. I had no idea that this was a common reaction to *Tristan,* and I became at length so agitated that I was relieved when the director called to the conductor through a little megaphone to stop the music.

The woman who was singing Brangäne had been delivering the off-stage warning in a voice that was almost inaudible. She complained that the strain on her vocal cords was so great that she could not sing in full voice until the performance. It could be then or now, she concluded defiantly. The *Herr Direktor* could choose. He turned to Uncle Ed.

"Which shall it be, Mr. Stillman?"

"Tell her to sing today," Uncle Ed snapped, and the rehearsal went on. Inexperienced as I was, I could sense that he had already taken hold of his company.

In a break, after the duet, Uncle Ed suggested a turn around the block. I was very proud to be on the arm of my handsome and distinguished uncle, and I admired the easy courtesy with which he raised his hat to any members of the company whom we passed, without interrupting the flow of our discussion. He asked me which I preferred, *Tristan* or *Lucia,* already knowing that *Lucia* was my favorite opera.

"Oh, *Lucia,*" I said promptly. "But *Tristan* is more interesting," I added, politely, suspecting his own preference.

"Interesting," he repeated thoughtfully. "Perhaps that's just what it is. Look down Broadway, Amy." We paused at the corner and gazed south at the great thoroughfare. "Look at all that gray dirtiness and listen to all that strident clamor and tell me if you really think our modern life corresponds to the tinkling tunefulness of Donizetti."

"You believe it should?"

"Well, don't you think there should be *some* relation between daily life and music? Or do we go to the opera just to dress up and see our friends?"

"But Uncle Ed," I protested earnestly, "shouldn't opera help us to forget all that dirt and clamor?"

"Spoken like a true boxholder! You'll be like the other dreamers in Number Seven, Amy. Your grandmother sighs for Edgar of Ravenswood, and even your Great-aunt Rosalie wants to immolate herself with Rhadames in a living tomb!"

"And I can be Carmen!" I exclaimed, feeling very adult to be joking about such things (particularly Granny!) with the older generation.

"I'm sure a very proper Carmen," Uncle Ed added with a chuckle. "Maybe even a rather severe one, like dear Lili Lehmann. She sings the "Habanera" as if it had been written by Haydn. I suppose, Amy, I sometimes feel that our life is such a continual fancy dress ball that I want — just for a minute, mind you, just every now and then — to slip into plain old clothes and be myself."

As I took in with a quick glance my uncle's rich brown tweeds, the maroon polish of his shoes gleaming beneath his spats, the red carnation in his buttonhole, the walking stick with the silver knob, I could not but wonder if *these* were his plain old clothes. "Does your *Tristan* 'correspond' to modern life?" I asked timidly.

Uncle Ed became immediately serious at this, more so than I could ever remember having seen him. "That's a good question, Amy. No, Wagner's operas don't correspond to modern life because Wagner didn't believe in modern life. Not in ours, anyway. He thought that it didn't exist, or if it did, that it was too trivial, too unheroic, too sordid, to be worth commenting on in musical terms. If a man was to write opera, it should be about valiant mythological figures, gods and goddesses, and if there weren't any gods and goddesses, he ought to create them. Think of it, Amy!" Here Uncle Ed's eyes really sparkled. We stopped walking, and he spread one arm in a broad gesture. "Ever since Shakespeare we have taken for granted that the artist must deal with mortal men, that his province must lie in love and compassion. You remember what Pope said: the proper study of mankind is man. But Wagner did what nobody has done in the whole history of art, except perhaps the ancients. If he was compelled to comment, he would create a world worthy to comment upon. He despised mankind, but did that stop him? He saw that the only beautiful thing in the world was death, and he made love to it in *Tristan*. Oh, Amy, when once you *feel* Wagner, there is nobody else. There is nothing else."

How vivid that moment is to me this day, more than sixty years after! For I saw things then that were beyond the comprehension of my years in a terrible flash of divination. It was not that I agreed with Uncle Ed. I didn't then, and, thank God, I do not now. But I *saw,* and the vision scared me. I saw into the awful emptiness of his soul, and I felt the well of pity bubbling up in my own. Because, you see, Mr. Styles, I felt that I had seen into something essential in the nature of my family, or at least of the Stillman side of it, something that Granny had all along suspected and that she fought blindly, without understanding. And this was it: Uncle Ed's elegance, his smartness, his whole air of exquisite maintenance was the same gallant but essentially futile effort to decorate the void of God's or non-God's neglect that he fancied he could detect in the tumultuous creations of Wagner. It all had to end, as it ended in *Tristan,* in a death that one could only pretend was a love death.

My shudder was barely perceptible, but Uncle Ed perceived it. He shook his head, apologized for his theorizing (always, in his opinion, "bad form") and led me back to the opera house.

"If Granny Stillman hears I've been trying to convert you to Wagner, there'll be the devil to pay," he said with a wink, as we took our seats. "If she asks you what was being rehearsed today, tell her it was *Les Huguenots.*"

Granny, of course, had not been born a Stillman, and she had none of their characteristics. She was a good deal tougher and less imaginative, and she was much more innately conservative. Where Father and Uncle Ed were by temperament aristocratic, she was bourgeois to the marrow of her bones. She had been widowed early in life and had managed her small inheritance so well that she was now able to maintain a house on Sixty-fifth Street and a shingle cottage in Southampton and to keep a butler and four maids. But always frugal, she depended on her richer sister for the luxuries of a carriage and opera box.

I look at Granny's photograph as I write, with the pale oval face, the high-piled, elaborately waved gray hair and the large watery, apprehensive eyes, and I think how she would stare at the liberties I am taking with her! Yet I have started this thing, and I have to make her understandable. Granny believed in the present, the present instant, the concrete thing before her eyes. Having said she was bourgeois, I will now say that she had a bit of the peasant in her. She accepted the mores of her New York as if established by divine decree. When her favorite niece lay dying, we were all surprised that she seemed wholly concerned with whether or not to call off a dinner party. But this was not from lack of feeling. It was from a deep-seated belief that doing the "right thing" was paramount to personal grief, and it gave an oddly impersonal quality to her snobbishness. She never scorned outcasts, any more than, conventionally anti-Semitic and anti-Roman, she in the least disliked or disapproved of Jews and Catholics. She simply would not pick her friends among them.

I believe that Granny loved Uncle Ed more than she had ever loved another human being (unless it was the rather shadowy figure of my long dead grandfather), but when rumors began to circulate that he had "gone over to the Germans" and even that he had "betrayed his trust," she found herself in an acutely painful position. She and her sister, Aunt Rosalie Belknap, were close with the peculiar closeness of their generation of siblings: they lived on the same street in Manhattan and on the same sand dune in Southampton and saw each other every day of the year. Aunt Rosalie, being older and cleverer and a great deal richer, dominated Granny, while Uncle Harry, who took care of her business interests, represented "men" in her respectful widow's heart. If the Belknaps were against the "new music," how could a Stillman be for it? How much less could a Stillman be for it who owed his very job to Uncle Harry?

Matters came to a head on the Sunday after that rehearsal, at Granny's family lunch. As in other brownstones of that period, the dining room was the one handsome chamber, always on the first floor back, shrouded in kindly darkness, high-ceilinged, with perfectly polished silver gleaming in crowded density on the sideboard and with high, carved Jacobean chairs looking like antiques under the crystal chandelier. When I inherited Granny's and put them in a good light, they showed up as bad fakes.

Aunt Rosalie, as was to be expected, led off the discussion. To tell the truth, I always found Aunt Rosalie, who dyed her hair a jet black and wore too many rings and bracelets, the least bit common, whereas Granny, even at her most worldly, was always totally a lady. Money sometimes had that effect on old New York. Granny may have owed her relative refinement to her relative poverty.

"They tell me young Damrosch is twisting you around his little finger, Ed," Aunt Rosalie began. "They say we're going to have nothing but darkened stages with earth goddesses moaning about time and fate."

"Oh, I think I can promise you a Rhine maiden here and there, Aunt Rosalie," Uncle Ed drawled in his easiest tone. "And we've installed some very curious machinery to make them appear to be swimming about under water. I think it might interest you to see it. Would you care to come down to the house one morning next week and let me show you?"

Uncle Ed could have his way with most women, even with Aunt Rosalie, but not when she was on the track of something. "It'll have to wait, I'm afraid, for I'm tied up all next week. But Harry and I would like very much to know what you're planning to tell your board when they find that all their lovely Traviatas and Aïdas have been traded in for a parcel of shrieking Valkyries. Wouldn't we, Harry?"

"Very much, my dear."

"Ah, but I'm all ready for the board, Uncle Harry, I assure you," Uncle Ed exclaimed, turning deferentially to the old white-whiskered gentleman. "I have ordered a new dragon for *Siegfried,* and you can't even object to the expense, as I've raised the money myself. It is guaranteed to send shivers down the hardiest spine. Fire and smoke come out of its jaws, and its eyes goggle hideously. I predict that even you, Uncle Harry, won't sleep through that scene!"

Uncle Harry grunted, and I giggled and Mother smiled, but there was a distinct feeling at the table that Uncle Ed was going rather far. Granny did not attempt to conceal her apprehension.

"I don't think that's very polite to your uncle, Edmund," she intervened, as if he were five and not forty-five. "After all, it was he who suggested your name originally to the board. He is going to bear the responsibility for what you do. *He* is going to be the one to face the boxholders!"

"I know that, Ma! I couldn't be more aware of it. But the day is also coming when Uncle Harry will be proud to have made me the manager. He will be known in musical history as the man responsible for the first all-star Wagner performances in this country!"

Uncle Harry looked so uncomfortable at this that even Aunt Rosalie saw that the conversation had better be changed, and we turned to the happier topic of who could be dropped that year from her ever-expanding Christmas party.

The struggle between Uncle Ed and the boxholders came to its crisis during a Monday night performance of *Tristan und Isolde* with the same cast that I had seen rehearsing it. I sat as usual on family parties in the front row of the Belknap box between Aunt Rosalie, who always occupied her special armchair on the left, and Granny. It was a trying seat, for I had to sit up as straight as they did. Aunt Rosalie even had a little cushion, as hard as a board, which hung down over the back rest to keep her from tilting. But what was far worse than the strain of the posture, at least to a music lover like myself, was the way, with a license as broad as their physical freedom was narrow, they exchanged comments about the opera across me in perfectly normal speaking tones.

In the second row were my parents and Miss Behn, one of those soft, chattering, semi-indigent old maids, always smiling, always looking to the "bright side" of their faintly illuminated existences, who attached themselves to the Aunt Rosalies of that era as pilot fish to sharks. And alone in a corner at the back of the box, a nodding Jupiter, Uncle Harry slept the sleep of the just fiduciary.

Why did they go to the opera? What took them, *every* Monday night, year in and year out? Could it have been only snobbery, as people believe today? I would be the last to deny that snobbery played its part, but it seems to me that there had to be something else, something deeper in the folkways of human communities. Monday night at the opera was like a village fair or a saint's festival. Society was still small enough so that one knew, if not everybody, at least who everybody was, and who were their guests and why. Many young people today do not know what this pleasure is. The impersonality of the modern city has destroyed it. But in New York you can still see a strange atavistic yearning for something not unlike it in the Easter Parade. What used to be a leisurely stroll of familiar figures in new finery down Fifth Avenue after church has become a turgid human river, overflowing the sidewalks and filling the thoroughfare to the elimination of all vehicles, a dense, slowly moving mass without origin or destination, drawn from the desolate suburbs, thousands upon thousands of women in silly hats, staring and being stared at, recognizing nobody and ignorant of why they are there, zombies seeking a lost ritual of community living that they will never find. Thank God my life has been largely lived in another day.

We arrived very late that night, to my distress but hardly to my surprise. Tristan and Isolde were already drinking the potion, and Granny and Aunt Rosalie were sufficiently diverted by the shouts of the sailor chorus so that no real ennui had settled in before the long entr'acte. In the second act, the love duet held everyone's attention, but trouble came, after the interruption of the lovers, with King Mark's long aria. The ripple of conversation through the boxes swelled to a gurgling stream.

I had done my homework on *Tristan* since the rehearsal, and I remember thinking that it was ironical that Granny and Aunt Rosalie's world should be most bored when Wagner was speaking most directly to them. For Mark sings of the day, which in *Tristan* is always compared unfavorably to the night. The day is reality: it is harsh and bright and garish. It is full of things that boxholders like to talk about: honor, loyalty, ties of blood. But the night, which to the lovers has become the only truth, is dark and lush and sleep-inducing. The night is death and love.

The chatter in the boxes reached a pitch that I had not heard before. It was actually difficult to catch some of Mark's notes. Suddenly, appallingly, silence fell with the unexpected downward swoop of the great curtains, the music stopped, and the lights went up. A tall bearded gentleman in white tie and tail coat strode quickly across the proscenium and faced the audience across the prompter's box. It was Uncle Ed. His high tense voice rang out in the auditorium.

"When the boxholders have concluded their conversations, the performance will be resumed. That is all. Thank you."

And he walked off stage as rapidly as he had come on. There was a moment of shocked silence, then a buzz of startled whispers, then some whistles and finally the roar of resumed conversation and a stamping of feet. The boxholders consulted each other indignantly; there were shrill complaints and some laughs. From the galleries came catcalls that might have expressed anger at the interruption or approval of the management. One could not be sure of anything in the general confusion.

In the midst of it all Uncle Ed appeared again, but this time in the back of our box where he took a seat beside Uncle Harry, for once thoroughly awake. Uncle Ed tilted his chair back and crossed his arms over his chest in the gesture of one who was prepared to wait all night. In a minute the entire diamond horseshoe was aware of his presence there. The issue was joined.

I am sure that that was the most terrible moment of Granny's long life. I had heard of her near insanity at the early death of my apparently charming grandfather, and I was later to minister to her in her desolation at the death of each of her two sons. But there is a compensation in the very fullness of the tide of love that creates the agony of bereavement; there is the luxury of memory always open to us. No such leavening existed that night for Granny. She could not even console herself that her most beloved child was showing an admirable courage in his isolation. It is always difficult for the conventional to recognize courage in what they deem ridiculous causes. Here was Granny, surrounded by the only world that she knew and admired, in the very heart of it and at its dressiest moment, and having to behold it united in an anger and contempt, which to her, alas, was a *justifiable* anger and contempt, by the perverse, misguided son who sat behind her with folded arms and icy countenance, identifying her and her family and her sister with his foolish fads. It was as if a respectable Roman matron, on a holiday matinee at the Colosseum, should have had the shock of seeing a son leap into the arena to shield some dirty Christian from a hungry and deserving lion. Granny's discipline was of the tautest, but I could see her jaw tremble as it only did in moments of the very gravest tension. Then, without turning to me, she touched my elbow.

"Ask your uncle to have the performance resumed," she murmured, as I leaned over to her. "Tell him I say: 'Darling, please.' "

It was in our family a lady's S O S, the ultimate appeal. I stepped to the back of the box, terrified to think that the eyes of the multitude were upon me, and whispered the message hastily in his ear. He nodded gravely, and in the second that I caught his eyes I read in them all of his gallantry and all of his defeat. He rose and left the box, and in five more minutes the curtain rose again, before a still chattering house, on the garden by King Mark's castle. It was then that I grew up — in a single minute — and felt at last the full tragedy of what had happened.

I did not see Uncle Ed again for many weeks. Father and Mother were angry with him for what they considered a public humiliation of Granny and Aunt Rosalie, and there were veiled references at our family board to his debts and drinking. When we lunched at Granny's he did not appear, and when he wrote to invite me to a rehearsal of his lavish new production of *Diana von Solange* by Ernest, Duke of Coburg, Mother replied that I was too far behind in my school homework for any more such privileges. But I followed sorrowfully every account of his new venture that I could find in the public prints.

The only way that I can explain Uncle Ed's extraordinary selection of *Diana* is that, having no basic training in music, he had responded to Wagner more with his heart and imagination than with his ear and that he did not have the critical apparatus necessary to assess the works of other composers. According to my father, Uncle Ed had hoped to appease the boxholders with a lighter kind of opera and to hold the loyalty of the Wagnerians with the introduction of another German music drama. The miscalculation could hardly have been greater. The boxholders were indignant at the notion that they wanted anything "light" and irritated by the suspicion that Uncle Ed thought to impress them with a royal composer, while the Wagnerians, ignorant of the very concept of compromise, were outraged that the tinkling score of an amateur should be heard in the same auditorium that had witnessed the master's work. Uncle Ed, however, calmly persisted in his enterprise with all the world now against him, and my father speculated in alarm at our breakfasts that he must be borrowing the extra expenses of production that the board had refused to underwrite. For Uncle Ed had announced to the press that *Diana* would be a grand opera at its grandest.

The opening brought with it a family reconciliation, and we all attended in the Belknap box. I think that Father anticipated the disaster and thought it was no time to be estranged from his brother. He was certainly right. The only thing that consoled me on the grim evening (grimmer even than the *Tristan,* for it was the only time in all my years of opera going that I heard extensive booing in that house) was that we were there with Uncle Ed. He sat in the back of the box throughout the performance, rigid and expressionless. No doubt he was heavily fortified by brandies. I hope so. When the lights went up after the final curtain, there seemed to be not even recognition left in those dead brown eyes, not a tremor in that rigid posture. Father gripped his shoulder as we filed out of the box, and Granny stooped to kiss the top of his head. He did not respond. But at least we Stillmans had stood together against the crass hostility of the boxholders and the Wagnerians. How superficial the old differences between the latter now seemed in the light of their noisy, stamping merger! And how that light showed up the basic vulgarity of each! I was proud to be with Uncle Ed in his boat even if it was a sinking one, and I turned to send what I hoped was a magnificent look of scorn over the house as I left the box.

I do not believe it was more than two days later that Father gave us the news at breakfast of Uncle Ed's resignation.

"I'm afraid it's a case of 'I quit,' 'You're fired,' " he said with a sad headshake. "He's going abroad almost at once. Your grandmother is terribly upset, Amy, and she finds it easier on her nerves not to be left alone with him. I think you'd better take the day off from school and spend it with her."

"But why is it hard for her to be alone with Uncle Ed?"

Father and Mother exchanged glances, and then he abandoned the subterfuge. "Well, I guess you're old enough to hear about it. Your uncle has run up some very serious debts, and he will find it cheaper and more convenient to live in Germany while arrangements are being made about them. Your grandmother can't afford to dig any deeper into her capital than she's already done, and she's afraid that he will try to persuade her."

I do not know if it was the restraint of my presence, but Uncle Ed certainly made no remark during lunch at Granny's that could even remotely be construed as referring to his financial exigency. Indeed, anyone watching the three of us in that dusky, silent dining room would have assumed that Granny was the one harassed by creditors. For all the reputed discipline of her generation, she made not the slightest effort at conversation, but simply sat there staring with tear-filled eyes at the errant son who was holding forth gracefully to me about the reasons for the failure of *Diana.* At last she interrupted him harshly.

"Haven't we heard enough about that sorry business?"

"Very well, Ma."

"I don't see how you can be so cold, so casual."

"I don't see how you can be so flurried, so emotional!"

"Edmund!" Granny cried. "I can't bear it! You know, my darling, that I would give you what you ask if it was fair to the others . . ."

"I know, Ma. Of course. Please! Remember Amy."

After lunch, when Granny had gone to her room for a nap (nothing ever interrupted that) Uncle Ed followed me down to the hall and helped me into my coat. It was a long red coat with some twenty buttons down the front, and in my nervousness and distress, I buttoned one in the wrong hole. Uncle Ed turned me around to face him and carefully unbuttoned it to button it again properly.

"It doesn't matter," I murmured. "I'm only going home, just a block."

Uncle Ed raised a reproachful finger. "It always matters, Amy. Remember that. It *always* matters. Those are the only words of wisdom (the only assets, in fact) that your departing uncle leaves behind."

And then, like Granny, I too broke down. I threw my arms around his neck and sobbed.

"Poor Amy," he said, stroking my hair, "life is going to be hard on you, too. Just remember what I told you about the buttons. It doesn't sound like much, and it's *not* much, but it may be better than nothing. If it's all you've got."

I ran out the door and down the stoop, and I never saw him again.

Three years later, when I was in Paris with Father and Mother, they went to see him at his hotel, but they would not let me go with them. By then he was intoxicated most of the time, and in a few more months his liver mercifully gave out.

As I learned later, too much later for my own good, he went first to Munich after leaving New York and there became finally disillusioned with Wagner and Wagnerians. The master's message was already being interpreted along narrow national lines in a way that was totally abhorrent to my gentle uncle. When an Englishman called H. S. Chamberlain convinced him that there was justification for this in the prose writings of Wagner himself, he left Munich and German opera quietly behind him. Uncle Ed was not one to publish or even to communicate a disillusionment. And, after all, how great a loss was *his* faith in Wagner? It was not the loss of it but the acquisition that had destroyed him. Without that raging music in his ears and blood he might have married happily, like my father, and raised a family. He might even have taken a regular job and finished out a normal lifetime as a graceful ornament to the world that had produced him. You may sneer, Mr. Styles, at the idea of this being so preferable an alternative, but you did not see the agony of what *did* happen that summer in Paris in my father's eyes.

My own story is only a sad postscript to Uncle Ed's. Without his example I might have faced the fact earlier that I did not have a voice for Wagnerian opera and reconciled myself to marriage and children. But the idea of a Stillman carrying on where he had failed became a fixation. I even believed that I owed it to him to sing the great roles as gloriously as he had dreamed of hearing them. Had Mother and Father ever divined this madness, they might have helped me, but it was part of my crazy integrity to tell them nothing.

After graduating from Brearley School, I refused adamantly to "come out," and I opposed my mother and grandmother so violently in every other plan which they proposed for me, that Father, always the peacemaker, at last had to take charge of the situation. He decreed that I should be allowed to study the voice under professional auspices. Of course, it went without saying that I should continue to live at home, but I was permitted to spend my mornings in the studio of Madame Grisi-Helsinka, to be ostensibly trained to appear in benefit performances on the concert stage. Of course, *I* was determined that I would make my debut as Sieglinde, but there was no need to throw it in my family's face until the time arrived.

My teacher scoffed at my Wagnerian pretensions and tried to turn me to operetta. My voice, such as it was, turned out to be nearer contralto than soprano. But there was still Fricka, Erda, Ortrud to be sung. I persisted in my lessons. For ten years I studied German opera, the same decade that witnessed the great popular triumph of Wagner in New York that Uncle Ed had predicted. The irony of my situation and the endless queries of my family drove me at last abroad where, at the age of thirty, I sang Ortrud for a road company in Rouen, my debut and my finale.

For a cable came, not of congratulation but of recall. Granny was ill. She had had a stroke which I was made to feel was not unrelated to the absurdity of my operatic career. Father had at the same time come down with a kidney disease that was to kill him, and as Mother had to spend all her time with him, she insisted that my place was with Granny. I debated my reply for a desperate week, and in the end I decided that Mother was right. I sailed home from Le Havre and spent seven dreary years with Granny until her death at the age of ninety-one. By then I was thirty-seven, and there was no further question of an appearance in opera. The family had won — or thought they had.

But I must insist on one point. Everybody has always taken for granted that I was talked into looking after first Granny and later Mother. They say: "Poor old Amy. She wanted to have her little fling, you know, but old Mrs. Stillman put a stop to all that. They preferred to have her a useful 'companion' to an indifferent opera singer." Everybody assumes that I was simply another of those weak-minded spinsters of the late Victorian era who bowed their heads submissively as they were cheated of their birthrights by selfish mothers and grandmothers. But it wasn't so. It cannot have been so! What I did, I did under nobody's persuasion but my own. I took a long clear look at my opera career and weighed it against what I could do for Granny. Had I had the voice for Isolde I hope I would have had the divine egotism and the courage to let Granny die alone. As it was I could not sacrifice the small consolation that I was able to bring her for the chance to sing second-string roles in third-rate opera companies.

But we had our moments, Uncle Ed and I. Who knows, as Robert Browning might have put it, when all is finally added up, if we will not have had as much as the others? It is more graceful, anyway, to think so. It is like keeping that twentieth button properly buttoned on one's coat. And so I am going to be glad for what I have had. I am going to be glad for my little night in Rouen, and I wonder if Uncle Ed, even in those sorry last years, was not occasionally glad that he had had the thrill of producing *Tristan,* if only to a golden horseshoe of chattering friends and relations.

Sincerely yours,
AMY STILLMAN

36 I